WHITBY ABBEY
PURE INSPIRATION

WHITBY ABBEY PURE INSPIRATION

An anthology of stories

ENGLISH HERITAGE

Whitby Abbey Pure Inspiration

Spiderwize
3 The Causeway
Kennoway
Kingdom of Fife
KY8 5JU
Scotland UK

www.spiderwize.com

ISBN: 978-1-907294-78-5

Contents

Introduction

When we launched our Pure Inspiration writing competition, we really did not know what to expect – after all, as a source of inspiration, Whitby Abbey has been influencing writers, poets, knights, artists and photographers for hundreds of years!

What we got was an insight into how different people perceive the Abbey, and a real sense that everyone who sees the ruins knows it has an unlimited number of stories to tell. Standing proud on the headland, the Abbey has seen so much over the generations and, with care, it can continue to stand proud against the wind from the North Sea.

And that is what makes this book so special. Every time a copy is sold, all the profit will go back into paying towards the maintenance of the Abbey; a virtuous circle where those who gained inspiration from the Whitby Abbey will help preserve it for future generations.

What you are about to read is a diverse anthology of stories, all of which feature Whitby Abbey in some form. Some stories made us laugh, others made us cry, and several sent shivers down our spines!

We hope you enjoy reading it as much as we've enjoyed compiling it. And when you've read it, don't forget to come back to Whitby Abbey for another visit. We'll look forward to welcoming you back.

Happy reading!

English Heritage's Whitby Abbey team.

Human Remains

By Sarah Ann Juckes
*Overall winner of the 'Pure Inspiration' writing
competition*

The jangle of the shop bell rolled to him through the dust of the back
room like a death rattle. Joshua scratched his beard, a sure sign of his
irritation. A customer. He knew what to expect next, and sure enough a
raucous conversation punctured his solitude. He growled into his paint-
flecked hands, his irritation escaping him, clinging to his skin and
itching.

In his years of residing in Whitby, he had learnt that silence was a hard
thing to come by in this town. Schooner horns blasted, carried on the
howling wind, accompanied by a crescendo of children's screams, the
screech of seagulls and incessant Yorkshire drawl of the locals. Even
buried miles beneath a mountain of stale dust, Joshua was haunted by
noise.

Upon his first visit to the tiny art shop, he had been surprised at the
strident nature of its interior. The exterior, somewhat removed from the
main thicket of the costal town, lay buried in the cliff-side, seemingly
disconnected from the bustle of the tourist shops.

The facade camouflaged perfectly with the cliff-side, fingers of moss
winding their way up the wet sides and clinging to the cracks in the
stone as if the earth and cliffs were embracing the little shop as its own.
Small, darkened windows and a narrow wooden door were all that
separated it from the Whitby shore. Joshua remembered seeing it as a
cave, his own fortress of seclusion from the tousling cobbled streets.

The shop was dim-lit with a faint tang of seaweed and wet rock that
seemed absorbed into the very beams of the building. The walls were
cluttered with various art supplies, paint, brushes, pallettes, all crammed

into every crook and crevice of the large wooden shelves. Stools, easels, and larger items encroached on to the floor like sea froth, supplies dangling from the low wooden roof like ratted seaweeds.

Joshua had been different back then. Shaven, smart, even slightly more susceptible to conversation. The shopkeeper of the art shop was the first man Joshua had made contact with upon his visit. The man was boisterous and overly jolly, his eyes set like pebbles in the sand, worn smooth and seamless by the tides. His flesh was wrinkled and torn, reminding Joshua remarkably of driftwood, his old clothes hanging limp off his bones like that of a scarecrow. Yet he radiated some strange energy that seemed to come from deep within the depths of his chest with his chuckle.

'Hello there! What can I do you for?' Joshua remembered the peculiarity of his posture, both wooden arms resting on the surface of the cluttered counter like an easel.

'Good morning. I'm fine, thank you,' Joshua had replied. He was never one for talking even in his younger years. Like his father, he preferred the whisper of a pencil on paper or the hush of a brush on canvas to any small talk. Yet this man would not cease.

'New to the area are we?'

'Yes,' he had replied, trying to inject a tone of finality into his voice.

'Ah, a tourist then! Staying long?'

Joshua flinched and itched under the name 'tourist'.

'Not long, a few weeks I hope.'

He turned his back on the old man, trying to drown out the chatter with thoughts of brushes and paint.

'What brings you to Whitby then son? Hoping to do a spot of painting are we?'

'Yes,' Joshua replied without turning.

'Sea views you after?'

Joshua sighed, finally letting himself be carried by the tides of the conversation. He hadn't the energy to fight it.

'The Abbey.'

'The Abbey hey? Oh, we get a lot of that here. A lot, a lot. Got some good ones here, I'll show you.'

The man lifted the clutter off his desk, peeling it away skilfully like a wet plaster, revealing a set of pale paintings detailing various views of the Abbey and its surroundings.

'I'm not here to buy. I'm here to paint.'

The old man smiled at him knowingly, as if finally understanding Joshua's temperament.

'Let me tell you something my boy,' he said with a mysterious smirk. 'The beauty of that Abbey when the sun rises and the day is still crisp with night... Ain't no painter alive that can capture that feeling, the pureness you feel in your very bones, and put it on a chunk of canvas.' His smile broadened. 'But you're welcome to try. Canvases are in the back room there.'

Joshua had nodded quietly and willingly followed his direction to the back room that he squats in now, three years later, scratching his tangled beard irritably as if he had fleas.

The old man had been right, and Joshua hated that. How he wished he had ignored him, as he does now. To have closed his ears and blocked-out all the old man's words like eyelids shutting out light. The shopkeeper's revelation was a curse, he was sure of it. Punishment for his unwillingness to comply to their first conversation. He would have been happy to have gone to the Abbey the next morning, paint one or two mediocre pictures that would have satisfied his dead father's dream and left on the train the next week. But no. Joshua's pride had absorbed the old man's words like a dry sponge, weighing him down with sodden expectation.

Three years he had been in Whitby, rising at 5am every morning from his pokey B&B room and climbing the 199 steps to the cliff top laden with easel, paints and canvases to take in the magnificent sunrise as it yawned over the horizon. He'd sat at every angle, even those on the neighbouring cliff tops. If it rained, he'd put up a cover and sketch anyway. For three years.

It haunted him. Its ruined shape was all he could see when he closed his eyes. He saw every stone, every blade of grass, every arch in his food, his sleep, even his fellow people became misshapen stone objects signifying the wet walls, the clouds, the ships in the harbour below. Charcoal, watercolour, pencil, acrylic, pastels, even Biro and chalk. Nothing Joshua did even came close to describing the gothic beauty of that Abbey as the first rays of day crept over the horizon.

The meditative state Joshua had tried to sink into in order to choose the size of his next canvas seemed pointless now the shop was filled with the echoes and shouts of the old shopkeeper and the willing tourist. He wrenched his fingers from out of his tousled beard and picked up five of his usual canvases.

'Perhaps one of these...' he thought. But after all this time, he didn't hold much hope.

He made his way silently out of the back room. When it became clear that this was the only art shop for miles, Joshua had learnt to sneak. He knew every creaky floorboard, every overhanging item ready to be knocked off with a clatter. He'd even learnt how to stifle the shop bell as he pushed open the door so as not to alert the old man to his presence and draw him out of his front room to conversation.

Today it was unavoidable seeing as the old man was already out on the shop floor with the excitable tourist. The shopkeeper did not look surprised to see Joshua. Joshua suspected he had become used to the mysterious change and silent notes left on the counter in a bid to avoid banter. The old man caught his eye and nodded in his direction. The tourist, slightly more surprised with Joshua's sudden presence, hesitated for a moment before reaching out his hand with a broad smile.

'Hi there. I'm Benjamin. Didn't know you were back there!' His abrasive American tang caused his beard to itch again. Joshua grunted, ignoring the man's outstretched hand and instead pressing the money on the desk for the canvases he held stiffly under his arm.

The American frowned and lowered his arm in embarrassment. Joshua pushed past him and opened the little wooden door with a tinkle to the harsh sea air. He knew he had been rude. But really, what was politeness? Politeness was annoyance, a rock in the tides. Joshua already felt washed in the currents, without crashing against the rocks. It was the Abbey: it consumed him. He knew he was obsessed. As soon as he'd laid eyes on the grand structure, he felt the compulsion to preserve it grasp him by the throat, dragging him down to his knees.

He felt it now too, brush poised over canvas, staring into the heart of the new day. The Abbey stood grandly above him, haunting the landscape like a cliff-top graveyard. Joshua loved every moss covered stone, every sun-flecked arch and barricade. He treasured the way the light jumped and played around the Abbey walls, chasing shadows like a boy who never grew up. Here, he felt a thousand miles from the red roofed cottages of the town below.

The blank slate before him taunted him. How was he to fill its empty page with such history and wonder? Even a photograph would only fictionally represent the mere sight of the Abbey on that fairytale morning. What of the sharp twinge of sea air? The squabble of the dawn chorus? The years of love and history that still echoed around the ancient walls?

He began none-the-less, trying to force the conjoined warmth of all these things down his arms and through his paintbrush, hoping it would somehow spray all over the page. Slow walkers wound their way over the cliff-top, pausing occasionally to wonder at the beauty of the view, a smile of ignorant bliss etched onto their faces. Occasionally, an inquisitive dog would rummage through his clutter on the hilltop, sniffing at his paint tubes and brush stubs before being called back by their owners.

Joshua squatted on a low stool, his largest canvas stood before him on an easel. An explosion of reds, yellows, greens and greys lay over a palette resting on his lap. Next to his water pot was a half-eaten sandwich, laid on a bed of cling-film, cool in the shadow of a pile of canvases.

He bent over and took another bite from his luncheon meat sandwich he had made from his breakfast platter that morning. The jellied meat squelched against the roof of his mouth, escorting him back to his boyhood fishing days with his father, a meat sandwich for lunch, half going in the river for bait. It never failed.

This was his father's journey, his life he was living. A week before his death, Joshua's father had grasped him suddenly by the hand after days of drug-induced silence, rasping his regrets that he'd never painted the Abbey before slipping into his final coma.

After the funeral, Joshua had not delayed taking up his easel and taking the train up to the old town of Whitby to fulfil his father's dream. He felt like he owed his father that much. It was he, he thought, that had given Joshua his painting skill. He would sit for hours on the hearth watching his father sketch and paint, his brush dancing on the canvas like a skater on ice. Joshua was ashamed that he'd let such lustrous pride take over this final act for his father. Everyday he told himself he would leave, but his own vanity kept him there like a fish caught in the colourful nets strewn across the harbour.

Joshua put his finished painting down on the grass with a sigh. It was another failure. He couldn't understand where he was going wrong. Every turret and stone of the nave was flawless, the light impeccable. But where was the feeling? He shoved the last of his fly-ridden sandwich hungrily into his mouth and felt the sigh of lost childhood speed though his veins. He hadn't realised his hunger. He closed his eyes and allowed himself to be transported back to the riverbank with his father; his only worry being what fish would be the catch of the day.

He was awoken lightly sometime later by a child's laughter echoing off the cliff face. He felt himself slowly being pulled to the surface of consciousness. He watched dozily as the children he had heard chased each other excitedly around the ruins, hiding behind broken walls and squeezing into groves. The sun's rays warmed his face and body, filling him with joy.

Almost in a daze, Joshua set up a new, smaller canvas on the easel and began painting what he saw. The sun was high in the sky now, nuzzling deep into every nook, illuminating the whole area with unseen beauty. He opened his ears to the sounds of the laughing children and let his fingers guide the paintbrush lazily over the page.

After over an hour of painting, Joshua felt a presence behind him and snapped awake. He turned to find an old couple, excitedly admiring his work.

'Wow, that's quite a picture you've got there,' one of them drawled.

Joshua blinked and looked at the canvas before him. They were right. It was... wonderful.

He was lost for words, awaking from a three-year dream. He picked up his brush and hurriedly continued, suddenly aware of the new beauty. He had drawn in the children playing in the turrets of the Abbey, tiny blurs of innocence and glee. Joshua had always erased all locals and tourists from his page in the past as if they were mere artefacts spoiling the beauty of the picture. He had been wrong.

When he had finished, he stepped back to admire his creation and a smile cracked over his face. It was perfect. It embodied everything he had ever felt whilst sitting in the shadow of the ruins. Carefully, he picked it up, tucking it under his arm and beginning to descend the steps, every one closer to home. At the bottom, he caught his reflection in a shop window.

'First thing I'm going to do when I get back,' Joshua thought, 'is shave off this damn beard.'

No Such Thing as Angels

By Mark Branagan

The only reason I went to Whitby Abbey was I had stopped believing in God. Stupid really - like continuing to patronise funfairs when you knew the coconuts were super glued to the shies, and the sickly goldfish given away as prizes by the shooting gallery were likely to die in a couple of days.

Losing my faith was going to be big deal to my stout Anglican family from Middlesbrough who ever since I was accepted for Durham University had been telling everybody: "Did well in his exams. He's training for the priesthood too, you know." Crisis would be a word all too apt.

My three years at Durham had got me a First. I could quit now and have the world at my feet. I didn't have to spend the rest of my life writing sermons and darning my socks to stretch the dismal pay. It was just a question what to tell the parents.

I needed some thinking time. Lindisfarne - Holy Island, beckoned. My fellow candidates for the priesthood said the pubs on the island never needed to close, provided the curtains of the window facing the mainland police station stayed shut.

I could buy some souvenir Holy Island plates, take them home to mum and dad, and break the news about me and God. So it might have been had not a headline in the papers caught my eye - Whitby Abbey Now World Class Tourist Attraction.

Whitby Abbey - I hadn't been there in years. It sounded like something to tell the parents - the birthplace of modern Christianity was now just another tourist attraction. I bought a cut price coach ticket that involved breaking the journey in Middlesbrough. Unable to face the family, I killed the two hour wait in the Civic Centre, where a Polish festival was going on.

I dozed in the main concert hall during a piano recital by a lovely young Polish girl playing determinedly to rows of empty seats. I tried to remember that God was everywhere but the only other person was a tramp snoring in the back row. He stirred as the recital hit crescendo. I looked at him, but he only winked and went back to sleep.

Seagulls circled the Abbey headland. I hardly recognised the place. The last time I visited the site the ambitiously named "Visitors' Centre" was a temporary building, which rocked gently in the offshore winds. It presented a potted history of the Abbey of which I can remember only one photograph - an eerie black and white shot of the black rocks at the base of the cliffs, awash with water. Haunting in its way.

Now there were new buildings, a smart gift shop. I browsed the book spines. 'Do Angels Exist?' was one title I leafed through in mild disgust. How could an English Heritage site sell such tripe? I scanned prices, determined that the attraction was going to confirm all my new found prejudices about organised religion.

Seeing no sign of my iconic photograph, I took a short walk across the site to see how the reality of peering over the cliffs measured up to the memory. It was cold and there was hardly a soul about, it still being out of season. A fence now guarded the cliff edge - Health and Safety, of course. Standing next to it, hands deep in his overcoat pockets, was an old man. I followed the direction of his gaze and sure enough, there they were - the black rocks, swished by the waves. A couple of hundred feet below.

The old fellow nodded. There was a terrible distress in his eyes. It was a pain I'd seen before.

Don't ever let anyone kid you that would-be priests don't get around a lot. In my experience those about to feel the pinch of a dog collar around their neck feel the urge to travel more than most. Ireland had been my second home in my student days. Hitchhiking; boarding houses. I was two days away from the ferry and a stopover in Clifton proved to be fortuitous. The landlady said she had an elderly German couple leaving tomorrow who would probably give me a ride almost all the way to the boat. As far as Waterford, at least.

The hitch went fine - until the end. I had found out the German had been a U-boat survivor, who had been torpedoed twice. My inquiring and insensitive mind made the mistake of pressing for details and he broke down: "I never really had a youth." I left him weeping at a café table in Waterford - sobbing about "bloody Hitler". I apologised to his wife who told me: "Don't worry about it. It does not happen very often." But I could not forget the misery in his eyes and started thinking - How can there be a God? If people are driven to such despair? That had started 'The Doubts'. God knows what I had expected to find at Whitby Abbey to stop them.

I nodded to the old man: "Some view, eh?"

He nodded back. "Yes though not one I care to look at for too long. Though that's another story."

"I'd love to hear it."

He tightened his coat. He smiled. "Sure. But let's go somewhere warmer." He raised his eyes to the darkening heavens. "Looks like a storm's coming in."

The café was empty. I memorised the price list. When my parents moaned about my new-found worldliness I wanted to tell them exactly how much a brew and a bun cost at Whitby Abbey. I went up to the counter and ordered two teas but the old boy loudly corrected me, saying he wanted coffee. Cappuccino, preferably. I changed the order. The girl did not bat an eye lid. Cappuccino it seemed flowed as freely in Whitby these days as malt vinegar on fish suppers. I set the cups down. The old man stuck his hand out - "I'm George Stubbings, by the way."

We shook. He said: "You seem troubled."

"So do you."

He smiled mischievously. "You tell me your troubles. I'll...."

"Why did you look so miserable just now when you were staring at the black rocks?"

"Because they remind me of another set of black rocks. From Italy during the war. And in nightmares."

I was puzzled. "Nightmares about the war?"

He shook his head. "From childhood.. Terrible nightmares. I could see these black rocks in the sea. I didn't know what they were. But I knew if I went anywhere near them. Well... something terrible would happen." His cup clattered slightly on his saucer. His hands were shaking - but we had been very cold.

"Anyway. I grew up. I went to University. The nightmares stopped more or less. In time, I came to forget the black rocks. I put it down to some piece of childhood insecurity. I had my whole life ahead of me. Then came the war."

For a moment he reminded me of my old U-boat survivor. That haunted look. The saucer clattered again, ever so slightly. "In 1943 I was a lance corporal in the Eighth Army. North Africa had ended in triumph and elements of the Eighth Army were recapturing Sicily. You know everyone knows about D-Day. But in '43 the Generals were seriously thinking about launching an invasion against the coast of southern Europe rather than across the Channel.

"We invaded Italy in September, five days before the Italians surrendered. During the first landings the Italians even helped unload the landing craft. Later many of them threw away their weapons and uniforms and vanished into the countryside. The joke was we would advance into Italy with an olive branch in one hand and opera tickets in the other. To be frank, the holiday mood had blunted our fighting edge."

His expression grew dark. "It didn't last of course. We soon ran into the Germans who had replaced the faint hearted Italians and over the next eight months they fought both us and the Americans to a standstill. By May '44 a stillness had descended over the battlefields. Both sides were regrouping, getting ready for better weather - and the push on Rome.

"My platoon was billeted at a seaside resort. There was a café and the Italians there treated us very well. The previous year the town's starving civilian population had attacked the local German anti aircraft battery and the Nazis sent in combat troops to put down the rioting. The civilians viewed the Germans for what they were by then - an Army of Occupation - not the "reserves" Hitler had told them.

"We arrived at night and slept in until afternoon when we decided to explore the place. We were determined we were going to have some fun. We knew the push was coming and we weren't looking forward to it. A Nazi propaganda poster showed the road to Rome paved with the skulls of Allied soldiers and we believed it.

"Being Desert Rats by trade, we weren't exactly sad to see the back of the Aegean winter. We'd fought in snow capped mountains in torrential rain which turned the ground to mud. Summer could not be any worse. There was just the heat, the hellish hills, gyppy tummy and septic blisters to put up with.

"Most of the time the only bathing we got was a sponge bath, using our tin helmets as a bowl. A 'Whore Bath', the Yanks called it. So when we started wandering towards the beach and saw the ocean - well, we kind of all went crazy."

The old man pushed his cup away. The storm was coming closer. "Blokes were pulling their shirts off. Getting ready to kick their trousers away. Packs and kit were being dropped all along the beach."

The old man paused again. The lightning popped, the thunderclap followed a split second later. The storm was directly overhead. He flinched at the bang. "Do you know what a linked minefield is?"

"No."

He sighed. "Man's devilishly clever when it comes to war. There are two types of minefield. One is designed to slow you down. Mines explode when you step on them. But they don't contain enough explosive to kill you. Just blow a leg off or a foot. Then two other chaps have to carry you to the dressing station. The idea is it takes three people out of the battle."

I nodded. All this was doing was confirming my opinion about the evil of man and wondering why on earth God would want to create him in His own image. More thunderclaps burst and he almost cringed. "A linked minefield is different. It is designed to eliminate an entire unit at a single stroke. When one soldier steps on a mine - the whole field explodes. These aren't the little ones that just blow a foot off. These are spring mounted so they shoot out the ground and explode in mid air and spray shrapnel everywhere."

The storm rattled the windows. The door banged as visitors came in to escape the downpour. "I would have died that day. Then I glanced ahead and saw the black rocks. I could see them clearly, sticking out of the water, a couple of hundred yards off shore. They were exactly the same as the rocks from my nightmares.

"I stopped in my tracks. I just stood there while the rest of them ran on. Then a couple of minutes later…."

I knew not to say anything - I think that was the priest in me. I just sat and waited for him to go on.

"Everyone was killed including the radio operator whose set had been blown to bits. I knew I had to get back to the town and get a message to Brigade HQ about what had happened. So I went back to the café because they had a phone."

The storm was receding now. All around us people were finishing their tea, and getting ready to go back to their sight seeing. The old boy looked me hard in the eyes. "Now we come to the really strange part.

"When I explained what had happened the café owner told me the funny thing about those black rocks was they only appear once every 30 odd years. When there has been a very unusually low tide. So what do you make of that?"

"I don't know."

"No. Neither do I. All I know is that I never had another nightmare about the black rocks again." The warmth of the café seemed to have crept up on us. He unbuttoned his coat.

I saw the dog collar.

"You're a priest?"

"Retired. But they still let you wear the collar. And strictly speaking I am still the Reverend Stubbings." He winked. "And I get to deliver the odd sermon."

After the war he had returned to England and joined the church, who gave him a living down South.

So what brought him to Whitby?

"I come here every year for my holidays. That's the trouble with seeing active service overseas. It does blunt your enthusiasm for foreign travel. I still like Italian coffee though. Could you fetch me another one? I'll pay."

I went to the counter. When I returned the chair was empty. I turned back to the counter and asked the girl. "What happened to the priest who was sitting with me?"

She looked blank. "Sorry. I didn't see you come in with anyone."

I could go on, tell you how I searched for that man and found no sign. But then I risk you getting bored.

A cough reminds me where I am. Not at Whitby Abbey ten years ago, but here in my church delivering my Sunday sermon.

The punch line did not rock them in the pews, the way it used to do.

My regular congregation had heard the tale on many a Remembrance Sunday to the point I once overheard my church warden complain to the organist: "The vicar hasn't just milked that story. He wants cheese out of it as well."

But my sermon never mentioned that while attending a church conference down south years later I did try to look the old boy up. He was long dead. His family was delighted I remembered him. The trouble was on the date my diary has us meeting at Whitby Abbey they were just as clear that he was on his deathbed hundreds of miles away at their local hospital.

What does it all mean? I don't know. Save to say I keep that book on Angels close, and reach for it every time I hear of a stranger, or strangers, who gives someone a helping hand - then vanish as quickly as they appeared. Because one thing I have learned about Angels - they're everywhere.

Ascension Day at St Hilda's

By David Craggs

14th October 1942

The German U-boat, U-115, captained by Heinrich Heckman, came up to periscope depth, its mission to observe the British North Sea fishing fleet. A thick mist, known locally as a sea fret, had rolled in from the sea and had already enveloped the coast. The captain needed a sighting, possibly Flamborough lighthouse or maybe even the ruined St Hilda's Abbey at Whitby. He had seen the Abbey many times before and used it as one of several reference points along the east coast.

As often happens with sea frets they momentarily clear in patches, and this happened allowing Heinrich to pinpoint his exact position. The sun had already set and the outline of the ancient ruin stood out against the already reddening sky. The U-115 was just three miles north east of the fishing town of Whitby.

Heinrich zoomed in on the harbour entrance and through the mist started to count the fishing boats as they approached after a day's fishing. As the submarine moved slowly forwards, driven by its silent electric motors, the sound operator found the 'mush' coming through his headphones confusing as the fishing boats manoeuvred into position to enter the narrow opening.

But, unknown to him, because its engines' sounds were being masked, the Royal Navy Destroyer, Magpie, having earlier detected the U-boat and trailed it at a distance, was about to strike. The Destroyer's sharp-eyed lookout had spotted the periscope in the thinning mist and its captain, Commander Bill Travers, decided to ram the submerged craft while it was at periscope depth.

With frightening speed the Destroyer moved in and the grinding of steel indicated that it had struck the U-boat amidships. Rising bubbles, followed by oil floating on the surface, confirmed a 'hit'.

As the Destroyer moved slowly away, Bill Travers glanced up at the ruined Abbey and observed a column of coloured light that appeared to be rising from its highest pinnacle. He saw it arc over and slowly continue to a point out at sea, just off the coast. A rainbow of course. The absence of sun and rain didn't occur to him.

Heinrich Heckman was incredibly lucky. As seawater rushed through the gaping hole, instantly drowning his crew, he found himself trapped in a rapidly shrinking pocket of air, with the conning tower hatch immediately above his head. He knew that there was only one way out of his predicament - as soon as the air pocket shrank to nothing he should be able to turn the wheel that tightly locked the hatch, ease up the cover and pass through it and up to the surface. It was a procedure that he had practised at the Kiel Training School back home.

One thing was in Heinrich's favour - the U-115 had settled on the seabed only twenty feet below the surface. Providing he could release and lift the hatch he would be able to make his escape, but he would only get one chance to do so. One thing was certain, he couldn't afford to panic.

Heinrich Heckman came to the surface like a cork. But was he any better off? The water was intensely cold and he was immersed in a sea fret. How long could he survive? A few minutes at the most.

Heinrich was not a religious man but, bearing in mind his hopeless predicament, he decided to pray, just in case there was someone 'up there' willing to lend him a hand. Maybe that 'someone' would direct one of the fishing boats towards him so that he could be rescued and treated as a prisoner-of-war.

Once again the fret cleared, but this time in a narrow 'channel' allowing Heinrich a glimpse of the ruined Abbey, still silhouetted against the now darkening sky. As he rose gently on the slight swell, his eyes focussed on the remnants of the once great building, he started to philosophise with his already confused mind - why, over the centuries, had people of all nations built such majestic buildings if there was no God to worship? It just didn't make sense.

Suddenly, he became aware of a faint glow, appearing to emanate upwards from the highest point of the ruined Abbey. The glow then seemed to intensify, displaying all the colours of the rainbow, and appeared to be slowly moving towards him. In a matter of seconds he found himself at one end of a giant multi-coloured arc of light, the other end being the Abbey itself. Was he dreaming it all? In his confused state he didn't honestly know, but suspected that he was. That was the way intense cold got to you just before you passed into unconsciousness, the final stage before death itself. The last sensation he could remember was being gently lifted by some invisible force. Seconds later he regained consciousness to find himself lying on a grassed area just in front of the Abbey itself. How he'd got there, he'd no idea.

But what to do next? That was the pressing question that now faced him. He was dripping wet and hypothermia was already insidiously creeping through his body. He had to move.

He chose to head inland and soon came to a main road, then a railway line. Across the line he could just make out a farm through the slowly dispersing sea fret. A farm meant barns, straw and warmth.

Just as he was about to cross the large yard, the farmhouse door opened and Police Constable Whitaker, who had been investigating a case of sheep rustling, emerged and headed for his bicycle that was leaning against the wall. He spotted Heinrich and shouted across: "Eh, you...identify yourself."

Heinrich's command of the English language was quite good, thanks to his crash course at the Kiel Training School. Wet and intensely cold, and realising that the game was up, he shouted: "Heinrich Heckman...Deutsch...I demand treatment under the Geneva Convention."

Constable Whitaker smiled and called back through the still open door. "Jake...better bring your shotgun...and make sure it's loaded...we've got ourselves a Gerry."

Heinrich then explained to the Constable how he had managed to escape from his stricken U-boat and had somehow been plucked from the sea and transferred to the cliff top close to the Abbey. The Constable of course, didn't believe a word. The only way to get from the beach to the cliff top was to climb a couple of hundred steps. But would the German have had the energy to make the climb, even if he'd managed to work out the route? The Constable doubted it, and yet he apparently had.

And so Heinrich Heckman was arrested and, as a prisoner-of-war, spent the next three years in a camp just outside York. Here he worked on the land and took the opportunity to learn English until he was fluent in the language. In 1945 he was repatriated to his homeland.

Bill Travers also survived the war and returned to his former job as a manager with the West Riding Building Society. But the love of the east coast and the deteriorating health of both himself and his wife, led them to move to the tiny village of Flamborough. The setting was idyllic and it wasn't long before their two young grandchildren, Becky and Joel, started to make regular visits, often staying for long periods during the school holidays. Bill had never told his grandchildren about the sinking of the U-115. It was an act in the past that he wasn't particularly proud of, but in wartime 'one did what one had to do'. The subject had occasionally come up in conversation between himself and his son, David, Becky and Joel's father, so they did know something about the incident.

14th October 2002

At breakfast one morning, which just happened to be the sixtieth anniversary of the incident, Joel suddenly asked: "Grandad...take us to Whitby and show us where you sank the German U-boat."

Without giving it a moment's thought, his grandad briefly replied: "Certainly not, Joel." He wasn't prepared to explain the reason why.

Then it occurred to him. Would going to the site, maybe even saying a prayer for the crew who had died so horribly there, make his disturbed mind feel a little easier?

He decided there and then to make the visit: "On second thoughts, Joel, yes we'll go...both you and your sister be ready to leave in half an hour."

He looked at his wife and she nodded approvingly, for she knew better that anyone how the incident had preyed on her husband's mind over the years.

And so an eighty year old Bill Travers, along with his wife and grandchildren commenced the journey to Whitby. Just before midday he parked his car on the large car park close to the railway station. Within a few minutes the small group of two elderly grandparents and two young grandchildren was crossing the swing bridge that spanned the River Esk and heading for the one hundred and ninety-nine steps that would take them up to the Abbey and the cliff top.

Heinrich Heckman, a year younger at seventy-nine, had been thinking along the same lines. Although his amazing escape from the stricken U-boat and his subsequent unexplained 'transfer' to the cliff top, had taken place many years ago, every day he thought about the incident. Before leaving this Earth he had to return to the spot where it had all taken place and try to make sense of what had actually happened. And so, knowing that the following day would be the 14th of October 2002, the sixtieth anniversary of the incident, he and his daughter, Helga, left their home city of Dusseldorf and headed for the Dutch port of Rotterdam. The overnight ferry would allow them to sleep and when they disembarked at Hull they would be fresh for their journey north to Whitby.

After parking, also by the railway station, Heinrich and Helga headed across the river and in the general direct of the Abbey, which they could see a couple of hundred feet above them. There must be some steps somewhere. A few minutes later they found them and started the long laborious climb. As Heinrich slowly ascended he tried to think back sixty years. Did he actually climb all these steps? No, definitely not. So how did he find himself on a grass verge in front of the Abbey when he regained consciousness?

After he and his daughter reached the last step both made their way towards the cliff top. Heinrich wanted to see the approximate spot where the U-115 had gone down. A casual observer, also on the cliff top, would have seen two groups - one of two elderly people and two young children, the other of an elderly man and a younger woman, possibly his daughter.

As if previously rehearsed, the two elderly men suddenly moved forward, away from the others and were barely a yard apart when they stopped five yards from the cliff edge.

Bill Travers spoke first: "Sea's very calm today."

Heinrich replied: "Yes it is...Unusual as we move into the winter months."

Bill immediately detected an accent in the man's voice: "You sound a long way from home."

"Yes...Dusseldorf...Germany." Without thinking, Heinrich then added: "I know these waters well...or did sixty years ago."

Bill immediately picked up on the comment. How could a German have been in these waters sixty years ago...unless he'd been on a U-boat or had bailed out over the North Sea from a doomed German aircraft. He decided to do a little probing: "Military man, then...last war?"

"Yes...U-boat captain."

This was all becoming too much of a coincidence for Bill. He had to know more: "Very dangerous...but you obviously survived."

"Yes, I did...but unfortunately my boat and crew didn't...they're down there." He pointed to a spot out in the bay: "I managed to escape through one of the hatches."

Bill now knew exactly who the man was for over the years he had collected memorabilia about the U-boats and this included a letter from the German War Archives which stated that the U-115 had been lost off the Yorkshire Coast on the 14th of October 1942. He was speaking to its captain, Heinrich Heckman. This placed him in a very difficult position - should he reveal his own identity, or should he keep that to himself?

He decided to do the former. It could do no harm. Besides, the incident had happened sixty years ago: "I was also in the area at the time, captain of a British Destroyer…we spotted a U-boat, trailed her and eventually rammed her." He paused, then apologetically added: "It must unfortunately have been the U-115…yours."

Heinrich nodded, but remained silent for there was nothing to say - certainly no point in ranting and raving in an accusing way. He then decided to tell his former adversary of his unexplained rescue, hoping that both could in some way work out what had actually happened.

But all Bill could do was to add that he too had seen the column of light directly above the Abbey, and had whispered a prayer at the time, hoping that at least some of the crew had managed to escape from the U-boat.

Heinrich then turned and faced the ruined Abbey: "Would you care to walk with me…perhaps even join me in a small prayer to the sailors who were lost on that day?"

"Yes…I would love to."

Both men stopped a few yards from the Abbey, bowed their heads then lifted their eyes to the highest point of the ruin and began to observe a column of multi-coloured light appearing to emanate from the pinnacle. It then arced over, split into two and slowly descended to where they were standing, eventually enveloping both men.

Both suddenly felt a tugging, as if some force was trying to lift them off their feet. Then it stopped. The light slowly retreated, finally disappearing into the pinnacle from where it had originally emanated. It was as if some superior force, God maybe, had decided that it was Ascension Day for them, and had then decided against it. Heinrich now knew what had happened on that day sixty years earlier. It too had been an Ascension Day for him, but only for the short journey to the top of the cliff. On two occasions God had decided to 'take him', then, for his own good reason had decided against it. When would the third and possibly the final time come, he wondered?

And what of the two men's relatives? What did they see? As it happened, nothing, for they had been fascinated by the antics of a couple of seal cubs out in the bay and had therefore been facing the wrong way. Little did they know just how close they'd been to losing their loved ones to a place much, much higher than St Hilda's Abbey at Whitby.

Broken Wings

By K. M. Lockwood

Dear Molly,

Hoping I find you and Ron well. Delighted with the paper - the cameo of Landry House is very tasteful against the cream. It is so important to attract the right sort of guest.

Such nice people recently – the Harrisons left a really kind comment in the guest book. It's all in the detail, like those toiletry baskets. They had the Lavender Bedroom – wasn't it over your way we found that lace tissue-box cover?

You know how much I enjoy a little sit in the Abbey? Well, the benches have gone 'for essential maintenance'. What sort of maintenance does a bench need, for goodness' sake? I suppose they want them varnished for the trippers at Easter.

Actually, I tell a lie. There is <u>one</u> bench left. What use is that? You never know who you might have to share it with. Anyway, I must go – the Butlers of Slough will here any moment wanting a nice pot of tea.

All my love,

Betty

Hi Sis,

Thought I'd give you an update about life in Whitby. I've found a brilliant stall in the market – Decadence – they'll take my cobweb chains on a sale-or-return basis. I'm getting quite adept at twisting wire into kooky shapes.

Tell Dad I'm truly grateful for the old drill. Does he like his remodelled surgery? I guess it's all glass and chrome (Yuk!) There's this amazing smell of bog when I'm drilling the jet – gloriously melancholy. Can't see him putting up with it – but Freyja doesn't seem to mind. The only smell she notices is fish.

Went up to the Abbey at sunset – all but one of the seats had gone. At least they'd left my favourite: the one with supports like branches covered in layer after layer of paint. I feel so close to Tobias there in the beautiful morbid twilight, surrounded by Gothic arches. I miss him so much.

If Auntie Gwen has got over my name change, do you think she'll come to the handfasting? Keep writing to me.

Blessed be,

Lucrece

Dear Molly,

Thank you for your lovely letter. Gilbert's busy with his blessed pigeons – keeps him out from under my feet. Mustn't grumble – been busy recently which is just as well seeing as Gilbert's pension isn't what it was.

Truth told I'm not so quick up those 199 steps now, but it is worth it. There's such peace up in the Abbey, and warmth off the sandstone. It glows in the evening light, I'm sure of it. Warms these old bones, I can tell you.

Still only one bench where I like to sit. This strange looking lass goes there regularly. She'd be about our Ellen's age, I think - hard to say with all that make-up on. Looks like Morticia out of The Munsters – or was it The Addams Family? It can't do her hair much good all that dye, either. Takes all sorts.

Must bob down to Botham's for some curd tarts before they shut.

Lots of love,

Betty

Hey Jude (you know I only say that to annoy)

No wonder I love the Abbey – I've just found out it's on a ley line with Lilla Cross and Foster Howe! We always knew it was a special place. The Celts call it a 'thin place' - I feel the spirit of the place soaked into the very stones of the ruins.

So much to paint: hidden faces, cadaverous shadows, and damaged traceries. Tobias will be proud of me – I feel so inspired.

I'm not the only frequenter of the Abbey: an old dear comes too. We share the lone bench – just. She sits in her pink outfits at one end, as far from me as possible. It's as though she believes I'll rub off like charcoal!

You have to hand it to her; she even wears pink rubber gloves to pick up rubbish on the headland. Can't fault that.

Must go, Freyja's mewing for her tea.

Blessed be,

Lucrece

Dear Molly,

We are all well, thank you. A bit quieter here – I even had time to go to a jumble sale yesterday. I found a peachy vanity set: cut glass in perfect condition. Makes you wonder why anyone would throw out something so tasteful. All's well that ends well, though. It looks lovely in the Apricot Bedroom –the one with a grand view of the Abbey when it's lit up at night. That Halloween girl was there – I bet she lives off benefits. Looks like she could do with a good feed. I can't see why a young woman wants to swathe herself up in black. I love to get back into my Spring pastels.

Fair's fair, mind you. I saw her the other day, long skirts, witchy boots and all, helping this young mum with her buggy up Church Lane. Quite why it's called a lane beats me. Only an idiot with one of those satellite navigation gizmos would try to drive up there, it's that steep. Kills the back of my calves – more suited to donkeys than people.

Anyway, a bit of a breeze has got up so I'll sign off before this ends up in the North Sea!

Love,

Betty

PS Gilbert asked how Ron's pond is coming on.

Greetings, Sis,

I wish you could see the Abbey right now – bone white traceries against a stormy purple sky. Francis Ford Coppola couldn't do better. I love it in the winter with the ice forming on the monks' pond – but long summer evenings can be ethereal too. Twilight really <u>is</u> longer in the North.

I saw 'The Pink Lady' at a rummage sale. Even her umbrella matched – not my style, but you have to admire the consistency. I found an old edition of Keats there. Can you believe it that there were still dried pressed flowers inside? So pale and fragile – the wings of some delicate plant spirit. My webs and paintings are selling well at Decadence – need to finish some more before Tobias arrives.

Blessed be,

Lucrece

Dear Molly,

Such excitement here! There I am, sitting on the Abbey bench, enjoying the last of the sunshine when this swan crash-lands on the grass. It must have caught a wing on the new television mast. Careered through the open nave and fell at our feet, poor thing. Just as well the Abbey's a ruin or it would have hit the roof, literally.

Well, you can't judge a book by its cover. That girl in black – Lucrece (what sort of a name is that?) whipped off her black stole when I explained what to do. Between us we had it soothed and pinioned in no time.

Her sweetheart, Toby, drove us all the way to the Swan Rescue place near York. He wears a top hat in broad daylight, I ask you! Gilbert had to do the guests' tea and cakes – I hope they didn't get food poisoning. I'll keep you informed about the swan's progress, anyway.

Love as always,

Betty

Greetings Judikins,

I don't suppose you know how to clean swan's blood out of a bombazine shoulder cape? Perhaps Carri at Dark Angel might. Betty (The Lady-in-Pink) and I used mine to pacify an injured swan.

Its twisted flight was so eerie and beautiful among the broken columns of the Abbey. Soft and white on the ground it lay like melting snow. Then it started writhing and hissing in pain. Talk about brave – Betty just leapt into action. Those things can break your arm, you know. She was so calm!

Tobias drove us to a Swan Sanctuary in Brandsby. Apparently <u>she</u> will take four to six weeks to heal. I've named her 'Björk' after the honking noise she makes and that dress! I would be thrilled if 'Björk' were free for the ceremony.

Blessed be,

Lucrece

PS There was this amazing pair of black swans with red beaks and eyes at the Sanctuary. How deliciously sinister would they look on a cake for the handfasting?

Greetings, Jude,

A brief missive today: I couldn't keep this to myself. I had a chat with Betty – the lady on the bench. We both wondered how 'Björk' was getting on. I mentioned my black swan idea. Turns out Betty's hobby is cake decorating! She is happy to give it a go, though I had to explain what a handfasting is.

Blessed be,

Lucrece

Dear Molly,

Just a quick update - our swan is doing fine - should be fit to fly by mid-June. Toby, her fiancé, offered to run me and Lucrece (the witchy girl on the bench) over to York. Wasn't that sweet of him? But I said the 'phone was good enough.

I've been invited to their 'handfasting' – a kind of pagan wedding, apparently. I must be daft but I said I'd decorate their cake. She wants black swans on it! They'd better not let any children eat the icing or they'll be climbing the walls.

Lots of love,

Betty

PS Glad she didn't ask for the Abbey!

Darling Judikins,

I'm writing this because my jaw's too stiff and sore to speak to you on the phone. You know a lot of this already but I need something to do, stuck in hospital. Thank you for coming to see your battered big sis – you must've driven non-stop. I need to write it all down – cathartic, I suppose.

I went up to the Abbey, usual time, usual bench. The new benches had arrived; all gleaming and varnished – Dad would approve.

I'll spare you the boring details of what the pond-life looked like – I told it all to the police anyway. I remember thinking what a poor quality tattoo one of them had.

They'd been there a while, going by the cans, ring-pulls and fag-ends lying about. I suppose I'd got the habit from Betty – I started picking up their litter. It wasn't far to put it in the bin. I can't recall a lot more. I know "Who do you fink you are?", "dirty mosher" and a lot of effing and blinding came into it. Estuary English - definitely not from round here.

Looking at the state of his duster coat, Tobias took most of the kicks before Betty turned up. He'd only brought my sketch book I'd left behind.

I used to chuckle at Betty's colour co-ordinated umbrella – not any more. She was a pastel-pink avenging angel. I'm sure the Abbey must have seen worse violence with the Vikings – but none so colourful! Seriously, though, it's good to think those skinhead creeps are just nothings in the flow of history.

All praise to the Goddess – I've nothing more than bruises really. It could have been so much worse.

I'm rather tired now.

Blessed be,

Lucrece

P.S. Wouldn't Tobias look rather elegant with a silver-topped cane to help him hobble around?

Dear Molly

Well, it's not every day you get to be a bit of a heroine. I just had to write and dwell on my moment of glory. It just isn't the same relaying it on the 'phone with Ken ear-wigging.

Bless her, that poor girl was only picking up rubbish. What right had those thugs to set on her? Toby was brave; he must've been black and blue from the kicking they gave him. I had to laugh – he seemed more upset about his top hat being ruined than his leg broken.

I didn't do much really – they just ran away like the cowards they are. My trusty old brolly must have hurt a bit. It was such a good idea to have it strengthened like Queen Mary's.

I'm just glad they weren't locals. Makes it more difficult for the police, I expect, but we don't have that sort of moron here. Must close - have to feed 'Freyja' - their cat.

Love,

Betty

Dear Auntie Gwen,

I hope you're mending well after your hip operation: I missed you at the ceremony. I'm fine, thanks. All my bruises have gone – which was almost a shame - some of the colours were so weird. I know; not your style.

Midsummer's Day came round so fast. It truly was a blessed time: I know you were there in spirit. The panne velvet cloak Judy found was ideal – it's pretty chilly on the East Cliff at sunrise, and Betty's cake was brilliant.

You've probably seen Dad's photos a thousand times already but I've enclosed a 'special' - a copy of the one I've put in the frame you sent. Thanks – you know how much I love Art Nouveau. Gilbert (Betty's husband) took the picture in the Abbey later.

Can you believe the swan turning up at that exact moment? Stretching out her exquisite wings to show us they were mended. Look at the light streaming through the arch behind. The guidebooks say it's St. Hilda in her shroud, but I prefer to believe it's the Goddess in her sacred mother aspect. We pagans were there first!

Whatever you think, it's a lovely shot. So kind of the Sanctuary to set 'Björk' free on the 21st. I know they were bringing her back to the Esk anyway – but the timing was inspired.

Thanks again for the frame and I hope you feel better soon.

Your loving niece,

Lucy (Lucrece)

Dear Molly,

The 'handfasting' went well, apparently – daybreak's far too early for me! But there was a nice do after. Gilbert took some snaps in the Abbey. Please find enclosed some of his 'masterpieces.' Took him a while to work out how to use his scanner/printer thingy, but there are one or two good ones.

Lucrece looked lovely – all brides do – if a bit odd. Not what I'd want for my daughter. What a surprise, her sister Judith and their father, Ian, are nice, perfectly normal people. I thought one on 'our' bench for or old times' sake would be nice. That lad of hers was thrilled with the top hat. They insisted on paying me handsomely for my cake. Must say I was pleased with how it turned out: the lustre effect really set off the black plumage.

The swan turning up was a big surprise. Whether it was 'our' one or not I can't tell, I'm no expert. But its wings did look heavenly with the Abbey as a back-drop. I think Abbess Hilda would approve – she always comes across as a motherly sort – and it certainly looks like she does in the one with the sun through the arches, doesn't it?

Anyway, no rest for the wicked – the schools break up soon and we've lots of guests booked in.

Love to you and Ron,

Betty

Dear Mrs.Nesbitt,

Thank you so much for Tobias's top hat. My father and sister really enjoyed their stay with you - 'home from home'. We were delighted with the cake too. I hope to see you up at the Abbey again soon.

Yours sincerely,

Lucy Holmwood (Lucrece)

The Ghost of Whitby Abbey

By Sarah Morton

The rough, sea-weathered wind ripped through the air, tearing at the girl's hair, intent on ruining the careful, meticulously placed curls and ribbons, so that dark bedraggled twists fell around her face. Her attire was neither time nor place appropriate, a full-skirted, flowing creation of lace and beads, which had once been white, and had once been breathtaking.

She stood amongst the Whitby Abbey ruins, the moonlight casting a flowered shadow on the dark grass as it gleamed through the old brickwork, the tall empty windows watching her with dead eyes. How had she come to be here? And why?

She stood still for a moment, gazing up at the brickwork as if seeing a ghost. It wasn't supposed to be like this, she knew that for certain, but she couldn't remember what it was supposed to be like either.

The sea wind pulled at her hair again, and she turned her head, looking for something, something that she had lost or forgotten. Something that she had to find. It wasn't supposed to be like this, she knew that.

She turned slowly, looking around her as if the very air might hold the answers she looked for, as if the taste of the sea breeze might return him to her.

Him? Was there a him? Was he what had been lost?

But as soon as the word left her tongue it was gone again, pulled away by forces she could not hope to understand.

A soft whisper stilled her, and she tried to listen. Tried to hear what this disembodied voice was softly crooning, but it was too faint, too fair, too soft to hear; thrust away from her by the hiss and crash of the waves against the cliffs below.

She heard another sound, louder this time. Was someone here? Had someone followed her?

Panic rising in her throat she began to move, picking up her once beautiful skirts and turning towards the Abbey, she would be sheltered there, the Abbey always protected the lost and innocent.

Ducking her head as she turned into the wind, she stilled as a sudden flash of lightning lit up the sky, closely followed by a rolling, grumbling, angry thunder call.

Had she imagined it? The figure among the old arches? Cast in shadow, but silhouetted by the strike of light that had shot from the sky? Was she running towards her enemy?

She dropped her skirts and looked around her again, waiting to see if she would see him again, feeling a fear in her chest that would not abate.

She pushed her stray curls away from her eyes as the first drop of rain touched her skin, raising her face to the sky as if God himself would see her and guide her, the spots of rain hitting her forehead like a natural baptism. The rain was a message that God was with her, and it gave her the strength to go on.

Lifting her skirts again, she moved over the rougher ground, trying to walk carefully so as not to injure herself where the ground was uneven, the slick stones hard beneath her slippered feet.

A second bolt of lightning flashed, illuminating the sky and making the Abbey's outline burn black against the sky, announcing its authority clearly, even though there was nobody but her to argue.

She had seen the man. She knew he was there, and he must know that she was there also. Did he mean her harm?

But then another thought came to her. She had lost something, forgotten something. Was it possible that he was what she was supposed to find? Or was he the one who had taken it from her? Stolen it away while she wasn't looking.

She moved closer to the Abbey, the weight of her wet skirts slowing her now. How was she to know who he was, and what he wanted with her? Was it safe to approach him?

She walked around the Abbey, leaving a wide stretch of ground between them in case he tried to come after her, looking for a movement or shadow that would give him away, but there was none. Nothing to give him away, no small sign that would let her know where he was.

How long had he been watching her? How long had he been following her?

She approached the ruins from the side now, hoping to spot him before he spotted her, wanting a brief sojourn from the assault of the wind and the rain, her legs hurting from climbing the hilly slope.

Should she be afraid of him, this man who watched her from the shadows? Did he mean to harm her?

The thunder rumbled threateningly around her and she dropped her skirts to allow her hands the freedom to brush her now tangled curls from her face, her ribbons long lost to the biting hands of the wind.

And then he was there, standing in front of her as if he had always been there, long dark hair pulled back from his face, his formal clothes wet and muddied.

"Take my hand!" he called, offering it out to her, his words sounding distorted, as if a barrier somehow existed between them. But she didn't know him, didn't recognise him, and could not be alone in this place with him with no means of protecting herself, no means of knowing what he intended to do with her.

She shook her head, stepping backwards as one hand held her curls while the other plucked at her skirts. She couldn't be here, she didn't recognise the man, so he was not the one she had lost, not the one she was looking for.

Turning she began to run, holding her skirts to stop them from tangling with her feet as her slippered soles ran across the moonlight coated ground, her fear and fright making her feet light over ground that she would once have stumbled across, rain running down her face like tears and dripping down onto her gown as she ran.

She looked back to find him following her, awkward over the terrain that she had somehow flown over, her feet as light as a cat's.

And then she was falling, her surprised breath escaping from her mouth with a strangled cry as she tumbled, her skin abraised and broken against the slippery ground, her mouth and nose filling with murky water as she found herself submerged.

The pond. She had fallen into the pond, as she had lost her way in the darkness.

Desperately she thrashed, trying to bring her head above the water to take the breath of air that she needed. But she was caught, the wet fabric of her dress pulling her under as she struggled, and the one remaining ribbon in her hair pulled down by a ghostly hand from the depths.

She heard the man calling to her, his cries muffled by the water, knowing that he would never get to her before the water claimed her, realising that he had been running after her to stop her from falling, to stop her from drowning, but he would never make it in time now, the light feet that she thought had been saving her proving to be her downfall.

She made one last attempt to pull herself free before her poor oxygen starved brain took over, drawing the murky water that surrounded her into her lungs.

And then it was over, and she was able to see herself, spoiled white dress floating out into the water, trails of dark curls, almost too dark to see amongst the dark water, tiny battered slippers still poking out at the water's edge.

The man came closer, too late to help, too late to intervene, and he tried to pull her cold, limp body from the water, spoiling his trousers further as he waded in to detach her from the thing that had kept her under, pulling her back to the water's edge where he cradled her.

Was he the one that she had lost? The one she had been looking for?

But then as he held her it came back to her. He was not the one who was lost, she was. Lost in the cold and the wind and the rain, bound eternally to make the same mistakes.

Slowly the storm thundered to a close, and the ruffled waters stilled, the scene at the water's edge slowly fading with the wind, until all that was left was an echo, a hollow cry of a long forgotten misadventure, forever returning to the scene when the weather was stormy and the moon full.

No one knew where she came from, where she was going to, or how she had got there. But it was always the same, the same lost girl, for a girl was all she was, barely sixteen, and the same shadowy figure calling out to her, trying resolutely again and again to save her, and always ending up alone on the edge of the pond, her spirit slipping away from him as he cradled her in his arms.

Eternally he waited for her among the ruins of the once great Abbey, hoping that the next time he would get it right, that he would save her, all the while knowing that it could never happen, that she would never be saved. Endlessly roaming the remains of the beautiful Abbey that had once made her feel safe, and had once been the scene of her demise. The ghost of Whitby Abbey.

A Pile of Old Rubble

By B.B. Bromley

He's becoming an old grump, thought Evelyn, taking a sideways peek at Ted. They were sitting in the sun opposite the East Cliff of Whitby with its imposing Abbey on the top. Yet Ted was slumped like a sack of wet sand. Something about his shoe laces held him mesmerised though Evelyn couldn't figure out what.

This decline into negative thinking and dreary behaviour was what most tried Evelyn's patience; after all, Ted was alive and healthy wasn't he? As he turned his saggy features toward her, Evelyn was reminded of a bloodhound once used to advertise dog food – what had been its name? Harry…? No… Henry: that was it.

"What time did the driver say we could go back?" he asked wearily.

"Ted!" Evelyn snapped. "We've only been here an hour."

"Remember it wasn't me that suggested we come in the first place."

"That may be true but let's make the most of it now we are here? We haven't had a day out for ages and look how lucky we're being with the weather."

"There's a rain cloud on the horizon."

"It's blowing away," said Evelyn knowing how Sisyphus felt rolling that stone up the hill. Lightening Ted's mood was impossible. "See the Abbey on the opposite cliff, Ted?" she tried, nodding toward it. "It's meant to be lovely up there. We could take a look once we get our breath back…maybe enjoy a cream tea?"

"Looks like an old pile of rubble to me," said Ted, sneering. Yet Evelyn knew the magnificent ruins were admired by many for their colourful history and painterly perspectives. "Bound to be overrated," he went on. "Worse still, they're over there."

"But the walk around the harbour will be lovely; it won't take us long and the view from the East Cliff is meant to be quite something."

"Anyway," Ted mumbled, distracted. "Why do you carp on about cream teas so? Your doctor's warned you about your cholesterol. Why not listen for once?"

You just don't get it do you, thought Evelyn. My silly old husband of forty-five years has forgotten how to live.

When the dirty looking cloud reached the harbour and a light rain began, Ted tutted in annoyance. "See, woman, told you it was coming toward us, not going away. Where do you suppose we can take shelter?"

"I say in those nice gift shops we passed."

"Hate shopping, you know that. Damn waste of time. That place over there looks comfortable; think I may wait in there while you browse or whatever you call it. And try not to spend all our money."

Following Ted's gaze, Evelyn was taken by surprise. He was staring at a rhubarb-and-custard striped construction reminding her of a small circus tent. A sign placed at the entrance said:

Madame Rominska

Hypnotist, Fortune Teller, Psychic Counsellor

Find your path and make your dreams come true…

Had he completely lost his marbles? Ted was the most cynical man Evelyn had ever met – he'd even put her off acupuncture once, rudely dismissing it as needlework for unemployed Chinese. But what Evelyn had missed earlier was the sight of Madame Rominska dashing out to buy a cup of tea. Like a cormorant watching a fish, Ted had witnessed the fortune teller's splendid curves and noted that Whitby had its attractions after all. Of course, he had no interest in such jiggery-pokery but if he had to sit and listen to claptrap for half an hour at least the view would be easy on the eye.

"Let's meet back here on the hour," he told her, more assertively than he had for some time.

When she'd finished browsing, as Ted called it, Evelyn made her way back to the harbour wall. Their bench was now occupied by a passionate young couple intent, it seemed, on retrieving lost objects from behind one another's ears. We felt like that once, thought Evelyn, sighing. It was too late for them now, what with Ted perched on some distant crag where he could only look down on others to harp and criticise. What had he said to her last Sunday when she couldn't find the roasting tin? "You're a mess, woman; you no longer know your backside from your elbow and that must be difficult these days as you've got double the backside." His words were sharp as broken glass yet he never knew how hurtful he could be.

But when Ted emerged from the hypnotist's tent, there was something very different about him. He appeared taller for a start; his chest broader. What's happened to him, thought Evelyn, peering more closely. It was Ted all right but more the Ted of yesteryear with his upright bearing and Gregory Peck cheek bones. His new deportment had given the effect of a face lift, replacing the bloodhound with an aging but well preserved Afghan. Evelyn experienced a flutter of longing, like a whiff of memory from her distant past. Once, her husband had made her feel quite peculiar as if she'd been filled with many volts of electricity. But with his shoulders back, Ted was again an imposing figure, like the naval officer of his early career. How handsome he had been in those days, all shiny buttons and an endearing penchant for spontaneous cuddles, especially after periods at sea.

Striding toward her, Ted beamed; his recently fitted dentures Hollywood-white against his pottering-about-in-the-garden tan. The sight of him smiling was a bit of a shock but not an unpleasant one. "Sorry I've kept you waiting, E; how do you fancy that walk up to the Abbey now? We'll have tea and a bun: my treat."

Evelyn could only smile hesitantly. Was this some sort of trick? Increasing her step to keep up with him, she took another sideways look. This time it was in amazement, not exasperation. Turning towards her, he smiled; ocean-tinted eyes refilled with their original depth and vision. Here was a man comfortable with the world. One, she could see, who admired and appreciated it. One who wanted to relish his last years on this planet with his wife beside him.

"So what did you make of the hypnotist?" asked Evelyn, catching two women giving Ted an admiring look.

"Not much to it," answered Ted with a shrug. "She asked what I would most like in the entire world - which I had to write down and secrete upon my person - and then I think I fell asleep."

"I see," said Evelyn though she didn't really see at all. But who was to argue if this was the result?

Reaching the bottom of the 199 steps that climb steeply to the Abbey, Ted turned to Evelyn and offered her his arm like the perfect gentleman. "Was thinking, E... I wouldn't mind being called Edward again. Can't remember why we shortened my name to Ted but I'm much more of an 'Edward'- don't you think?"

"You are now, dear," Evelyn replied, remembering how his affectionate use of 'E' had been lengthened to Evelyn at about the same time his 'Edward' had been reduced to Ted. Maybe that was when it had all gone wrong. Still, what a smashing day this was turning out to be. With 'Edward' helping her climb the steps, Evelyn reached the top without stopping. When they passed a couple coming the opposite way, also with arms linked, each of the couples acknowledged the other as happy twosomes do.

After a refreshing pot of tea and too many buns – which Edward insisted upon, saying, "Why not? We only live once!" – they strolled over to the Abbey. Edward immediately fished out his guide to Whitby which he'd just purchased in a flurry of interest and started telling Evelyn the history of the ruins. If he'd been a dog his tail would now be wagging. "Do you know it's remarkable how many times this place has changed hands?"

"Really, Edward?" she said, distracted by a notice standing nearby:

Member of staff required to help with enquiries and visitor orientation. 20 hours a week - would suit a retired lady or gentleman.

I should enjoy that if I lived here, she thought, loving the sounds of the seagulls and the sight of two handsome, tan cows standing in the meadow behind the Abbey. Whitby was getting into her blood in the way some places are wont to do. But aware that Edward was speaking, she turned back to her husband.

He was eagerly turning over a page of his guide book. "Do listen, E, this really is interesting. Apparently, the Abbey was originally founded by a princess from Northumbria but was destroyed years later by the Vikings..."

"Uh huh..."

"Yes; but then the site was taken over by the French, only the church was considered inadequate for its needs. That's when the building that stands here today was erected, to accommodate the requirements of the clergy."

"So what happened to this, then? Why's it in such ruins?"

"Old Henry VIII had it dissolved in 1538."

"Torn down you mean? Oh, weren't they dreadful in those days! What happened then?"

"The site was handed over to the Cholmley family and they built the house where we just had our tea."

"Lucky them, it was a nice cup of tea."

"I don't think they had much to do with your cup of tea, E. Oh, and it says the family had to live in the Abbey's lodgings and gatehouse till their own place was finished. How would you fancy that, then?"

"Long as the sheets were clean I wouldn't mind!"

"They wouldn't stay clean for long if we were in them," said Edward with a twinkle.

"Ted! I mean, Edward, you're a devil."

"Better the devil you know that the one you don't!"

All this daft talk was making Evelyn feel strange. She was getting the absurd notion she fancied Edward again, like in their early days when they'd wined and dined before going home to celebrate something much more important - each other. Gazing at him, Evelyn wondered if she'd been too quick to criticise. He really was quite the charmer, taking her hand here and there to guide her. When she wanted to get a better view of the harbour, where they'd sat earlier, he helped her onto a large stone.

If only there were somewhere quiet to go, away from the throng...

Then she had an idea; a daring and frivolous one. Ted would almost surely laugh at her suggestion but Edward, her reinvigorated Ted, would possibly take the bait...

"Dear," she started, flirtatiously. "I've had a thought... You may think it's rather daft..."

Yet when she told him, Edward was keen as a horse for sugar. "That's a great plan, E! Let's get back down those steps and take a room for the afternoon; I saw plenty of B&B's. We've bags of time before the coach goes."

"Anyway," said Evelyn, more daring by the minute. "Who said we even have to go back today? We don't live that far away; we could always take the train home tomorrow..."

"Spiffing idea, young E. I say we get moving quickly, while the kettle's still on the boil."

With that, they hurried to the bottom of the cliff with fire in their tails. Who said only the young had fun?

In less than ten minutes they had booked a room, paying in advance and not telling the landlord they might only need it for a couple of hours. It was a cosy room with a generous double bed afloat in an ocean of chintz. The perfect room for an afternoon liaison. Edward pushed open the casement windows to allow in the salt-sweet Whitby air. Spring really had sprung. Evelyn felt a pang of sorrow for all the other pensioners on the trip who were probably dragging around the gift shops or having one of those dreadful lunches where they have nothing to say to each other. Poor them for not having the same vaa-vaa-voom: the same joie de vivre! Yes, a zest for life is a marvellous thing, thought Evelyn, slipping under the covers as Edward finished his ablutions in the en suite.

But when, after fifteen minutes, Edward still hadn't reappeared Evelyn felt an ominous chill. His naval background had instilled in him the virtues of cleanliness but how clean did he need to be? A slight roughness could be attractive. "Edward?" she called but got no answer; at least, not a proper one. The only sound issuing from the bathroom was a series of Neanderthal groans.

Feeling cold, Evelyn pulled the bedspread about her shoulders and made for the en suite. Opening the door she found a sad but not unfamiliar sight. It was Ted, not Edward, sitting on the edge of the bath. Half-way off one foot was a sock but that was where he had given up undressing. Something had stopped him from going further in the way a clock winds down or a crane runs out of power. His usual air of disinterest had returned, bristling incongruously against the bright and breezy bathroom with its flotilla of jolly ship ornaments and pictures.

"Oh no, Ted, what's happened to you?" ventured Evelyn. But even as she asked she knew it was hopeless; that Edward – the man with whom she had just spent the last three hours - was once again the Ted she felt saddled with.

"I've been wondering how I got here," he mumbled. "Don't remember coming to a hotel. We haven't paid for it, have we?"

"Oh, Ted..." was all Evelyn could manage. She knew what would happen now, that they would wait for the coach and that would be that. All hope of love's second wind would go home with them. Looking down, Evelyn noticed a slip of paper on the bathroom floor and, picking it up; read it in dismay. Really, she should have guessed sooner. It said (in Ted's handwriting): Sitting here, looking at Madame Rominska, I know if I had half the chance I'd be thirty-five again, if only for a few hours...

So that explained everything. Her husband had been hypnotised to have whatever he wished. And though they'd had a heavenly time together it had come about by accident, from his desiring another. Was this something she could live with; his not having wished for her especially? Coming to a sudden decision, she looked him squarely in the eye. "I'm going back to the Abbey, Ted, though I know you won't understand."

"But it's just an old pile of rubble…"

"I'll give you rubble. It's you that's in ruins. I've a job I need to apply for and I'm certain you can find your own way home."

'Come quickly George Fenchurch, you won't believe your eyes!'

By Matthew Willis

George Fenchurch put his hand on the rail at the foot of the Abbey steps, he didn't feel like he had the energy tonight but he wasn't going to let that stop him. Almost every night of his life in Whitby he had come up these steps, it was like an obsession. It was a special place though, the Abbey, and he liked it at night.

He put his foot on the first step and started his climb. His father used to bring him up here when he was really young, before he was allowed to do it himself. The menfolk in his family seemed to appreciate their solitude at times and he was like the rest of them. George remembered how as a teenager he used to run up the 199 steps, bypassing the tourists and locals egging him on.

Tonight though was quite a struggle. He stopped to catch his breath halfway up. He hadn't had to stop before for at least twenty years. He ran a liver-spotted hand over his bald head; his brow was speckled with sweat beads. 'Come on old man' That's what Lucy would've said, George encouraged himself as he picked up his pace and continued his routine.

George could feel his heart beating a snare in his chest. Maybe I should go back? The thought crossed his mind. 'NO!' he scolded himself. He slowed down a little but persevered. Nearly there now. The dark ruins of the Abbey loomed in the distance. They never failed to take his breath away but this time more than normal. He doubted whether it was just the sight of this mythical place.

George sat down on a bench at the summit of his climb. The night was beautiful, not a cloud in the sky and millions of stars twinkled down on his seventy-three year old face. He reached in to his coat pocket for a quick sip of whisky. His daily reward for his heroic ascent.

George made his way into the Abbey grounds; he knew every contour beneath his foot like the back of his hand. The Abbey walls towered above him mighty and powerful. World famous landmark withstanding all weather conditions on its mighty perch upon the cliffs. How he had dreamt all his life to see it all in its original glory. To whizz back in time to witness its construction.

A sudden sharp intense pain shot through George's chest and up and down his left arm. George cried out in pain and fell against the ancient stone wall. Wave upon wave of hurt surged across his chest and he slumped onto the grass and onto his back. Through tears he saw the beautiful night sky and at the bottom of his vision the most impressive remaining piece of the Abbey's structure, the Rose Window, a bright star shining through its central point.

As he lay on his back on the cool grass in sheer agony he felt someone beside him touch his hand. He grimaced and started to ask for help but as he turned his face towards his possible saviour he was lost for words as Death gripped his heart harder. A girl of about seven or eight grinned down at him. Long, curly blonde hair cascaded down her back which she kept out of her face with a blue band. George was startled but remembered another girl who she resembled sixty-five years ago.

His dad had quite a good haul from his last trip at sea and had given him a little extra for his pocket money. Even though George was a keen saver he couldn't resist the rum and raisin that Old Mr Hughes made and sold in his homemade fudge shop. The way the fudge was so creamy and melted in his mouth was addictive. He'd just been telling Mr Hughes about his father boasting that his last trip out had caught him enough fish and crabs to feed the whole of Whitby for a month. Mr Hughes had been his ever enthusiastic self and laughed and nodded in all the right places. George had just put his money on the counter and was in the process of putting his fudge in his school satchel when the bell on the door rang and a girl ran into the shop. George flinched at the sudden intrusion and he dropped his fudge all over the floor. Cursing quietly to himself he crouched down to retrieve it when Lucy Walker, a girl from his school who had never spoken to him before, grabbed him excitedly by the hand and yelled, 'come quickly George Fenchurch, you won't believe your eyes!'

George looked wild-eyed at Mr Hughes who returned his gaze with equal bewilderment and chuckled as Lucy half-dragged George away from his shop.

'Quick follow me!' Lucy cried as she pulled him along by his hand, her long blonde hair blowing along behind her as they ran towards the Abbey steps.

'What's going on? What's going on? This better be good, I've dropped my fudge.' George complained as he tried to keep up with her as she ran up the stone steps as if the devil was on her tail.

All she said in reply was, 'hurry up, this is better, the fudge will be there tomorrow, this won't!'

As they climbed the steps as quickly as they could George kept noticing Lucy glance over her left shoulder in the direction of the harbour. What's going on?

Finally when they reached the top George thought she would stop but Lucy ran past St Mary's church and stared and pointed down over the harbour out to sea.

George didn't need to ask what she was pointing at, it was impossible not to see.

Over the water about two, maybe three miles out to sea was a gigantic water spout. It looked like a huge thick white snake stretching up out of the sea and into the clouds. As water looks beneath the surface when it goes down a plug hole only a million times bigger. A small fishing trawler rocked perilously close to it. They could only imagine the terror of the people on board.

He stood beside her open-mouthed, too shocked to blink let alone speak.

Lucy leant to him but with her eyes still mesmerized by the colossal spout. 'Isn't it magnificent?' she said and squeezed his hand.

George couldn't find the words to describe how magnificent it was; he just stared gob-smacked at the beautiful freak of nature.

After a while, much to their disappointment, the water spout dispersed and vanished into nothing, first severing its connection with the sea and then slowly evaporating. It was only then George spoke, 'it's a good job my dad went fishing yesterday!'

Lucy giggled at him and the rest of the daylight hours they spent running around St Mary's and the Abbey grounds chasing one another and talking about the giant water spout. Lucy told him all about Dracula and how the boat that brought him to England docked here in this very town. George sat and listened intently, hanging on her every word but at the back of his mind was concerned about the outcome of his rum and raisin.

George looked at the girl beside him, she looked exactly the same. The pain in his chest was constantly reaching a new crescendo. He felt like he had a spear through his heart, pinning him to the ground. His vision blurred and the stars above his head swirled into one another like drops of cream stirred into black coffee and he passed out.

He sat with Lucy Walker on a picnic blanket. The sun was glorious and the weather not too hot, but it was one of those days where you could get sun burnt without even feeling it. They had been going out since they were in their teenage years. He had surprised her with a picnic lunch for her twenty-first birthday. She hadn't changed much from the first time he came up to the Abbey thirteen years previous. She still had her pretty beautiful blonde hair and still wore a blue band to tame it. Excitement fluttered in his belly as he watched her nibble a piece of pork pie. George filled two glasses with white wine and offered one to his girlfriend. 'Well, happy twenty-first birthday Lucy,' he said as they chinked glasses and drank through smiles. 'I've got you a little something to commemorate our first official meeting; you can have your other present later,' he said with a wink and withdrew a brown paper bag from his jacket pocket.

Lucy's eyes lit up as she took the bag and opened it, 'ha ha ha, rum and raisin fudge! It should be me buying you some. It was me who made you spill yours!' she leant forward and kissed him on the cheek.

George pulled his hand from his pocket and felt his heart beat quicker, 'give us a bit then.'

Lucy offered the open bag and George delved inside and plucked a piece of the creamy brown produce and held it between his thumb and forefinger. Lucy smiled and drank her wine.

'Are you not going to have some?' George said impatiently, toying with his nugget of fudge, 'Mr Hughes made it this morning.'

'Oh well George you know how I'm watching my figure but I suppose one piece won't hurt.' Lucy slid her slim fingers into the bag and as if bitten by a snake recoiled and covered her mouth with her hand. The bag fell to the grass spilling a few fudge pieces.

George's heart stopped. Icy invisible fingertips crept down his spine.

Lucy lowered her hand and revealed the biggest smile he had ever seen her give. She reached into the bag and withdrew the engagement ring.

Without giving him enough time to even propose she sprang across knocking food and wine everywhere and on top of him planting the hardest of kisses on his lips. 'Oh God George, yes I will marry you, yes yes yes!'

They lay together for hours making shapes out of the clouds and unbeknownst to them at the time, getting burnt red like lobsters by the afternoon sun.

George regained consciousness and tried to prop himself up on one elbow but it was useless, the pain too intolerable. He wondered where the little girl's parents were, someone that young shouldn't be out at this time of night on her own. Turning to face her he finally realised who she was.

Fifty years later to that date Lucy had died.

George had laid out a tray of fruit, natural yogurt, tea and toast and slipped quietly into their bedroom using his back to shield Lucy's gaze from her special birthday breakfast treat. He turned round with the opening words to happy birthday on his lips when he saw her and felt himself shatter from the inside out. Lucy lay on her back half beneath the bed sheets, her eyes glazed over looking slightly to George's left. There was no life in them at all.

'Oh dear God no!' was all that he could say as he carefully placed the breakfast tray on the dresser. Lucy would tell him off if he spilt it on the floor. He knelt by the bed and touched his hand to her cheek, it was soft but cold. One hand hung from under the duvet and George clung to it and pressed it against his face. Tears followed. After calling for an ambulance he sat and mourned for his beloved Lucy.

The pain was easing now and the stars looked down where George Fenchurch lay in the ruins of Whitby Abbey. An old man lying clutching his chest, his face ashen. 'I wonder how many people have died on this land, on this very spot,' he whispered as he felt himself get weaker and weaker. The girl to his right squeezed his hand as if to reassure him. He gazed up at the brightest star that shone down on him through the centre of the Rose Window, his favourite piece of the Abbey. As the star got brighter George's pain subsided completely and everything other than the Rose Window grew darker. The star seeming to be the light at the end of a very very long tunnel. He knew it was the end for him. The girl helped him to his knees and George stepped out of his earthly body. He was dead. He turned to the girl who held his hand and smiled. Lucy Walker smirked down at him excitedly and pointed up towards the bright light of the shining star, 'Come quickly George Fenchurch, you won't believe your eyes!

One Year On

By Kirsty Ferry

It's raining, and I've been sitting here for what seems like hours. I can feel my hair sticking to the back of my neck and my rucksack is propped up by my feet, leaning on the bottom of the gravestone. It's one of those table sorts of tombs that look like big, cold boxes. I don't know who I'm sitting on and I hope they don't mind. I tried to scrape away the green stuff covering the name to see, but even when I managed to claw a few marks into it, the storms and the gales that blow off the North Sea have eroded everything. I spent the next fifteen minutes or so picking the green stuff out of my nails and wishing I'd brought a nail file or something, because I've ended up snapping a nail and had to chew the jagged bits off.

I'm not sure how long I should wait here, really. I've wandered around the church and the Abbey, and scrambled over the stones. I've stood at the east end and looked up at the huge pointed arch, craning my head back until I went dizzy. I've eaten a bar of chocolate from my rucksack and had some Pepsi. The Pepsi fizzed up everywhere when I opened it, because the bottle had been bounced around in the bottom of my rucksack all day.

There looks like there could be another wave of rain coming in, and the whole town seems dark and grim. The rooftops are all shiny, reflecting the odd bit of watery sunlight and I remember reading somewhere about 'ramshackle rooftops'. I smile a bit, because now I can see what they meant. The rooftops are all higgledy-piggledy, marching down the hill into the town and from here it looks like they are all different – different heights, different widths, different everything.

I ram my hands with the chewed fingernails and the flaky black nail varnish into my pockets and shiver slightly as the wind picks up and whips around me, bringing with it the smell of fish and chips and warm cafés from somewhere down the hill. From my seat on the tomb, I can see the Magpie Café across the harbour, black and white merging into a horrible grey as the drizzle wipes across it like a dirty dishcloth. There are still a few straggling families queuing outside it and I swallow a lump in my throat as I wish I was there with them. Maybe even with my Dad.

I know my Dad is here somewhere. The last birthday card I got from him, nearly a year ago, had a Whitby address on the envelope. Mum threw it in the bin after tearing it up and scrumpling the bits into a hard little ball. I waited until she'd left the room, and I pulled it out again. I smoothed the ball out, laid the pieces together again and read the address. Then I took it upstairs, copied the address into the back of my diary and hid the bits of the envelope inside one of my books. I've brought my diary with me. I thought I could write about my visit to Dad, record all the great things we would do together and then I'd have a record of it forever. Because if Mum finds out – or should I say 'when' Mum finds out, because she's bound to realise I've gone by now and I did leave a note for her - I'll not be allowed to do it again. I've even switched my mobile phone off, just in case.

I don't know if I should just get up from the gravestone table and start walking down all those steps to the town, or stay here a bit longer. I push my hands further into my pockets and hunch over. The Abbey seems a really peaceful place and I kind of think if I leave here and all the calmness the monks left behind to find Dad's house, the spell will be broken and the Abbey won't be so peaceful anymore.

'You OK?' I hear a voice from behind me and I jump. I turn round and see a boy standing behind me. He looks really eerie, because the mist is rolling in from the harbour and it's billowing through the big empty holes where the Abbey windows used to be. He's dressed all in black, right in the middle of it. He's about my age, I think. Maybe a bit older, like seventeen or something. And then I realise he's all in black because he's a Goth. Black shirt, black trousers, black boots with huge silver fastenings and a long, sort of flowing black coat. His hair is black too, but he's got amazing sea green eyes and he's smiling at me. He's got his hands in his pockets too, but I know if he pulled them out, he'd have black fingernails, just like me.

'Yeah. Thanks,' I say, and turn back to face the harbour. The tourist boat is coming back in now, and the sails are flapping about in the wind like huge bat wings.

'You sure?' he says and I hear him mushing through the wet grass to come and stand beside me. 'Fantastic view,' he says. 'I love it here. You mind if I smoke?'

'Hmmm,' I say. I don't really care one way or another. I kind of wish he'd go away and leave me alone, but on the other hand, I kind of want him to stay and talk. The last conversation I'd had was with the conductor on the train. His machine had bitten a clean edged '2' in my ticket as he punched it, and I zipped it into my rucksack to keep it safe for my return journey. Whenever that would be.

The Goth Boy is rolling up a cigarette. He lights it and the end flares like a tiny firefly in the mist. He inhales deeply and blows out a perfect smoke ring. He sighs.

'I know; I shouldn't,' he says. 'But hey.' He moves closer to me and leans on the tomb. I can smell his aftershave, something sharp and lemony, combined with the smoky smell. 'You're not from round here, are you?'

'No.' I shake my head. 'I'm visiting.'

'Ah – you with family?' he says, looking around the graveyard. 'Hope they don't mind me talking to you.' He smiles suddenly, a flash of white, straight teeth. His sea green eyes crinkle at the edges. 'You maybe don't see so many of us where you come from. Plenty of us here. Goth capital of Yorkshire,' he says with a laugh. 'Have you seen her yet, then?' he asks. I'm thrown by the sudden change of subject.

'Who?' I ask. 'Seen who?'

'Abbess Hild. Or should I say her ghost. She's supposed to appear in the window at the west side and wander round the Abbey. She used her enchanted whip to lop the heads off all the snakes in Whitby. Of course, if you believe all that, you'll see the phantom coach and horses that stop outside the church as well.' He shrugs his shoulders. I can't help myself, and I laugh.

'I don't believe in ghosts,' I tell him.

'Excellent,' he says, and grins at me. 'Now, what are you doing here? I can't see anybody wandering around and it's nearly closing time, so I'm guessing you're on your own.' He flicks what's left of his cigarette into the grass and it fizzles out. But he's right. I hadn't realised how late it was getting. The sun, what there is of it, is starting to set. It's dropping down in the sky behind me and it's going to fall behind the hills. There are a few sickly rays struggling through the mist and trickling through the empty windows. Suddenly, I don't think I want to be here that long after dark, and I shiver again. I poke at my rucksack with the toe of my boot. The bag falls over with a soft thud. I stare at it, without really seeing it.

'Allow me,' says Goth Boy and bends over. He leans the bag against the stone and stands up.

'I'm going to my Dad's in a minute,' I blurt out. 'He lives here.'

'Oh! Whereabouts? Sorry. You must think I'm really rude. I'm Adam, by the way.' He holds out his hand.

'Lucy,' I tell him. Awkwardly, I hold my hand out. He laughs and clasps it. His hand is cold, but he shakes mine firmly. 'Lucy. Like the girl in Dracula. You've come to the right place then.' He grins. 'I don't bite, you know. I may look like I do, but really, I don't. So. Your Dad. Where did you say he lived again?'

'I didn't,' I reply. But I lean over and open my rucksack. I pull my diary out and dust off some bits of fluff and chocolate crumbs. My mobile looks at me accusingly and I quickly zip the bag up again.

'Here,' I say, handing the diary over. 'I copied it from my birthday card envelope. But I don't know how to pronounce the first bit properly.'

Adam takes it off me and studies it for a minute. He nods.

'Lucy – what does your Dad do?'

'He's an artist,' I tell him. 'He's got a studio and he's working with the jet and stuff. He said he would make me a necklace, all out of Whitby jet. My Mum wasn't happy. She said he was all talk.'

Adam looks at me and smiles.

'I'd make you a jet necklace,' he tells me. 'Match your nails perfectly.' He winks. 'Great look, by the way.' I smile again and relax a bit.

'I don't normally wear it,' I tell him. 'But I thought if I was coming down here I might blend in a bit. You know?' Adam shakes his head.

'Never blend in,' he tells me. 'Be individual. It's better that way.'

'But you're...' I sort of point to him and I can feel myself blushing. He laughs.

'I'm what?'

'Well – like – a Goth or something.'

He looks down at himself and makes a little startled noise.

'Good Heavens, so I am. Something is about right anyway.'

That makes me laugh again, and he winks at me.

'I'm me. You're you. You're Lucy. Don't be like Lucy in Dracula and get dragged into something. You don't want that.'

'I suppose,' I say. I start chewing my ragged nail again. The black has practically all gone from that nail now and I sigh. 'So do you know where that street is then?' I ask. 'My Dad's street?'

Adam closes my diary and hands it back to me. He smiles again, but this time it's different – more sort of sad and grown up.

'Afraid not,' he says. I feel my heart sink into my boots and puddle there like a dead thing.

'Oh,' I say. 'No idea at all?' Adam shakes his head. 'I've lived here all my life,' he says carefully. 'I know every street, every alley and every close up and down this town. And I know the old bits and the new bits and the bits in-between.'

'But not that bit?' I say. He shakes his head again.

'Never heard of it.'

'But – my Dad. He wouldn't just – like – make it up, would he?' I say. Even to myself, I sound really stupid. 'It sounds like a real place,' I say, my voice catching.

'Caedmon is a famous poet. He's got links with the Abbey. That's where he got the name of the street from,' Adam says.

'But - the jet? My necklace...' Adam looks away over the harbour, not meeting my eye.

'Jet is really famous here as well. It's the kind of thing you could read about in say, a guide book. Or on the internet. Or notice if you're just passing through here on your way somewhere else.' He brings his gaze back to meet my eyes. I can feel the hot tears bubbling up and Adam goes all swimmy whilst they threaten to burst out of my eyes and run down my cheeks. He looks away again, giving me time to wipe my face with the back of my hand. My nails look stupid now. And I want to go home.

'So you don't think my Dad is here, then?' I manage eventually. Adam shrugs his shoulders.

'I don't know, Lucy,' he says. 'I honestly don't know.'

I hunch up even more. The light has almost gone now and the rain has started to come down heavily, battering the tombstones and the Abbey and leaving shiny trails down Adam's leather coat. I wonder if it rained when my lying, selfish Dad sat in a pub scribbling a load of crap onto a birthday card he'd bought in a hurry, because he realised my birthday was coming up. I think of my train ticket in my rucksack and my home and my Mum who must be going through hell today. The tears run down my face properly now.

'Want some company back to the train station?' Adam says, reading my mind. I nod.

Adam walks me back to the station. He takes me down the hill, through the town and doesn't say anything when we pass all the jet workshops. He crosses the bridge with me and points out a couple of little boats to me in the harbour, which he knows I don't really care about. He waits with me on the platform until my train comes, and makes sure I get on it.

I sit down in the corner of a carriage, and prop my rucksack up next to me. The window is all steamed up with the rain and the heat of the bodies in the train. I rub a patch in the steam and see Adam standing on the platform. His hands are stuffed in his pockets again. Nobody takes any notice of him as he watches me and waits for the train to pull away. Someone has left a newspaper on the seat next to me. It's boring, but will last me until I get home; take my mind off facing Mum. The headline catches my eye. One Year On – Whitby Remembers.

It goes on to relate the story of a blaze at a club in Whitby, one of these basement places Goths hang out in. There was one death. They've got a photo of the victim in the article. I sit up and press my face to the window. Adam takes his hand out of his pocket and waves at me. I wave back. He nods and winks. I look back at the newspaper, read a couple of lines and look back at the platform. Adam has gone. I settle back into my seat. It's just a co-incidence.

I don't believe in ghosts.

A Twist in the Taste

By Ray Clark

Ut quod ali cibus est aliis fuat acre venenum

Margaret had simply vanished.

Frank had only stopped for his morning paper. On leaving the shop, his wife was nowhere to be seen. He'd searched Baxtergate in a mild panic, which had soon turned to abject fear after he had also scoured the Upper Harbour, the beach, the shops and everywhere else he could think of without success: desperately questioning everyone he'd met whether or not they had seen a woman fitting her description.

Margaret's missing brother had been their reason for visiting. The details of Phillip's demise had been sketchy, confusing. His car had plunged over a cliff. It had not been reported stolen. He had not been driving. His body had never been found. The police had been mystified as to why a happily married man with two children, a well paid job and a stable home life could simply cease to exist.

Margaret had wanted to spend every weekend at the resort after the incident - convinced she could unearth some clue that the authorities may have overlooked.

Frank had tried to persuade her otherwise for obvious reasons. He'd understood her grief: suggesting perhaps her brother was no longer the person she'd known when they had been children. Phillip had married, raised a family. They'd grown apart. She would only torture herself by spending the rest of her life searching for him. He remembered his remark causing a blazing row, marriage threatening, because Margaret had taken it out of context.

The near deserted resort of Whitby had once again reached the end of a long, demanding summer season. It was early evening and Frank was standing on the bridge overlooking the harbour. The working boats had finished for the day and the evening pleasure cruises were taking over. The pungent aromas of sea-air infused with fish and chips and salt and vinegar invaded his nostrils: the haunting cries of the seagulls a constant reminder that they were here to stay, unlike Margaret.

Where could she be? How could a fully-grown adult simply disappear without trace? Hadn't anyone seen her? She must have spoken to someone!

It had been a long, hard struggle. He'd done exactly as Margaret had wanted to; spent most of his weekends travelling back and forth from their home in Leeds: badgering the police, scanning newspapers, and talking incessantly to anyone who would listen. So far however, every avenue had drawn a blank.

There was still no trace of Margaret. No one recalled seeing her on the day, or since: almost as if the place harboured a dark secret: one that reduced people into silence? Maybe it wasn't the resort he thought.

Frank glanced at his watch and realised he had lost all track of time. He needed a newspaper and strolled over to the shop.

He smiled at the girl behind the counter and they exchanged pleasantries. As well as buying the nationals he bought the local rag, glancing at the front page in anticipation. He seethed when he saw the headline and the story that followed:

The Seaside Herald

MANOFEE PIE!

Humans ... an Alien delicacy...

An undercover report received last week has damning evidence that the small port of Whitby has been infiltrated by aliens who have more than a passing interest in the human race ... we have in fact become ... a part of their food chain.

(Details - page 3).

Inside, the continuing story suggested their base was a vault underneath the Abbey: the report substantiated by a number of locals having reported flashing lights above the ruins some months previous.

Frank dropped the paper back on the counter, mouth agape: his stomach churning.

"Who prints this crap?"

The girl glanced at the tabloid. She seemed embarrassed. "The editor, sir."

Frank blew out a sigh. "Prints The Sunday Sport as well, does he?"

"I'm sorry?"

"Well look at it: human-eating aliens for crying out loud. It's up there with the aeroplanes on the moon and London double-decker buses in the North Pole. I lost my wife here, for Christ's sakes! I don't think I've ever once seen an article about her in this local piece of shit he calls a paper! Would it hurt him to concentrate on human interest stories?"

Frank didn't wait for a reply. "No! It wouldn't. All he's interested in is selling newspapers and it doesn't matter how he does it!"

"I think it's called freedom of speech, sir," replied the girl, cowering into the corner behind the counter.

"Freedom of speech?" repeated Frank. "We'll see about this!"

Frank almost flew out of the shop, turned up Bridge Street and then left on to Church Street, stopping only when he reached The Black Horse. Inside, he ordered a stiff whiskey, downed it in one.

Sensing the drink had not calmed him he left the bar and stepped out on to the narrow cobbled street, almost into the path of a car.

The blaring horn sharpened his senses. He glanced up quickly: panicked, stumbled, and fell back in one quick movement.

Embarrassment turned to anger and he hauled himself up: dusting down his clothes he cursed under his breath. When he finally took notice his surroundings were different.

He was in a strange alley - one he hadn't seen before. He didn't like it and wondered where in relation to the rest of the resort it was. He thought he knew every inch of the town, but the passage was new to him.

It was Victorian, in a small cobbled setting, at the end of which stood a shop. Frank glanced upwards but there was no name. He stood back a little, stared at the article in the paper and then peered into the alley again. A shiver turned his stomach. The bloody thing went straight towards the Abbey – in fact – underneath, as the paper had suggested.

Although an air of must prevailed, it was clean and litter-free with none of the usual half-eaten fast-food cartons scattered around most towns.

Frank's initial fear subsided and he strolled towards the shop. The clicking of his heels against the cobblestones echoed loudly. The further he went, the colder it became.

He was surprised when the shop turned out to be a café, or to be more precise, a small but elegant restaurant. Stone coloured vertical blinds hung in the window, matching the colour of the exterior brickwork. He glanced up at the sign: A Twist In The Taste. Underneath, in brackets, it read: "We cater to your every need."

The glass was so clean he was able to study his reflection: the view afforded him a sorry sight: a middle aged man dressed in a drab grey suit whose weight had plummeted so that his clothes hung like rags, the result of which he noticed was a slight stoop. His head of healthy black hair had first receded before falling out: what remained was now grey.

A sudden movement in the window caught his attention. The man he saw was tall: perhaps mid-forties with slicked back hair. His impeccable attire was evening dress and although he seemed too graceful for a waiter, thought Frank, that's what he appeared to be.

A long, skeletal finger beckoned him inside.

Against his better judgement, he opened the door and entered, his curiosity piqued.

"Good evening, sir," said the waiter.

"Evening," replied Frank.

On the inside, the establishment was pristine. An aroma of fresh bread prevailed, and another smell he couldn't quite place ... exotic, spicy even. Eight tables and chairs were all neatly set with new tablecloths and cutlery. Decorating the walls were a variety of oil paintings, mostly of what he took to be the town from a bygone era. In the background, he recognised the music as Glen Miller's Moonlight Serenade.

Frank chose a table and the waiter passed him a grey folder menu with the insignia of the restaurant embossed in gold lettering on the front. Although he'd had little or no intention to eat on entering - and quite why he had remained a mystery to him - he had to admit he was hungry ... starving almost. It suddenly dawned that he hadn't had a decent meal for a week. All he'd done was pick at sandwiches.

Frank studied what turned out to be an appetising selection, though he couldn't claim to know any of the dishes on offer: Rump Siélou; Roast Leg of Tar' Gamtré; Breast Amiré ... the list seemed endless and the tantalising smells wafting their way from the kitchen were indescribable.

The waiter eventually returned and Frank ordered the roast leg, marinated in ... whatever: he couldn't pronounce it. He hadn't had leg of lamb for years.

Frank had calmed down and while waiting for the food he listened to the background music and reminisced: his wife would have liked it here. He glanced around, surprised there were no other customers.

The food came on a plate the size of a dustbin lid because the joint of meat was colossal. He tried to imagine the size of the sheep but couldn't.

After the meal - half of which he left - Frank ordered one of the speciality coffees.

Little time had passed before the waiter returned to the table.

"Forgive me for saying, I couldn't help but notice your pained expression, sir." Without being invited he sat opposite. "Is there anything I can do to help?"

"Not really," replied Frank. He glanced upwards and it was only then that he observed the pallor of the waiter's skin. His complexion was ashen, very unhealthy. Considering he worked in a restaurant, it was a poor advert.

"They do say a trouble shared is a trouble halved. We're not busy, and I would be more than willing to listen."

Frank sipped the coffee. It tasted herbal, with a tinge of mint. The inner feeling of warmth as it slipped down mellowed him.

He continued to stare at the waiter's lop-sided grin. He was absolutely daunting: and Frank didn't like his gravelly sounding voice either.

He took another sip of his drink. The more he had, the more he wanted. It really did taste good!

Time passed and Frank was on his second cup when he opened up about Margaret's disappearance and the intolerable period he had spent searching for her: diligently driving to the coast every weekend.

"If only I could see her again." Frank's voice broke.

The waiter leaned forward and touched Frank's hand. "Tell me, what would you give?"

Frank recoiled a little at the man's touch. "What?"

"I asked, sir, what would you give just to be able to see her again?"

"What kind of a question is that? What would I give?" He stared at the waiter. "Do you know something?"

"I don't know anything, sir. I simply asked what you would give. We often say it but rarely mean it because we know it's not a position we would be in."

The waiter smiled innocently.

"Oh ... I see," replied Frank. "I'd give anything ... everything I have ... just to see her again, to know she's all right, that something bad hasn't happened. Even if..." Frank found his thoughts difficult to voice. "...even if she didn't want me!"

"Everything you have?" mimicked the waiter. "Your home ... your car, maybe?"

"Of course I would! What do you take me for?" Frank was struggling to keep a lid on his emotions but they were all over the place: one minute he was up and hopeful: the next, down and defensive.

"Your life?" asked the waiter, casually.

Frank felt the colour drain from his face. He neither found the question nor the waiter's behaviour threatening but the way in which it had been delivered was so calm and clear that Frank's testicles shrunk, his groin tingled and his throat closed somewhat. He suddenly realised that apart from a lack of customers he'd seen no other staff.

The man pulled back. "I'm sorry, I shouldn't have said that. You don't look at all well, sir."

Frank found his comment amusing. "I'm just a little tired. I think I need some fresh air."

The waiter then pressed something into Frank's hand, squeezing it, like his mother would have done with a shopping list wrapped around the money when he was younger.

"What's this?" he asked, yawning, struggling to stay awake.

"When you're better, sir, please study the card. They may be able to help."

Frank yawned again. He really needed that sea air.

"If you wait a moment, sir, I'll help you out."

The waiter headed for the door but Frank's world suddenly darkened.

When Frank woke up the first thing he noticed was the intense cold. In fact, it was freezing!He rubbed his hands up and down his arms despite his lethargy. As he tried to stand, every joint in his body seemed locked and cried out for mercy.

"Jesus Christ!" muttered Frank. A cloud of white breath filtered into the air.

He grew more alert and studied his surroundings.

"What the..?" The room was littered with people: all hung on rails, in various states of decomposition - some missing whole limbs. The discovery sent shockwaves through him. Frank lurched forward and bumped into one of the bodies.

"Oh, Jesus..." He recoiled, repulsed at the thought, still wondering where he was.

As he backed away from one body he ran headlong into the next.

One he recognised.

"Oh, dear God, Margaret..." Frank howled with pain.

Fixed to Margaret's head was a card.

His eyes were drawn to his own card. They were identical.

The card read: A Twist In The Taste. Underneath, in brackets, it read: "We cater to your every need." It even had a 'Use By' date.

Frank struggled desperately to contain himself as he bolted towards the freezer door where he noticed the deep scratch marks...

The newspaper article about human eating aliens suddenly came flooding back to him.

He turned and screamed and then stopped screaming as his throat constricted when he spotted Margaret's left leg was missing. Sickening realisation hit home as he also became aware that Roast Leg of Tar' Gamtré had simply been an anagram of his wife's name.

Ut quod ali cibus est aliis fuat acre venenum

What is food to one is to others bitter poison

Lucretius (c. 95-55 B.C.)

The Beachcomber

By Ann Madden-Walsh

Soon it would be dusk, time to follow the path down through Caedmon's Trod to the winding Whitby streets below. The Abbey walls loomed forebodingly above Hannah's head, magnificent, crumbling relics of a bygone age. Most of the visitors had gone, heading off to the car park by the ticket office to make their journeys wherever. Hannah wasn't ready to leave as she huddled against the cold stone wall of what was once the Abbey nave. She sat cross legged pressing her body into the column making herself as small as possible a subconscious attempt to make herself part of the Abbey.

This is where it had all begun, two years, three months, seventeen days and six hours ago. This is the place she had met him, this very spot. Hannah had come to sketch the Abbey, a hobby she was pursuing on a solo-backpacking trip as she took a gap year between college and university. Most people went to exotic climes for their gap year but Hannah had decided that England had much more to offer. She had just completed the Coast to Coast walk and was about to embark on the Cleveland Way from Filey. She never managed the Cleveland Way because on this very spot on that very day her life had changed forever.

Hannah had been sitting on the stump of the column, busily sketching the Abbey ruins oblivious to all around her, trapped in her own singular world, when a shadow suddenly appeared across her sketch pad. Hannah turned her head to see where the shadow was emanating from, a simple turn of the head which would change her life forever. There he was; tall, rugged, sun tanned with piercing amber eyes. His hair, an unkempt, tousled mass of sun kissed champagne blowing gently in the warm sea breeze. He swiftly perched himself on the fractured column by her side and offered her his right hand.

'Sam,' he announced, in a soft lilting voice with a slight hint of an Australian accent, 'that's pretty good. Are you an artist?' pointing to the sketch.

Hannah took the outstretched hand and shook it gently.

'Hannah,' she replied, 'and no, it's just a hobby of mine.'

'You should take it up professionally. You're good.'

Hannah smiled but didn't offer a reply. She was doing what she did best, working out a scenario for the Adonis sitting by her side. Surfer, yes he had to be a surfer, the looks, the accent said it all. Hannah had become big on people watching. A skill honed on her journey from St Bees to Robin Hood's Bay. Travelling alone with no real human interaction other than the odd cheery hello from other walkers, she had passed the time creating whole new lives for the people she met on the way, from the dreary local history buff to the couple of history teachers having an extra-marital affair. If she wrote the stories down that she had created for the people she had met she would have a best seller. Sam had to be a surfer.

How wrong she had been. On this very spot two years, three months, seventeen days and six hours ago she had learned that Sam was in fact a Geologist. Newly graduated from university with a BSc in Geology with Palaeobiology, Sam had rented a small cottage in Runswick Bay and was pursuing a career in beachcombing. All that education and Sam had decided to comb beaches for a living. He hadn't made a bad job of it though. He earned enough to keep a roof over his head and feed himself, supplementing his income by working in a local pub in the evenings. As the sun began to set over the bay Sam had offered Hannah a bed for the night. Totally against her better judgement Hannah had taken up the offer and even now the tent stood against the wall in the porch of Sam's cottage where she had placed it on that very first day.

The morning after that first meeting Sam had taken her down to the bay and had showed her the myriad objects of value that had washed up on the last tide. Sam mostly collected fossils, which he sold to shops along the coast, a hit with visiting families. Sometimes he found large pieces of jet and iron stone, which he sold to jewellery makers in Whitby. Occasionally he would find flotsam fallen from sea going vessels which he would sell to whoever was prepared to buy. His metal detector was an asset to his business as he would trawl the beaches for coins and jewellery dropped by the holidaymakers.

From that morning onwards Hannah also began her new career. She would collect attractive pebbles that she polished and made into jewellery, selling the finished products to the local tourist trade. She also sketched the beautiful coastline around her. Sam would create driftwood frames for the sketches, the finished product also sold to tourists. Their goal in life was to be able to make enough money to rent a small shop in Whitby from were they could sell their wares.

And so it was. Hannah and Sam became a couple. To the locals in the bay they were the new age couple from the fisherman's cottage on the hill, all free spirit and weird ways. An impression they had created themselves when Sam had decided that the only way to dress was in long khaki shorts and misshapen T-shirts and that daily shaving wasn't strictly necessary, often sporting a face of fine dark blonde stubble. Hannah on the other hand had grown her hair and it had become a mass of long brown unkempt curls reminiscent of a Botticelli painting. She had taken to wearing long gypsy skirts and cheesecloth blouses unless she was beachcombing . Then she would wear a pair of Sam's khaki shorts folded up at the legs, tied around the waist with a piece of orange twine found on the beach and sporting a pair of large green wellington boots. Yes, to the locals they were free spirits. Together they were one. Hannah and Sam were soul mates of the highest degree. They were joined together by an invisible bond. Since that very first day, on this very spot they had never spent more than a couple of hours away from each other. That had all changed one day and nine hours ago.

Hannah lifted her head and looked at the ever-looming ruins around her. Soon she would be confronted by the Abbey security, who would usher her away from the ruin so they could close for the night. Hannah would go. She would show willing but as soon as the security had gone she would scale the wall on Abbey Road to sit once more on the spot where they first met. Oh how she needed him at this moment, how she needed him to tell her that everything would be all right. That she could survive without him. Tears welled in her eyes as she began to re-examine the events of the last thirty-three hours.

The previous day had started as normal. Sam, as usual, had brought her a mug of steaming tea in bed. He had set it down beside her and hurried to the small shed at the back of the cottage to check his equipment for another day of beachcombing. He had been excited, as there had been a fierce storm the previous evening meaning lots of finds would be out in the bay waiting for him. He wanted to start early before anybody else got there first. Hannah had suffered a fitful sleep in the night. The storm had kept her awake most of the night so Sam had told her to stay in bed and he would see her in the bay when she was ready.

Hannah had fallen back to sleep and had lain there for another three hours when she was awakened by the ringing of her mobile phone. She had sleepily answered the phone to hear Sam excitedly telling her to bring him his crowbar and truck. The truck he had made himself from wooden planks washed up on the beach that he had fitted with axles of an old railway truck with large pneumatic tyres. He used the truck when he found large objects on the beach. It was easy to manoeuvre along the wet sand as the tyres bounced over the rocks. Hannah had dressed and wheeled the truck down to the beach. She hated doing this, as the road to the beach was steep. She thought it would be far easier if Sam fitted breaks to the truck so they could ride it down there.

As she had neared the beach she had seen Sam way out in the bay hammering away at something by his feet. She had slowly dragged the truck towards Sam and as she got nearer she had noticed a pattern on the rock Sam was hammering at. Sam had looked up from his toil as she stopped the truck near him. He was hot and sweat was dripping from the hair on his forehead, the hard labouring had reddened his face.

'Look Hannah,' he had said excitedly as he drew away from the rock, 'look what I have found.'

Hannah looked at the rock, jutting from its surface was a huge fossil. She hadn't a clue what it was but Sam seemed to be in awe of his find. She could make out certain features of the fossil like backbones and toes but what it was, she hadn't a clue.

'It's complete Hannah,' Sam gushed, 'a complete pleseosaur, not a big one I'll admit but complete all the same.'

'But it's too big,' Hannah replied, 'you'll never get it out before the tide comes in.'

'I will if you help, please Hannah this is my big discovery. I could sell this for…well the Americans will pay a fortune for it on e-bay. Just help me get it out.'

Sam hacked away at the rock around the fossil, trying to break it away from the nodule it was attached to. Hannah had helped him to force a crack through the base of the rock. They had toiled and sweated for what seemed ages as the fossil began to move from the rock beneath. Sam placed the crowbar under the fossil and moved it away from the underlying rock. Together they began to slide the huge rock onto the truck. The rock was heavy and it needed both their strength to move it. After what seemed like an age the rock was on the trolley and ready to be moved to the beach. That's when Hannah had looked up and screamed.

They were standing on a tiny island in the middle of the bay. The tide had come in and they hadn't noticed. Soon the tiny island would be under water. Sam looked up when he heard Hannah's scream. He pulled her to him.

'Don't worry, don't worry,' he reassured, 'we can get back it isn't that deep yet'

Hannah had started to paddle out to the beach. Sam started to pull the truck.

'Just leave it Sam,' Hannah screamed.

'I can't, this is our fortune.'

The water was getting deeper with every step and very soon Hannah felt herself swimming. She had looked back at Sam to see him struggling with the truck.

'Leave it Sam,' she called, just as a large wave engulfed her and transported her to the shore.

On the shore she had sat and looked out into the bay. The island was gone; the truck was under water. Where was Sam? She stood and scoured the sea. She couldn't see him anywhere. She turned and raced up the steep road to the cottage to call the coastguard. The coastguard scrambled a helicopter to search for Sam. That was 25 hours ago and still she had not received word.

By this time Hannah knew that all was lost. If Sam had been all right he would have found a way of contacting her. She knew she had lost him. Two years, three months, seventeen days and six hours after their meeting she now realised that she would see him no more. She would have to live the rest of her life alone. The grounds of the Abbey were now silent. Only the whistling of the wind through the ghostly glassless windows could be heard. Hannah threw herself down on the column stump and cried softly into her arms. Her hair tumbled over the cold rock like sinewy snakes. The folds of her skirt danced over the sides of the column in the wind.

She heard a noise, footsteps coming towards her, two men, one with a familiar, soft, Australian accent.

'She didn't stand a chance, if only she had waited she could have climbed on the truck with me and she would have been saved. Funny how the coastguard thought it was Hannah who called them though. Seems whoever called gave her name and our address.' Sam related to the security guard.

'Maybe she telephoned them from the shoreline before...' the guard suggested.

'No, she was found on the beach with her lungs full of water, she was already dead when she reached the shore. Anyway thanks for letting me in. I just needed to be here for a while. This is the spot I first met her'

Sam sat on the column beside Hannah as the guard moved away to leave him in grief. Hannah lifted herself up and sat staring at him. He was crying. The sun had gone down and the spotlights around the Abbey made dark eerie shadows on the grass. Hannah tugged at Sam's sleeve.

'Sam, I'm here,' she whispered.

Sam brushed at the sleeve she had just tugged and looked up at the looming apex of the Abbey.

'Please God,' he pleaded, 'take care of her. Tell her I love her.'

Hannah stood in front of him blocking out the view. Sam stood up and walked straight through her towards the waiting guard. He shuddered as he suddenly felt a cold shiver. Hannah watched as he walked away as she suddenly realised what had happened. She wasn't scared. She felt happy knowing her love was safe and sound.

'Take care, my love,' she called 'if ever you need me I'll be here.'

She looked around at her new home, sat down on the base of the column and waited for his return.

Decision at the Abbey

By Tom Benson

Matt was a few miles from Whitby, but could clearly see the impressive stonework of Whitby Abbey high on the distant headland. In modern times it was simply referred to by some as a ruin, but it was a majestic ruin. As he looked at the sun shining on it and the clear blue sky behind, he imagined it spectacular in its heyday, complete with stained glass windows.

Matt's task was simple enough, but the 27 year old Interior Designer knew from experience, a tight schedule can destroy a plan. When still two miles from Whitby the traffic started to back up a few hundred yards. It struck him that there were outside forces working against him in his quest. If necessary, Matt had already decided he would park up and run the last mile or two. His 'one mile' time wasn't what it was at school, but with the right incentive, which he had today, he could push himself. He lifted the long blonde hair out of his eyes and promised himself yet again that he'd have his hair cut shorter.

He glanced up once again at the building on the skyline. So near, yet, so far... then turned to look to his front and slammed on his brakes to avoid hitting a man in a motorised wheelchair. The old boy shouted something and waved a clenched fist. Having successfully avoided any more road traffic trauma the young Scotsman drove towards the Marina car park. It was reputedly the easiest to find a space. Only when he was parked did he consider the 'Pay and Display' aspect of his decision. He raked through his pockets and as he did, found himself looking up at his goal. The old Abbey ruins seemed to be beckoning him and taunting him simultaneously. He had agreed to set this thing in motion and now wondered if it was such a good idea after all to put a deadline on it.

Matt pushed the money into the slot of the parking ticket machine. He had just enough change for three hours so couldn't afford to have a coin not accepted. One of the coins fell through three times, failing to register. Matt looked up at the Abbey for whatever good it would do as he said, 'Please...' The coin dropped in.

A quick look at his watch told him that he should still make it in time, but he knew he couldn't afford to dawdle. He was a typical Taurus. A life in good order, good at timing and when the chips were down, he was resourceful. He found himself constantly planning ahead. As he strode to the mini-roundabout and turned right towards the bridge he couldn't help but look up at his destination again. It held a strange magnetism for him. Was it simply the impending meeting – if he was in time, or was it something more mysterious? On reaching the narrow drawbridge he realised for the first time just how busy Whitby was on a fine day. What stood out more than the numbers was the lack of any urgency. For most people this was a relaxing day out to a historic fishing town, which had by way of a main attraction a particularly well-known and beloved ancient monument. For some people a visit to the Whitby Abbey was akin to a pilgrimage. Matt's 25 year old girlfriend Elizabeth was a history graduate and revered the place.

Once over the bridge Matt headed left and slowly made his way up through the small Market Place. It was becoming apparent to him that time was slipping away rapidly. The more he tried to speed up his progress, the slower it felt he was moving. He was wearing leather soled shoes and having difficulty keeping his footing on the smooth cobbles of the very narrow Church Street. It felt as if he was swimming vertically against a sea of humanity, against the tide. Running wasn't an option now, but the frustration of trying to move faster was telling mentally, if not physically.

Matt reached the junction at the base of Tate Hill and turned right to take in the sight of the 199 steps he had to climb. At the base of his next challenge Matt was not pleased to see a large group of schoolchildren setting off up the steps, three abreast, with their two teachers in attendance, both attempting to give an impromptu history lesson.

'Excuse me...excuse me...excuse me...' Matt was trying to move up the steps quicker and couldn't work out why he felt as if he was treading water.

'Stand back children...' a young lady said, 'this gentleman will show us how to go up the steps quickly...apparently...'

Once clear of the children and the unimpressed teachers it was clear what the issue was with the steps. They were wide, so it was difficult to negotiate two at a time, but they were also low in height, which meant it felt as if an actual step up wasn't being taken. Matt's frustration was increasing with every lengthened, half step. At the 47th step there was a platform of sorts and he stopped briefly to look up at the ascent. He wondered if he should take a run at the remaining steps, but dismissed the thought and started out again steadily.

Arriving at the top was a relief but it was to be short-lived. Matt looked at his watch. He had just over seven minutes to make the deadline. Looking to his left he took in the tiny, quaint St. Mary's Church and adjoining small graveyard. He made a mental note to visit them both later. He looked ahead at the perimeter wall and thought all he had to do now was make his way along to a gate and he was there. A few metres further he reached the gates, but they led right and onto the Hard Garden situated to the front of Cholmley House. Matt quickly went through the gates glancing up to his left, now in close proximity to the ruins of the Abbey. Ahead of him through the gates was the impressive sight of the Borghese Gladiator. The bronze statue stood there on its plinth in the centre of the cobbled garden, as if challenging Matt on his quest.

Matt obeyed the signed request not to walk across the ancient cobbles and instead jogged around the smooth pathway to reach the entrance to Cholmley House. This building had been converted to be the Visitor Centre and entrance to the Abbey and grounds. As Matt made his way around the path he tried to remember where he'd seen the impressive gladiator statue before. In a few strides it came back to him, it was a copy of the original. He glanced back at the statue just before he entered the building. He had seen it in Paris. The original marble statue dating from 1611 was on display in the Louvre.

'Nearly there.' Matt murmured, looking up at the Abbey as he went into the house. His heart sank as he saw a group of tourists asking a multitude of questions at the cash desk. He glanced at his watch. Five minutes. He pulled his wallet out to pay his admission then looking at a young lady in a red shirt, he thought again. The words 'English Heritage' emblazoned in white across her shirt struck a chord. He pulled out his membership card and showed it to the second cashier. Inside a minute he was on his way with a gracious smile, an audio guide and a handy leaflet.

Matt took the steps up to the next floor three at a time which surprised all the other visitors. He ran along the length of the large room passing the impressive large audio visual display and the informative glass display cases of artefacts. Later, he thought. No time to look at his watch now he decided and ran as fast as he could. Straight on out through the glass doors at the end and onto the ramp. He'd reached the well-kept grass before he remembered once again he was wearing leather soled shoes. As he tried to run he found himself slipping in his frustrated efforts to gain speed. A glance at the leaflet as he'd gone up the stairs had told him the Abbey pond was at the distant end of the ruins so he now sprinted as best he could. Matt had to reach the end where the chapel would have been situated. His breathing was erratic when he reached the end of the building. This wasn't due to the running itself, but the continual slipping as he concentrated on keeping his balance at speed.

Matt reached the end of the Abbey and stopped. He turned left, close to the far wall of the massive ruins and for the first time since leaving his car he attempted a smile. Standing with her back against the wall of the Abbey was Matt's girlfriend, Elizabeth. Her long, perfectly brushed auburn hair was draped over bare tanned shoulders and contrasted with the pale blue of her knee length summer dress. Matt thought she looked both ravishing and elegant, but more importantly worth the efforts he had imposed on himself.

Elizabeth glanced down at her diamond studded Cartier wristwatch and her right eyebrow raised slightly which Matt knew was a good sign. As

Elizabeth looked at him and smiled, Matt reached into his pocket, dropped down on one knee and opened a tiny red box.

'Elizabeth Cholmley...will you marry me?'

'Of course I will Matt.' Elizabeth said. She smiled broadly and held her left hand out as the most important person in her life stood up and slipped the diamond ring on her finger. She said, 'Romance for me is all about time, place and who is sharing the moment. Would you like to tour Whitby Abbey, my favourite historic monument before we go to lunch?'

St Hilda's Embrace

By Paula Readman

Coming back may have been the wrong thing to do, but somehow it seemed so right at the time. I wait here among the weatherworn ruins of the Abbey for my much beloved Esther whilst all around the sounds of the seagulls keep me company. They circle overhead their calls echo between the ruins while far below I hear the sea crashing against the shoreline. These all too familiar sounds bring back such happy thoughts of my time spent with the woman I love, and whom I long to be with once more.

For a brief moment, I break my vigilance and look up at the delicate stonework. Each stone, lovingly crafted by the hands of men, placed one upon the other to show their love to God. Though now in ruins, the Abbey has stood here for eternity, and still it echoes with love for the Holy Father. For most, it's a grand sight to see. However, for the likes of me, Robert Wicking, a sailor by trade, these ruins have always told us our journey is safely at an end once we're back in the shadow of Saint Hilda's. At Sunday school, I'm sure I learnt that the Abbess Saint Hilda was once a Northumbrian princess, but my memory is a little hazy now, and my only thoughts are of my longing to be with my own sweet princess, my darling Esther.

Ever since our first meeting many years ago, Esther and I have strolled among the ruins, in all kinds of weather. Here we would talk about our dreams of what our lives together would be, and soon it became our favourite haunt. I can still see that first meeting as clearly as I see her now coming along Church Street with our two fine grown-up sons and our beautiful daughter. Closing my eyes, I can feel the warmth of her touch and, above the salty air, I can smell her own sweet perfume like the scent of the wild flowers she loved to gather from meadows around the Abbey. These memories are so clear to me.

Our first encounter was on such a day like today, blue-summer skies and the warmth of the sun made the horizon shimmer in a dancing haze. It was the first fine day after days of heavy stormy weather. When the awful weather finally broke, the relief among the fishing folk flowed up from the harbour and spread through the town as at last the boats could set sail. I remember with such clarity when I first set eyes on her. I was busy working on my father's boat and paused to straighten my back and there she was, such an unspeakable beauty. With such poise and dignity, she carried herself so tall and straight, with a basket of mussels on her head as she came up from the beach. The light sea breeze took liberties with her hair, pulling it from under her bonnet and giving me a glimpse of its copper-red beauty. I nodded my good morning as she passed me by, and my reward was such a pretty smile.

Every day, I watched for her bright smiling face among the lasses who worked the shoreline until I found enough courage to speak to her. To me, she was too fine a lass for the likes of me. My heart had never beaten so quickly for any other, from that day to this, when Esther agreed to step out with me.

It was to the Abbey we went, to stroll among the ruins. Here she gathered up the golden buttercups, the white mooneye daisies, and the meadowsweet from the pond edge while swallows skimmed and twisted overhead, and the lazy cattle dipped their heads to drink and softly moo in contentment. I knew in that moment, as I sat and watched her with no doubt in my heart, I wanted the feeling of serenity forever. Once the sun began to dip on the far horizon and the shadows of the ruins grew longer, our afternoon spent together was over too soon. I took her hand in mine, and we walked slowly down the 199 steps, hoping each would last an eternity. As I stand here now, watching and waiting for her, my soul lifts with delight, as soon I shall be able to take her in my arms again after we've been parted for so long.

One of the hardest decisions I made was to allow the sea to come between us. On that day, I took Esther to walk among the ruins to tell her of the decision I had made and to my delight, she told me, she understood. She said it was God's way of testing our love for each other.

I kissed the top of her head, and the sweet clean smell of her freshly washed hair made me never want to let her go. I took her small hand in mine and kissed the back of it and while I stared deep into her sea-green eyes, I pledged my heart to hers, promising her as soon as I returned, by the next fall, to marry her.

Now I was earning a little more money, we could start saving for a place of our own. Neither of us wanted to live in the crowded little houses, as our parents did. I wanted the finer things in life for us, and began to work hard learning a new trade. While we were apart, I wrote to her every day telling her of all the things I was learning, and seeing on my voyages around the world. Spending only a little of what I had saved, I sent her a parcel of fine yellow silk to make her wedding dress. To my surprise, Esther wasn't idle either; she informed me excitedly in one of her letters from home that Mrs Anderson who owned the drapery shop in Skinner Street had offered her employment after seeing her fine needlework.

Autumn could not come round quickly enough for me. How happy I was to see her when I came home, knowing we were to be wedded. My parents and Esther's had planned everything, such a simple, but beautiful affair. All along the steps to the church were the smiling faces of our family and friends, everyone happy to know we were right for each other and to share our wonderful day.

I can see many of those same faces now, older but still recognisable, following behind my family. It's good to see them here today, and I'm glad they want to share this time with us too.

The thing about Whitby folk is the sea, it's in our blood, and the air we breathe. It can bring us all together, and so easily pull us apart, but neither of us can survive one without the other, but on days like today with the sun shining, we all stand together.

Soon, with our hard work, Esther and I were settling into our new home overlooking the park. On our last evening together before I had to set sail again, we walked among the ruins and talked about my going away. I was broken hearted; it would be six months before I was home again. By the time, I returned Esther was heavy with our first child. I'm pleased to say when it came time for my farewells I knew my Esther no longer waited alone for me as she cradled our newborn son, William.

Though each journey I made brought us the finer things in life, I felt I missed out on so much, seeing my beautiful daughter, Lucy with the laughing sea-green eyes, taking her first faltering steps, and my youngest son, Robert, singing in our church for the first time. How my darling wife found the time to run the drapers after dear old Mrs Anderson passed away, and look after our growing family I shall never know. In her letters to me, she always made light saying it helped to pass the time until I came home again.

Setting sail for home on my last journey, I could not wait to see my family. We were favoured with fine weather, which expanded our sails like the wings of a bird in flight. Bowling along with us, the white trade clouds swept across a windy blue sky slowly turning day into night. As our long and uneventful, but prosperous journey ended, the 'Good Company' carried my crew and me ever closer to our families. With a young moon watching over us and our night watchmen familiar with the constellations safely guiding us homeward we all began to relax and enjoy this restful time. I took to my cabin to finish some neglected paperwork. While I worked, I could hear the buzz of the froth at the bow and the hum of the canvas overhead. After what seemed like mere moments, I was disturbed by the ship's cabin boy, who came to light the lanterns so I could continue to work into the night. Looking up, I could see on the far horizon the faint traces of daylight, which lingered there. After the lad bid me good night, I settled back to work. Then without warning, the ship pitched. I heard a night watchman call out. Coming aloft, I was shocked to see how much darker the sky seemed than I had expected. No stars were visible and the air seemed to weigh heavy on me. My first mate said, "We're in for foul weather, Captain."

A loud cracking sound split the night air and ricocheted around us as lightening lit up the night sky. At first, the sails began to flutter lightly as the ship rose and fell. Each time we rose up, so the sails joined in the dance with the racing clouds until the strength of the winds seemed almost to rip them from us. I called every man to the deck as the seconds became minutes and the storm gathered speed and velocity. A shout went up as the first of the rain began to fall and with it, squally showers, which took our words away. I looked toward the direction my first mate was pointing and across the sea; I could just make out the familiar outline of cliffs and Saint Hilda's Abbey. To know we were so close to shore, but still three miles from safety was maddening. It all happened so quickly, as we realised we were not the only ship in distress that night. At first, we hoped the storm might burn itself out, but the rise and fall of the ship told us that wasn't about to happen, as she swung right before the swell. We heard the screeching of a whirlwind racing along the surface of the water. The driving winds turned the sea into a heaving mass, which seemed to boil up and soak the deck with a furious sheet of foam. All around, the masts creaked as the rigging sang out under the strain. One moment the wind seemed to be driving us to the shore then it changed direction, losing us much of the ground we had covered; it took us further out to sea. As my men fought with the sails, it looked as though we could be winning unlike the other ship that battled to make it to the safety of the harbour. We watched in horror as the sea claimed what was its to take, as the other ship left it too late to lower its sails and disappeared from view only to reappear as a mass of floating debris.

I called out trying to make myself heard above the thunderous sounds of the sails as the sheets snapped and cracked all around us. Tired and soaked through there didn't seem to be anything we could do to help the struggling men we saw in the water apart from offering our prayers up to God himself, though it felt as though he had deserted us. High above us on the cliffs we saw hundreds of flickering pinpricks of lanterns among the ruins.

Out of the darkness of the sea, a lifeboat appeared. We watched as the open-top lifeboat rose to a sickening height and then came down, down, down to disappear amidst the waves only to reappear moments later. While we watched the bravery of the lifeboat men, we'd taken our minds off our own peril. Our ship seemed to rise up with the next large wave as it caught us astern. We all braced ourselves as the ship crashed down as though it headed for the bottom of the sea itself.

Feeling neither fear nor wonder, a thousand thoughts travelled through my mind during the time I found myself under the icy water of the North Sea. As the pull of life dragged me from the deep, I gulped in air then on seeing what had become of my ship I felt myself giving up, as all seemed lost to me. Then from out of the darkness, I swore I could hear the sound of someone calling to me above the rising waves. I felt the warmth of strong arms around my waist and my nostrils filled with the scent of wild flowers.

I'm not sure what happened next, but all I know is today my Esther is coming to meet me. Ah, at last, she's here and looks as beautiful in her wedding dress, as she did on our wedding day so long ago, with her copper-red hair hanging softly around her bare shoulders. Taking her in my arms, I whispered, "My sweet darling, at last, we are together once more."

"Oh, Robert, I knew you would be waiting here for me. Come, we must let the children know..."

Kissing her urgently, I whispered, "Esther, I'm sorry, there's no time. Saint Hilda is waiting to receive us into her embrace."

In the churchyard below the Abbey, Lucy wasn't sure what made her look up. Sensing something, her brothers followed her gaze.

"What is it, Lucy?" William and young Robert said in unison.

Through all that remained of the high façade in the north transept of the Abbey, with its mounting tiers of three long slits of empty windows, they could see beams of dancing sunlight. It filled the north aisle with colours as though the nine windows were once again full of brightly, coloured stained glass. Crowning the top with its delicate stone tracery the rose window seemed more noticeable against the setting sun. Feeling her heart miss a beat, Lucy clung onto her brothers' arms to stop herself from falling, "At last," she whispered, "they've found each other."

Solemnly, the Vicar tossed the soil onto the coffin and said, "Ashes to ashes, dust to dust..." Lucy knelt and dropped the garland of wild flowers she had gathered from the Abbey's ground onto her mother's coffin.

The Treasure Hunt

By Jane Harlow

The first few clues had lead them up into the north-west of the country. At lunchtime on Saturday the teams eventually gathered at the White Lion, Pickering, having followed the clue "WILLIAM HENRY, DISCOVERER OF PHOEBE (Meet at White Lion for lunch)". The idea of the treasure hunt had started as an acorn in the Golden Eagle one night as they were relaxing after the weekly pub quiz. Their aim this weekend, now it had come to fruition, was to follow ten clues, without the use of the internet, taking them on a journey through some of the finest countryside in Britain.

There were twenty one people involved, five teams of four, Legal Eagles, Too Many Cooks, White Collars, Academia and Saga Louts. The man who had set the clues, booked the accomodation and was driving ahead, was Arthur, Dave's cellarman at the Golden Eagle. Becky and James, both in the police force were accompanied by the landlord Dave and his new girlfriend, solicitor, Helen. The other teams consisted of civil servants, a team of caterers from a local sandwich shop, and two cars full of retired couples who were the favourites to win based on their collective experience and knowledge.

The late Autumn weather had been kind to them so far. Although they had left Derbyshire in the rain on Friday morning, the low black clouds had soon cleared and a crystal blue sky had accompanied them all the way up to Yorkshire. They had stopped at a cosy, oak panelled hotel in Doncaster the night before and an early start after breakfast had lead them up to York, Thirsk and then Pickering. After a break and a late lunch at the White Lion, Arthur gave out the next clue and they set off in convoy towards Scarborough for their overnight stay, marvelling at the sunlit brown and yellow leaves of the trees as they drove along the edge of the moors. After checking their bags in, the five teams began to relax. Some of them walked along the deserted sands enjoying the last of the afternoon sun. Others trawled their way round the shops, looking for local produce to take back to Derbyshire. A few of them visited the Rotunda Museum to look at the preserved skeleton of the Gristhorpe Man, found locally and believed to be an ancient British chief who had lived around 500BC. Later in the evening, the teams enjoyed a fabulous dinner at the hotel, relaxing afterwards with drinks and coffees, congratulating Arthur on a job well done so far and looking forward to the next day's challenge. They had already been given their next clue, "FIND THE HOME OF THE EARLY ENGLISH POET WHO ALSO LIVES IN PHILIP'S KINGDOM IN THE ANCIENT WORLD". In the lounge they separated into teams again, scratching their heads and making lists of all the English poets they could think of. Helen came up with a few useful suggestions for various King Philips of Spain, France and Portugal, but they were no nearer to solving the clue as they retired to bed. Long after midnight they drifted off to their respective rooms to clear their heads with sleep for the Sunday ahead.

Helen shivered, pulling her Goretex jacket tighter around her. She stopped and watched the first of the fishing boats emerging from the sea fret with their night's catch. The pre-dawn hustle and bustle of Whitby was stirring as men stepped out of the shadows waiting to tie each boat in the fleet safely to the harbour wall. Each skipper picked their way carefully between the boats moored behind the harbour walls and worked their way back to their spare lobster pots and nets dotted along the quay, tired after their night's work but relieved to be safely home for another day. Barrows containing empty wooden boxes were wheeled along the quay and the catches were slowly sorted, unloaded and cleaned ready for the morning's fish-market at the bottom of the quay. A small boy ran along to the end of the harbour wall, straining his eyes into the mist, waiting for the last of the boats to come back. He wrapped the empty sack he was carrying around his neck to keep the damp off his chest as he shifted from foot to foot.

Helen strode off round the corner into a quieter area, searching for her mobile phone in her bag. She phoned Dave to tell him to get out of bed and come and look around the market for some fresh fish to take home with them. As she hit the call button and put the phone to her ear she glanced up at the street sign, Bagdale. The dialling tone faded as the unmistakeable sound of horses' hooves grew closer and she was forced against the stone wall of an old cottage to make way for the carriage. "Sorry Miss," the coachman shouted as the horses wheeled off round the corner to the quay. Disorientated, she stepped back into the road again, realising that the concrete beneath her feet had turned to cobbles.

The small cottages lining the street were in total darkness. So too, she realised was the street, no street lamps at all. Perhaps the electricity grid was down, she thought. Suddenly, running towards her, she saw a street urchin dressed in rags, he was the boy from the quay, his sack now a quarter full of crab and lobster from his uncle's boat. "Miss, can I interest you in any crab or lobster please?" showing her the opened sack. He sold the catch door to door in the town every morning.

"Er. No thanks, I'm on holiday here, just staying overnight".

The boy held her gaze, looking puzzled. "Where do you live, Miss?". She explained that she was a lawyer in Derbyshire and she and some friends were on a treasure hunt for the weekend which had brought them up to Scarborough. The boy asked what a treasure hunt was and she told him it was a game of clue and problem solving, guiding them from place to place until they got to the end of the game and the theoretical treasure or prize. He looked at her clothes and the phone in her hand. "Who are you staying with?" Helen pointed across the harbour at the hotel she could no longer see. The boy fell quiet for a moment, then looked up at her again. "Do you think you might be able to help me, Miss? It's just that my father is leaving on the clipper for Canada today. You may have seen it moored in the bay? He works on the ship as a map-maker. They boarded last night and are rowing the last provisions over now, ready to sail at first light. My mother has a book of poetry she would like him to take for company on the journey, but no more personal possessions are allowed on board. Could you have a word with the bosun for me and see if I can get it on board to him?" Helen considered what the boy had said for a minute then took the book from him and walked back with him towards the quay. It was inscribed inside the cover "To my darling John, this poem goes with you all. God speed you back to me and Jake. Take care on board. I will pray for you. Your loving wife, Esther" The book was creased open at the chosen page.. "Caedmon's Hymn".

Helen looked towards the clipper moored out in the bay. By now it was getting light and the last few wooden crates of provisions were being lined up on the quay ready to be ferried out to the ship by rowing boat. Helen spotted a man who seemed to be organising the transfer. "Excuse me please, Sir. This young boy would like to get this book of poetry out to his father who is already on board and sailing on the ship. Do you think you can send it over to him in one of the boats, please?" The bosun looked at Helen, at her trousers, her shoes, her thick jacket and her shoulder bag. He hesitated, just for a moment, then shouted one of his men to get the book into the next rowing boat. "Make sure this book gets to John Joseph Blackmore, map-maker on the Majestic. Tell him his boy sends it." He looked back at Helen and the boy, rubbed his eyes, and turned away to continue with his work.

"Come on Helen, it's 8.30, they finish serving breakfast at nine." Helen turned away from the bosun, and began to wake up. She looked pale. She had forgotten most of the dream but was quiet and thoughtful throughout breakfast trying to piece it back together. They enjoyed a last coffee and on Arthur's advice, the hotel manager sent them off up the A171 towards Whitby. They were headed for tourist information first, but stopped to look around the grounds of a local church on the outskirts of the town. The congregation was just emerging into the Autumn sunlight after the bone-chilling Sunday morning service. As they wandered around the gathering crowd of locals and headed amongst the gravestones, Helen's eyes were drawn to a large cenotaph just off the central walkway. "To all those men lost at sea on H.M.S Majestic," the list of names below included John Joseph Blackmore. Helen cried out as the full memory of her dream came back to her. She looked further and the bottom of the cenotaph bore the inscription "He first created for the sons of men, heaven as a roof, the Holy Creator."

As they walked down to the local tourist office with Becky and James, Helen explained to Dave how she had dreamt about the boy and the book of poetry. The tourist guide knew immediately which poet they would be looking for. "That will be Caedmon of the Abbey, he was reckoned to be the first recorded English poet. His only known remaining work is this Hymn," and she showed them a transcription. "That was the inscription on the cenotaph, Dave, it's got to be him. It must have been some kind of sign." They went for a coffee and sat with pen and paper, thinking hard, trying to work out the puzzle. "It's got to be an anagram" said Becky, taking the pen off James. Five minutes later she had it, Macedon, an ancient kingdom she had heard of. They raced to the nearest bookstore and searched the dictionary for Philip. "Yes, here it is, Philip II, ruler of Macedon from 359BC. It must be Whitby Abbey, the answer must be up there."

They strolled up the hill and had a good look around the ruins, reading about Caedmon, the shepherd, turned poet, who was attached to the Monastery during the Abbay of St Hilda (657-680), and how the Abbey was attacked by Vikings in 867AD, but finally destroyed by Henry VIII, during the dissolution of the Monasteries in 1540, remaining in ruins to this day. They eventually found Arthur's last laminated sign on one of the walls. He was waiting for them with a big grin on his face. "Congratulations guys, you've found it," handing them an envelope with their prize, £100 and five free drinks each back at their local, the Golden Eagle. Within the hour the other teams started to arrive and after congratulating and commiserating with each other, started to descend the hill again to enjoy Sunday lunch at the fisherman's pub by the harbour before their journey home. As they made their way down to the town, Helen looked down the hill, then to her right, beyond the harbour walls and for a brief moment, saw H.M.S Majestic still lying there in the mist.

The Abbess's Tale

By Shelagh Wain

Whilom there was an abbess, Hild by name
And worthy was she of her widespread fame
Noble by birth, and yet by nature too
Her rule as abbess holy, just and true.
The house she led stood on a headland high
Open to God's world – land and sea and sky.
Streoneshalch, 'tis said, means 'Beacon Bay'
Hild's holiness shone out, just like a ray
Illuminating all Northumbria
From Humber up to Tyne and Tees and Wear.

Now at the time we speak of, two events
Occurred together, and, between them, lent
Still further lustre to this house of God.
As well as scribes and scholars, those who trod
With sandalled feet, who worked with book and pen
There was a need for other types of men
To tend the beasts, to plough and sow the land.
And one of these was Caedmon, a stockman
Much valued for his skill with animals.
But Caedmon had a weakness. In the hall
When men began to sing and play the harp
Caedmon would flee outside into the dark
Of shed and stable. Forced to leave the feast
He found his comfort with the humble beasts
For Caedmon was tone deaf. No single note
Of tuneful music ever left his throat.

One night, he looked up from his bed of straw
To see a tall man standing by the door.
'Caedmon, please sing for me.' 'I cannot, lord.'
The tall man smiled, the words were just ignored.
'Sing out in praise of God, and his Creation.'
Then Caedmon sang, and to his great elation
His voice rang out, melodious and free.
Next day, the gift remained. Excited, he
Reported to the reeve, who was in charge
Of all the Abbey lands. A man both large
And pompous, Ethelred was filled
With self-importance. 'I must go to Hild
And tell her of this news – she'll want to know
That one of my men has been honoured so.'
Then he turned to Caedmon: 'Well, come on.
And by the way, you'd better have a song
All ready, just as proof.' Poor Caedmon trailed
Behind the reeve. What happened if he failed?

The Abbess cut short Ethelred's effusions.
She valued him, but still had no illusions
About his ways. "A miracle, it seems!'
She smiled. 'So, Caedmon, what does all this mean?
We'd better hear a song – you make a choice.'
The stockman coughed, then shut his eyes. His voice
Flowed pure and clear, like that of which he sang:
The first, unsullied, loving state of Man
Dwelling in Eden, tending plants and flowers.
Hild listened, rapt. She knew then that his powers
Had come from God. She turned to Caedmon. 'Brother
This house needs you to join us.' 'Holy Mother!
I am not worthy..' 'Nonsense! You will sing
Of all God's works; in that way, you will bring
The Truth to simple folk, for they can learn
From your sweet melodies. You'll help them earn
A place in Heaven. Your place is now with us.'

Ethelred spoke, and tried to make a fuss.
He did not wish to see a mere cowherd
Raised up to such high status, but his words
Counted for nothing. He was sent away,
Grumbling, and muttering 'She'll rue this day.'

Meanwhile, far off, among the good and great
An argument arose about the date
Of Easter. Some believed the Pope in Rome
Knew what was right, while others, here at home
Followed the Irish ways. These men had taught
King Oswy, but his son, King Alchfrid, thought
The new scholars knew best, as did the Queen.
To settle matters, everyone was keen
To gather priests and bishops from the whole
Of England for a synod - and the role
Of hostess to this group would go to Hild.
'For,' Oswy said, 'this meeting here will gild
The good name of your Abbey. Kings and priests
Will come here to debate – and then to feast.'
The Abbess bowed acceptance, though she guessed
The real reason: her Abbey was the best-
Defended site in all of Oswy's realm.
No foe could here creep up and overwhelm
The grandees, undetected. On all sides
The view was clear for miles. So, satisfied
King Oswy left her to arrange it all:
The bedchambers, the seating in the hall
The food (as we know, even holy men
Enjoy some good rich feasting now and then).

Back at the farm, the reeve was now without
A stockman. He employed an idle lout
By name of Bradda, nephew of his wife.
A bad mistake, for soon his easy life
Would get much tougher. Bradda did not care

A toss for any of his beasts, and where
He could, avoided heavy work. For days
He milked the cows too late, and was amazed
That they were noisy, fractious, and in pain.
He never knew that each one had a name.
To make them move, he beat them with a stick.
And so their milk, which once flowed rich and thick
Grew weak, and thin, and scarcely filled a pail.
Young Bradda told the reeve a sorry tale.
'It's not my fault,' he said, 'your useless herd
Should be replaced at once, you take my word.'
'Just get out of my sight,' his uncle said.
He dared not sack him, for upon his head
Would fall the wrath of Ermengild, his wife
A woman well-versed in marital strife.
But still he needed butter, cheese and cream
To feed the synod. It would be a lean
And meagre feast the way things were
And as for Hild – he dreaded seeing her.

The preparations now were under way
So when the Abbess called him in one day,
To ask about supplies, he could not lie.
'The cows aren't giving milk – I don't know why.'
Hild raised her eyebrows, slowly. 'Is that so?
We must find out. I think we'd better go
And see the byres.' She rose and strode away.
And came on Bradda, sleeping in the hay.
'Young man, you need to learn that cows, like men
Thrive best on loving treatment and, till then
You cannot work here, at least, not alone.
Ethelred, you must supervise this youth
And make him a good stockman, for, in truth
It's both his fault and yours that we are short
Of milk.' The reeve scowled, knowing he was caught
Between two fearsome women, and that either

Could make his life a misery. 'They'll mither
Me to death. I can't take any more!'
Ethelred glared at Bradda, feeling sore.
'You useless lout! Now thanks to you, I must
Rise before dawn, and work till after dusk
As if I were a ploughboy. Well, you'll learn.
If I must suffer, you will in your turn!'

Back at the Abbey, Hild, while trying to grapple
With her problem, slipped into the chapel.
'Lord, You who turned the water into wine
I pray to You for help. Please send a sign
To show me how I may provide this feast.'
Just then the Abbess heard, beyond the east
Window, the voice of Caedmon, singing clear.
She smiled, and went outside. 'Caedmon, come here.
I need to ask you – when you first compose
Your music, would you say that it arose
Complete in every way, or must you hone
And sharpen it, like blades on a whetstone?'
'Why, Holy Mother, though my gift's divine
As I believe most humbly, yet I find
That as with all God's gifts, mankind must work
To make the best of them. I never shirk
From practising my music, to improve
My skill.' 'Oh Holy Lord, You move
In most mysterious ways!' the Abbess cried.
She smiled again. 'Dear Brother, do not chide
Me if I ask a favour; for you can
Perhaps save our good name. Now here's my plan.'

The day came when the great men all arrived:
Two kings, Oswy and Alchfrith (and their wives)
Three bishops, Colman, Agilbert and Cedd,
And many priests, all needing board and bed.
No problem, for the reeve could now provide

Cream, cheese and butter. No-one was denied
His rightful share, because the milk was flowing.
The cows lowed gently in their cowshed, knowing
They would be treated well. Caedmon, their friend
Was there again to soothe them – not to tend
Them as a cowherd, but to sing and play
His tuneful music. In there, every day
He worked on his new songs, and, in so doing
He made them sleek and happy; and their mooing
Echoed his harp in counterpoint. The peace
And harmony was good, not just for beasts,
But also men. For Bradda slowly learned
To be a proper stockman, so he earned
His place; Ethelred's skin was saved at home;
The Synod, thanks to Wilfred, followed Rome
While thanks to Hild's wise counsel, on its hill
The Abbey flourished, and it does so still.
For many visitors from every nation
Will find here beauty, peace, and inspiration.

Tapestry

By Melanie Walpole

Rising stiffly, and fighting against the pain in her swollen fingers, Meg turned towards the window. The October sunlight splintered on the water as the breeze whipped up small wavelets. Fishing boats were leaving the harbour, and Meg knew she must return to the tapestry to weave them some fish to catch. It was hard to coax her twisted hands to work, and Meg felt every one of her 75 years pressing down on her as she struggled with the weight of responsibility for the people of the town, and the disappointments she had had to overcome. First her daughter had died as Lily, Meg's granddaughter, was born and now, at 24, Lily refused to believe in the power of the tapestry.

From her cottage on the hill, Meg could see the small seaside town below her, and the people who had been her life's work. The tapestry she wove was more than just a picture; it was the very fabric of their lives, and Meg was the keeper. Usually she would weave them in or out of the tapestry, recording the normal pattern of life, but now she was preparing for a cataclysmic event. Even as she allowed herself a brief rest, some of the threads began to work loose.

Glancing up the hill, Meg could make out the warm ochre stonework of the Abbey walls reaching towards the bright sky. Visitors flocked around, chattering and taking photographs, unaware of the devastation which could soon be unleashed, on All Hallows Eve.

One man, however, seemed different to the others. He was alone and totally absorbed in his search, constantly checking his position against an old sketch in his hand. He began to walk quickly through one space between the broken walls when he stopped abruptly. No one noticed that he physically couldn't walk through the gap, even though others could. Checking again, he managed to pick out the faint maze pattern in the stone doorway. Ben knew he had found the gateway, but now his hardest task would begin. Leaning against the low wall he gazed across the houses, then closed his eyes and began to concentrate. He let his mind drift out, seeking.

Sighing as she went back to her work, Meg reflected on the fortunes of Whitby and its people. It had been 500 years since the gateway had last opened and the dark ones had come through. That had been a terrible time for the people of Whitby as the dark ones had taken their minds, but, in the battle that followed, the Guardians had defeated them and closed the gateway. Many had tried. The Christians had built their strongest buildings over it, recognising the place of power, but their defences were always weakened. The Guardians had constantly shielded the gateway and one of Meg's ancestors had been here even before the Abbey was built, but they did not always have the strength to stop the dark tide rising, even with the full power of the Abbey at its best. Stories of the opening had remained, surviving in legends of witches and wizards, vampires and ghosts. Stories used to frighten the children, but which Meg knew may become reality again soon.

Suddenly Meg felt a flash of pain across her eyes. Tendrils of thought began to seep into her head. Quickly she closed her mind. She had been careless, and someone had tried to read her. As the pain faded, she reached her own mind out to it, seeking the origin. She had to be careful; had to find out as much as she could without giving anything away. It was hard work. The seeker was experienced and very well defended, and the attack exhausted Meg. She lowered herself slowly into a chair.

"Nan," Lily came towards the kitchen where the tapestry brooded on its loom. "There's someone here to see you. Are you decent?"

Meg heard the laughter in Lily's voice and then the footsteps coming through to the back of the house. She covered the tapestry with a sheet, not wanting a stranger to see its threads unravelling.

"This is Ben Walker, Nan. Ben, this is my Nan, Meg Carter."

As Ben came towards her, Meg could feel her headache starting again. This was the man who had been seeking her. She took a step backwards. He stopped.

"I'm sorry," he said quietly. "I needed to get to you in a hurry. I found the gateway."

"I know." Meg was abrupt.

"We need to work together to keep it closed. I'm like you, a Guardian. I've been sent to give extra support. We recently noticed what's happening and didn't think you'd need help as there are two of you, but the forces below us are strong now. I'm sorry we didn't realise how serious it is. What defences do you have?"

Lily had made tea and heard the tail end of the conversation.

"What! Don't tell me you believe this too. I can't seem to get away from this ridiculous idea. It's the 21st century. This just isn't going to happen."

Ben was clearly shocked by her words, looking at her with disbelief. Abruptly, he stopped to focus, closing his eyes. Meg slammed her mind shut. Lily gasped as the full force of Ben's seeking hit her. He was so strong, she couldn't move until he had finished, then she leaned on the table, holding her head.

"Oh. What was that?"

"I'm sorry it hurt," He didn't look very sorry. "I had to do it quickly. I didn't realise you weren't helping with the tapestry, and I thought you may have crossed over, but now at least I know the truth."

"You did that? You read my mind? How can you do that? It's not possible."

"Sweetheart," Meg answered, "You have to understand that there are things we can't explain but it doesn't mean they're not real. Our friends are in danger. He did it because he's here to help us."

"How do you know he's not lying?"

Ben smiled as he looked at Meg.

"Oldest trick in the book. She checked me out while I was seeking you. I forgot how experienced she is."

A ghost of a smile crossed Meg's face as she removed the sheet from the tapestry. "Well now we know, we'd better get prepared."

All Hallows Eve dawned slowly. The sun seemed to take its time, finding Ben already at the Abbey. He was laying a piece of amethyst each side of the gateway, to increase the protection.

Patchy clouds scudded through the sky on a freshening wind as preparations were made for the celebrations. In the annual festival, the Abbey was blessed in a ceremony lead by a girl from the town. She was the festival queen, and with her attendants, she laid flowers around the grounds of the Abbey. Significantly, she also sprinkled water from a jet bowl across what Meg now knew to be the gateway. The people of Whitby had been unknowingly guarding it themselves with their ritual, and despite the true meaning being lost over the years, they still did their best. Meg wondered if it would be enough.

Her hands were too stiff to work the tapestry now, so she had spent the last few hours making Lily check and recheck the threads, making sure they were in place and the tapestry could not change to allow the gateway to open.

"Make sure they're tight," she grumbled at Lily's slow work. "You need to be quicker, there's a lot to do."

"Its fine Nan, now you go get ready while I finish off."

Meg reluctantly left her to it.

As the sun began to set, the queen was surrounded by her giggling attendants and they began the procession up the 199 steps to the Abbey, passing the cottage on the way.

"Hurry Lily, they're almost here."

Lily closed the door behind her as they set off up the steps, then felt in her pocket.

"My phone! You carry on Nan, I'll catch you up."

Leaving the front door open, she ran upstairs, grabbed her phone then rushed back down, slamming the door behind her. The slight movement in the air was enough to disturb the sensitive tapestry, and a hurriedly added thread from the gateway slowly drifted to the floor of the empty cottage.

Meg had to lean heavily on Lily for support as they walked slowly up the hill.

"Where's Ben?" she managed to say as they rested at the top.

Lily, too, was beginning to worry.

"He went to the museum this morning to get something he said he needed. I hope he's okay."

"He should be, he has more protection than most. Come on, we need to hear the blessing."

Meg worked her way slowly through the crowd. She needed to check on what Ben had done.

"Oh no." Her gasp was almost inaudible as she saw the gateway.

"It's ok Nan. It's where Ben put the amethyst, it's there."

But Meg just shook her head. She could hardly talk.

"No. It's....gone. Something else is there."

Lily tried to see what had replaced the amethyst. Malachite. A dangerous stone in the wrong hands.

She looked round fearfully, but everything seemed normal except for the sky, which had darkened too quickly. Storm clouds had gathered and hung heavily above them. Before the queen had laid her first bunch of flowers, fat raindrops were squeezing themselves from the clouds.

Lightning flashed and thunder followed. The storm was close.

"Quickly, we ought to get the girls out of the rain," the Mayor shouted, but no one needed any encouragement as they hurried back to town and the Festival supper. It didn't seem to matter that the ceremony was interrupted. Only Meg and Lily remained, both of them held by the power that was emanating from the walls around them.

"Oh." Meg gasped again. Lily looked at her, and then followed her gaze. A man sat on the wall to one side of the gateway. He held the jet bowl above his head, and as they watched, he brought it down with enough force to shatter it on the Abbey wall. The shards glittered as they flew outwards; away from the gateway. For a brief moment, the only sound was his tormenting laughter.

Heavier rain then, like grey rods falling from the sky, surrounded them. Once more, lightning whiplashed through the clouds, but this time it was right above their heads. Thunder tried to rip the sky apart and Lily felt a tremor in the ground beneath her feet. More lightning was hurled at the Abbey walls. There was a sharp crack. The foundations split. A deafening crash came with the thunder and the gap widened. Lily stared in horror at the narrow black fissure between the walls. The gateway was open.

A sound, not unlike a satisfied sigh, could be heard above the noise and a heavy black smoke was briefly visible, until the rain drove it back to earth. It lay, like a greasy stain, at the edge of the gap. The smell hit her next. The fetid stench of all pervading evil coating the air.

Lily felt them before she saw them. Fear was making her heart race and each beat began to pound in her head as the pain came. Every pulse was probing agony, stabbing deeper each time. She couldn't think. Her mind was giving up and something else began to take control. It made her look towards the gateway, and stopped her from screaming out loud.

The man beside the gateway raised his hands aloft and they heard his triumphant shout.

"They have come. At last, they are free."

The stuff of nightmares started to emerge. Long black fingers hooked the edge of the crevice before dark, hooded shapes and shadows hauled themselves out. Each one was weak and stooped and translucent, but they edged their way forward to touch the malachite, drawing strength and energy from it. Lily could do nothing but watch as dark fog spread insidiously into her very soul.

As the shapes reached the Abbey walls, each became solid; took human form as the cloaked and hooded figures from childhood, but these were much more threatening, and very real.

A soft hiss rose from the figures as a bigger, bulkier shadow emerged. This one picked up the malachite and stood, taller than the rest, incredible power radiating from it. Lily felt forced to kneel and worship this deity, but recognised the need to fight it, and struggled to stay on her feet. As it focussed its gaze upon her, her knees began to buckle.

Meg, more prepared, still had control. This was the fate which awaited the people of her town. Their minds would be taken over even though their bodies would survive to be inhabited by this terrible force. She sobbed from the pain of its probing, but refused to give in. Gasping for breath, she fought the evil which emanated from it. The figure seemed surprised by her resistance, and halted before her. Suddenly Meg bowed her head and the figure howled its triumph, but Meg had noticed someone approaching; fast.

The man, intent on watching his dark lord's triumphant return, hadn't seen what Meg had. Ben ran straight at him, and a bright flash showed Lily the black rod in his hand. It was the ancient wand, fashioned from jet, which had always been kept in the museum. Without hesitating, he ran the wand, like a sword, through the man. The shadow figures turned with a cry of dismay, as their life giving force dropped to the ground. Ben leapt onto the hidden maze and, holding the wand in both hands, raised it above his head.

A blaze of lightning fractured the sky immediately above the Abbey and hit the wand. Light radiated from it and bathed the Abbey walls. The malachite shattered as the rays hit. The thunder roared its anger, the clouds hurled bullets of hail downwards and the ground shook. There was an anguished cry as the dark ones diminished, their leader returning to a wisp of shadow before being sucked into the crevice. The gateway slammed shut.

Ben was surrounded by a blaze of light from the wand. It held the light for a few more minutes before letting it soak away to replenish the Abbey's strength. Lily could only watch as, exhausted, he collapsed onto the grass.

All Saints Day dawned bright and clear with everyone wondering how the lightning had shattered the bowl, but not struck the Abbey.

"Someone up there must be looking out for us," they said.

Three exhausted people had been up most of the night repairing the tapestry and tending, amazingly, to only slight burns. As they sat on the Abbey walls watching the people from the town going about their normal business, they allowed themselves a smile.

A Haunting View

By Lin Whitehouse

The journey was spontaneous, although she had thought about going back several times. During bleak moments - of which there had been many over the years – when she wanted to feel some familial warmth, she would plan a trip, but she was never sure if the reception would be friendly or hostile, or indeed whether they would still be there, it was a risk she hadn't been able to contemplate, until today.

This morning, Lucy had woken early with an unexpected pleasant feeling of calm. She lay for a few moments trying to find the cause of the serenity that infused her body and mind. But after a few minutes of silence she was seized with a maternal fear. Almost too afraid, she crept to the side of her daughter's bed, suddenly realising why she felt so rested, it was the first night since Maisie had been born that she hadn't woken during the night.

Too scared to speak she looked for signs of life and focussed on Maisie's face, the bright blue eyes were closed, shut tight, the lips of her rosebud mouth were parted but motionless. Lucy prayed silently, to a God she wasn't sure she believed in, but one who had accepted her prayers several times before, when her inexperience as a mother guided her to, and as Lucy's eyes strayed over the little girl's limp body, to her immediate relief, she saw Maisie's chest rise and fall.

Lucy's wide mouthed smile welcomed Maisie's yawns as she shrugged off sleep. Nothing was wrong save for the fact Maisie had slept through the night, a milestone Lucy thought should be celebrated and without further planning, which might deter her from going back, Lucy readied them for the journey.

As she'd thought about making the trip so many times before, the train timetable was imprinted into her memory. With an urgency as yet not experienced, they made their way to Paragon Station, with Maisie wrapped up well against any unexpected chilly coastal breeze. The rhythmical sounds of the train calmed Lucy, and she pointed out forgotten landmarks to her daughter who, enjoying her first ride on a train, was oblivious to her mother's simmering angst.

It seemed they had arrived too soon. Lucy was not quite ready to retrace her steps in this place that was familiar, but also foreign to her now. Seven years she had been gone, seven tormented years. Would coming back make a difference? Would she be able to address her demons, lay them to rest? Only time and nerve would tell.

Clutching Maisie's hand, they disembarked the train and headed towards the harbour. Maisie complained of being hungry and Lucy produced a biscuit to stave off the pangs of a forgotten breakfast.

'We can get some chips later,' she said, then wondered if she would find the resolve as memories of a home life that she would rather not remember flooded her mind.

'Let's climb up to the Abbey, shall we Maisie?' But Maisie didn't look enthusiastic. 'There's only 199 steps,' Lucy countered, 'I expect we can get some ice cream at the top.'

A mother's bribery was always persuasive, and the two of them mounted the first step. Although she held her daughter's hand firmly, Lucy was too mindful of what she might say - if she saw any of her family – to notice that Maisie was stooping to retrieve some of the coins left in piles at the edges of each step. Too young to understand the coins were left by people to raise money for the upkeep of the Abbey, she sang, contentedly to herself as she gathered a pocketful of change.

The young man, pleased to feel solid ground under his feet, bounded up the steps two at a time, bending at the top step to deposit a handful of coins onto a growing pile. He turned and gazed down to regain sight of something that had attracted his attention. Among the people climbing towards him was a young woman. Even from that distance Aidan could tell she was beautiful. She moved slowly, mounting each step and waiting for a little girl, who clutched her hand, to follow her. It amused him to see the little girl selectively collecting coins from the piles of donations on the steps.

The pair progressed slowly; almost wearily it seemed to Aidan, until at last they reached the top. He stepped back to observe them a while longer, knowing he had to find an excuse to delay them.

'Ice cream, ice cream, mummy,' Maisie said, holding out cupped hands filled with the stolen coins.

Lucy turned with a hostile movement when she heard someone laugh close by.

'I'm sorry,' he said. 'Forgive me for laughing, she just looked so funny.'

'Did you think I'd let her keep the money?' Lucy snapped in response.

As she persuaded Maisie to replace the coins, Aidan remarked on the haunting beauty of the Abbey.

'When I saw the ruins rising up on the headland, I had to drop anchor and investigate,' he said.

'Anchor, anchor' Maisie repeated, clapping her hands.

Aidan explained he had been sailing from the South West of England for the last ten days and nothing had tempted him to come ashore, until now.

Lucy scrutinised the young man as he recounted the story of his journey. She took comfort from his tale and was pleased to listen to the soothing tone of his voice.

'Good job you didn't get washed up like Dracula did,' she laughed, feeling little pricks of excitement tickling her temples.

'Do you know Whitby then?' he asked.

She nodded, giving away too much by her veiled eyes. She wasn't used to a man's company, her one and only previous encounter had resulted in a pregnancy, unwanted at the time, but she had learned to cope and would not be parted from Maisie under any circumstance. Unlike her own mother who had abandoned her, just a couple of days old, left in the hospital waiting for her grandparents to claim, like a parcel left at the collection depot.

Lucy's story unfolded, falteringly, as she walked around the ruins with the man who had introduced himself as Aidan. They walked slowly behind Maisie who skipped along contently, crouching at the knees to inspect loose stones dotted along the route. Then they began to descend the steps from the Abbey and Maisie, who was now tired, balanced on Aidan's wide and welcoming shoulders. As they reached the last step, Lucy revealed her own mother's shame of being pregnant out of wedlock.

'It was a big thing then,' she said, her voice tinged with a sadness she had not allowed to escape before.

Outside the fish and chip shop she used to call home, she explained the kids at school had said she smelled like a battered cod. No matter how many times she had washed, she couldn't disguise the smell of chip fat. Although they were quick to take the bags of scratchings she handed out, the kids had still tormented her, it had prevented her from forming any lasting relationships, and prompted her to leave as soon as she was able, without a backward glance.

'Chips, mummy chips.' Maisie said.

'Do you want to go in?' Aidan asked her softly, concern exposed openly in his temperate manner.

Lucy shook her head, she felt safe being in Aidan's company, but didn't feel ready to face her demons, not yet.

A Changing Wind

By Maureen Chapman

The wind changed direction, freshened and began to blow towards the high cliffs at the same time that the tide turned and the waves steepened, driving the small fishing boat under its red sail towards the safety of the river mouth.

'We've made a good catch today,' said Conn to his nine year old son Fitch. The gasping fish fell from the newly hauled net into the well of the clinker built boat.

'They've lit the cooking fires up at the monastery,' said Fitch, his mind occupied by his grumbling stomach and the thought of hot food. As lay servants, they shared in the communal life of the busy double house ruled by Abbess Hild, using the Rule of St Columba of Iona

'Aye, the light is fading and rough weather is coming,' said Conn glancing up at the thin plumes of smoke bending in the strengthening breeze. The sounds of lowing cattle and the voices of busy men and women carried clearly across the choppy sea. Seabirds, racing out from the cliff ledges met the boat and circled hopefully above it all the way to the river and the landing beach beside the monastery jetty. Then they waited for the cleaning of the fish and their evening meal.

As Fitch helped his father pull the boat up onto the grassy bank in front of the fishermen's cottages, a whirl of movement across the river caught his eye.' Look dad, there's a rider come to the ferry crossing.'

Outside the ferryman's cottage, a tall, blond nobleman was dismounting from a tired, sweating horse. The ferryman himself appeared, followed by a youth who ran to attend to the horse. After a brief conversation, the ferryman rowed the stranger across the deep river to the jetty. Once landed the messenger hurried up the long, steep, zig-zagging path to the monastery above.

'That's one of King Oswy's men. I wonder what's up?' said Conn.

A neighbour came out of his hut. 'He's in a hurry. Is it war or something?' said Wulf. The ferryman shrugged his shoulders and rowed back across the river.

'We'll find out soon enough. Let's deal with the fish and get them into the smoke house. I'm more than ready to eat,' said Conn.

'There should be room for your fish,' said Wulf looking at the size of the catch. 'I caught a couple of good sized salmon myself in the river earlier. They're smoking right now. I'll give you a hand. The dinner bell will go soon.'

Before long they were interrupted by a monk who came hurrying down, calling for everyone to come and hear the news. A little group of people came out from the other cottages, all fishermen or sailors and gathered round him.

'King Oswy and his son, King Alchfrith have called a Synod to be held here at Whitby as soon as the delegates arrive, which could be quite soon. The summons went out early from York and Bamburgh. We are expecting at least fifty or more guests.'

'Let me guess, you want us to catch more fish to help with the feeding,' said Conn.

Brother Lucas grinned. 'I knew you would volunteer Conn.'

'What's a Synod?' asked Fitch.

'It's a gathering of churchmen to debate important matters and lay down the rules for people like us to follow. They plan to settle the Easter question as well as other matters like the tonsure.'

'Ha! That's a bit of religious rubbish,' said Wulf, spitting on the ground. 'The Queen and her son Alchfrith and his court are still fasting for Lent while King Oswy and his court are celebrating the feast despite the friction. I thought these Christians were supposed to live in harmony.'

Brother Lucas rubbed his chin. 'I know. It's a difficult situation. The King was brought up on Iona in the Celtic/Irish tradition while the

Queen grew up in Kent and the Roman tradition. It's going to take all of Mother Hild's skills to deal with this one.'

'Mother Hild is very wise. She will do it,' said Fitch with conviction.

The grown-ups smiled at his innocence.

'Anyway, we have many guests coming who will need feeding. The carpenters are erecting some temporary shelters and the woodcutters will be going out at first light for more timber. Some livestock are being slaughtered and the hens have been told to lay more eggs and the rest of us are running around in circles tripping over each other.' Brother Lucas laughed at the thought. 'Seriously, we need plenty of fish and the visiting ships will need help to enter the river safely and find secure mooring places.'

It's a pity we couldn't have a pond or something stocked with live fish. The smoke house will barely take anymore fish and the salt is running low,' said Conn.

'Now that's an idea we could take up after the Synod. I think we have a back-up supply of salt somewhere, and I'll get the woodcutters to fetch you plenty of oak chips for the smoking,' said Brother Lucas. 'Just do your best lads.' A bell sounded in the evening air. 'Time to eat. Are you finished here?'

'A few minutes more. You can rely on us Brother Lucas,' said Conn. Quick hands completed the work and they all hurried up for their evening meal.

It wasn't long before the guest boats began arriving. The fishermen, experienced in the ways of the tides and currents, helped each boat to its mooring place and had comradely chats with the visiting seamen. A couple of trading boats arrived as well, sensing an opportunity to buy and sell. Stalls were set up on the meadow beside the ferryman's cottage and trade was quickly underway, with stewards sent to buy provisions for the kitchens, scriptorium and the infirmary. The ferryman was kept busy rowing customers back and forth across the river.

A well-used boat came in carrying Bishop Colman and his group of monks from Lindisfarne, Iona and Ireland. Dressed in thick, brown woollen robes and leather sandals, wearing the Celtic tonsure, they were greeted by Mother Hild herself, waiting on the jetty for them. Behind her stood a small group of lay servants who hurried forward to carry the two painted wooden chests, containing the Bishop's robes, silk cape and palladium up to his quarters.

'Welcome my lord Bishop. Was your journey a good one? How are the brothers at Lindisfarne? Are you prepared for the debate? I'm longing to hear all the news.'

'My dear lady Abbess, thank you for your greeting.' He indicated the chests. 'I do dislike all the pomp and ceremony but on this occasion it is necessary. First I must greet these fishermen and give them my blessing. Do they know the stories of the first disciples, now apostles, who were fishermen? Have they heard about our Lord's miracles performed on the Sea of Galilee?' Bishop Colman launched into a short story telling session and then blessed each home and its occupants.

Fitch was full of awe, still feeling the tingling as the Bishop's hands had rested briefly on his head in blessing.

'No doubt you are busy braving the seas to catch fish for us to eat. May the Good Lord who rules the winds and the waves keep you safe and fill your nets.' Then chatting away, the group went up informally to their quarters.

After a couple of wet days, the Latin churchmen arrived from Kent and Gaul. Dressed in fine clothes, they disembarked from their comfortable ships and stood on the jetty wrinkling their noses at the stench of fish. They coughed when smoke was blown over them by a fitful wind. Ignoring the waiting fishermen and lay servants, they turned to greet Hild as she waited patiently for them.

A very large quantity of boxes and chests were being unloaded and the lay servants began carrying them up to the guest quarters, staggering under their heavy burdens on the slippery, muddy slope.

'My lords, I trust you had a good journey. You should find your guest quarters comfortable. I will escort you there myself. Bishop Agilbert, I trust you had a good stay with King Oswy? Wilfred, it's good to see you again after your long stay in Rome and Gaul.'

Wilfred bowed briefly. 'Mother Hild, I hope you have prepared well for our victory and the re-organisation of the churches in Britain,' he said formally.

Mother Hild frowned. 'But the debate has not yet begun. Surely it is wise for all to listen to each other and find some peaceful way to make a final decision. After all, we all serve our Father in heaven and his Christ. The decision should be in harmony with the Holy Scriptures and not our own desires.'

There was a lot of muttering among the churchmen in Latin. Hild understood their words and, rarely for her, looked angry. With cold courtesy she led the way up to the monastery.

The churchmen, all wearing the circular Roman tonsure, formed themselves into a procession behind a very large, ornate silver cross carried by a junior churchman. Chanting psalms, they processed up the slope, sliding a little in the mud. On one tricky corner of the zig-zag path, a monk fell and later a chest was dropped, spilling the contents out into the mud. Wilfred was furious.

The fisher folk stood and watched in silence.

'I wonder what life will be like if he gets control,' said Wulf. 'I think I would go back to being a pagan.'

'Lets go catch some decent fish. I don't want to let Mother Hild down. I pity her, I really do,' said Conn.

While they were out on the sea, they spotted the royal boats sailing in. 'More difficulties for Mother Hild even though they are family. Oh, Fitch, the net feels heavy. Quick, we don't want to lose the catch.'

When Conn and Fitch returned, squeezing in among the many moored boats, the sound of men at work made them look up. A group of burly workmen were creating steps on the difficult parts of the path.

Wulf came over to help with the catch. 'Apparently there's a lot of talk about the fine stone streets of Rome and the many grand marble buildings. We are the barbaric northern outpost in comparison.'

'But Mother Hild has ordered the building of the monastery very well. It is much superior to any of the villages,' said a surprised Conn.

'Well they have tried to sweeten her with costly gifts of books for the library and silken embroidered vestments and altar cloths,' said Wulf, raising an eyebrow.

'That won't sway Mother Hild. But King Oswy is to be the decider so I heard,' said Conn.

The debate was long and the raised voices could be heard some distance away. Everyone was tense and busy with the duties of hospitality. Hot meals were brought down to the fishermen, as their long shifts, governed by the tides, meant irregular hours and a lack of sleep.

Then the debate was over and a decision was made. Brother Lucas came down, very upset and angry. 'They have over-ruled Bishop Colman and make him look foolish. They called us stupid for following the rule of St Columba and said that we must repent of our errors and obey the Latin disciplines. They frightened King Oswy into a bad decision. Wilfred is so clever. We are to speak Latin in our worship.'

'But we can't understand Latin,' said Fitch.

There was a commotion on the path above. Bishop Colman and his retinue came hurrying down, followed by a distressed Mother Hild.

'Get the boat ready. We sail as soon as possible.'

'Please Bishop Colman. Take time to think this through,' pleaded Mother Hild.

'My dear lady, you must make your own decisions for your monastery. He has thrown me out of Lindisfarne and insulted our St Columba. I must go back to Ireland with those who chose freely to come with me. Where else can I go? Such arrogance, such ambition.'

He has some good points. The Celtic church is disorganised and we do need to change some our ways. Why can't we work together?'

But Bishop Colman was adamant and soon the boat left with a few extra monks on board including Brother Lucas.

It wasn't long before a jubilant Wilfred and his group of churchmen paced majestically down the slope with much holy chanting followed by sweating servants and the heavy luggage.

'Conn, are you going fishing?' Mother Hild asked after Wilfred's party had departed.

'You want to come out onto the water?'

'Yes. The monastery will manage without me for few hours. I need to clear my head, do some thinking and praying.'

'Fitch, fetch the sheepskin for our Lady.' It was placed on the bench, while Fitch sat in the well of the boat and Conn stood, guiding the boat out to sea.

Conn took his boat to the usual places, but the sea was empty. He caught nothing.

Mother Hild came out of her reverie. 'No fish Conn? Why?'

'It's a big sea and we are very little. I think the wind is changing, with bad weather and an offshore wind on its way. The tide is still on the ebb. The fish go further out to sea and into deeper water, where we can't follow.'

'Look Dad, the smoke is bending over. The wind just changed.' Fitch pointed up to the cliff top.

'Right, we go home my Lady. I daren't lose you at sea. In the church's storm we need you more than ever.'

Conn used all his seamanship, tacking back and forth to reach the safety of the river in the face of a strengthening off shore wind.

'You had to zig zag, as our cliff path does to fight against the elements,' said Hild. 'The church is caught in a storm, but we can use all our skills to deal with it, and the Lord who rules the waves and the winds is in control of us all. Conn and Fitch, thank you so much. I have learned much from you today. One thing I must do is introduce lessons in Latin for everyone, but we will continue to use our Saxon language too. Our world has changed, so different now to when I first came here and we need to change too.'

A bewildered Conn and Fitch watched Mother Hild go joyfully up the slope.

'What did we say?' asked Fitch.

'I don't know, but I'm going to miss Brother Lucas.

Peace

By Barbara Huntley

The black and white coach parked neatly in a space on the car park. Thirty boys tumbled out, ignoring instructions to walk quietly and not run. 'We've two hours to spend here. Save your energy for the choir competition later!' Michael Boyd, their choirmaster, shouted after them. His assistant, Peter Boyce, laughed as the boys glanced at Whitby Abbey and rushed for the steep stairs leading down to the town. There was food down there, and shops, let alone the challenge of the steep stairs. 'Bet I can get down there first!' one boy shouted. 'Run, Dracula is after us!' another one shrieked.

Only one boy headed for the Abbey ruins. Jim Venables, son of their vicar at St Mark's Church. He was ten years old, fair haired and slightly built. Peter and Michael watched him slowly head for the ruins.

'He's so quiet. Did you hear the other boys teasing him on the way here? ' Peter said.

Michael nodded. 'Yes, I stopped them but I heard them whispering about him. He's scared of his own shadow. I wish now I hadn't asked him to sing that solo tonight but he's good, really good.'

'I know, but will he do it?'

'If he does we could win the trophy,' Michael added.

Peter grinned, 'and that would be brilliant!'

Michael laughed. 'I know. I know the choir could win – but it all depends on Jim.'

'Come on, let's look around the church and then go and get a cup of tea. We can look at the Abbey a bit later.'

117

The Abbey ruins were majestic, rising up tall and grey in front of a clear blue sky. Swallows swooped low chasing flies. A lark sang in the sky. It was a perfect day, Jim thought, as he wandered around the ruins. It was peaceful there. He was a sensitive boy who shrunk from noise and fuss. Every one said he took after his dad. He liked quietness and was glad the boys had run off without him. They had been teasing him on the coach for the last hour, laughing at him for being the vicar's son and whispering about him and saying Dracula would get him. He did not believe them but he felt scared of what was going to happen in a few hours' time, worried about the solo he was going to sing. He had sung solos before, but never in such an important competition. He knew that everything depended on him, Michael had told him often enough. The other boys said he had not got the guts to sing and that he would mess it all up. He would like to prove them wrong.

He sat down on the grass a short distance from the Abbey. The green grass had been there for centuries he told himself. Like the ruins. He fiddled with the little stones in the grass and thought about the Abbey, so tall and solid and mysterious. Years of prayer and history, as his dad would say. It looked as if it were reaching up to heaven. Life was one big worry, he decided. A tear rolled down his cheek and he brushed it away impatiently with the back of his hand.

A slight movement made him look up. A boy a bit older than him was standing there. A boy with a mass of dark curls who was barefoot and wearing a dark grey dress with a leather belt. They smiled at each other shyly. Jim wondered who he was, he looked as if he were dressed ready for a play. He remembered what his dad had told him about being polite and said 'Hello, I'm Jim. Are you going to be in a play?'

The boy grinned and looked puzzled. 'A play? I don't think so.'

Jim said 'I'm visiting here. What's your name?'

'My friends call me Caddy. I live here.'

'Do you? Where?'

Caddy waved his hand vaguely and said 'Just over there, behind the Abbey. I live in a stable and look after the cattle.'

Jim could not see anything but ruins but he did not comment.

'Why are you looking so worried?' Caddy suddenly asked.

Jim told him about the teasing and the solo and the competition and Caddy nodded his head wisely. 'I know how you feel. We sing songs after work and we all have to sing something. My mind went totally blank one day and the others laughed at me. The men I work with get a bit drunk at times.'

Jim looked at him curiously 'Did they ever stop laughing at you?'

Caddy nodded. 'One day I was so upset I ran back to the stables and God spoke to me in a dream and gave me a new song to sing. All about creation, it was. God gave me lots of poems to sing. When I woke up I went and started singing and people thought it wonderful. I enjoyed singing after that and I sang to lots of important people.'

Jim stared at him, not sure what to believe.

'Come with me.' Jim followed Caddy into the centre of the Abbey.

'Look up.' He said and Jim did.

Caddy laughed. 'Think of the sky as the Abbey's roof, put there by God the creator.' He swung round to face Jim. 'Sing to the sky, to God and to me,' he commanded. Jim felt himself going red.

'Sing here?' he asked.

'Yes. Sing your solo. Let me hear it. There's no one else here.' He added.

Jim obeyed. His voice rose up clear and pure, seeming to go up past the ruins to the blue sky. He somehow felt part of the Abbey, it felt good.

Caddy grinned 'I know your choir will win the competition and it will be thanks to you.'

'How can you know that?' Jim asked.

'I just do. You're brilliant!'

A bell rang. Caddy stood up. 'It's time for me to go,' he said.

He bent down and picked up a smooth grey stone. He then picked up a sharp stone and scratched a cross on the grey one. He held it in his hand and muttered a few words in a language Jim did not understand and then handed it to him.

He looked at Jim 'Take this stone. I have blessed it, so it is special. Remember Jim, sing because God gave you a voice to sing with. Enjoy yourself singing. Forget about the listeners. You'll be fine.' He gave him a friendly punch and disappeared towards the Abbey.

Jim looked at his watch. Time had passed quickly and he had only half an hour before the coach left. He must buy his mum and dad a postcard of the Abbey, he decided and hurried to the English Heritage shop. He chose a view of the Abbey and took it to the counter. A smiling lady took his money and put the postcard in a bag.

'Had a good time, pet?' she asked. She had watched him wandering around the Abbey. He had looked lonely when he went to sit on the grass by himself and she had felt sorry for him.

'Yes thank you,' Jim said politely 'I met one of your actors and we had a long chat.'

'Actors?' she asked surprised. She had not seen him talking to anyone.

'Well, he was dressed up,' Jim said 'in a grey dress, bit like a sack, with a leather belt'

The assistants called across the room to her friend, 'Emily, have we any actors around today?'

'No.'

'He said he was called Caddy by his friends' Jim told them. 'I told him I was scared about singing in a choir competition later and he talked to me and now I don't feel scared at all!'

The assistants looked at each other and frowned. 'Caddy? You couldn't have met Caedmon,' Emily said. 'You must've fallen asleep and seen him in a dream!'

Jim shook his head and shrugged. He had never heard of Caedmon. 'All I know is I met a boy called Caddy. He was nice to me. I expect he's a good actor. He told me he was a well known poet, but I suppose he was boasting. I must go now. I am needed. I have a solo to sing!' Jim told them importantly. He heard the assistants laughing as he ran off, but he did not care.

Michael and Peter watched as Jim hurried across the car park. They smiled at him as he clambered on to the coach and he beamed back at them.

'Okay Jim?'

'Yes, I met a boy who told me we would win.'

'Did you fall asleep and dream?' Peter asked laughing.

Jim shook his fair curls, 'No. He was real. The assistants in the shop mentioned a young man called Caedmon, they seemed to know about him. Have you heard about him?'

Michael caught Peter's eye and then looked at Jim. 'We must really get going! I'll tell you more about him another time.'

'I'm ready to sing now,' Jim told them. 'Caedmon said I was to think about God and sing for Him.' He had already decided not to mention the grey stone but held it firmly in his pocket.

As the coach left the Abbey Jim looked for Caedmon. He thought he saw the shadow of a boy running around the Abbey but the wind blew and it was no longer there. Must be imagination, he told himself, and turned his thoughts to the coming festival. He clutched the smooth grey stone. He knew that he was going to do well and they would win, Caddy had said so.

And they did! People heard Jim sing and a whole new world opened up. The choir made records with Jim as their soloist. They sang in churches and cathedrals around England. Jim was no longer scared, but sang confidently and enjoyed it. Michael told him about St Caedmon and he did not know what to believe. How could he have met a boy who lived centuries before? A boy who was also bullied. A boy who could sing because God gave him the ability. Was it a dream or real? But he had the grey stone with a cross on it – how could he have got it if it was all a dream? How could he have carved a cross on a stone in his sleep?

Three years later Jim arrived at the Abbey with his father. They crossed the car park. Jim's heart was thumping with excitement. What would they find there? He fingered the stone in his pocket. He wanted his dad to find the Abbey as helpful as he did.

Rev. Venables was heavy hearted. His wife had died two months before and he felt so miserable he could barely speak to anyone. He felt he had all the cares of the world on his shoulders. The Bishop had told him to go away for a bit and Jim had suggested Whitby. His father had just shrugged. He did not care where they went. The sun shone in a blue sky. Jim watched the swallows flying backwards and forwards and heard the skylark high in the sky. His dad barely noticed them.

The Abbey was as beautiful as ever and the ruins, mellowed by years of prayer and love, seemed to link earth with heaven. Jim led his father to the middle of the Abbey and they looked up at the cloudless blue sky. The grass moved gently in the breeze. Then Jim heard a voice singing quietly, and realised it was coming from the ruins. He looked for the boy in the grey dress with a leather belt, but there was no one there. The sound soared up above the ruins to the sky and beyond.

'Can you hear it dad?' Jim asked.

His father nodded, speechless as he felt peace and strength flowing into him. The peace that passes understanding, that he had preached about so often from the Bible. Now it was true for him. He felt he could face life again. As he went back to his car he smiled at his son. He started up the car as he quoted 'Well Jim, 'God's in his heaven...All's right with the world.'

The Clouds of Whitby

By Stan McReady

The great library of Cambridge University was adorned with aged books that soaked the air with a distinctive 'smell of knowledge'. The huge reading tables filled the room, sitting at one such table was a 14 year old girl, whose name was Jayne. She revelled in history, especially that which concerned ancient Britons; the Celts and Druids firing her imagination.

Today she was helping her father, who was the head curator at the British Museum. He had once been a renowned archaeologist, recognised throughout the world for his works on Druidic Briton. The bond between Jack and his second daughter Jayne (one of a twin) was strong; she admired him tremendously; and he in turn was only too happy to impart his knowledge.

The current thesis Jack was working on, was entitled 'British Abbeys' (known to Jack affectionately as the 'Abbey habit') and focused on monastic and Abbey life throughout the ages; this being the reason for the visit to the university library.

Jayne's curiosity for the day centred on the works of the Venerable Bede. Most of his work associated with Whitby Abbey and after six hours of relentless reading, the lids of her liquid blue eyes became heavy. Weary, tired, inevitably her head began to sag, finding solace in her folded arms. Jayne slept.

Within a blinking of an eye, she was abruptly awoken by the sound of the manuscript monitor she was using, beeping, warning her there remained only five minutes of viewing credit. She looked at the screen, to her amazement words started to jumble, and specific letters appeared to be jumping out at her, giving the impression of a 3d image puzzle.

Subconsciously Jayne picked up her pen from the desk and started to scribble down the letters as they flashed into view.

UNTOFTREONAEFHALCHFHALLYEFEEKETHTHINETRUTHE

As quickly as it had begun, it stopped. Jayne looked at the letters in complete bewilderment. She had no idea what they could mean.

A voice startled her, saying "Unto Streonaeshalch Shall Ye Seek the Truth."

"What did you say?" she stuttered turning to look at her father.

"Roughly translated it says. Go to Streonaeshalch and you will find the truth," he said sitting down beside her.

"I don't understand," replied Jayne rather perplexed.

Jack pointed to the screen and explained "You must remember the Vicar of Dibley, when Alice was reading from the old Bible. The letter 'F' was pronounced as an 'S'."

"How can I forget?" replied Jayne smiling.

"What I would like to know my dear; is why you wrote that?" Jack asked inquisitively.

"I don't know. The letters just seemed to jump out at me on the screen."

"I see, you know I really should be making a visit to one of the Abbeys as part of my work, how about a trip to Whitby."

"Why Whitby?" replied a bemused Jayne.

"Because Streonaeshalch is the ancient Gaelic name for Whitby."

The following day Jayne and Jack set off at around midday and made their way northwards towards the East coast of Yorkshire.

"I'm glad it's only the two of us, Dad. I couldn't have coped listening to Janice moaning all the way. There's no Dolce & Gabbana in Whitby."

"Now, now we don't know that for sure. I am sure there are hundreds of shops for your sister to indulge herself in," laughed Jack. "Anyway your mother was relishing the thought of another few days with Janice." He raised his eyebrows.

"How much will that cost you?"

"About two weeks of washing up?"

Both of them laughed at the prospect.

They approached Whitby around dusk. The Skyline of the town was etched by the receding sunlight glazing the ruins of the Abbey. "Look Dad, it's awesome. I never thought it would be this stunning."

"You know pumpkin; I am ashamed to say I have never actually been here. I am amazed. Look; that must be St. Mary's Church over there in front of the Abbey. I believe Bram Stoker took inspiration for his novel Dracula from the surrounding area."

"I can see why, it looks quite spooky."

Jack and Jayne smiled to themselves. They were ready for adventure and glad they had come to Whitby.

"You know the first Abbey was destroyed by the Vikings," said Jack.

"Didn't you say it was rebuilt again after 1066," asked Jayne.

"Yes, it was by Reinfrid. He was a soldier monk. It lasted up until Henry VIII," replied Jack. "The place really is steeped in history."

Jack turned the next corner and parked up in front of the hotel. "We are here. Come on. I could eat a horse."

"Not if I eat it first," chuckled Jayne. "Can we go up to the Abbey tonight Dad?"

Jack gazed at the ruins in the dusk laden air and sighed deeply "No my dear, tomorrow will be soon enough. Anyway it is dark and I don't have my garlic. But fangs anyway."

"Dad, that's really corny," smiled Jayne.

Jayne and Jack rose with the sun. They were the first diners of the day.

"So where shall we start Dad?"

"I think we should have a look around the church and the cemetery. Then finish with the Abbey and museum, if that's alright with you?"

Jayne nodded and smiled, as she took another bite of her bacon butty.

"By the way Jayne, I have asked Mr. Charlton to meet us up at the Abbey. I hope you don't mind. He is a respected local historian, and a bit of an expert on Whitby. He may be able to give us some help in looking for what ever it is that holds the truth!"

"Should we tell him about the message?" asked Jayne.

"No pumpkin. I think we should keep that bit to ourselves. We don't want him thinking we are a couple of nutcases do we?" laughed Jack.

By the time the local clock had struck 9.00am, the pair had begun their ascent of the steep 199 steps, which snaked up the south cliff towards St. Mary's Church, and the Abbey ruins. As they neared the top of the stairs, Jayne could see rows upon rows of concrete headstones poking through the cliff edge, like tiny soldiers defending the church and Abbey. Almost on cue, as they reached the final step, the sun burst through the clouds, and Jack thought to himself what a fine way to spend the day. It was certainly better than trudging around shops with his wife and other daughter. A slight pang of guilt went through Jack's mind as he visualised his poor wife having to put up with Janice.

"Good morning Jack." came a cheerful tone, which shook Jack from his thoughts.

"Good morning Bill. How are you?" replied Jack, turning around to face the direction of the voice. "Jayne this is Mr. Bill Charlton. The gentleman I mentioned to you at breakfast."

"Hello, Mr. Charlton. Pleased to meet you."

"Call me Bill chuck, everyone else does. Now what can I tell you about this wonderful place. It's breathtaking don't you think?"

Both Jayne and her father nodded.

"Now the Abbey was founded in AD657 on the site of what most archaeologists believe to have previously been a Roman signal station?" said Bill as they walked together.

Jack nodded. "Yes the Synod of AD664 was founded here. It's believed they used to debate the date of Easter and such like."

"Wasn't the body of St. Hilda buried here?"

"That's right," said Bill surprised. "She was the first Abbess."

"My Daughter's done her homework," laughed Jack.

"I would love to discover something we don't know," Jayne sighed.

Bill smiled and chuckled to himself "I see a relic hunter."

Jayne looked at Bill and smiled not knowing what else to say.

"Well there is jet in the hills yonder and I'm betting that you could find ammonite down on the beach head. Many fossils have been found down there, even pterodactyls. Now if all that fails, well there is always fish and chips. Now that's what I call real gold."

Jack and Bill laughed, but Jayne was not amused. She didn't like being patronised.

Jayne made a polite excuse and left the two men to their discussions and walked down one of the many paths in the direction of the Abbey. She gazed westwards towards the calm North Sea; its smell filled her nostrils, and closing her eyes took in another deep breath.

She opened her eyes feeling a charge of energy invigorate her body and continued to walk down the length of the Abbey. She walked past the north and south transepts, gazing at the crumbling columns as she made her way towards the nave.

A voice boomed out to Jayne. "Did you know that these graves date back to Anglo-Saxon times, and are remnants of the first Abbey?" It was Bill pointing at the gravestones.

Jayne turned and loudly replied, "Yes I know that, thank you."

She carried on, wandering about for a long while, fascinated by a land that seemed to define the very fabric of time itself. Jayne let her mind wander, imagining what it must have seemed like when it was full of song, majesty, pomp and ceremony. Gazing at the columns, transepts and gothic framed window arches, she contemplated what it might be that she was looking for.

Her search took her eventually to the edge of a tranquil pond; a little way from the ruined site itself. The water's surface lay so still and the sky so clear and from where Jayne was standing it magically reflected the eastern wall of the Abbey giving the illusion of a huge X. Jayne thought to herself X marks the spot! Could it be that simple?

A chill crept up Jack's spine, making the hairs on his neck bristle. He looked up towards the sky. A dark cumulous cloud appeared to have formed. It was racing at a most unusual speed. He scanned the horizon for more, but there were none like this. The grey cloud appeared to be perfectly circular and it seemed to use the other clouds in the vicinity as camouflage.

Jack turned to Bill; he was also looking at the sky. "What is that?" he asked Bill, but Bill was too intrigued, to reply. Jack felt a sense of foreboding. Where is Jayne he thought. Jayne was nowhere to be seen. He called out "Jayne, Jayne."

He felt a knot turning in his stomach and watched with trepidation as the strange object in the sky, cast its shadow upon the ground. The round silhouette swept across the cliffs of Sandsend and approached the western side of Whitby. It climbed effortlessly up the steps bathing the concrete sentinels as it made its way towards the Abbey and …..Jayne. There she was… alone and unaware.

"Jayne" he bellowed. But he knew she was too far away to hear him. He franticly ran towards her, leaving Bill behind. The circular cloud-like craft stopped abruptly and hovered above her.

She remained staring at the reflection on the pond, when the extraordinary cloud dwelled upon her and did not notice the beam of light that pulsed from it, fully encasing her. It completely cut off her world and opened up another, in which images of times gone by flashed before her.

Bombs began dropping around her, she saw the Abbey being hit. Then came the Tudor knights, destroying the Abbey, killing monks and nuns in their path, which merged into images of Reinfrid, standing in awe of his perfect building. Then there came visions of Vikings, pillaging, ransacking, destroying the Abbey and reducing it to rubble. Images seemed to slither over each other and pour into a new scene. The Abbey was then again whole, only for a while, then. Blood flowed over the land, yet the Abbey withstood the Danes.

After that there was peace, tranquility. She saw monks and nuns tending to the gardens around the Abbey, each one disappearing as the Abbey "unpicked itself" stone by stone until just the foundations remained. Jayne could clearly see a labourer carrying rocks and laying them on the wall of the Abbey. Then a woman dressed in a white gown appeared and smiled. She walked serenely towards Jayne, she spoke and continued to walk right through her.

All was then still. The tube of light vanished and the circular cloud merged back into the heavens.

Arriving at the edge of the pond, Jack shouted, whilst catching his breath. "Jayne! Are you all right?"

"I...I...don't know," said Jayne still stunned.

He held her in his arms for several minutes. "It's alright now, pumpkin. It's all over. It's gone." He released her from his grip "It stopped right above you. Frightened the life out of me. You are ok, aren't you?" Jack reached for Jayne's hands which were fully clenched through fear. Jayne slowly unfurled her left hand and Jack took it softly and held it reassuringly.

"Now let me have your other hand sweetheart."

Jayne slowly lifted her right hand. Unfurling it, both Jack and Jayne gazed at the small gold necklace nestling in the palm of her hand. The chain contained an exquisite small enamelled shield. It was emblazoned with a crowned black bird adorned by a single blue tail feather.

"Where did this come from? It looks to me remarkably like a coat of arms from the court of King Leodegrance. Nevertheless it appears to be very old..... Very old indeed."

"I was just staring at the reflection in the pond. The sun just disappeared. A light came from nowhere, I just couldn't move. I saw the Abbey as it was. It was like I travelled through the Abbey's history. It stopped when the Abbey was being built. I saw the men building it. Then this old woman in a white gown came to me she was talking but she walked right through me as if I wasn't there. Then you grabbed me."

"What did she say? Take your time," said Jack gently. "Try to remember it word for word."

"She said, now the truth shall be known. With the coming of... Well I wasn't too sure what she said then. It sounded like tartar sauce."

"Mmmm," mused Jack as he rubbed his temples "tartar sauce."

"I didn't see her give me anything. I don't understand it Dad. What just happened?"

Jack looked pensively at Jayne and asked "Could she have said, Tarturus?"

"Yes, I think so. I think that's what she said, Tarturus," replied Jayne. "What is it? What does it mean?"

Jack replied "are you sure that's everything you heard?"

"She said something else. Something like "restore my name." What does it mean? I don't understand." Jayne was confused.

Jack turned his gaze away from Jayne and rubbing his chin replied "I'm not sure, my child......... I think it could mean a visit to STONEHENGE."

By the Pond

By Jessica Rogers

"There is a legend that a white lady is seen in one of the windows of Whitby Abbey ruins."

I see why he fell in love with this place more than with me. I guess my long luscious blonde locks, don't compare with the tall, wide pillars with the shades of blue, brown, green and grey. My small hazel eyes aren't as dreamy as the richly painted glass inside of the building. Every spare moment we spent together. I remember spending many late nights beside the beautiful pond with him, admiring the breathtaking view whilst having a picnic of freshly baked bread and cheese.

We used to do everything together. We had some sort of connection, which made me feel quite flustered and made my stomach churn. The way he looked at me, sent shivers through my spine and made my legs want to melt on the floor.

He wasn't particularly attractive. He had long brown hair filled with many loose ringlets and his face wasn't symmetrical. But to me he was perfect. No matter what anyone else said.

It all started by the pond outside the local Abbey. I usually went there to recollect my thoughts. One day, I saw a stranger was sitting in my usual spot. He was throwing pebbles into the water. I was about to walk away and then he turned around. There was an instant bond. I suddenly felt that I could trust him. I sat down beside him. We got talking. He kept on complimenting me on the white dress which I was wearing. When it started to turn dark, we then had to part but promised each other that we would return to the same spot the next day. I came home with a wide grin upon my face and every day since then I have gone to the lake. Until this day came.

I came to the pond as usual however he was nowhere to be seen, only a piece of parchment. It was left on a patch of grass in our regular meeting place. Written on the note was:

'Sorry. Dad has sent me to be a monk. I have realised my true calling.'

No "I love you" or "I will miss you" just "sorry". My heart was completely broken and beyond repair. The first thought, which rushed inside my head, was that I should go to the Abbey and declare my love for him as there may be a chance that he will change his mind. Maybe I could even become a nun.

I walked to the Abbey, my pace quickening as I drew nearer. Mother thought I was off "reading" again. In my hand was my heart and I was prepared to give it to my beloved.

Now I was by the pond. Close enough to see that something was happening inside the Abbey. Monks, nuns and commoners were running away from the building, shouting, "Save yourselves, the Danes are here!" A huge black flag was towering above the Abbey tower. I had to run faster than I ever had done before, to save my life.

Sprinting to warn my family back home, I felt betrayed that he had left me. Though mostly I felt like that I had done more wrong as I left him there to perish. I will never forget leaving my love to save myself.

My family all ran as quickly as possible away from our home. The whole time I couldn't stop thinking about him and how I chose to save my life over his. I acted as if my deep mad love for him never existed. Didn't our time together mean anything to me?

Looking back, I still don't understand why he left me to become a monk and why I left the love of my life, to save myself. Now, married with two children, I still live in the past. I gaze into my husband's eyes but I never had with him the same feeling that I had once before. When my sixteen-year-old daughter told me she had found love, I fully supported her. I have experienced true love and I want my daughter to be happy with whomever she has met.

My husband however has different views. He wants her to marry a man of great status. He thinks she is too beautiful and talented. He always comments on how she is the spitting image of me, when I was younger. That was when he first met me, after my family and I ran away. We stayed at our relatives and he was the son of one of the neighbours. He always followed me around and then asked my parents for my hand in marriage. We couldn't refuse the offer as we had little income, only just enough for starvation rations for all of us. He was wealthy, noble and very caring.

I usually let him have the final say in our household, however in this subject I put my dainty little foot down. We have agreed to let my daughter bring home the man of her desires. I wish I had the man of my dreams, or at least to see what he has doing now. I have never entered Whitby Abbey since it was destroyed by the Danes.

Today is the day when I meet my daughter's beau. I put on my favourite white dress, the one that I wore on the first meeting with my loved one. She giggles nervously and has lost her appetite – even to my homemade bread with foreign cheese (a special treat). It reminds me of my feelings when I was in love. I can't fight it any longer, I have to let go, stop holding on to the past. Focus on my family. That's where my morals lie.

A loud knock echoes through the house. My daughter jumps up from her seat and goes to answer it. What I would do to have that feeling of excitement again. I have to find out what had happened to my dear loved one. My daughter re-enters the kitchen on the hand of an elderly looking gentleman. My loved one. My George.

He's alive, was the first thing I thought. Then I suddenly realise he is my daughter's suitor. We were supposed to look alike, but I didn't realise how similar we both were. Any memories of the feeling of love have now shattered. He had fallen for my daughter and judging by the expression on his face, he didn't recognise me.

The pain I felt inside was like no other that I had felt before. It was a sharp pain that struck deeply through my heart. My head became dizzy and all I could see was a white light.

Suddenly, I was in the Abbey beside my favourite pond. The pond where I first met George and the pond where he broke my heart. I know he still loves me. I'll just remain here until he comes and says those three important words.

I will never give up waiting for him.

Generations

By Caroline Hindson

If any pilgrim shall come from distant
parts with wish to dwell in the monastery...
he shall be received for as long as
he wishes.
The Rule of St Benedict

"About time, Grandpa," Emily shrieked gleefully when her Grandpa Arthur announced that as a special birthday treat he would tell her and Benjamin the 'special' story.

Grandpa removed the crystal stopper from an antique port decanter and poured himself a measure. The old man lowered himself into his favourite Chesterfield wingback next to the open fire and made the usual show of getting comfortable on the well-worn green leather. The movement caused him to tilt his drink slightly. Quick as lightening, he rescued a drip of the exceptional vintage with his finger and touched it to his tongue.

The children settled cross-legged on the soft hearthrug and waited patiently, enthused by the familiar ritual of story time. The fire glowed orange and crackled pleasantly. The scene was set.

Grandpa took a sip of the garnet-coloured liquid and began. "This is no ordinary story," he warned, "this time you need to pay especially close attention because I'm going to give you a mission."

Two large pairs of dark eyes returned his gaze expectantly. "Do you both know who Henry VIII is?" Arthur asked.

"He's the fat king who killed his wives," returned Emily.

Arthur nodded sagely and aimed an enquiring glance at his grandson.

135

"He had syphilis," offered Benjamin.

Arthur arched a bushy eyebrow. "Good, you both know your history," he continued, concealing his amusement. "Well we'll begin the story during the reign of Henry VIII. As you may already know from school, Henry decided to close the monasteries and nunneries in England so that he could take their money and pass the land on to his friends. Tonight's story begins in Whitby Abbey where you had your school trip last week."

The dark eyes widened in anticipation. They had both had great fun recreating the Abbey and listening to the talking heads of Bram Stoker and Brother William.

"14th December 1539," Arthur commenced dramatically.

"Do the voices," the children begged.

Grandpa smiled conspiratorially, then in an anxious tone cried out: "Abbot, the King's Commissioners draw close with the deed of surrender."

The twins' expectant expressions morphed into delight.

Arthur continued in his own voice: "The Abbey's community had gathered together in the Great Hall. Abbot De Vall's authoritative voice sliced through the rumble of anxious monks." Grandpa's tone became commanding: "Go with Brother William to the Chapter House immediately."

The old raconteur paused for a sip from his goblet before continuing. "Brother William began herding the subdued group out of the Great Hall. As they filed past him, Abbott De Vall seized a dawdling monk by the habit. 'Daniel, come here,' the abbot whispered, 'quickly, there's no time to waste.' They hurried towards a doorway at the end of the South Aisle. In seconds, the abbot had gained entry with a misshapen iron key and was racing up the staircase within. Daniel held back, acting as lookout. Following a brief commotion from above, Abbot de Vall reappeared clutching a package wrapped in timeworn red brocade fabric. Indicating the entrance with a nod of his head, the abbot spoke urgently: 'Get inside. Check above the doorway for a stone sticking out further than the rest.'

Obediently, Daniel entered the confined area and groped the stone surface until he discovered the protruding stone. 'I've got it,' he yelled back. 'Push on it,' commanded the abbot, 'push hard'. The stone moved easily beneath Daniel's powerful shove, producing an instant rumble of something heavy moving. They watched the base step pivot slowly aside to reveal an additional staircase descending beneath the Abbey. The abbot thrust his precious bundle into Daniel's arms and bade him conceal it under his habit. 'Now, make haste down the staircase to Mr Fisk's shop, lad. Deliver that package to him directly, and don't come back. Your uncle Fisk will look after you now.'

As he gaped at the hole, Daniel heard the door close behind him. Then Abbot de Vall's strong hands were manoeuvring him toward the dark opening until he smelled the dank air rising from beneath. The young monk sought reassurance once more in the abbot's compelling eyes then deftly he began to descend. Daniel saw that the staircase stretched far below him. Every now and again it seemed to twist in a new direction and in places the walls revealed strange carved letters which he could not decipher.

Far above, he heard the deep dragging sound of the slab shifting back into place. The abbot would now hasten to rejoin the brethren before he was missed. The valuable relic they guarded was on its way to safety in the nick of time, and the realisation spurred him on.

Gradually, the incline became less steep until the steps ended and Daniel found himself in a long tunnel. After what seemed like an age, the passage ended at an ancient wooden door bearing further illegible writing. With no apparent means of entry, Daniel inhaled the thin air deeply, and with the confidence of youth knocked twice on the door. Mr Fisk answered the door to Daniel and ushered his nephew inside a smallish room with no windows and a roaring fire, barring the door closed behind them. Floor to ceiling shelves lined the walls, containing hundreds of leather-bound volumes in a range of autumn colours. Uncle Fisk was tall and pale, and he was receding at the temples, a bit like your old Grandpa." Arthur stroked a hand across his pate. "Mr Fisk accepted the heavy package and rested it on a pockmarked wooden writing desk to free it carefully from its once fine wrappings." Grandpa retrieved his port glass and circled the rim with a long crooked index finger, making it sing. "What do you suppose was inside?" he challenged.

Emily and Benjamin were hanging on every word. "Was it a book Grandpa?" Emily ventured, gaining an impressed nod from her brother.

"Well done. Yes it was a very special book," Grandpa replied. "In those days, the monks were the best educated members of society and they made records for future generations. This tome contained records of Whitby dating back centuries. But more importantly, it held her secrets."

"Is tome another word for book, Grandpa?" Benjamin interrupted.

"Yes, well done," Arthur praised, "a tome is a large and often important book. Now where was I? Oh, yes, Mr Fisk removed the red and gold cloth to reveal a magnificent illuminated manuscript bound in leather-covered oak and secured with brass clasps. Inside, the first letter of each page was larger than the rest and decorated in coloured ink. That type of letter is called a rubric.

"Anyway, Mr Fisk was loyal to Abbot De Vall, and he promised Daniel a home in exchange for his help in keeping the Abbey's book safe. In time, he confided in Daniel about the book's heritage and taught him to read the words so that he could learn the history within. Daniel discovered that the task of recording Whitby's history had begun with the first Abbess, Hilda, in the year 657.

"In the centuries that followed, several attempts were made to destroy the book but all of them failed. The monks hid it well," Grandpa swept his right hand to the side, "even creating their tunnel to evacuate the book in volatile times."

"Why would a book like that be so important?" Benjamin wanted to know.

"Why would anyone want to destroy it?" added Emily.

"Well, it is a very ancient book, children," Arthur explained, now approaching the crucial part of his story. "The book contains not only the only true record of Whitby's history, but also information that could be very damaging to the town."

The children exchanged puzzled glances. "What kind of information?" Benjamin asked.

"Can you remember listening to Bram Stoker's talking head in the Abbey Museum?" Grandpa prompted.

"Yes, he wrote Dracula," answered Benjamin.

"He was inspired by Whitby," added Emily.

"He certainly was," Grandpa agreed gravely. "What I'm about to tell you might at first be a little frightening, but I'm afraid you have to be told. After all, it is part of your heritage. Bram Stoker wasn't merely inspired by Whitby, children. He was a member of the Golden Dawn, a secret society which met in the town. They were interested in the occult, which means things like magic and the supernatural. It was after one of these meetings that Stoker discovered the inspiration for his so-called fiend, Dracula. Stoker gathered ideas for his new novel by exploring Whitby's narrow alleyways and haunted corners. One evening his curiosity led him to St Mary's churchyard. He was following the path to the Abbey when he encountered a harrowing scene. A young woman sat slumped on a bench among the gravestones. Stoker stopped short, filled with concern. To his dismay, a sinister black figure suddenly loomed over the stricken form. The figure immediately sensed Stoker's presence and lifted its deathly white face toward him. Even from a distance and in the pale moonlight, Stoker realised that this was an ancient vampire. Its black eyes locked on his, flashing crimson with fury. Chilled to the bone, Stoker backed away, unable to drag his gaze from the vampire. A feeling of intoxication washed over him. An irrational thought occurred: perhaps he should approach the creature. What harm could it do? Panic welled inside him as he felt common sense deserting him."

The children cuddled into each other for comfort in the growing tension. "What did he do?" said Emily.

"This was a man who had studied European folklore for many years," Grandpa explained, "he knew exactly what to do. Summoning all of his resolve, he thrust the malevolent suggestion back at its sender with such vigour that he broke the creature's hold over the young lady and caused it to stumble and cradle its head. Stoker would surely have perished had the vampire not been feeding, but its attempt to entrance two victims simultaneously had been too ambitious. Stoker fled for his life, fearing that the devil himself would come after him. However, he did manage to reach his lodgings safely. He immediately protected himself by hanging a crucifix around his neck and garlic flowers at his windows. In the morning, he resolved to use his journalistic skills to uncover all he could of Whitby's dread goings on and expose her dark secret to the world in his next novel. In the course of his discreet investigations, he was soon directed to our family."

This revelation elicited simultaneous intakes of breath from the twins.

"Our family has been trusted to hide the truth of Whitby's vampires for centuries," Grandpa confided. "When Daniel and the abbot rescued the book, they saved it from certain discovery by the King's Commissioners who would have ransacked the Abbey for its treasures. Our ancestors knew that once people found out the truth, they would stop visiting; they would send in armies to hunt down the vampires. My own father entrusted me with this book," Arthur seemed to conjure the ancient leather-bound manuscript from thin air. "It has passed down the generations and one day it will pass to you two."

The children's faces darkened as they discovered their legacy.

"Stoker must have been fearless and determined to approach our ancestors the way he did," Arthur continued. "His interest in the Occult made him receptive to ideas others would dismiss as mere nonsense or imagination; he had uncovered Whitby's illusion. What is more, he came armed. As head of the family, my father had no choice but to propose a deal."

Benjamin looked suspicious. "But Mr Stoker was going to tell the secret, Grandpa," he pointed out.

"That's true, but my father spotted a way in which they could both benefit. You see, it was clear that our town was already beginning to attract interest from groups like the Golden Dawn. The family were uneasy about people with inquisitive minds and receptive imaginations being drawn to Whitby's dark and ruined splendour. Stoker hinted that the Golden Dawn had already developed a fascination with vampires. A fascination which had not only prompted Stoker to begin research for Dracula, but had also provoked his late night visit to St Mary's graveyard. We were very lucky that he was alone.

"Well children, I'm sure you'll agree that the town's veil of secrecy was beginning to slip and that it would only be a matter of time before others would guess the truth. Fortunately, despite Mr Stoker's passion for the Occult, his sole motivation had always been simply the pursuit of the truth. He had fallen in love with our town and didn't wish to see her disgraced or destroyed," Arthur explained. "He agreed that by working together he and the family could create a smokescreen; a myth based on reality to obscure the truth. Stoker would learn accurate details for his fictional Dracula, but he could never reveal his source. What is more, he understood the price he would have to pay for breaking this agreement.

"And look how well it worked. Vampires remain the stuff of fiction and the tourists keep coming, oblivious to the risks they take, even delighting in our little town's sinister associations. So tell me, children, didn't our gamble pay off?"

"But what about the victims, Grandpa?" Emily asked, imploring him with her unusually dark eyes.

"Oh, don't worry about that my dear. There will always be victims." Her grandpa flashed a meaningful smile, "as long as the tourists keep coming."

Jet

By Jenna Warren

The nine year old boy looked up at the Abbey. From this angle, the ruin was a dark silhouette against the dawn sky. A rose window, deprived of glass, stared down at him like a great eye.

It looks like a skeleton, the boy thought. The skeleton of some giant beast. But at the same time there was the sense that it was a living thing, a thing with memories, waiting to wake up.

'Do you know what this is, son?'

The boy had been so lost in his thoughts about the Abbey that he was startled by his father's voice. He turned to look at him. His father held up a small piece of shiny black stone.

'Jet,' said the boy. It wasn't likely to be anything else. 'Whitby jet.'

His father smiled. 'That's right. I'm going to carve your mother a pendant from this piece of jet. It will be the shape of an oval, with a picture of the Abbey carved into it. Do you think that sounds like a good idea?'

The boy was unsure about this. Ever since Prince Albert had died and Queen Victoria had started wearing jewellery made from jet in remembrance, the stone had been in great demand. His father was a renowned craftsman, but most of the jet pendants in his shop were tiny. He looked at the Abbey again. It seemed a very big thing to carve onto a pendant. He wanted to express his doubts to his father, but he decided he should be kind to him instead. After all, you could make beautiful things out of jet, and his mother would probably love a piece of jewellery of her own.

'That sounds like a very good idea, father,' he said.

'Your mother loves the Abbey. When we were married, we visited the Abbey on our honeymoon. That was when we decided to settle in Whitby.'

The boy sighed. His father was dwelling on the past again. The boy found this mildly embarrassing.

He preferred to think of the future.

Michelle was tired. It had been a long journey, but at last she was home.

It was strange that she still thought of Yorkshire as her home. After all, she hadn't lived here for many years. She had moved to France with her parents when she was seven. At the age of eighteen she had returned to England, and had attended university in London. She had lived and worked down there ever since. Her parents still lived in France and most of her childhood friends had left the area a long time ago, so she had never had any reason to return to Whitby. Until now.

That evening, standing near the Whale Bone on the West Cliff, Michelle looked out over the old town which she had often visited as a child. Then she allowed her gaze to travel up the opposite cliff, following the route of the 199 steps, until she was looking at St Hilda's Church and the Abbey.

She realised that she was clutching the jet pendant around her neck. The pendant was the shape of an oval, suspended from a silver chain. A small impression of Whitby Abbey was carved into the jet. She could remember Aunt Emily telling her all about it. Michelle's great-grandfather had made it for her great-grandmother as a gift to celebrate their wedding anniversary. Aunt Emily wasn't sure which anniversary, but she knew that the great-grandmother had been very taken with the pendant. There was even a very old photograph of her somewhere, standing in front of the Abbey, and wearing the Abbey pendant around her neck. To Michelle, the pendant seemed impossibly old. After all, it had been made long before she was born.

Perhaps tomorrow she would visit the Abbey, after she had fulfilled her other, more important task.

She turned away from the view and walked the short walk along the promenade back to her hotel.

The next morning Michelle was awoken by the harsh cries of the seagulls. After a quick breakfast, she wrapped herself in her winter coat and scarf and headed for the old town.

It was packed, as usual. As she crossed the bridge she had to swerve to avoid other visitors to the town. It was even more crowded near the gift shops. She was glad when she finally ducked down an alleyway and found the cottage. There was no doorbell, so she knocked on the wood.

The door was opened by an unexpectedly old lady. For a moment, Michelle did not recognise her.

'I'm sorry,' she said. 'I think I've got the wrong address...'

But now the old lady was grinning. 'Michelle? Is that you?'

'Aunt Emily!' Michelle exclaimed. She recognised the voice. 'Yes, it's me. I was in the area and I thought I'd come to visit you.' Michelle was good at lying. She always had been.

'How lovely,' said Aunt Emily. 'I haven't seen you for...My, it must be ten years. How are you? Do come in.'

Michelle followed Aunt Emily into her cottage. She saw immediately that very little had changed during the last ten years. There were still crocheted antimacassars on the backs of the chairs, and the old watercolour painting of the Abbey still hung in pride of place above the open log fire. The house smelled the same too. Michelle could smell burned wood, smoked kippers and the salty, refreshing tang of the sea.

There was something else, too. A copy of Michelle's graduation photo. She cringed in embarrassment for her younger self.

Aunt Emily sat down in an armchair and gestured for Michelle to be seated on the sofa.

'I'll make some tea in a minute,' she said. 'But first I want you to tell me why you've come to visit. It's lovely to see you, but it's a bit of a surprise.'

Michelle felt ashamed. 'I'm sorry I haven't visited in such a long time. But the thing is…I suppose I felt guilty.'

And Michelle laughed nervously.

Aunt Emily looked at her with those wise, sympathetic blue eyes. 'Whatever for?'

'I have a confession to make,' said Michelle. She swallowed hard. This was the moment she had been dreading. 'When I was a little girl, I stole something from you.'

Aunt Emily's eyes went wide. 'What?'

Michelle withdrew the jet pendant from beneath her coat.

'My goodness!' Aunt Emily exclaimed. 'I haven't seen that for years.'

'That's because I took it. I'm so sorry. Can you forgive me?'

Aunt Emily looked suspicious. 'What happened, exactly?'

'Do you remember that time I came to visit just before I moved abroad with Mam and Dad? I must have been seven.'

Aunt Emily nodded.

'We were here for a whole day. That morning you'd taken me up to see the Abbey, and I loved it.'

'Yes, I remember.'

'And when we got back here you showed me some old photos of the Abbey. And you showed me the pendant. Then you went into the kitchen to see to the tea and left me looking at it.'

'Yes.'

'I'm not even sure why I did it,' said Michelle. It was absurd, but she suddenly felt very close to tears. She would be forty next summer, but she still felt a twinge of shame when she thought of that awful day. 'I'd never stolen anything before, and I haven't since. But there was something about that pendant…I was fascinated by it. It was almost as if it was from some strange, distant past which was calling to me. I suppose that sounds silly.'

'Not at all. The past is a great source of fascination to so many people. Just look at all the visitors who come to the Abbey every year.'

'And I was also thinking about moving away from England,' Michelle continued. 'I thought I'd miss everything, and I suddenly thought I would miss the Abbey most of all. So I took the miniature Abbey to remind me. I slipped it into my trouser pocket and hoped you wouldn't notice it was gone. Then I felt guilty, but I knew I couldn't say anything because I'd get into trouble. And then after that it never seemed like the right moment to return it. For several years I forgot about it completely, and then one day last week I was sorting through some stuff when I came across it again, lying at the bottom of a drawer, almost as if it wanted to be found. I'm so, so sorry.'

Michelle stopped talking and looked down at the floral pattered carpet. There was a brief silence.

'You were very young,' said Aunt Emily. 'I forgive you.'

'But it was an awful thing to do.'

'If it's any comfort, I knew you must have taken it, but I didn't ask for it back.'

Michelle looked up at her. 'Why?'

'I would miss you. I didn't want us to part on bad terms. Listen, Michelle. It was wrong to take the pendant. But sometimes we have to let the past go.'

Aunt Emily patted Michelle's hand. Michelle removed the pendant from around her neck and handed it back to her Aunt.

'Come on,' said Aunt Emily, after another awkward silence. 'Why don't we walk up to the Abbey while the weather's still nice?'

They walked together up the 199 steps. Michelle was surprised that her Aunt walked up them with such ease. Aunt Emily saw her looking and smiled.

'I walk up here every morning,' she said. 'It keeps me fit.'

They reached the entrance to the Abbey. Michelle paid for admission, but Aunt Emily had an English Heritage Membership card. Then they walked towards the ruins and looked up at the empty windows.

'Beautiful,' said Michelle. 'I know we should look to the future and all that, but it's nice to preserve a bit of the past, isn't it?'

Aunt Emily smiled. Michelle noticed she was wearing the jet pendant around her neck. The silver chain, slightly tarnished, shone dully in the sunlight.

Later, when they were having tea back at Aunt Emily's cottage, Michelle noticed that the pendant was missing.

'Your pendant's gone,' she said. She was suddenly frightened that Aunt Emily would think she had stolen it again.

'Oh, so it is,' said Aunt Emily.

'Maybe the chain snapped,' said Michelle. 'It was very old.'

Aunt Emily shrugged. 'I wouldn't worry, my dear. Perhaps the pendant has found its way back to the man who made it. He's buried in St Hilda's churchyard, you know. Your great grandfather.'

Michelle did not reply to this. What could she say? Aunt Emily just smiled and sipped her tea.

The tourist looked at the exhibit in the glass case. Then he consulted his guidebook for an explanation.

'This Whitby jet pendant was found in the grounds of the Abbey on the 3rd July 2200. If you look closely, you will see a likeness of the Abbey carved into the jet, although the design has been partially worn away. The pendant is thought to date from somewhere in the late nineteenth or early twentieth century. It was possibly sold as a souvenir to a twentieth century visitor to the Abbey. Our researchers are seeking to confirm this.'

The man looked closely at the pendant. He could just make out the carved likeness of the Abbey, but it was difficult. It was strange, the idea that someone had made this, long ago. Their intention had been almost lost in time, but the Abbey itself, yet more ancient, still remained.

The man left the Visitor's Centre and wandered towards the Abbey. Its stones were weathered, but he found this oddly comforting. Everything was so shiny these days. Buildings seemed to consist of smooth surfaces, elegant in their way, but not as imaginative as the Abbey.

He had liked the Abbey pendant. Perhaps he could buy one in town, for his wife. But perhaps not. Genuine Whitby jet was getting rather hard to come by these days. If such a pendant existed, it was bound to be very expensive.

Never mind. He would persuade his wife to visit the real Abbey with him the next time he came. He was sure she would like it.

She had always loved to dwell on the distant past, even though she had never been there.

They still could not afford that time machine.

Love at First Bite

By Alison Austerberry

The rain lashed against the windscreen as I drove along the motorway. Seeing the signpost for Whitby I breathed a sigh of relief, grateful that I had almost reached my destination. I felt excited, yet somewhat nervous, unable to explain the strange compulsion to visit the North Yorkshire coastal town; especially on a late Autumn's evening. I had been inexplicably drawn there by forces unknown.

A text message flashed onto my mobile and, as I quickly glanced at it on the seat, I saw it was my friend Jill wishing me a good weekend. Maybe, she hoped, I would meet the man of my dreams even though I had no wish to having not long come out of a long term relationship. It was then I noticed the date...30th October. Tomorrow would be Halloween. I realised then it was the Gothic Weekend in Whitby, an event held twice yearly in April and Autumn. I intended to visit Whitby Abbey the following day and to do some sight-seeing as I had never been before. I planned to take some super photographs.

Dusk was falling as I parked in the car park at the top of Robin Hood's Bay and, taking my luggage from the boot, made my descent into the pretty fishing village that reminded me of Clovelly in Devon, another magical place I loved. A shiver ran down my spine as I thought of smugglers in secret passageways. The fog become denser as I got nearer the sea and I quickened my pace. I could hardly see in front of me. I heard laughing and a group of people appeared in front of me, clad either in fancy dress for the night or for the gothic event - I wasn't sure - but they were certainly fitting for such an evening. I paused, then asked them the way to the Station Hotel. One of the group, a dark haired man with piercing blue eyes, pointed to a white rendered building just across the road, just about visible in the mist.

"Thank you," I said, mesmerised by the colour of his eyes.

"The pleasure is all mine," he replied, holding back from the rest of the crowd.

For the second time that evening I felt as though somebody had walked across my grave.

Glad to get inside a nice cosy environment, having settled in my room, I made my way down to the restaurant and bar where I enjoyed a hot bowl of homemade tomato soup and some cheese rolls, followed by a nice glass of red wine. Pumpkin faces lit the room and several children dressed as witches, ghosts and wizards were watching a special live haunting TV show. I noticed the group I had seen earlier come in and settle down in a corner of the bar and then I noticed the man with the blue eyes sitting alone at a table.

How strange that he sat alone and not with his friends. I tried not to stare and hoped that he would look up and smile but he didn't. He spent most of the time simply staring, almost sadly, into space. I wondered what was going through his mind and why he was so sad. He had certainly taken the trouble with his gothic outfit, I noticed. He could give Johnny Depp a run for his money, I mused. After my second glass of wine I decided I would approach him - just to be polite - and paid a visit to the ladies' room first.

On my return, however, he had vanished although his other group of friends were still there. Feeling a little disappointed I sat down with my drink and just enjoyed the evening listening in to other snippets of conversations, watching the television before finally making my way to bed. I was feeling tired with the sea air already. Once in bed, I decided to read for a while and plan my following day's itinerary. I opened my guide book for Whitby and turned on the small television. I was thrilled to see that, by coincidence, Bram Stoker's Dracula was just starting. How apt. I had always loved Halloween time as a child, and enjoyed it still. I settled down to watch the film but the red wine took effect and I must have fallen asleep. The next thing I encountered was the smell of bacon frying elsewhere in the building.

It was a glorious morning, once the mist had risen. After a hearty breakfast, I walked to get the bus into Whitby, deciding to leave the car in the car park due to the busy gothic festivities. Arriving in town I was met by hundreds of people - and some pets - dressed in gothic clothing. I got out my digital camera and started to snap away, certain I would get some decent photographs. I had a busy day planned, so much to fit in, and beyond the swing bridge I could see my ultimate attraction, the ruined Abbey. I would save that until last.

I had an enjoyable day doing all the usual tourist things including visiting the Captain Cook Museum, the monument and the Bram Stoker Dracula museum. There certainly were lots of monsters, werewolves, and vampires too. After all, it was the eve of All Hallows.

It was in a back street, just after lunch that I saw him. The man with the piercing blue eyes. I saw him enter a building, alone, still dressed in his dark gothic outfit. He was obviously here for the weekend. Feeling brave, and curious, I followed him into the strange looking place with effigies hanging on the walls outside, thinking it was some kind of gothic museum.

It turned out to be a bar, as I later discovered, called The Hellfire Club. I had never seen anything like it and was in awe at the food menu: Devil's Pie, Dracula's Delight. And then a voice said, "Have you seen something you like...?"

Before I turned round I knew it was him. Almost speechless, I turned to stare at him. He was now smiling and I found myself melting into his eyes. "Allow me to get you a drink maybe?" he asked.

I allowed him to buy me something called "Bloodfire", which I assumed was merely red wine. It came in silver goblets. We took a seat at a table in a dark corner. What was I doing, in such a place, with a stranger?

However, as the wine filled my veins I began to relax. I sensed he did too. He began to chat a little, asking my name, where I was from. I asked him if he was here for the weird weekend, as I called it. He merely nodded. I did notice that he seemed to avoid answering some of my questions - like where he was from. However, he told me his name was Adam Lord. It suited him. I said I admired his outfit, that it was very authentic. He asked if I was hungry. I found I was ravenous so he ordered us meals and I enjoyed liver and kidneys in red wine, whilst he devoured a rather raw steak, with the blood oozing out.

Later, we made our way into the streets and I was surprised to see how quickly time had passed. Glancing at the clock I noticed it was almost 4pm and that the night was drawing in. I wanted to take some more pictures and, as we walked around the various attractions, I snapped away, thankful that my flash was working. I took lots of Adam too - when he wasn't looking - although he caught me once and didn't seem too happy. It was as if the light hurt his eyes. Even so, I was enjoying myself and very much wished I had dressed up for the occasion.

At 7.30pm he suddenly said he had something to do. Would I meet him later? I realised I hadn't even seen the Abbey yet. He suggested I meet him there later. How later, I asked. Midnight. Something made me stop in my tracks. He could be anybody and did I want to be there at midnight with him? Yet there was something about him and, after all, it was Halloween, the place was full of people and there was an event going on outside so I felt fairly safe. Just before he left, he got hold of me by the shoulders, took my face in his hands and said "Please, Maria, meet me. At the Abbey, at 12. It is a special night. And you are special. I knew the moment I saw you. Do you believe in love at first sight?"

At that moment I did.

I sent a text to Jill saying I had no idea what was happening but I had met somebody very special, a cross between Johnny Depp and Richard Gere. I got one back: "Just be very careful".

I needed to kill some time. I decided to get myself a gothic outfit, to join in, and blend in. There were several shops still open with fancy costumes and silly witches hats but I wanted something special. For Adam. Eventually I found a dark velvet floor length dress on a rail, with ruffles around the cuffs and neck, complete with a velveteen cape. It was a little expensive but what the heck. Out came my credit card. As I waited to pay, I also picked up a beautiful gold cross adorned with jewels; probably fake looking but attractive none the less. Perfect for my new outfit. Feeling happy with my purchases I nipped into a cafe and changed in the toilets, applied black kohl to my eyes, reddened my lips and unclipped my long chestnut hair from the confines of its ponytail. I was pleased with my reflection. I hoped Adam would be too. I could not wait until midnight.

After some time wandering around the streets I began to feel a little tired. It was quite cold and I pulled my black cloak around me, my other clothes and belongings stuffed into my bag. I spent some time chatting to a group of revellers who told me they visited Whitby twice a year. They loved visiting the magical place.

As midnight approached, I began the climb of 199 steps to the Abbey. I began to feel a little apprehensive, especially since crowds were breaking up and there were fewer people around. The wind was blowing and it was beginning to rain. Something dark fluttered in front of my face. All I knew is that I was being called and that he would be waiting for me. I approached the Abbey ruins, sinister against the night sky. Then I saw him. Looking magnificent in his cape, his silhouette outlined against the sea. I knew why I had come. Love at first sight.

"My love," he called as he took me in his arms, "I knew you would come. We are meant to be. I have never wanted anybody so much. Please. Be my bride!"

As I melted into his arms, the wild wind whipped all around us and, somewhere in the distance, a clock struck midnight. Adam's lips came down on mine and he led me to a sheltered area near some gravestones, where he gently laid me to the ground. I gave way to wild abandoned passion as I had never known in my life.

Afterwards, we lay still. He caressed my face, brushing my hair, his piercing blue eyes burning into my very soul. My neck felt a little tight and I pulled the chain and touched the jewelled cross at my neck when suddenly he let out a cry:

"Arrrgh!" He held his arm against his eyes, shielding them from me.

"Adam, what's the matter?" I exclaimed.

"Arrgh. Get away! Get away!" he shouted.

He ran away from me into the night. Vanished – without a trace. I sat on the cliff top for some time, calling his name, chilled to the bone, but he didn't return. I don't remember much about my journey back to Robin Hood's Bay. All the way back to Manchester I couldn't stop thinking about him. Was it a dream? Did it really happen? When I looked in the mirror I knew it did. I could see the visible bruising on my neck. I tried to be adult, sensible about it. A modern girl. That's what happens, sometimes, with a stranger.

Eager to upload my photos I summoned Jill round for a bottle of wine and to show her my photos. I confessed all about Adam: "Just wait till you see the photos." I was surprised my bruises had faded quickly though and I felt a little disappointed.

"So where is he then, your brooding goth?" Jill demanded. "I think you made it up! " she added as I made us some pasta in the kitchen.

I came to look at the PC, but was surprised: "I took lots of photos," I said.

"He was on this one" pointing to one taken by the Abbey. " And this one...."

But there wasn't a single picture of Adam.

"Sure you didn't imagine it, it being Halloween?" asked Jill. "All that talk of vampires! I know what a wild imagination you have."

Could I have imagined it all?

As the weeks followed I tried to analyse what had gone on. Who was "he"? A figment of my imagination? A ghost, a vampire? I didn't have any answers but the whole thing played on my mind and made me feel sick to the stomach.

None of it made sense until I was sitting in a doctor's surgery several weeks later and heard her saying, "Congratulations! You're expecting a baby. It is due next Summer."

Then I knew that Adam was real....that our love was real and I was having his child.

The smell of frying bacon suddenly became stronger. I opened my eyes to find myself staring at the blank TV screen, the Whitby guide book lying on the floor beside the bed. Something washed over me, both relief, and sadness. I got ready for the day ahead, and went downstairs, Jill would laugh when I told her my dream. I should never eat cheese near bedtime.

I sat down to a hearty breakfast, in preparation for the day ahead in Whitby. I did all the things from the early part of my dream but when I entered the building which had been the Hellfire Club I laughed to myself. What an imagination I had. It was just an ordinary wine bar. Feeling decadent, I ordered a Bloody Mary and sat down in the dimly lit corner. As I took a sip, a voice said, "Is this seat taken? May I join you?"

I looked up to find myself staring into a pair of piercing blue eyes.

The Brightest One

By Dorothy Reed

Adult Category Winner

I'd got tired of looking for her in the sky.

Mam said Deidre was one of them, the stars I mean. She said she was the brightest one and too good for this world, so what did that make me? I wish mam wasn't sad. I strained my eyes every night and asked God to let me see our Deidre as the bright one but I never did. Danny Mc Coy said it was all a load of rubbish, I was beginning to wonder. Danny had a brother up there, he also had been too good for this world so I felt better, knowing I wasn't the only one.

Danny and I went to the same school (we were both named Danny) not far from the river and the stadium. We had been warned off the river ever since Jimmy Burke had fell in last Summer holidays.

Jimmy was now also up there in the sky with our Deidre and Danny's brother, I wonder how many can go up there before it gets full up?

There was one more day before we had six weeks off for the Summer. I forgot about stars and sadness stuff for a while and began thinking of Whitby and Lucky. I'll tell you about Lucky in a minute but Mrs Lynch is walking right towards me, and I'll have to say hello, because she tells mam all kinds of stuff about me and Danny, and our Eileen and Cathleen are best friends with her girls.

"Yes, Mrs Lynch, I'm fine and looking forward to the hols, and yes I'll be keeping out of mischief you can be sure. Is your Declan coming out to play just now?" I said all this in the hope she wouldn't find anything to tell me off about, and didn't really want to play with Declan, he was a real pain in the neck, honest!

Mrs Lynch was the priest's housekeeper (nearly a saint she was, I think) and her face was a sort of ginger colour (pan stick stuff our Eileen said it was). Mam said we should feel sorry for her, having no husband, he'd gone off with some fancy woman. (Me granny said never to trust a Cork man, or fancy pieces that wore American tan tights.)

None of us kids liked her or Declan but we had to keep on the good side of her.

"Declan is at home with tummy pains, he's eaten far too many pea pods, so no Danny Ross, in answer to your question, he won't be coming out to play," Mrs Lynch said all this in one breath while lifting her eyes up to heaven. I couldn't believe my luck. No Declan and no interrogation from the mammy either!

Every holiday I go to Aunty Lils near Whitby Abbey. Her husband, my Uncle Jamsie, works around the harbour helping the fishermen unload, he used to be a "big shot" in Harrogate council until the redundancies got him. Now he does odd jobs, but he's happier than ever. We go on adventures all around Whitby, one day we climbed all the steps, all 199 of them, just so we could look down and pick out landmarks, sometimes we would talk about smugglers and Captain Cook at sea on his ship "The Endeavor". Once, I let a balloon float into the sky with my name and address attached. Uncle Jamsie said you never know what might come of it. I'm still waiting; however whatever we did was fun and exciting.

Now I'll tell you about Lucky. He's mine, well almost as good as mine, at least when it's holiday time.

Lucky is a horse, actually he belongs to a man who lives in an old caravan in Whitby. He rescued him from a gypsy who said he was a runt and that he should have been at least 14 hands but as he didn't make the grade he was going to be put to sleep, Johnno kept him, was good to him and now he lets me have Lucky for the holidays. Tomorrow I will walk and groom him... we talk Lucky and me, (sorry Lucky and I, mam says I've to speak proper), about all kinds, well I talk, but he understands, honest he does. I told him about President Kennedy getting shot in

Dallas and about our Deidre being up there in the sky with Danny's brother and Jimmy Burke. I've told him I can't find her even though mam says she's up there. Lucky knows all my thoughts and I'm certain he understands them.

Whitby harbour was busy, it had stopped raining. It rained "cats and dogs" all the way from Wylam earlier that day. All the families were there, the atmosphere was lovely, just like when the hoppings come to the Town Moor, the smell of fish and chips and burgers making you want to stay forever. On the other side of the harbour, about half a mile from the Abbey I saw Johnno's red caravan.

"Hey, Danny boy, look at this poster here, there's going to be fireworks tomorrow evening in Whitby Abbey. Wouldn't you like to see them eh?" Uncle Jamsie knew I loved fireworks and always bought me a huge box on bonfire night even though Aunt Lil didn't like me to have them.

"Thanks Uncle I'd love to see them, can we go after I've sorted out Lucky?" He nodded and just then I thought I was the happiest boy in the world, going to see my horse and then fireworks at Whitby Abbey all in one day. Uncle Jamsie told me great scary stories about the headless lady who roamed Whitby Abbey in the moonlight, he assured me it was true until he got ticked off from Aunt Lil so I was sworn to secrecy not to mention it again. He made me swear while he winked at me.

The rain had made way for lovely sunshine, no evidence of the previous day's clouds. This was real six-week holiday weather! My bedroom window looked out onto the field at the back of the cottage. I got up and went downstairs counting all the days I had left of the summer hols. Mam always laughed at me when I did this, she never understood that each day was precious and as soon as it was over it meant one day nearer to September and school. I shuddered at the thought. We were having breakfast listening to the shipping forecast, I loved to hear all those names, Cromarty, Dogger Bank, Finisterre, exciting names all of them, when the knock on the door came. It was Johnno. He asked Uncle Jamsie if I was in. I got up from the table and aw Johnno was upset, I could tell, he was wringing his hands together as if agitated." Danny boy, I need to tell you straight out son, Lucky is in a bad way... he has some kind of pneumonia I think, the horse man from the village has been and doesn't hold out much hope, I'm sorry lad but I think I will have to let him go, it would be kinder I think, but I needed to tell you first."

I could hear the words but they were making no sense, I thought I was dreaming.

Nightmare things...

"Noooo, please nooooo... you can't do that," the voice screamed out. It was my voice, hardly recognisable. I pleaded, and cried. I wanted to be there, I had to do something. My heart was pounding, as if it were going to burst, I had to be with him and if only I could get to him I knew he would be ok, something told me that..

I don't recall how I got there, or how long it took. Lucky was shuddering and sweating, rasping sounds coming from his throat and chest. I pleaded and bargained with God to let him live, not to take him from me, not like he took Deidre from mam, from us.

I rubbed him with towels, I washed him gently with cool water and tried to get him to drink and all the while I talked to him. His breathing was quick and uneven and he was struggling, desperate for breath. Johnno looked on, helpless. "Johnno, please help him, do something," I wailed. Johnno had some foul smelling grease based ointment and decided we would rub him down with that, and in the meantime filled an old steel barrel with water, boiling it on his small stove." The steam might help him lad, sure enough we have no other hope."

We decided to try anything, so we covered Lucky in a huge blanket and sort of guided the steam from the boiling barrel right into him under the blanket...

Hours passed, I was exhausted from rubbing him down, the steam still being directed into the blanket. Lucky was slipping away, I felt as if I was too. I laid my head next to him, I could feel his exhausted, laboured breathing, I became one with him in some strange way. I was drifting, just like he was.

We were galloping, the wind was in our path, we were near to the Abbey, no one was around except some hooded figures near St Hilda's. Lucky made a noise. We stopped... He sensed danger before I did. There was chanting, strange singing, church type noises like when it was special feast days or Holy days. One of the hooded figures came towards us, Lucky backed off, I stayed still on his back. The hooded man spoke softly, offered Lucky his hand and said not to be afraid, he nuzzled the figure who was stroking and whispering in his ear. The man was named Caedmon and he was dressed in brown flowing garments, and all the while he spoke gently. Suddenly there were fireworks, and the sky lit up. Caedmon was still stroking Lucky's neck and telling me it would all be alright and to trust the sky, he kept on repeating that, I wanted to ask him where he had come from and what he meant but as I tried to reach over to him, he seemed to slip away. He was gone.

I moved my aching legs and slowly realised I had fallen asleep. It was dark; Johnno was by my side, Uncle Jamsie also. I jumped up. I remembered the whole sequence of events now... Lucky was still lying there but now he was struggling to get up, shaky and still making strange noises from his throat. Lucky had come through... he was on the mend. Uncle Jamsie said he had come through the crisis, just as the fireworks started in the Abbey. How could I explain the strange things I had seen? Had I imagined them?

Johnno was still cleaning him down, and he was drinking water. We had survived. Lucky looked at me. We had a bond now that no one could break,

I looked up into the sky. The brightest star in the whole of the galaxy was shining down on us, Mam would be pleased, I had seen what she told me was there. Caedmon was right... I had trusted the sky.

Prophetic Whispers

By Amy Clarke

Life is exceedingly tedious. Each new face that stares at me chants the usual compliments. For years now I have wished the human race would stop admiring my body, no longer stare at the long walls and golden brick that have formed me.

Was it not better in the past? At least then I was no tourist attraction, but rather beloved by my brothers as they whispered to me in the darkness, pouring out their emotions like the steady trickle of rain, dripping into my foundations, through the stone and earth. I hold their secrets still. Modern man with his synthetic fibres and electronic wizardry does not know, and shall not know the secrets I hold in my belly, until it is time; until my stories are told.

The sea air blusters through my skeleton, salt fizzing against bones of brick. It coursed downhill, over the precipice to houses beneath, my breath flooding the crowded streets. Blowing wild and untameable, it rattles windows and doors, clawing at the occupants who lie huddled within. One, I remember, did not cower but sat nearer, gazing out at an austere and wind-warped landscape. She sighed, and her faint breath fogged the glass.

Mary Lockhart turned reaching for her shoes and, slipping them on, walked from the room. The Coastline Hotel was far more than she had hoped, with polished wooden floors, bright fires and historical pictures framed and displayed in each room. The eyes of her predecessors watched her move through corridors, monochrome ears listening to the click-clack of heels. Pushing open a heavy door she moved into the dining room. A roar of sound bubbled forth, swallowing her dainty steps in a chaotic rumble of voices, chairs squeaking; china clinking; drinks slurping. The warm scent of tomatoes and herbs drifted over their heads, curling in the air. A waiter rushed over and ushered Mary to her seat, elaborating vastly on the day's specialty, glancing at the empty chair opposite. She tried not to notice his extra wide smile, his false laugh and hungry eyes.

Running her hands over the smooth white cloth, Mary perused the menu, luxuriating in her situation. Sitting there, alone, made her feel quite confident, a new sense of independence seeping into the pores of her skin and trailing round her bloodstream. It was daring she thought, liberating, to be unknown in a place. She could become anyone, do whatever she fancied and no one was there to scold her, or tell her she was wrong. It felt like she had been a caged bird, now free. Soon the waiter returned, to pour her wine. She watched the crimson liquid crash and swirl in the glass, brought it to her lips delighting in its rich flavour.

Candles were lit, lights switched on, casting a gentle golden haze over the room to combat the growing dark from outside. The thick night spread over the headland and enveloped the labyrinthine town.

A rush of rain moved in from the sea, like a wave in itself, cascading towards the houses. The Coastline Hotel was pummelled with the downpour, shooting waterfalls from its roof. Mary stared at the blackness, at small rivers of water coursing down the window panes. Suddenly the sky flashed white and the whole town was visible, thrown into sharp relief, and stark, frightening colours. A booming crash ripped through the peace. Mary jumped, her hand knocking carelessly into a glass. It fell and cracked on the table. Red wine spilled like blood over the cloth, dripping down to the floor as she dabbed at it frantically with a napkin. Behind her someone started laughing, "Now that won't do at all."

Mary spun round, angrily, "Excuse me?"

The man on the table next tohers smiled, "I'm sorry, I simply meant that you can't eat at a wine-soaked table."

"If the waiter brings me another napkin I'll be perfectly fine."

"Don't be ridiculous," he said, signalling to the maître d' himself, "you can sit with me."

Mary frowned, "I couldn't possibly, I don't want to ruin your evening."

"You won't. We may as well eat together, seeing as neither of us has any company," he chuckled, "unless you've got a knight in shining armour stowed away in your room?"

"No, unfortunately not."

He nodded, gesturing to the spare seat, "There you are then. I'll try not to bore you."

Mary hesitated, her fingers clenching and unclenching in her lap as she fought with her fear.

"Please? At least then you won't stain your dress," he said.

She sighed, and moved to sit opposite him as the waiter fussed about with cutlery and plates. They ordered their meals and Mary watched the member of staff scurry away.

"Well," her companion said after a measure of silence, "allow me to introduce myself, I'm William Lawrence."

"Mr Lawrence."

"Please, just call me Will."

"Very well" Mary said, shaking his hand, "I'm Mary Lockhart."

"Lockhart? That's an unusual name."

"I'm an unusual person."

He laughed, smiling at her as their food was brought, the steaming plates laid before them. "And what brings you to this neck of the woods Mary Lockhart? Family? Friends?"

"Neither, actually, I came for work."

He raised his eyebrows, "Work?"

"Yes. I'm a writer; I came to … get a feel of the place," she said, conveniently hiding the true reason for her trip. In theory she was here for her occupation, yet the journey was hardly necessary. In truth Mary had come because of a dream, a waking phantasm that goaded and cajoled her into leaving the pretty little village she called home. Whitby felt like destiny – she had the impression that she was fated to be here, under my shadow.

"What is it you're writing?" Will asked, leaning forward in his chair, "A history of the Abbey perhaps?"

"Nothing so intellectual; I write fiction, most of the action takes place here so I wanted to be certain I could describe it properly."

"That's very dedicated of you." he smiled, and his warm brown eyes sparkled in the candlelight.

Mary blushed, the colour of roses blooming under her skin. I suppose she thought him handsome. "Thanks," she said "although I haven't explored very much, I've not even seen the Abbey, yet."

"That's dreadful."

"I know," she laughed, "you see, I'm not that dedicated at all really."

Will looked down at his meal, picking at the food meditatively, "I hope you don't think I'm being rude here but I just wondered...whether, perhaps, you'd like to visit it with me tomorrow?"

Mary blinked. "The Abbey?"

"Yes. Only if you'd like to, of course; feel free to say no."

"No – no not at all, I mean, I'd love to."

"Really?" he grinned, "You're sure?"

"That's what I'm here for."

"Excellent." He smiled again, and Mary mirrored his expression. They sat there for a moment, until embarrassment flooded forth and they hurriedly focused back on the meal.

Outside the storm raged on, flooding the roads in torrents, and churning the sea into a tortured lather. Flashes of lightening illuminated the sky, masking the town in sheets of fire. The wind continued, pressing in on the small hotel, ghosting through the smallest of cracks. A waiter came to remove the dishes as the lights flickered, drowning the room in temporary darkness. Mary shuddered. "How long can this keep up?"

"It'll get worse before it improves."

Mary turned away, staring into the storm. She leant closer, and her breath quickened, misting from her mouth in delicate clouds. "There's something," she murmured, "there's something out there."

"Mary? Mary, are you alright?"

She turned back to see Will's concerned face. His voice sounded far off, hazy and distorted.

"Is something wrong?"

She shook her head, glancing back to the glass, "I have bit of a headache. I think I'll go to bed now, if that's ok?"

"Of course."

She fumbled in her bag for her purse, but Will placed his hands on hers, "Dinner's my treat."

"But –"

"I'll pay. I did spoil your solitude after all."

"Thank you," she rose, "I'll see you in the morning?"

"Yes definitely."

She smiled and walked from the room. Will stood and watched her go. Around him the candles sputtered out.

Mary tossed fretfully in her sleep. Her eyes darted behind closed lids, and a cold sweat beaded across her forehead. Her dark hair spilled over the pillow like tangled seaweed. A voice filled her head, a moaning lament calling her name.

'I'm here, Mary. I'm waiting for you. Just here, over here.'

She curled into a foetal position, clinging to the bedcovers.

'Mary. Mary? Can't you hear me? I'm here.'

Groaning she rolled to the other side.

'Run Mary. Run. Run!'

With a gasp she leapt into the waking world. Her skin was damp and frozen as ice. The evening dress crumpled around her body where she had slept in it, too fatigued to change. She looked with surprise to the open window, its curtains tugging ferociously at the rings which bound it. She could have sworn it was closed. The night called and she turned to see my shadow, high on the headland, a tall ominous figure staring down. A kind of nervous fever possessed her senses, and she bolted, wrenching the doors. The rain quickly soaked her clothes, and the cold stung her lungs so she struggled for breath. A skylight swung wide and Will leaned out, "What are you doing?" he called, "You'll be frozen out there!"

Laughter bubbled in Mary's chest as she pelted along the street, her bare feet slapping against the concrete. She ran on and on, never relenting, never slowing as the storm whipped her face. Her dress snarled about her legs fighting to restrain, and tearing in the process.

When she reached the cliff top she wanted to sing for joy, heart swelling in her chest. Here amongst the long grass and the bleak sky she felt like the heroine of a novel, a fantastic creation of bravery and beauty. Looking to the iron clouds Mary stretched up, trying to reach them, to brush the heavens with her fingertips.

She heard shouts behind her and glanced back. Will was running after her, his hair black with water and slicked to his skull. "Mary come back!" he cried, "What are you doing up here?"

"Can't you hear it?" she yelled, her voice echoing over the bay, "Can't you hear it calling?"

"Mary, what are you talking about?"

"It's there, just there!" she shouted, sprinting towards the Abbey ruins, towards me. Mary fled through the arches, her hands brushing the wet stones as she passed. The green smell of the rain swirled around us, enveloping the scene, guiding her trembling form to where my secret lay. She ran along the cloisters into my hortus conclusus, my once enclosed gardens. There she collapsed into the grass and mud, scrabbling at the earth with frantic fingertips. The moon shone on her hunched form, casting tall shadows. Will caught up with her, "What are you doing?" he touched her shoulder, "Mary?"

"Help me," she said, "help me dig."

Without another word he moved the soil away, mining into undisturbed ground. Mary sent the dirt scurrying like pebbles off a precipice, as I guided her frantic hands. Eventually instead of earth and rock their fingers felt something rough and hard. They tugged it loose and she pulled from the earth a small wooden box. Shaking, she removed the lid, emptying the contents onto her lap. The ancient folds of material moved away and Mary found herself touching peeling leather. She stared at it for a long time, before impatience won through and she opened the medieval book. Its pages were illuminated with the bright pictures and flowing words of my brothers, my monks. Will shielded the masterpiece with the box lid, protecting it from the rain. Mary gazed at the contents, her attention fixated by another wonder. Inside there was one loose page. She pulled it to the fore. On the thick cream parchment were four words; two names: Mary Lockhart & William Lawrence. He looked at her then, wonder shining in his eyes. She smiled.

Behind them the sun rose, casting hope and light upon the harbour; the pink promise of a new beginning. I sighed, and my breath was carried off by the westerly breeze.

Steps to the Abbey

By Christine Richards

199 steps to what? They called for me to climb, but would they take me to a life of joy or a life of pain? Only 199 stairs.

My stomach was still churning from the boat ride. Or was it from the fear of what awaited me at the top of the steps? I looked up, but couldn't see the top or Whitby Abbey which I knew was on the headland overlooking the harbour. I could see the huge structure before the boat entered the harbour, but it disappeared as we docked below it. Beyond the stairs waited the man who would be my husband.

"Lord, let him be a kind man and let his love for me be true," I whispered as I fingered the cross he sent in one of his letters. He had carved it out of a stone taken from the Abbey ruins. The words I'd received from him were caring and gentle, but I'd seen similar words in the notes my father had sent to my mother. He was a brutal man and had killed the woman who had given me life. He was an uncaring man who had sent me here to the highest bidder regardless of my desire to marry the man I loved. He wanted nothing more of the burden of my living in his house.

The last letter from the man I knew only as R. George Montgomery was crumpled in my left hand, the same hand which held my cloak together. In it were directions to meet him. My right hand lifted my skirts to avoid falling as I climbed the stairs. With this letter had come the money for new dresses and a stateroom on a ship bringing me to Whitby. How would this man react when I arrived with only two gowns instead of the dozen he ordered father to get? What would he do when he learned I'd slept in a hammock in the hold of the ship instead of a bed in a stateroom? Would he punish me for disobeying his orders? Or would he understand it was father's doing and not mine?

One of the stones beneath my feet shifted. I grabbed the railing, wishing it was Robert; wishing he was catching me the way he did when the stone turned as I walked though the city gardens. His grey-green eyes bored down through mine, all the way to my heart, and he saw the pain and misery within. His arms kept me safe as he carried me to a bench. His gaze was so intent I don't think he even saw the bruise on my jaw. He didn't speak that day. He set me down and fetched me a cup of water. Sure I was safe; he turned and disappeared between the couples walking among the flowers.

My father only allowed me to leave the house on Tuesday afternoons. The rest of the time I had to be ready to serve him immediately upon his call. But on Tuesdays a friend came to visit and he always sent me away. Each week I went to the gardens and after the day I almost fell, Robert was there. It must have been three or four weeks before he spoke to me. His words were hesitant and halting. At first I thought he might be mute, or partially so, but as the weeks progressed I realized he was painfully shy. He spoke mostly of the flowers or the weather. Occasionally he would ask something about me, but he never mentioned himself.

After a time he started bringing me gifts, usually a bouquet of flowers. Father always wanted to know where I'd gotten them when I came home. I didn't want to lie so I told him in the city gardens, but I didn't say that Robert had given them to me. He wouldn't have approved of my meeting anyone. He wanted to know what I paid for them, but I said I found them. I was forbidden to have any money. I looked forward to each Tuesday afternoon when his friend came and eagerly waited for the order to leave. The seasons came and went. Sometimes when it was very cold, father would ask me how I found live flowers in the gardens. He didn't seem to care when I said they were just there.

A child running from his mother pushed me out of the way. He bumped against the wrist father had bruised as he threw me onto the ship. I cried silently in pain. Father taught me never to make a sound when I was hurt. I reached into my purse and pulled out the paper holding some of the salve Robert had given me. It was the last of the ointment. I wouldn't have any if I got hurt again. I didn't know what it was. It was gritty with grey, green and brown chunks. I rubbed a little on my wrist just as Robert had soothed it over numerous injuries on our Tuesday get-togethers. We'd been meeting for about three months the first time he pulled a paper out of his jacket and covered a place on my neck with it. Then he folded the parchment and placed it in my hands. The pain was gone. After that he always brought it and sent me home with what was left after putting it on the injuries he could see. I think he knew there were more beyond his eyes.

I stopped to rest. The stairs were so long. The clouds had parted and the sun was shining between them. I let my hood fall back and my cloak fall open. The brown-grey waves in the harbour turned to blue sparkles. The breeze blew my hair and cooled the sweat from my climb. There was freedom on the wind, freedom from my father.

I turned and started up the stairs again. Above me I could see a church. I checked the letter despite having memorise it while I was on the ship. Up the stairs, past St. Mary's church and the tombstones surrounding it, continuing up the hill to Whitby Abbey, and through the Abbey ruins to the nave entrance where R. George Montgomery would be waiting.

A few more steps and I saw the tops of the tombstones. I grabbed my cloak and pulled it around me, but it didn't warm the chills running though me. The large markers were black, as black as the granite in the gardens the last time I saw Robert. I was telling him I was worried we wouldn't be able to continue seeing each other. When father's friend came today, she didn't look happy and the last few weeks, when she left after I returned home, they were arguing. As we walked though the shining jet arch, I saw a reflection flash across the stone and Robert fell beneath many blows. Father battered him to the ground and dragged me away, leaving him unmoving surrounded by red blotches glimmering on the rocks.

He threw me into my room and locked the door. I sat on the floor and pulled the parchment of salve of my bag and spread it on the bruises father left on my arms. The brown, grey, and green granules reminded me of Robert's touch and of his eyes. Each night for over three months he slipped a jug of water and a loaf of bread inside. I kept track of the days. Did Robert wonder about me when I didn't return to the gardens? Was he even alive? Did he even want me after the way father had beaten him? Was I too great a liability, too great a danger? Father never spoke to me during those long days. There was no communication until the night before yesterday when he tossed several letters on the floor along with two new gowns. He told me to pack and the letters were from the man who would be my husband. I would be leaving in the morning. As I read the missives, one for each week I had been locked in my room, I remembered the words my mother had shown me from my father before they were married. I didn't understand the mention of gifts of jewellery when all I found was this stone cross. I wondered if this R. George Montgomery was false and going to change as my father had.

As the sun rose, I dressed in one of the gowns and waited. I held the bag with my meagre possessions. The door burst open. Father yanked me from my room and dragged me to the harbour. He handed my ticket to the man at the bottom of the gangplank, threw me at his feet, turned and walked away without a word. I knew I would never see him again. I was left with the letters, wondering what this man would look like, how he would act, and if he really wanted me or just a wife.

I walked though the cemetery, keeping my eyes on the stones beneath my feet. The tombstones held too much fear and too many questions. Would I be killed as my mother was? Was my sweet Robert lying cold beneath such a marker? I could see the Abbey ruins above me. Were these fallen stones and bare spires an omen? Was my life to be as barren and useless as this building?

I looked once more at the letter signed R. George Montgomery. I neared the back side of the Abbey and walked toward the nave and the entrance. I could see a man's back. He was leaning against an empty arch. Beneath my feet was a mixture of green grass with brown and grey stones. I forced myself to breathe and to keep walking. The man turned and I knew God had answered my prayer. Robert George Montgomery, my beloved, waited for me with open arms.

Abbey Ear

By Sally Brown

'Sans sang je ne peux pas respirer'

It is nearly 3.25 pm and Hannah Jerome waits on the platform at Whitby train station. She stamps her feet up and down in her high, black lace-up boots and thrust her fists into her pockets of her short black denim jacket blowing out silently and slowly through pursed lips. Her body language was typical of a cold Winter's day but slightly incongruous on the hot Summer afternoon it actually was. As if suddenly aware of this, she stopped stamping and turned her face to the sun. Her sundress was new, halter-neck and bright yellow and, in that respect, was the most exciting thing she had worn for the past eight years. The very ordinariness of it was a novelty to her and therefore, bizarrely, it felt the opposite. Being a goth since she was 15, she'd dressed entirely in black or occasionally purple for the last eight years. She ran a tentative hand through her long hair tucking it behind her ear. Looking at it, she has the strange sensation that it belongs to someone else. Instead of the glossy jet-black, gold and copper strands are falling through her fingers. The sight of the pale hair shining in the sunlight makes her smile. She had taken out her studs in her eyebrows, tongue and upper ear and her nose ring, leaving only the small diamond stud on her right nostril that matched the small studs in her ears. But the most dramatic change had been her face. No covering of thick white powder, no heavy black kohl eyeliner on her upper and lower eyelids and no black lipstick. Instead she had applied a little blusher to her cheeks, a blue sheen of eye shadow, a thin line of dark green eyeliner. The only black had been a few strokes of mascara and the lipstick was now a shiny reddish-brown. She realised she had hid behind the heavy makeup like a mask. Even her own father had done a double take when he had opened the door to her when she'd come back from Uni transformed. 'Finally emerging from her dark chrysalis into the beautiful butterfly I always knew she was' he had proudly

shown her off to his friends down The Walrus & The Carpenter. She
had thought it quite poetic for a down-to-earth baker. The black coffin
shaped handbag she usually had slung over her shoulder had been
replaced with a multi-coloured cloth bag, the only concession to her
goth following, a couple of her favourite band badges. She turned round
so that she could check out her reflection in the Whistle Stop Café
window. What would he think of her new image she wondered? She
could see him in her mind's eye, pushing back his long black fringe,
craning his neck to catch a glimpse of his precious Abbey. She stood
with her back to her. She knew it was stupid, but she'd long ago thought
of The Abbey as just a ruin on the hill. 'Abbey' had become such a
strong presence she felt her even when she wasn't in Whitby. She could
understand that as an artist it was about as dramatic and inspirational a
landmark as you could get, but his endearing fascination was now
bordering on obsession.   He'd painted it from a dark silhouette
overlooking the harbour to an imposing close up, each stone lovingly
replicated with intricate detail. His final piece, for which he had passed
his Fine Arts Degree with a distinction, had been an oil painting from
across the pond at night under a full moon. The imposing stone façade
reflected in the still waters was dramatic and chilling. She knew he had
painted it over and over again because some of his canvases were stored
in the corner of her room. One of the pictures she thought was even
better than the one he had finally submitted but she thought she knew
why he had rejected it. She just had to pluck up the courage to ask him,
to find out if her nagging anxiety was justified or plain paranoia. She
went to bite her short, stubby chipped black-varnished nails before
realising that these too had been transformed. She fanned her hands out
to look at them. As with her hair, she felt as if she was looking at
someone else's hands. They weren't the hands of an up and coming
sculptor that was for sure. She couldn't imagine sinking the long talons
into the wet grey clay. They were just a temporary amusement but one
she thought Tom would like. But what about the rest of her radical new
look? Her biggest fear was that he would get off the train and just walk
right past her. That the 'special connection' they thought they had would
turn out to be only skin deep. The sun blazed down but suddenly she felt
chilled, and sensed a person behind her, standing too near. A smell of

damp and heavy, musky perfume, a rustle of clothes, a shape of blackness and a whisper formed by bloodless lips blown in her right ear 'He will not recognise you.'

She whirled round in fury to glare at a young family clutching seaside paraphernalia and a small toddler in a buggy. 'Bloody wasps!' she mumbled attempting a weak smile as she wafted her hands in an effort to give credence to her lie. The Abbey caught her eye before she turned round. It was she told herself, pure imagination that she thought she could see a lone, black figure looking back at her from the ruins. She jumped violently at the ear-piercing whistle and looking down the track, a plume of smoke told her that the steam engine was approaching. As it slowed into the station, a crowd of tourists and steam fanatics surged forward to take photos of the front and the driver obliging leaned out to pose for his adoring public. Her stomach lurched as the train finally came to a stop in a cloud of steam as if exhausted. Doors started opening and people emerged squinting into the sunlight. And then emerging through the smoke like a gun-slayer in a cowboy movie, there he was. He must have been baking in his leather trousers and long black coat that swung out behind him but in every way, he looked the epitome of cool.

'Tom!' she screamed running towards him. He stopped in his tracks clearly bewildered. She took hold of his hands and looked at him intently.

'Hannah?' he ventured 'Is that really you?' he sounded utterly incredulous.

She didn't reply but drew him to her and flung her arms round his neck to give him a long, hard kiss.

'What do you think?' she asked going to kiss him again but he gently disentangled her arms from around his neck and held her hands at arms-length looking her up and down.

'Definitely my Hannah' he grinned down at her. And then he said the one thing she didn't want him to say.

'But I didn't recognise you.' Suddenly she heard a low teasing laugh. She was just tormenting herself, hearing a mocking 'I told you so' chuckle; it was all in her head she told herself.

Tom looked at her quizzically. 'A sexy new laugh as well, is there any of the old Hannah left?' He said it lightly but she could sense his disapproval.

'Don't you like it?' she asked, the question more an accusation. 'I just wanted to surprise you with the new me' she broke away from his hands and did a little twirl. And then it dawned on her. He had heard the laugh too.

'I rather liked the old Hannah' he mumbled but she just stared uncomprehendingly. 'You heard it too!' she whispered 'You heard it too!' Tom took her hand and walked so quickly up the platform she had to run to keep up. Emerging from the booking office into the sun he stopped abruptly dragging her. 'Tom!' she shook his arm but he wasn't looking at her. His true love was reflected in his eyes as he looked up to the ruined Abbey.

They sat at the window table of the Abbey Steps Tearooms, Tom gazing up at the stone steps that led to the Abbey as if it was the stairway to heaven. Hannah stirred her chocolate milkshake with her straw absentmindedly while they waited for their toasted sandwiches. Tom nursed his black coffee and fiddled with the sugar packs in the middle of the table. A substitute for the cigarette that she knew he craved. He'd managed to smoke three already from the train station and now he was twitchy for another. Or maybe he was just anticipating the conversation they had so far delayed. They'd dropped off his stuff at the flat above the baker's shop with the inevitable embarrassing enthusiastic welcome from her dad. She supposed she shouldn't complain but it always amazed her just how much her dad liked him. She'd thought he'd take one look at his long black hair, numerous piercings and tattoos and roll his eyes in despair. But now she came to think about, initially he done just that. When Tom had first visited, her dad was finally selling-up after years of trying to find a suitable business down in Bude, Cornwall. It was Hannah's birthplace and she was delighted that they were finally moving back. They'd arrived to find him surrounded by boxes and her late mother's huge wardrobe in the small sitting room. How he had managed to get it down the narrow steep stairs she couldn't guess but he was complaining of an aching back. Anxious about the move and in pain, she realised it was probably not the best time to introduce Tom. Her dad had avoided them for the first few days, civil to the point of rudeness. Determined to win him over, Tom had taken him on a long session down the pub and had somehow convinced him that the only way to see the Abbey was on such a moon lit night. She had laughed at the sight of the two of them staggering into the night sky up the 199 steps that led to the Abbey. The next day she'd been woken up by a strange thumping sound and on opening her bedroom door had seen Tom and dad struggling up the stairs with the wardrobe. Her dad had a plaster over his right ear, apparently he'd fallen over up at the Abbey and had a nasty cut. But despite that, he'd been in a fantastic mood. Not only did her dad think Tom was 'a fine young man' but to her horror, he'd suddenly decided he wasn't going to move, he wanted to stay in Whitby.

'I just don't understand!' Hannah hissed at Tom when the waitress had gone. 'How come you could hear that stupid laugh as well? Tom, there was no one there!' She watched as he took a big bite of his cheese and tomato toastie.

'Tom! I've been thinking. There's been an awful lot of weird stuff happening.'

'What weird stuff?' Tom asked as he took a swig of coffee.

'It's that bloody Abbey!' she said tilting her head in the direction of the steps.

Tom shrugged and raised his black eyebrows as he took another big bite of his sandwich inviting her to explain.

'My dad for instance' she said 'One minute he hates you and is all set to move, then he goes up there with you…' she stabbed her thumb over her shoulder '…and the next, he thinks the suns shines out of your backside and decides to stay here, why? What happened to change his mind?'

'Must be my powers of persuasion' Tom grinned and draining his cup, swung it up at the waitress for a refill. 'I said I thought he must be mad to leave here, he obviously listened.'

Hannah shook her head. 'It's more than that.' She broke off a small piece of her sandwich.

'Why didn't you submit the oil painting of the Abbey with the black figure of a woman standing by the pond? she asked softly.

Tom slammed down his cup hard in its saucer and glared at her. She felt her stomach flip with fear and lust.

'Why didn't you?' she persisted 'when it was probably your best piece' she paused 'and why when she was standing right next to the pond didn't you give her a reflection? Is that the reason why you didn't submit it, because you forgot to put one in?

Tom shook his head and then leaned across the table at her. 'Of course I didn't forget!' he exclaimed. 'Violetta doesn't have one!

The Abbey Crafts Shop was busy. She lovingly looked over the replica china Abbeys she had made and turned to admire Tom's paintings that covered the walls. He'd painted some of the Abbey as it might have looked like before it was a ruin. The gaping windows now glazed with coloured glass depicting an amazing picture of William the Conqueror punishing the Scots for cannibalism. The grounds were full of monks and nuns, their reflections perfectly mirrored in the still pond. Except for one. They were so beautiful, so real, it was difficult not to believe it was a true record and not just out of his imagination. She glimpsed her pale face in the big gothic mirror. Her black hair had been cut into a short, spiky haircut that suited her. Mrs. Tom Delaney. She couldn't believe they'd been married for nearly three years. Today was the anniversary of his proposal. She couldn't believe they had argued, they never argued. She had for some bizarre reason wanted them both to move to Bude. The thought of leaving Whitby now made her shiver. He'd left a note on her pillow 'Find me, keep me, refuse and lose me.' The stone stairs seemed to be illuminated in the moonlight and she still remembered the sensation of gliding up them as if on a conveyor belt.

She felt the little nick in her ear. It was smaller than Tom's and her father's but like them, it itched from time to time. But she knew the cure, as did most of the local people who suffered from 'Abbey Ear'.

Moira had bought the little Abbey on the last day of their holidays. She'd endured a week of biting winds and gusting gales and vowed to never return to Whitby. But something had compelled her buy the little china Abbey. Sometimes when she looked at it she imagined she could see a small black figure.

'Do you want to go to Majorca next year love' Steve asked 'I know you didn't enjoy the holiday?'

Moira looked up at him as if he was mad. 'No way, I want to go back to Whitby.'

In Ruins

By Neal Barrett

Adult category runner-up

An Introduction

"You obviously want a story if you're reading this, very well, I'll tell you one. But there are a couple of conditions: it has to be a scary story, in fact, the scariest one I know, and you have to cut my grass, it's so long it's starting to irritate me.

"Do we have a deal? Good. Make yourself comfortable then, and hold on to your trousers, this story's so good it may well blow them off."

Part I

"Edward Gourmand was a very boring man, he liked routine and was not fond of surprises. He was rigid and precise like a robot, a very boring robot. He used strange phrases like 'thinking outside the box', he drove a car that was too big for most parking spaces and he 'did' lunch.

"At the time of our story Edward owned a big business, which specialised in buying desirable land and doing obscene things with it, like building shopping centres or gyms or coffee shops or all of these under one terrible, Godless roof.

"On this particular afternoon, Edward was in his home town of Whitby to oversee his most ambitious project to date: the construction of a multi-purpose international convention centre. He was at the very site, he sat on the base of a nave pillar, closed his eyes and tried to daydream, the sort of thing normal people do when they're content. But Edward couldn't daydream, it meant losing control of his mind and he never lost control. He also knew that he should really see his mother while he was in town. Nothing particularly daunting about that you would think, but it hung over Edward like a dark cloud. He had not spoken to her for months, had not visited her for years. He was far too busy for that kind of thing. He knew he should try harder, she was the only person who attempted to keep in touch, everyone else had tired of texts being ignored, birthdays forgotten and visits missed, they had long since faded away. Not that he really cared, all he needed was his mobile phone, his bank manager and his architect, that was enough to make him happy.

"He took a cursory look at his surroundings, centuries of splendour soared into the sky above him, saints and sinners, sanctuary and sacrilege, but he was oblivious. Instead, thoughts of his convention centre leapt through his mind, who could resist such a glorious building?

"Well, apparently the locals could, and the holidaymakers, and just about everyone really. They seemed to be quite attached to this old ruin and didn't want to see it blown to smithereens and replaced by a stainless steel and glass hexagon.

"Not that he was worried, the contract was signed, 'Money shouts louder than any fish fryer and tomorrow, my lovely, it's adios amigo,' he said aloud.

"His phone began to ring, it was his mother. She did not stop reaching out to him, despite the sadness she felt every time she thought about how little he must care.

"He rejected the call.

"Everything OK? Do you like my story so far? Good, I'll continue.

"Edward reached step 86 before he remembered he had left his car keys in the site office. He berated himself for sloppiness and bounded back up towards St Mary's. He was a fit man, but the thought of an escalator crossed his mind, the clients would appreciate some blue sky thinking, he thought to himself. He pulled out his phone and saw the missed call from his mother, he huffed and called his architect, but there was no answer.

"The sun was low and Edward's shadow crept long and lean over the ground on the headland. His phone rang again, and once again his mother was dealt the humiliation of her only son rejecting her call. Edward looked around in the lazy light and his imagination flickered. Earthy tones shimmered against the bright blood sky, faces appeared in the ruined walls and the stones expanded and contracted like the vast scales of a giant desert snake, he felt unnerved. The office was tucked away by the North Transept, still out of sight. He ducked and weaved underneath some scaffolding and through the opening in the north wall onto the grass clearing, where he was struck on the head and fell to the ground with a thump.

"He winced as he opened his eyes, it took a moment before memories bounced back. Beside him lay a bucket, on his head an egg, medium in size, it pulsed with pain. His first emotion was anger..........

...........actually I have an idea, it makes far more sense for Edward to tell this part of the story, it did happen to him after all! You don't mind, do you? Please, don't be put off by the picture I've painted so far, he has changed a great amount since the day I took him.

"Edward, come here, please. I'm telling your story to this charming person and I've just reached the scary bit, you know where -"

"Stop, please, I only want to hear this story once, whether it's from my mouth or yours and, besides, you'll ruin it for our audience!"

"Quite right. Well, you've just been hit with the bucket....."

Part II

"It did not take long for me to realise something was wrong. I was in the corner of the choir, a long way from where I was hit. I looked around for an assailant, but saw nobody. Then an eerie feeling began to tiptoe up my spine, I was being watched. I could sense it. I got to my feet and studied the choir, the crossing, the nave. Nothing. I was shaking with fear, I realised the eyes were not in front or behind me, but above.

"It took a few seconds to summon the courage to look up, the sky was red, the pallid moon ghosted into view and the twisted faces of hundreds of gargoyles pushed their way out of the walls above to stare back at me. They studied me, each pair of eyes different from the next, some were wide and insane, others piercing and cruel, but they all shared one thing: hate. I had never felt as despised as I did at that moment. Then their mouths began to open and their lips quivered, I had no idea what was happening. Their faces filled with rage and the ground beneath me shook. I realised they were screaming, but their was no sound, the headland was silent. I looked around to see the walls bulging like huge veins, the whole Abbey seemed to be moving. Suddenly the faces swarmed towards me. I ran, like never before. I aimed for the cloister, but I was not quick enough, arms began to grow out of the pillars, all reaching for me. Back into the nave, I saw the western doorway closing like a huge, broken jaw. I had one last chance, the doorway in the north wall. Arms reached upwards and outwards from the bases of the great pillars which stood in the way, but I had no choice. With all my might I threw myself forward, somehow I made it.

"Ahead of me the doorway was closing, but not fast enough, I was through and onto the grass. There was only one place left to go, as I ran I rummaged in my pocket for the small brass key that would unlock the door of the office. Out of the corner of my eye I could see the faces making their way over the top of the choir wall and down towards me.

"At last, I was inside with the door locked behind me. I did not get the chance to catch my breath before the palm of a stone hand slammed against the window with a thud. I searched my pockets for my phone, I needed to call for help, but it was not there, something else was in its place. I pulled out my hands to find them covered in soft grains of cold, damp earth.

"At that moment a second hand slammed against the window, then another and another, until the last of the half-light was lost.

"Words can't describe how frightened I was, the Abbey was alive. I screamed at the hands, pleading for mercy, asking why this was happening. But no response came. I was about to crumble when a light flickered into the dingy room, I knew instantly what it was, there was only one thing that it could be. A hand had pinned my phone to the window, the screen was bright and it took a few seconds for my eyes to adjust.

"As I moved closer I could see that a photograph was displayed, it was of me as a boy on the beach at Sands End. Another image flashed onto the screen: a girl from a different time, working in a field, picking onions from the ground. The work looked hard, but her spirits are high, she smiles at the camera. The next image was familiar, a lady on a picnic blanket in the shade of a weeping willow with a Moses basket by her side. The same woman appeared in the next photo, this time she has a young boy on her lap. I realised the woman in the picture was my mother and the boy was me. She looks at me with doting eyes, while I look at the camera. Another image of her watching me playing football, faint lines have started to show at the corners of her eyes. She looked different.

"The phantom slideshow continued for some time, showing pictures of my mother throughout her life. It settled on one taken a few years ago, she is at my Uncle Frank's birthday party. Despite the celebrations, she looks sad. Needless to say I wasn't there, I was in a meeting.

"It had been a very long time since I had cried, but it did not take much to pull the tears from my eyes as I slumped to the muddy floor in the lonely, stuffy cabin.

"I spent a wretched night seeking forgiveness more fervently than I had chased any business deal. I had realised long ago that I wasn't close to anyone any more, the only people I socialised with were work colleagues, I could not call them friends. I had left my family and true friends behind some time ago. It was not a conscious decision, it just seemed to happen, I did not really think there was room in life for relationships and business, so I didn't try to keep anyone close, I did not need friends to make money.

"Sorrow washed over me, maybe I had not left them behind after all, maybe they had left me behind.

"One thing was for sure, the situation I was in was desperate, I was surrounded by stone hands and I had nobody to save me, literally. If the phone was inside the cabin who could I call for help?

"I had slipped reality by this point and I shared the small hours with my first crush, some of my clients, long forgotten school friends, my project manager, dead grandparents, architects, and nieces and nephews I had never met, and all the while my mother looked on. She should have been the one constant in my life, while these people walked in and out, but I had pushed her away, she had also become someone passing through. I desperately wanted to call her, I needed to say so many things, things I should have said a long time ago. I hoped it was not too late.

"Time drifted by unseen, I did not notice that the morning sunshine had slipped between the fingers until my eyes began to sting. In the confusion of the night I had completely forgotten about the hands, and any fear I had of them. I walked over to look at my phone, the image of my mother had changed, she looked like she had done when I last visited. Sat on a bench in the early morning sun, her lips crept up at the edges and she squinted into the distance looking content and peaceful. A weight lifted from my shoulders, I felt as if I still had a chance to make things right. I would not stop trying until she forgave me, but she would surely forgive me in the end, I was her son after all. Isn't that what family did? Forgive and forget. I could not wait to call her.

"After a few seconds the screen went black and the hand backed away. My phone dropped from view and light flooded into the room. This was a sign, I knew what I had to do. Other hands followed, gliding away gracefully and disappearing back into the walls of the ruins, until I was left with a view of a perfect morning, the sun rising behind the buildings which stood on the edge of the headland. I walked out into the warmth and gazed at the sparks on the sea. My phone began to ring, I plucked it from the soft grass. A bright green telephone flashed on the screen above the name of my architect. I smiled, my mother would understand if I took a quick call. We were going to be so close that she would understand all about my business and she would support me, we would support each other. That is the way it would be, we would be there for each other in the future through thick and thin.

"I pressed accept and raised the phone to my ear, thoughts of the escalator rushed back into my mind. I did not have time to speak before a hand grabbed me by the throat and dragged me towards a huge gaping mouth.

"The last thing I remember of my life outside these ruined walls is the sight of hundreds of gargoyles, their mouths twisted in screams, watching as the Abbey swallowed me alive.

An Ending

"I've stood on this headland for over 1,000 years and have tried to show countless wicked souls the error of their ways, some learned their lesson, most, like Edward, didn't. Now he's just another stone face, with eternity ahead of him to ponder why I took him from his world.

"Don't worry about him now, though, he's doing very well. In fact I've just given him a prime spot at the top of my west wall, so he can watch the waves. I may be in ruins but the view from there is still good.

"How was that for a story then, eh? Not too bad, I hope. Now, about that long grass, please can you cut it today, it's really starting to tickle me around my cloister."

Trouble at t'Abbey

By Suzy Travers

Jonathan Duck had a lucky streak about him. The voyage from London was short but bumpy and he was relieved to be back on solid ground. He waited at the end of Bridge Street as per his instructions and at precisely ten to ten Hannah Harland left the house and made her way down the street. She undertook this journey so regularly that she wasn't taking a great interest in her surroundings and so she failed to notice Jonathan, first watching her from the other side of the street, then following in her footsteps. He had only minutes to intercept her before she reached her Aunt's shop where she undertook some work behind the counter. He had already considered the 'customer' option but he preferred that they have less of an audience. Just as they were approaching town he crossed the road to catch up with her.

"Madam, excuse me?"

She stopped short and turned around to see who was addressing her.

He bent down in front of her to retrieve a handkerchief from the pavement.

"I think you dropped this," he said ever so gently and sweetly.

Hannah's initial response was the honest one, "Oh no. I don't think so. That doesn't look like mine." It looked new, beautiful white lace edging. Expensive.

"Oh," he said. He sounded disappointed.

Hannah looked around. There was no one else nearby it could have belonged to. She thought perhaps there would be no harm in accepting it.

"Well, actually, may I take a closer look?"

"Of course." He remained reserved, polite.

She pretended to examine it with care.

"I do believe" she said, after a moment, "that this is one of mine. I so seldom carry this one around with me that I failed to recognise it at first. Thank you sir." She tucked it into the corner of her bag.

Will was waiting for Hannah outside the shop at six o'clock as usual. Hannah suppressed a smile. Will Storm was waiting for her on a Thursday come rain or shine. Poor Will, thought Hannah. Her Uncle worked him hard and he was grateful for the job. Too grateful. He regularly worked on, shut up the shop. His ma saw Will as their shining light. And here he was, waiting for Hannah as usual.

"Will!" Her voice was warm, her greeting sincere.

"Thought I'd try and catch you," he said, still slightly breathless from running to be there on time.

"Glad you made it," she said and she took his proffered arm. Slightly taller than her female contemporaries she almost matched Will for height.

"How are you Hannah?"

She smiled to herself. Should she tell him of her date? He would surely be jealous. Yet there was no one else she wished to tell.

"Will?" she began coyly.

"Yes."

"May I tell you a secret?"

"Yes," he answered slowly. "Sure."

"You mustn't tell Aunt Margaret," she warned.

"Where you off to now young lady?"

Hannah sighed. Not Aunt Margaret. Her mother's sister. Well meaning to be sure but increasingly cramping her style. It seemed these days that Aunt Margaret was there anytime she wanted to go out anywhere.

"Will, Auntie." She smiled serenely. "I said I'd meet Will."

"Will Storm?" sniffed Margaret even though she knew quite well which Will Hannah meant.

"Yes Auntie."

"Aren't you and he getting a bit old to be running around together?"

Hannah laughed. "Oh Auntie, he's my friend. He's always been my friend."

It was true that Margaret and Will had run around together for years, and that no-one batted an eyelid to see them together.

Margaret changed tack. "How's his apprenticeship going?"

"Oh, good," said Hannah. "Only another year or so to go and then he'll be ..."

"Hmm" said Margaret sniffing.

"Excuse me then Auntie," said Hannah seeing an opportunity to leave.

Margaret shifted slightly to let her pass. "Be careful."

"Aunt Margaret!" she giggled as she stepped past.

"Jack, Jack," she heard the sound of her Aunt's voice making a beeline for her step father in his workshop. She smiled to herself.

"Jack?" Margaret crept around the doorframe of the workshop.

"Yes Margaret, I am in here," Jack admitted.

"That girl is dressed up to the nines."

"Ah," said Jack. He was well aware that Hannah was of an age where she would attract suitors but he was half hoping that Margaret would manage this on her own.

"Who is she with?" he asked.

"She says Will Storm," said Margaret.

"You don't believe her?"

"No," said Margaret. "She'd never dress up like that for him."

Jack felt himself grow a little greyer at the temples if it was at all possible.

"Then who?"

"I don't know," said Margaret. "And that's what worries me."

"Margaret..." began Jack.

She cut him short. "Jack... I know she's not really yours but sometimes I think you hide too much behind it."

He sighed.

"She's Mary's and that man's. Maybe she's a touch of his arrogance about her it's true, but you'd hate to see her fall as much as I would. She needs a tighter reign. Just because that selfish cad deserted Mary it doesn't mean we should give up on Hannah. She's a fine young woman Jack, and she could make a fine match. Not poor Will Storm, though doubtless he's got his hopes up over the years. We need to pick someone for her, a decent match."

Jack would have preferred to have ignored Margaret as usual but he knew she was right. Hannah might be ignorant of the facts of her true parentage, but she deserved his support.

Jonathan Duck was a good looking man and he was well aware of the effect he had on women.

"Hannah my dear" he said and he moved to take her gloved hand and kiss it. She felt herself reddening slightly under his gaze.

"A successful day?" she asked remembering that he had said he was here on business.

"Well," he laughed coyly. "That remains to be seen." He was flirting with her, she realised. "Although now you have joined me I think that I can conclude that yes, overall, it has been a successful day." He smiled at her.

"You look beautiful Hannah," and he meant it. For she had dressed herself well, making the most of her natural charms. Hannah was surprised that Aunt Margaret hadn't made more of it.

"Where would you like to go?"

"Well?" she realised she had presumed that they were aiming for the Abbey but that actually they didn't need to go there at all. Her gaze began to shift from the steps back to the town.

"I've heard a lot about this Abbey of yours, but I haven't yet chanced to see it up close."

She looked back at him,

"Oh, well, we could take a stroll up the steps then, if you like?"

"That would be lovely. You could be my guide."

"May I?" he asked. Hannah hesitated but then took up the offer of his arm.

"I don't know a lot about the Abbey although I have walked around it many times."

"Tell me what you do know."

They began to make their way up the 199 steps.

Will Storm was watching them from his hiding place in the street below the steps. Although it was growing dark Hannah Harland was still recognisable as the street lamps caught the light of her chestnut hair. At the sway of her skirts as she took each step in turn, Will was enchanted. He almost forgot why he was there. "Oh Hannah," he sighed, disappointed. "You shouldn't be seen out alone with him. You don't know nowt about him." What did he want with Hannah anyway? She was pretty it was true, and her step father was still making decent money in the carpentry trade. But why would this stranger from London want her? Was she just a passing fancy? A passing fancy like him could ruin her.

As the silhouette of the couple began to fade from his view as they neared the top of the steps Will began to move once more towards them. 'Forgive me Hannah' he thought. He knew she would be furious if she caught him spying on her. He caught them by the door of St. Hilda's. He'd had to duck and creep across the churchyard using the gravestones for camouflage. "Sorry," he whispered to each inhabitant in turn as he made his way across. He crouched close by; just close enough to hear their conversation drift across on the evening's breeze.

"So you're saying that in the 9th century Danes sacked Whitby and destroyed much of the Abbey then?"

"Well that's what I was told. I don't know my history as well as I should."

"It's nice to meet a young girl with some brains."

Hannah flushed. "Well everyone knows a bit about the Abbey. It's stood over this town for so long. You grow up with it."

The full moon was now bright in the sky and they had enough light to see a fair way around them.

"Come," he said, offering out his hand. "Let us take a stroll."

Hannah paused slightly at the out-turned palm. To take his arm was one thing, his hand quite another. This wasn't Will Storm grabbing her hand and pulling her down the street to look at something. From his hiding place Will saw her take his hand and begin to walk with him. To follow them now would risk them seeing him for sure although he could use the ruins of the Abbey to duck behind as required. Anyway, he really was sure that Hannah wasn't thinking straight and that surely being spotted by him was better than her doing something foolish.

Jonathan paused under the ruins of the nave.

"Hannah," he said abruptly.

"Yes?"

"I should be frank with you," he paused. "I didn't bring you here for a romantic rendez-vous."

"You...didn't?" her voice faltered, uncertain.

"Hannah, what do you know about your past? Do you know about your father?"

"My father, you mean my real father? Not Jack?"

"Your real father Hannah yes," he sounded impatient.

"His name was Thomas. He died before I was born. Mother never spoke much of him."

"Ashamed?" queried Jonathan.

"Oh no," said Hannah. "Why would she be that?" She looked at him. "He wasn't very successful I know. When he died she was penniless, which is probably really why she married Jack so quickly." She put her hand to her mouth aware that she was being slightly disloyal.

He tried another tack. "Hannah, where did you get that ring from?"

He pointed to the jewel on her index finger.

"Well this was mother's."

"Where did she get it?" he asked.

"Oh I don't know," said Hannah. "It's just some old trinket."

"Girl, that gem's worth a small fortune, and any jeweller in Whitby worth his salt could have told you that." His tone was harsh now, disbelieving.

Hannah flushed.

"Ah," he said. "And you have been told it before haven't you?"

Hannah had. Years ago when times were hard before Jack's business took off she'd taken it into a jeweller and been rather taken aback when he asked her where she'd got it from, at first not believing it was hers, and then, being a kindly soul, telling her it was worth rather a lot more than she'd imagined.

"What's all this about?" she asked, suddenly angry.

He sighed.

"Hannah. Your father 'Thomas' is alive and well and living in London."

She gasped.

"He was never married to your mother. He met her whilst here on business."

He let this news sink in.

"Like you?" asked Hannah. "On business."

He laughed drily. "Sort of Hannah. He's a rich man your father. He didn't know about you, but then he came to know of you last year. Your Aunt Margaret's got a bit of a mouth on her. Draws a bit too much attention to your family."

"It's not a good thing?" she asked aware of the irritation in his voice. "I'm not a good thing? To him I mean?"

"Hannah," he looked a little sad now. "You're very bad news I'm afraid. You see, your father is Thomas Challoner. He's standing to become an MP. He's married into a very distinguished family and although childless, he wouldn't want news of your existence to get out."

"You came up here to tell me this didn't you," she asked touching his arm gently.

He pulled away at her touch.

"Hannah. I'm sorry but I just can't let this news get out. I'm here for more than just to tell you. It's my job to keep this, you, under wraps. You simply can't exist."

Her pupils grew large as she began to realise his words. She started to turn to move but he anticipated her and grabbed her arm. From his hiding place Will saw him move and he knew he had to act. He ran towards them shouting her name.

"Will!" said Hannah. She sounded hysterical.

"Hannah, what's wrong?" he asked.

"Oh my," said Jonathan as he pulled back. "You do realise you're spoiling a rather romantic moment?" He got down on one bended knee.

"Oh!" said Will who was taken aback. He glanced at Hannah.

"No" she said. Whilst Will was looking at her Jonathan had jumped back up and turning on his heels he ran towards the cliff edge.

"Will!" said Hannah. "He came here to kill me!"

"What?" Will was torn between staying with her and pursuing Jonathan. "Get help!" he said, and he ran after Jonathan. He made his way across the field to the west of the Abbey. Jonathan was running dangerously close to the cliff edge. Will realised that Jonathan could only get back via the churchyard so he began to head for it to cut him off. Once back in the old town there would be myriad alleys and passageways to hide in, maybe even a ship due to leave port. Will had to catch him here.

As he ran towards the gravestones Jonathan was no longer fully in his line of vision. Will sprinted the last stretch and then looked to his right. He stood hunched over, hands on hips, catching his breath. There was no one out there anymore. No one. He scanned the area around the cliffs. There was no way that Jonathan could have got across the churchyard without him noticing. He heard a commotion behind him. It was Hannah with a passing man.

"Where is he?"

Will pointed towards the cliff edge. "Last time I saw him he was running across there. He's gone. He's just vanished."

Hannah clung to Will's arm. "Where could he have gone?"

"There's only one way from there," said the man. "Down."

Oceans of Time

By Cheryl Spencer

Kate Everton was fed up.

The headaches had started again. It was always around the same time of year, and Kate could never get to the bottom of it. She'd seen so many doctors since the headaches had started back when she was eighteen, and now, ten years later, she still had them every Autumn and nobody could figure out why.

Recently she'd come to realise that they were always bad after a recurring dream she had of being in an old fishing town, where she'd be in a cottage at the foot of a ruinous Abbey, doing day to day things, and then, in the dream, she had felt dizzy and fallen down, only to wake up safe in her own bed. The dream was always the same. And it was always the same era – a hundred years or so before she was even born. Sometimes she swore she could smell herrings being smoked.

Whitby Abbey showed up clear on the horizon as the herring boat Joe Fisher was on sailed in rough seas towards home. This fishing lark was alright once you got used to it, he joked, but in reality he loved the sea and had come from a long line of fishermen before him. Joe's boat, the Valhalla, was a small fishing vessel and he'd got a place on it as a boy, partly because he was so keen to go to sea and partly because his father knew the captain. The sails were battered and the stink of herring never left the boat, even though it was washed by the sea a thousand times in ferocious weather. Joe didn't mind the smell, but he wasn't so sure if the pretty girl who lived nearby, Catherine, would take to it so well. Still, she was a sailor's daughter, he reasoned, so surely she wouldn't mind so much, and he smiled as he thought of their walks around the old Abbey together.

He had asked her shyly one day if she would like to go for a walk and they'd strolled up the great curve of steps, past St Mary's church where they all went on Sundays, and over to St Hilda's Abbey. Overgrown and ruinous as it was, Catherine and Joe loved it. They chatted for hours about what the glass might have looked like in the windows, which were now mullioned gaping holes open to the elements, or what the hymns must have sounded like in such a huge building. They talked about where they thought people might have lived and worked, where they might have prayed, all the time taking in the giant stones that once were part of a long gone monastic life on this remote headland.

Kate had never been to Whitby. She'd seen it, on TV, but never been. And yet, sat in her poky flat in a dreary northern city after a long and tiresome day in her office job, she knew that Whitby was where she was in the dreams. She decided, ridiculously, she thought, to go to the town and see if she could find the cottage. Kate wasn't one for what she called hocus-pocus, but she was getting to the point where she was willing to try anything to cure her headaches.

Joe's boat was going out again. The weather was rough, and the fires being stoked in the small cottages weren't keeping much dry or warm. The herring fleet had work to do though, and they went out regardless of whether the fire at home had dried their clothes from last night or not.

He decided to take a walk to the church to say prayers. His father and grandfather before him had done it many times in rough weather, walking up almost two hundred steps to the church perched above the town. Maybe he would see Catherine on the way....oh, how he loved her! He wished with all his heart that her father would return from sea soon so he could ask him for her hand. He had it all planned; what he would say, how they could live with her father and help him as he got older, how they would manage on their meagre earnings. Catherine mended fishing nets down on the quay with other women and girls to earn a few pennies, and he always smiled when he brought the nets back onto the boat because he liked to think Catherine had touched them.

Joe went to sea that day not looking outward to the ocean as he usually did, but back inland towards the town. The Abbey was the last thing you could see for miles after everything else had faded into the distance, and he kept his eyes fixed there until that too disappeared. Catherine lived in a cottage at the foot of the cliff that the crumbling stones from a bygone age sat on, and as long as he could see the ruins, he could see her.

Kate had thought Whitby a lovely old place and had spent days wandering the streets, getting to know the town. She had, this morning, climbed wearily up the steps to the Abbey, and had spent until way past lunchtime wandering around in the Autumn sunshine, looking at the arches, the windows, the Saxon graves and the pillar bases, and wondering why she felt ill at ease. After a while she'd gone to the church a little way off, and sat in complete silence in the dim cool, starting to feel peace with herself. But then an overwhelming sadness had come over her and she felt she had to leave.

Restless, she walked down the steps again, cursing herself for not enjoying the view, and suddenly stopped dead in her tracks near the bottom. In front of her was a row of old fishermen's cottages, and her head exploded in pain so sharply she had to sit down on the steps. Had she found the place in the dream? What did it mean?

'The Valhalla's lost!' shouted a man on the fish quay in a broad voice, 'Lost! They said she wunt make it back in after that last storm battered 'em all. I told 'em to make repairs on 'er, I did, but no! They're gone! Gone!'

Amidst the din from the fish quay and the noise of the rest of the returning herring fleet, nobody saw the young girl wipe tears on her apron and continue mending nets. Her heart was breaking, but the net wouldn't when she had repaired it. No more lost at sea, she kept whispering to herself. No more lost. She'd keep the nets strong and do her bit. But nobody noticed her, they were all hollering at another boat that came limping in from the same storm, sails flapping and torn, mast creaking unhealthily. Catherine couldn't bear to look.

Kate sat on a bench underneath the archways in the Abbey later. She remembered reading that the arches had fallen, intact, from a higher point in the building somewhere and had been placed, still intact, next to the boundary wall, with benches in the newly-formed alcoves. It seemed a quiet place to try and think.

She knew that cottage down the hill from her dreams, but she didn't know why. An old man came hobbling over, and asked her if he could sit on the seat for a while. Kate obliged.

'Lovely afternoon,' he said cheerily.

'It is,' Kate replied. She took the plunge and asked him about the cottages before she'd even realised it.

'Ah, them. Theer's a sad tale ter be teld abaht them, lass.'

'There is?'

'Oh aye. There were a lass what lived there, a long time back. She chucked 'ersen off t'cliffs o'er yonder,' he said, indicating with a bony finger to the headland over the wall.

'She did? Why?'

'Lad she loved dint come back from fishin' one day. 'E went aht ter sea and drahned when 'is boat went dahn in an ahful gale.'

'When – when was this?'

'Oh blimey, must be 'undred years or so nah, lass. They buried 'er in t'churchyard dahn t'road.'

Kate was intrigued. 'Do you know her name?'

'Oh aye, everybody does. 'Er name was Catherine Elliott.'

Catherine sat alone that night, with no candles to light the cottage and no fire. The wind howled around the chimney pots, but she didn't notice. Joe was dead. That was the only thing she noticed. She looked at her hands, already work roughened at the young age of eighteen, and tears spilled down her cheeks as she realised he would never put a wedding ring there. In despair and grief, she ran out of the house, tripping over her apron and her long skirts as she stumbled up the steps to the Abbey.

Kate scanned every gravestone she could find. Her head was pounding, her thoughts unclear, but somehow she had to find the headstone, although she'd no idea what she was going to do when she did.

Meanwhile, a man who had been to Whitby many times before was paying his entrance fee to get into the Abbey grounds.

'Back again so soon, James?' the guide asked.

'Yes, but only to look around this time. I haven't brought my sketchbook today.'

Catherine had reached the Abbey. She ran blindly from one part of it to another, shouting Joe's name as loud as she could. In the wild weather her voice was small and carried away too quickly, but she couldn't stop. She ran out to the headland edge to face the full brunt of the incoming gale and screamed at the top of her lungs.

'Why? Why did you take him? Cruel, cruel sea!'

Kate had found the headstone. It was overgrown, plain and held a name and dates. Then she realised the date of death for Catherine Elliott was...good lord. One hundred years ago tomorrow. Kate's heart raced. What now?

James, the man who'd gone to look around the Abbey without his sketchbook, felt ill. He couldn't describe it, never could. Of all the times he'd been here though, looking for something but not knowing what, and putting it down to an artist's restless nature, this was the time he'd felt most sick.

The sun went in. Clouds raced across what was becoming a leaden sky. The wind direction turned. 'Storm coming,' he murmured to himself.

Catherine held out her arms wide and closed her eyes. In an instant she had taken a deep breath and fallen forward, over the cliff edge.

Kate shot bolt upright in bed in her hotel, sweating and shaking. It was past midnight, and the storm was howling around the town. Rain battered her window. At first, she couldn't remember what she'd dreamed. But now...oh....oh, no...

The cliff near the Abbey.

Falling.

Kate threw on some clothes and ran.

James couldn't sleep. He was walking the empty streets in the middle of a gale and was soaked to the skin. The locals, if they saw him, must have thought he was mad, but he didn't care. It, whatever "it" was, was happening, he could feel it.

Kate's headache was making her feel sick. She ran across the bridge that spans the Esk river and started up the cobbled streets past jet shops and trinket stores that led to the Abbey steps. Her head felt too heavy for her shoulders. The rain and wind drove her back. The cobbles were uneven under her feet. But she kept going.

James suddenly realised he was on the wrong side of the river and started to run towards the bridge.

The pain in Kate's head blinded her now, coursing, intense pain that made her stop and cry out. Near the cottages, so vivid in her dream, she collapsed in the middle of the road in agony. She knew now.

James crossed the bridge and ran up the cobbled streets, buffeted by the wind and rain.

And then he saw her. Crumpled in pain and despair in the deserted street, she was sobbing hysterically.

'Catherine?'

Kate looked up, startled. Even in a howling gale, his voice seemed right next to her. 'Oh my God,' she whispered, '….it's…it's you.'

James smiled and looked at her closely as he helped her up. She had the same look in her eyes and her face was exactly as he saw it in his mind.

Catherine Elliott, reborn years later as Kate Everton, had found Joe Fisher again, albeit he was called James these days. 'I found you,' she smiled.

And then she realised her headache had gone.

The Dream Visitor

By Daniel Hurst

The boy's eyes shot open.

He glanced around the room, not entirely sure what it was he expected to see. He was in his room and could make out the shape of his wardrobe and desk in the dark. He could see 'that' jumper, the one his Nan had got him for Christmas, draped over the back of his chair. He'd had to wear it yesterday during a family meal. It was a sweet present but, with his 14th birthday approaching, wearing knitted jumpers was certainly not a step towards the street credibility he one day hoped to have. That chair was likely to be its home for a while, or at least until the next time Nan was coming to visit.

Turning his head to the right and straining his eyes he attempted to make out the blurry red numbers next to the bed. 3:43 am.

It must have been a dream he thought to himself, as he rolled onto his right side and attempted to get comfortable again. The moonlight was streaming through the curtains, making the room seemingly brighter now. His eyes were adjusting to the dark.

It seemed so real though.

He ran it over in his mind, trying to remember everything that had just happened.

I'd been outside. It had been dark. I'd been alone. At least I had been but I soon had company. A visitor. They weren't from around here; in fact they weren't even from this planet. It was definitely a dream then. They'd told me something. I had tried to get a proper look at this stranger but I couldn't, it was almost as if they weren't there at all.

He rolled back onto his left side, hoping to drift back off to sleep but still running the dream through in his mind.

The figure was wearing a long black robe that covered their entire body. They moved quickly, gracefully, almost hovering off the ground. They didn't scare me though. No, they were strangely comforting. It was like I knew I wasn't in any danger.

He sat up and pushed the white tangled sheets from his body. Swinging his legs to the side he forced his tired body out of bed. He reached for the empty glass sitting on his desk and he slowly made his way to his bedroom door. Quietly, so as not to disturb his sleeping family, he gripped the door handle and slowly pulled it down, praying the rusty hinges wouldn't squeak as the door opened. He felt his way down the hallway with his spare hand against the wall, its presence reassuring him he wasn't about to fall. It was still extremely dark and although his eyes were adjusting he didn't quite trust them enough yet to confidently make the journey unaided. Reaching the bathroom he filled his glass with water from the tap and took a long, refreshing sip.

Then he remembered.

The stranger had told me to meet him tomorrow night at Whitby Abbey.

He stared at the 199 steps leading up the cliff towards the Abbey.

He had been here on numerous occasions. It was almost mandatory that his school organized at least one trip a year to the historic site. These steps were definitely familiar. This time it felt different though. This time he wasn't sure he should be making his way to the top. The prospect of being stood amongst the ancient ruins as the clock approached midnight suddenly didn't appeal all that much. The Abbey was certainly spooky in appearance, looking like it could easily be hiding the ghosts and ghouls of the underworld. He wanted to be back in town, the town which contained the safety and comfort of his bed, the bed he was now over a mile away from. There was a clear sky overhead and the full moon was sitting brazenly, boldly right in the middle of it, illuminating the crumbling stone, forcing all the ghastly creatures out of their hiding places. This thought made him feel a little better. He'd never been up here on his own before, never mind at night.

Maybe this wasn't such a good idea.

He knew it had been a dream. He knew that dreams weren't real and that they were just another place for his wild imagination to run even wilder. But this dream had been different.

It had felt so real.

The stranger in the dream had given clear instructions and he was following them so far. This was why he hadn't been able to concentrate all day at school. This was why he had sneaked out of his house while his family were lying in their warm beds. This was why he now found himself preparing to slowly move his feet onto the steps and walk up the hill.

He felt unsteady as he climbed, a deep breath accompanying the placing of one foot after the other. The air was still and cool. He had been freezing when he left home. Wearing his smart brown Winter jacket and black cotton gloves had been a good idea. Now though he was beginning to get warm. Small beads of sweat began to form on his forehead.

Peeling off his gloves and pulling down at the jacket's zipper he welcomed the cool air as it hit the parts of his body previously wrapped under warm layers of clothing. He knew it wasn't the physical activity of walking up the hill that was making him sweat.

It was the mental activity of worrying what might be waiting for him at the top.

The grass was slippery underfoot and his trainers made squelching noises as he advanced towards the Abbey. It had rained earlier, typical January weather. The uneasiness with which he walked on this slick, muddy surface only added to the feeling of unease he was already feeling in the pit of his stomach.

Here I am he thought to himself, I'm here to meet you so show yourself.

There was nothing. No stranger in a robe hovering towards him.

Maybe mum and dad were right; maybe I need to stop living in a dream world.

Then he saw it, in the distance. Initially faint, but slowly the light grew stronger, gradually becoming brighter than all the stars that surrounded it. It seemed to snake across the sky, a wobbling, shaking, glowing ball.

Was it a plane?

He certainly hoped not with the way it was moving. If so, the pilot was certainly struggling to keep it under control. He couldn't hear an engine though and on a night as quiet as this the sound from an aeroplane's engine nearby would certainly have carried to his ears.

What was it?

Who was it?

The fluorescent object in the sky was slowing down, moving in a more controlled manner, but only just. It was still a good 100 metres away from him and he strained his eyes, trying to figure out what on earth it was. All he could see was light; it was like a flying miniature sun.

It had stopped moving now.

It was just hovering.

Now it was carefully, extremely slowly, dropping towards the cliff top below it.

Whatever it was it was landing, right here, at Whitby Abbey.

It had stopped again, a few feet off the ground, still and calm, in stark contrast to the crazy, almost reckless manner in which it had arrived. Then the light went out. He ran his eyes around the scene in front of him. Seconds ago there had been a ball of light floating just yards away.

Where had it gone?

Looking down all he saw were the long menacing shadows of the Abbey reaching across the grass towards him. The moon was giving out just enough light so as to capture perfectly the framework of what remained of the ancient landmark. He could see pale patches on the grass, where the moon's beams broke through the gaping space where the windows of the Abbey once were. The old resilient stonework around these holes however formed a much darker image on the surface of the cliff, the crumbling building's every detail highlighted by the midnight illumination.

Then one of the shadows moved.

He almost jumped out of his skin.

Turning his head right, he scanned around for whatever caused his heart to skip several beats.

Standing no more than five yards away was a figure in a white robe, silent and still.

The boy wanted to start moving away from the stranger, start making his way down the cliff and back towards the safety of his bedroom.

But he didn't feel afraid.

Instead the more he stood in the light of the full moon, high above Whitby, amongst the shadows of the famous Abbey, he felt calm and increasingly at ease.

"Who are you?" the boy said. It was the best he could come up with given the circumstances.

The figure moved slowly towards him. It was then he noticed whoever was in this robe was floating, hovering inches above the damp grass.

Just like in the dream.

And this person was short. They must have only been a child themselves.

"OK, I'm not afraid," the boy stated calmly "I just want to know who you are."

"I'm from your dream," replied the disguised figure, in an accent the boy didn't recognize. "Thank you for coming."

With that the stranger, arms raised, pulled back the thick white hood that covered their head and the moonlight hit their face, revealing the secrets of their identity. It was a young boy, perhaps in his early teens. He had short white hair, and a pale complexion. His eyes were a cold shade of blue. His nose seemed a little too big, like it was out of proportion with the rest of his face. Other than that he seemed to be quite normal.

At least as normal as you can get for someone who originally met you in a dream and now here they were standing in front of you in real life, exactly where they had told you to meet them.

"My name is Nova" said the pale boy, stretching his arm out towards the boy, a hand emerging from inside the baggy robes.

Surprising himself with his confidence, he held his hand out and accepted the peace offering, shaking Nova's hand.

"I'm Matthew."

Nova's skin felt unusually warm Matthew noticed. After all, they were standing on a cliff top at night in the middle of winter.

"This is weird," Matthew said "I dreamt about you last night. You told me to meet you here, at Whitby Abbey, tonight, and now here you are. How does that work?"

Nova turned to face the stonework ruins of the Abbey, his skin looked shiny, almost shimmering as it bathed in the light of the moon.

"That's how we contact humans Matthew." Nova explained "We meet them in their dreams, it's safer that way."

"How you contact humans?" Matthew questioned slowly, now even more puzzled but at the same time growing more excited by the second.

"I haven't got much time," Nova said urgently but still with a friendly tone, turning back to look at Matthew. "I've taken my parents transporter and I'll be in a lot of trouble if they notice it's missing."

Before Matthew could ask what a transporter was, Nova pointed to the sky. "That bright light, a few minutes ago, I'm sure you saw it. Well that was me, trying to land."

He had a cheeky smile on his face for a second as he talked.

"Anyway I came to you because I wanted to ask a favour."

He started to reach inside his robe, pulling at something, trying to get something out.

"This is so cool," Matthew chattered excitedly "I knew I wasn't imagining it, I knew someone was going to meet me here tonight. My parents and teachers are always saying I have an overactive imagination, when I tell them about my dreams and when I write my stories and when....."

"Matthew," Nova interrupted "I'm sorry but I don't have much time."

During his excited rambling he hadn't noticed what Nova had pulled out of his robe and now held in his left hand. It was a shiny silver triangle, and it had a black hole in the centre of it.

"What is that?" Matthew asked, curious because he'd never seen anything like it before.

"It's a camera," Nova explained "I know they are different to how yours look but they work the same."

He demonstrated by holding the triangular object up to his eyes and pointed it at the Abbey. Matthew heard a quiet click and then saw a brilliant flash of green light.

"You've come all this way to take pictures?" Matthew asked, unsure as to exactly how far 'all this way' was.

"Back in my star system, at school, I am studying your planet and as part of my project I have to get pictures from different landmarks, and I have to be in these pictures to prove I actually went there."

Nova held the silver futuristic looking camera out to Matthew. "Please can you photograph me in front of the Abbey?"

Matthew took the camera and held it up to his eyes. He looked into the back of the triangle and saw a world of colour. The image of the Abbey through the lens looked bright and colourful, not at all how it looked in reality in the dark of the night. Nova positioned himself in front of the Abbey and looking straight into the camera, his bright blue eyes widening, he smiled. Matthew wasn't sure how to actually take the picture when suddenly there was a loud clicking sound and a dazzling flash of green light.

"Thank you" Nova said excitedly, grabbing the camera from Matthew's hands and turning back towards the direction of where the transporter had landed.

"Wait I......" Matthew started but Nova, hood back up again, was floating off into the night. Then he stopped and turned.

"Thank you Matthew, I'm sure you have lots of questions but I have to get home now. If you would like, I will visit you in your dream tomorrow night and we can talk then."

"That would be great" Matthew happily replied, as if he made a habit of talking to people from other planets in his dreams.

Nova disappeared as quickly as he had arrived. Then Matthew saw the bright light again in the distance, rising slowly and unsteadily before whizzing off deep into the black blanket of the night sky. He was alone again, breathing heavily, in the shadows of the Abbey.

I can't wait to go to sleep again he thought to himself.

Where Earth Meets Sea and Sky

By Jill Dalladay

"Well done, son! A proper Freddie!"

Josh shrugged. He wished dad would stop trying so hard. It was a compliment; Flintoff was tough, carrying on with his bad leg. But it didn't make sense because Flintoff was going back, while he would never bowl again. That's what the surgeon said when he'd twisted the back-to-front ankle the right way round and sawn the toes off the other foot. Better face facts, Josh. Find another passion. Still made him sick to remember it.

As he dropped his crutches and collapsed on the grass, his mother bent to help.

"It's OK, mum. Don't fuss!"

"Sorry!" she flushed and switched to spreading the rug and opening the rucksack. Good. Pizza and a choc bar. He chewed in silence, feeding titbits to the dog and thinking the eternal thoughts. He could never go back to school now, after more than six months off. Spiky'd start one of his fights. Spots would take his place in the first team, and he wasn't nearly as good a bowler as Josh. Sarky Tanko would have a field day. And he'd have to take it all lying down. Screw that drunken idiot in the Merc!

"Josh, don't overdo Racey. It's not good for her." Mum nagging again, and he couldn't escape it. What was there to get better for? He'd always wanted to be a cricketer, given it all he'd got. He wasn't into levers and engines, like dad. Absolutely useless, he was, a total pain.

"OK if we wander round a bit? Want to come?" Mum in casual mode as she bagged the rubbish.

"No."

"No what?" Dad, sharp as pins. You'd think he'd let up a bit now.

"No ..." Josh sighed heavily, "thanks. You go. I'm fine here. Wanna leave Racey? And the ruck?"

"Right, thanks. Like to have a look at this book about the Abbey? Bought it on the way in. Here," dad pointed to the open page, 'this is where you're sitting, more or less. Halfway along the church. Cloisters over there."

"Wouldn't know, would you?" Josh looked round as he leaned back against the warm stone. Grassy mounds, stumps of pillars, fragments of steps. Unless he twisted right round, of course.

Over the fields from the caravan he'd seen the arches and pinnacles outlined against the sunset. Close to, they wore fantastic patterns. Chiselled by some phantom carver with the shakes, he fancied. And the stones were incredible; red, gold, orange, blue, not at all the plain grey he'd expected. He leaned back further, tracing the nearest pillar up, up into the sky, where it leaned to touch another, not quite making it, leaving a blue space where the birds flew through.

He'd wanted to come here all the time they'd been on holiday, but not until he could make it under his own steam. More of an effort than he'd admit, though, hauling himself up that lane. He felt whacked. Slithering down onto one arm, he stroked the dog and looked at the pictures in the book: bald-headed monks, pages of writing with funny pictures in the margins, a plan of the buildings with a garden in the middle, cattle in the fields, and miniature figures at work. Ah, here was the church with the tall pillars meeting at the roof – that would be his pillar – and lots of robed men, chanting, probably. No women to fuss, lucky old monks!

His sweat was drying cold and the sun was weak. He zipped up his hoodie and curled down on the rug where the north wind couldn't reach him, hugging the greyhound for warmth. When you shut your eyes, you could hear better; he'd noticed that before, in the hospital. Seagulls above, that was easy. Someone walking by with a scratchy audio commentary. A kid crying. And a kind of twittering. Probably his 'vacuum-bird' whizzing around after crumbs, wagging its tail. Behind him, the waves shushed, in, out, like the world breathing. And he could just catch the faint ringing of a bell…

Must be calling the brothers to church. They'd be padding along, heads bent under their hoods, and arms tucked inside their sleeves.

But not this one. His skirt was hoisted into his belt and he stood, scraggy legs planted apart, arms sticking out of wide sleeves so as to get a good grip on the horns. It was time for the Autumn slaughter, when the animals which couldn't fit in the byre were killed and salted as winter food.

"Not my calf!" Josh pleaded. "Dad gave me him. Runt of a bull for a runt of a boy, he said. No good for anything. So he won't be any good for you either." He had his arm round the little bull's neck, as he'd so often done in the dip in the cliffs where they went together, away from all the jibes and taunts.

"Exactly why he'd be right for me," the monk smiled, stroking the beast almost lovingly. "All your brushing's made his coat soft and supple. A special beast for a special purpose."

"What d'you mean?" Josh tightened his grip.

"Come and see. Leave him here for now."

"Sure he'll be safe?" Josh could see the field hands, under the direction of other monks, separating the cattle and leading some into the yard.

"Quite sure." Pulling his robe down, the monk turned up the slope. Josh hobbled behind, reluctantly at first, then with curiosity, towards the headland where the mighty Abbey reared into the sky. Through the great gate they went, the old man fitting his stride to Josh's limp. To his surprise they climbed the steps into the church which he'd only seen from outside. His eyes were drawn upwards to those tall, narrow windows. From inside, they dazzled him as they let through the light to paint flower-meadows on the paving. High up at the far end stood an altar glowing with gold, a huge book open on top. Stunned by the magnificence, Josh stood gazing.

"This way," murmured the monk, shuffling ahead and lifting a latch with an echoing clang. Josh followed into a square garden alive with bird song and the pungent scent of plants. Round the edge was a covered walkway with arches. Some very old monks were dozing in the sun, others stood reading at desks or hunched over their work.

"This is what I do." The old man drew the boy to a desk and took his hand, touching it to the vellum lying there. "This page is about Our Lord riding into the city. Our books are the most precious thing in the whole Abbey."

"Not the church?"

"The church gives glory to God, of course, but it's for men's use. This ..." he smoothed the work lovingly, "this is the word of God himself."

The boy stood fingering the manuscript, stroking the surface, admiring the blue, clear as the sea on a cold day, and the green brighter than Spring grass.

"Lovely," he breathed.

"As lovely as I can make it," the old man gave a wry smile. "I try to do justice to the material God provides."

There was a pause.

"My calf?"

"It could be your calf," the monk looked him straight in the eye. "Then he'd never be baited by dogs, or beaten when he grew old and cantankerous. In a way, he'd live forever. Some of our books are more than ten generations old!"

Josh was silent.

"I'm not sure." He knew the little calf was doomed; they only kept back a couple of breeding bulls. But how could he give it up?

"Don't worry. I won't take your calf unless you're willing. God wouldn't want a stolen gift. Come, I'll walk you home before Vespers."

"Have you always lived here?" Josh's eyes were everywhere.

"For many years. I grew up on a farm like you, too lively for my own good. Broke lots of the pots I was supposed to be making. One day my father gave me to God and the Abbey took me."

"Gave you...!"

"It turned out for the best. Hard at first, mind. As well as potting, I had to memorise psalms and learn to read. For all my rawness, they took me as I was. In the end, I came to accept myself. Something about the place. It has a way of lifting you."

"Holy, you mean?"

"That too, but..." They were at the top of the slope and the old man stopped to think. "Generations of good people have lived here and that creates an atmosphere. I think it's that." He walked on thoughtfully, supporting Josh under the arm. "But it may be where we are."

"Winds blowing away the rubbish?" Josh was thinking of the farmyard.

"Mm, perhaps," the monk smiled, stopping again and gesticulating with his free arm to show what he meant. "Look there, sea stretching to the very rim of the world. And there, a half-circle of hills. And here, where earth meets sea and sky, the Abbey stands like the needle of a sundial, drawing all eyes to the light."

He let his arm fall and turned to face Josh. "You could do things here, you know. With your hands and your head. If you ever need sanctuary. Your feet wouldn't matter."

The old man gripped his arm, shaking it eagerly ...

"Wake up, Josh! It's coming on to rain. Dad's gone to fetch a taxi." It was mum pulling at his arm. "Come on, Racey! Wake him up!" She took the dog's lead and held out the crutches. "Shall I help you?"

"Mm." Clutching her arm, he heaved himself up and swung a few strides to loosen up. He leaned heavily on the end pillar, kicking each leg in turn while she folded the rug. His hands were cold and the stone felt warm. Looking up, he saw clouds scudding past the top of the pillar so fast, it made him dizzy. He shook his head and moved crabwise round to the opposite side. Straight off the North Sea, the wind blew cold in his face, lifting his hood right off and blasting his hair sideways like a pennant.

Where earth meets sea and sky. At the very edge! A terrific place to be! On the horizon the moors looked sharp, hills folding behind each other in layers for miles. Almost at his feet, the red roofs of the little town began to gleam. He felt the first heavy drops on his face and lifted it up, enjoying the sensation. A fishing boat was racing for harbour and a black cloud bowled low across the bay towards him, churning the top of the water like a hydrofoil. Up here, he had a sense of power, of freedom.

"Yoohoo!" he crowed, waving a crutch at the cloud, "Yoohoo!" He looked round. No one was taking any notice; they were all running for shelter.

"Yoo-oo-hoo-oo! Hoo-oo!" All the tight knots inside him were exploding and the wind instantly whipped them away.

"Come on, daft head! You'll catch your death!" Mum stumbled towards him, hand outstretched, just as the downpour struck.

"Mum! It's awesome! Look! From up here, even the rain seems low! Masters of the world, that's us! Yoo-hoo-oo!"

"You go carefully," she laughed. "It's slippery in the wet."

Together they edged down the slope and met his dad, panting uphill with an umbrella and a wheel chair.

"Here, Josh! Get in! I know you hate it," he turned the chair round and held it firm, "but they've kindly lent it for quickness, and it'll save your mother getting drenched. Be quick!"

Back in the caravan, Josh sprawled as usual along one side of the sofa, listening to the rain drubbing on the roof, while the dog curled near his 'pots' and dad sat beside him, reading the paper. Three damp sweaters steamed gently over the stove where mum was cooking the tea. Josh rubbed a hole in the condensation on the window and looked across to the familiar outline, stark against the storm. Had he really been there? Was that what the Abbey was truly like?

"Dad, could you pass me that book? Please?"

A companionable silence fell.

"Da-ad."

"Yes, Josh?"

"I've been thinking."

"Oh, dear!" Dad smiled.

"No, seriously. When we go home…I was wondering…could I use your computer a bit? Things I want to find out. About the Abbey and that."

"Enjoyed it, did you?"

"Mm. Cool. Wouldn't mind going back."

"Well, we've another day or two."

"See, I thought I might do a kind of project. Off my own bat. Something to show when I'm able to go back to school."

His parents looked at each other.

"Fine, son." Dad's voice sounded funny and he gave Josh's shoulder a squeeze. "Anything to help."

"It'd be a new start," Josh said self-consciously, "sort of."

The Last Visit

By Jacqueline De Linford

I can remember vividly that stormy day; the sea was wild and great waves crashed against the fishing boats, and the picturesque confines of Whitby harbour. None to be seen but the fool hardy and those who earned their living by casting nets into the sea providing us land dwellers with feasts of fish. We had become accustomed to our Friday dinner plates full with the edible delights of the grand sea. Anyway, today was my birthday Adele Westoner, 21 today, 31st of October 1976, and I had collected my birthday cake, ordered from the prestigious Ashley's high street bakers. The huge waves washed the streets ahead of me and I tried my best to dodge each one of those torrent splashes. It was quite daunting as a step too near to the harbour's edge could see me and this beautiful creation, now securely tied with blue ribbon in a multi-coloured box, swept away into the tide. Luckily both cake and I made it safely back to Beauchamp Avenue, the home of my grandmother.

Grandmother's home was situated at the brow of the hill. It was an idyllic image; a two storey Georgian style house, with ivy growing on the walls and an overgrown garden filled with wild flowers. I loved its untidiness and array of colours. If you gazed high over the roof and towards the sky, you could view the eerie silhouette of Whitby Abbey, high on the cliff, proud and alone, overlooking the bustling harbour of Whitby and watching the ships sail in with cargoes of exotic goods, from continents far away. What wondrous tales, the bleak Abbey walls could tell, if only stone could speak. I had lived in this privileged place since I was seven years old, since my parents had died abroad in a freak accident. I missed them terribly, but grandmother was kind, knowledgeable, and generous to a fault; she spoiled me terribly but I'm not complaining.

I took the key from my pocket struggling to hold the cake while I turned the key with wet cold hands and entered grandmother's house. The front parlour was decorated with balloons and banners, and grandmother was in the kitchen. I could smell the sausage rolls cooking on the stove;

"Glad to see that cake is in one piece!" exclaimed gran, "We didn't have luxuries like cake in the shape of champagne bottles, in war times you know!"

Grandmother always went on about war times and the lack of bananas, chocolate and silk stockings and the general lack of everything. She compensated by hoarding everything she came across nowadays including tins of food, some over 10 years old.

"Waste not want not" she would say. Quite honestly I think gran enjoyed her war days; they gave her an excuse to nag.

"Reckon I will put this cake out on the table with the candles and the champagne, and then, change into my party dress grandmother. You know the surprise dress you bought me?"

"Yes good idea, you run along. Everything else is done now," replied grandmother.

Entering my bedroom I couldn't distinguish whether I was filled with depression or elation. There was the gown, hanging outside the wardrobe, my party dress as grandmother called it. What the hell was that? On inspection I found it to be a two piece outfit of deep purple velvet, a huge full skirt, circular to the floor, with tiered panels, and trimmed with roses of the same fabric. The jacket was tight fitting, open lapels and two buttons at waist level, and underneath was a silk boned basque. The basque was pretty I was not sure about the rest of it; also the strong smell of mothballs was a bit off putting. I suspected it was Victorian and once the property of my great aunt, Arabella Westoner. Oh well I thought my birthday is also Halloween, and I had nothing else to wear in its place. I pulled the costume on with great discomfort, realizing how tiny great aunt Arabella must have been. She had lived over 100 years ago. Her grave lay in the cemetery of St Mary's Church, positioned next to that eerie Whitby Abbey. I was told she had died from a rare blood disorder, that she was very beautiful and that her hair colour and skin were similar to mine. There was a headdress with the costume, so I undid my pony tail holding my long golden tresses of hair which hung to my waist, brushed the hair and rolled it into tidy chignons. I fastened the hair onto my head with the black crystal flower, held on two silver pins. The ornament sparkled, and I presumed was made from ancient Whitby jet, as I know aunt Arabella was of good breeding. I felt like a goth in the costume and, well, Whitby is goth town, maybe grandmother had better taste than I thought.

Downstairs the tables were laden with pastries, beers and wines - there was something to please every taste. Balloons were hanging from the ceiling and a banner with "21" on it. I was delighted and dying to taste the food.

"Oh thank you grandmother!" I exclaimed.

"This is so lovely"

With that the doorbell rang,

"I will get it grandmother. It must be my first guest."

My heart started to pounded, as my mind strayed to the school heart throb David Falworth De Cressy. Could this be him at the door? Handsome, rich, arrogant I hadn't seen him since my school days, but my old friend Peter had promised to pass on my invitation. My thoughts ran away, as David was of high society, and unlikely to call at my humble abode. My step quickened to the door. On opening the door my face dropped. It wasn't David; it was Luci and Mona Anthony, the old school gossips. Self important - they always appeared at the best parties.

"What are you wearing girls?"I exclaimed. Dressed in white shrouds and long black cloaks of velvet with strange metal bat necklaces, their skin was pure white, with lots of black eye makeup.

"Well it is Halloween, not just your birthday. We couldn't decide what to wear."

Mona replied with that upper class snorkling laugh, the grunt of a pig. Mona had been mocked for her unsavoury laugh at school. Showing the girls through, I couldn't help but notice the foul smell of her breath.

Then the arrival of friends John, Veronica, Michelle, Paul, and Peter. Unfortunately no David. I could have guessed he would not come. I turned up the music, playing a collection of Abba, Queen, Led Zeppelin, mixed in with a few songs from the 30s to keep grandmother happy. We all tucked into the buffet and giggled into the night. We had a great time dancing and singing along to the music. Things were winding down when Peter came to my side "Oh yes Adele. Happy birthday! I nearly forgot, David Falworth De Cressy asked me to give you a message. He wants you to meet him tonight at the old Abbey. He couldn't make the party tonight. Anyway you are to meet him at 11.30 to receive a special gift!"

"Oh wow!" I replied. Could this be true? David Falworth De Cressy, having designs on me. Peter interrupted: "Are you really going to meet him in the Abbey ruins? What a place for a first date! I think the bloke is a freak!"

"Of course I'm going Peter. I must find out what his gift is for me and, well, I am honoured to get a date with such a prestigious guy."

"Then I must accompany you to the ruins" replied Peter. Peter was such a gentleman - if only he was handsome and dashing instead of being so geeky, always with his head in a book offering loads of unwanted information, hiding behind those horrid professor glasses, and unkempt hair. All I could think about was my liaison with gorgeous David Falworth De Cressy. His name rolled on my tongue, wild and broody like the foamy waves of the sea.

The birthday party had come to an end, all my guests had left happy, and I was elated. Grandmother had gone up to bed early, tipsy, and full of sausage rolls. She would not notice Peter and myself leave the house into the darkness, off to the meeting at Whitby Abbey.

Peter had brought that stupid old rucksack, all patches and grimy, on his back, it went everywhere with him, not even leaving his books behind for a party, he was such a scholar. It was foggy, and we proceeded down the hill towards the harbour past the wild waves of the sea, and towards the 199 stone steps up to the Abbey. It was unnaturally quiet, and we had only passed one family of people trick or treating. We dropped a few coins in the children's cauldron and continued. The steps were daunting and slippy but this was an adventure, so we kept on going,

"Do you really have to meet this David fellow Adele?" asked Peter. "He is such a creep, and this spot is haunted you know? I mean who on earth arranges a date next to a cemetery?"

"Shut up you're only jealous!" I replied.

"At least you have me to protect you!" he replied. I laughed, mocking Peter's ability. So did Peter. We had reached the top and could see the eerie silhouette of the Abbey across the surrounding field and the wall surrounding the Abbey grounds. The wind was gale force high up there and the sea roared below.

I indicated for Peter to leave me and walked on leaving Peter dawdling somewhat worried looking by the steps while I went to my liaison with David. Checking my watch I was fifteen minutes early. Getting my breath back on one of the benches in the cemetery grounds of St. Marys Church, I could view Whitby harbour, the lights in the houses below, the boats at sea and the wild sea battering spray even this far up the cliff face. I could taste the salt in the foggy rain on my face, never had I seen such waves. Shuddering I heard a voice from the bench behind me. I looked around to see a beautiful young woman, dressed much the same as me in Victorian costume. Her pallor was white, with huge pale blue eyes and golden tresses of hair,

"Hello" I said. "I see you got your costume from the same place as me. Was it an heirloom too?"

The moon shone around the young women and beams of light surrounded her. She looked angelic in the strange light. Her costume was black satin and she wore a matching bonnet. She spoke, "Don't go to the Abbey, there is great danger there."

Shocked at her reply, she continued, "I am great aunt Arabella Westoner; there are secrets hidden here. The undead have returned to Whitby, they want revenge. My sister, Luci, was the vampire's first victim over a hundred years ago, and my spirit visits here every Halloween since that time, to find an ancestor of our blood line to set her free to find peace. Run dear niece or you will find a fate similar to Luci."

I gazed at the moon to make sure I wasn't dreaming or hallucinating. Looking back at the bench, Arabella had vanished.

Shaking with fright I decided to leave that place and ran past the tombstones and through to the Abbey. Stopping for a second to catch breath, I felt a deathly cold hand on my shoulder. Fear and dread set through my soul.

"You came my darling" whispered a familiar voice. I gasped with relief - it was David. Relief turned to horror - his pallor was deathly white, and his eyes were like burning torches, red and bulging, his pupils black. His once groomed hair was now a dishevelled, black mane dripping with blood, and glowing against the moonlight. He wore a long black cloak and a frilled shirt. I shuddered away from the horrid sight, and I escaped the icy claw. I was horrified; David was a vampire, and this was no Halloween costume, it was a real nightmare.

"Be mine Adele!" he exclaimed holding out the clawed hand. "Join us. I need your blood to gain full strength; your ancestor was Luci the vampire, first victim of my uncle, the Prince of Transylvania, who landed on these shores a century ago. You will become immortal if you join us."

Two ghostly voices harped the same message from behind a tree. "Join us Adele" cried the two figures, in white shrouds. I realized these were my two friends Mona, and Luci, bearing long fangs and blood stained shrouds. Their eyes like hungry animals approaching me, crying "We need your blood, join us."

I screamed until I choked, frozen to the floor in horror, I could not move. At that moment Peter appeared. He jumped in the space between me and the vampires, the vampires retreated hissing. Peter pulled the old rucksack from his back and, on opening it, a number of wooden stakes fell to the ground.

"You can't kill me!" snarled David. "I am descended from the Transylvanian Prince of vampires and Adele will join me in my lust for blood. She is a Westoner in ancestory. She belongs to me by birthright".

"Then it is fortunate for Adele that I am descended of Van Helsing, the born slayer of all vampires. Accept your fate Falworth De Cressy!"

Peter picked up a stake and lunged forward with it, but missed. The stake had struck through the heart of Mona, causing the deranged vampiress to explode, leaving nothing but a pile of ashes. Luci reached out her talons, screaming like a banshee, pulling my hair from its bun, holding my tresses and drawing her teeth near to my throat. Her breath was even fouler than earlier, smelling like rotting meat. The pure silver hair pin of great aunt Arabella had penetrated the hand of Luci, her hand began to burn. Steam flowed from the hand as it shrivelled, rotting up her arm, flesh dropping away into a mound of putrid, stinking, carrion. The rest of Luci's body followed suit and Luci was gone. Peter and David Falworth De Cressy struggled. Peter held the wooden stake firmly, they were nearing the cliff side and Peter was losing the fight, All of a sudden the battling waves formed the wings of a bat, they surrounded Falworth De Cressy in a vortex. Peter thrust the wooden stake into the vampire's heart. He began to bubble, and the ghostly apparition of Aunt Arabella imposed itself over the bat face. Falworth De Cressy was engulfed by the wave rotting in its path disintegrating into beads of foam; this was the vampire's last visit to Whitby.

Day-bright, Dark Night

By Sophie Barr

The wind was chilly today, thought the girl Eoforhild as she made her way down the slope to the postern gate. A month or more after the Summer Solstice and she could feel the season beginning to turn. He was there, as ever, waiting. Waiting for her? She could not be sure. She was sure, however, that she volunteered far more often than she ought to collect the Abbey's tithes from the town of Whitby.

"Daegberhdt, is that you?" Eoferhild called, hoping yet slightly dreading an affirmative answer. As a novice nun she was not supposed to form friendships with anyone other than fellow men and women of the cloth, but Daegberhdt managed to tempt her away from her promises of silence. His name meant 'day-bright' and with his fair hair, sparkling blue eyes and wicked smile, he made the most glum days seem cheerier.

"Good morning Miss Eoferhild!" he grinned back as he handed over a pair of baskets. "Fresh eggs, bread and of course some fish – you religious folk certainly eat well!"

"We require sustenance in order to dedicate our lives to the Lord" she responded primly, trying to hide the faint blush beginning to tinge her cheeks. Failing that, she grabbed the baskets and hurried away with slightly more haste than was seemly for a young woman on the cusp of her life as a bride of Christ. As she made her way back up the hill towards the comforting familiarity of the Abbey and its outbuildings, she tried to ignore the sensation of the young man's eyes following her path, and smiled inwardly at the thought of his knowing look.

It was the year of our Lord 867 and life in the Abbey of Whitby continued along its familiar routine as it had for the past two hundred odd years. Eoferhild had been a member of the small community of monks and nuns for the past seven years since her father drowned at sea and her mother died soon after, some said of a broken heart. An only

223

child without any known living relatives, she was taken in by the religious community and rechristened Eoferhild in honour of the venerated Saint Hild who had ruled the Abbey with kindness and piety a century and a half earlier. Her duties were not irksome, she lived in more comfort than many of the townsfolk and never went hungry, so why did she feel this niggling sensation of something wanting? As an orphan of only five years she had been described as 'fey' by one of the older nuns on her arrival at the Abbey, waking in the night hours with screams of terror. How could she tell the kind strangers who took her into their midst that she dreamt of her father's drowning, of his pale corpse being assaulted by nameless monsters from the deep? These nightmares continued throughout the wild and windy winter of her sixth year, during which another dozen fishermen from the town had been lost at sea. Thankfully her dreams had become more peaceful as she settled into life at the Abbey, yet of late she had been waking once again in the small hours, frightened and alert, afraid of she knew not what. The dreams themselves may have been lost in her subconscious but the feeling of disquiet, almost foreboding, persisted until matins.

Matins was where Eoferhild headed after depositing her baskets at the Abbey kitchens. Any lingering thoughts of Daegberhdt and his bright blue eyes were dispelled with the rhythmic chanting of the monks and nuns at prayer. The church was so peaceful, thought Eoferhild, as she knelt among the new-strewn rushes to pray. It truly seemed as if nothing would ever disrupt the tranquillity of Whitby's religious community. She could almost see the path she would follow in her mind's eye, growing serenely old in the service of the Lord, praying for the souls of the villagers and the fishermen lost at sea, tending to the herb garden to the rear of the scullery until it was her turn to be buried beneath the green turf of the headland. Eoferhild lost herself in these imaginary visions until she felt something tug at her thoughts, becoming more and more insistent until she was jerked back to reality and, startled, looked around her for the source of this intrusion. Yet everything was as it should be. The comforting murmur of people at prayer, the calling of the seagulls and the far-off crashing of the waves at the foot of the high cliffs. Eoferhild became more aware of an uncomfortable sensation, of a force unseen pressing down upon her, until she felt the very walls and rafters of her beloved church were closing in on her. Unable to take any more she leapt up and fled the growing oppression within the room, ignoring the surprised looks of her fellow nuns and, feeling almost as if she were starved of air, ran out into the courtyard.

She stared around her, looking for a reason for her discomfort. Unable to see anything amiss, and still feeling sorely ill at ease, Eoferhild left the Abbey enclosure by the seaward gate and half-walked, half-stumbled along the cliffs away from the boundary fence. After she had walked briskly for a couple of miles or so across the sheep-nibbled grass of the headland she felt her head beginning to clear, although her uneasy sense of foreboding remained. Her frantic pace slowed to an amble, and she eventually came to a halt, turning to face the horizon. Many folk who lived along the shore feared the sea and the relentless tug of its many currents and tides, but Eoferhild loved its ever-changing moods and hues, varying from the palest blue to a deep iron-grey. She always felt peaceful when she listened to the sound of the waves pounding the weather-beaten cliffs and found a kind of solace for her soul when she thought about how the waves had always crashed against these cliffs, and would for all eternity, unknowing and uncaring of the tiny humans who lived so close to its depths.

That sense of peace was, however, unattainable on this particular day.For quite a while she stared mindlessly at the horizon, noticing the contrast between white tops of the waves and the deep cobalt blue of the sea. "White horses" her father had called the foamy tops of the waves and she smiled at this recollection. Some time had passed before she became aware of an intruder between the sea and the sky. Far distant, but approaching quickly with the full force of the wind in their sails were half a dozen boats. These were like no boats Eoferhild had ever seen. The fishermen of Whitby built small, round tubs that nobody would dare take beyond the lee of the shore for fear of being tugged away by a baleful undertow, these magnificent ships were long and sleek, leaping through the waves like graceful serpents with their sails billowing around them, the masts rising and falling in tandem with the vertical motion of the surf. As they approached Eoferhild noticed the hideous grimacing figures mounted at the prow of each boat. She began to smile, thinking how similar they were to the carved stone gargoyles which adorned the beams of the church, until the realisation hit her that these boats were not approaching her home with any form of friendly intent. Why, these must be the dreaded Norsemen! Tales were told on dark nights of the pagan men from barren lands to the north who crossed the seas, killed, burned, looted and, leaving a trail of misery and destruction in their wake, sped back across the watery expanses to their homeland. Eoferhild had thought these were only rumours, thought up by mothers to discourage their children from straying too far from home, but she had not thought to see evidence before her very eyes in the calm vicinity of the Abbey. The Abbey! She must warn everyone! Cursing her wandering mind that had led her so far from home, she hurried back along the cliff tops, breaking into a run as she saw the longships had disappeared from view – they must have reached the town – she ran headlong into a rabbit hole, fell, knocked her head and drifted into blackness.

A few moments later – or was it a few hours, how could she know – Eoferhild awoke and in a second of horrible clarity remembered the reason why she had been so hurried. A second later the unmistakeable acrid smell of burning reached her trembling nostrils and she thought she could hear screams. The monks and nuns! She must get to the Abbey before the sea-borne marauders. Scrambling up off the salty turf Eoferhild sped off towards her friends, indeed all the family she now possessed, hoping and praying to reach them in time.

As she closed the gap between her frantically running self and the solid, familiar wooden palisade of the Abbey enclosure, she began to shout. She wasn't aware of consciously forming words, or sentences, just screaming words of danger and fire, whipped away on the wind. Panting, she darted through the seaward gate, left ajar – by her departing self, a few hours previously? Hoping so, she ran down the slope towards the low cluster of buildings. She was too late. An unidentified nun ran shrieking in her direction, only to be hacked down by a fearful warrior whose blade glinted in the sun, the nun's scream abruptly cut off as her head was severed from her body. Everywhere Eoferhild looked was carnage and bloodshed. Smoke began to rise from the church; all around her were screams, death rattles and the war-whoops of the terrible creatures spewed forth from the savage north. In a part of her mind detached from the awful present Eoferhild realised she could not remain unnoticed for a second longer. Yet she remained numb, unmoving, frozen into absolute stillness. This state of petrified shock saved her life. For amongst the bloody slaughter of men and women, the screeching and wheeling of the seagulls, the fire and destruction, who would notice a small brown figure stood stock still against the wooden palisade. One of the metal-clad Norsemen was on the very point of turning in her direction when a giant roar in a foreign tongue sounded over the din. Eoferhild did not recognise the utterance, but it was the Norse word for gold. Gold, silver and jewels were the main reasons behind the fearsome raids on the Anglo-Saxon coastline and these the Abbey at Whitby had, not in abundance, but enough to tempt the warriors from wholesale slaughter towards the church storeroom.

Eoferhild gathered her wits about her enough to sidle out of the gate and crouch low behind the wooden fence. Perhaps the wood was too damp to burn, or perhaps the beautiful gold crucifix studded with jewels and the smaller precious objects distracted the formidable sailors from the north, but the palisade fence was the only part of the Abbey that survived intact. And Eoferhild its only inhabitant. As dusk fell, and the remainder of the ships' crews descended the hill laden with plunder and a few livestock carcasses slung over their shoulders, she crept from her hiding place and wept as she surveyed the destruction and ruin of all she had known and loved, all that she knew. As she stood in the middle of the enclosure, her vision blurred by the tears that clung to her eyelashes, she caught a movement in the corner of her eye. A figure was approaching. Too caught up in her grief to run, she stayed where she was, waiting for the Norseman to reach her, waiting for death. But instead she felt comforting arms around her, soft fingers wiping away her tears, and a pair of warm blue eyes looking into hers.

"It's me, Eoferhild, my love. You're safe now. Come with me."

A few months later, the town of Whitby was beginning to recover from the horrific attack that had left so many dead and so many more impoverished. The Abbey, however, was not spoken of. The ruin sat atop the hill and blackened timbers stabbed the sky like a crone's accusing fingers. The townspeople crossed themselves whenever they accidentally happened to glance in its direction. Great evil had taken place on that fateful day, but the greatest evil in their eyes was the callous murder of the monks and nuns, peaceful beings who had tended to their flock with kindness and guarded their immortal souls. Who would now baptise the newborns and pray for the dead? On a moonlit night people muttered that they heard ghostly screams coming from the hilltop and saw shadowy figures flit amongst the ruins.

Eoferhild was still shaken by the calamitous events of the raid and, while Daegberhdt and his family were kind and welcoming, she still suffered terribly from nightmares. One day she set off alone up the hill to the ruined Abbey. Daegberhdt watched her leave but sensed her need for solitude. Up the slope she climbed, the grass grown long and unkempt without the Abbey's sheep to graze it, those sturdy creatures with their matted coats and enquiring eyes had been victims of the raid along with so many others. Panting slightly, she reached the scene of devastation where once had been a place of such spiritual peace and wellbeing. Blackened rafters and ashes the colour of bone. The year had definitely turned. Gusts of wind from the sea had a definite nip and the leaves were fading from vibrant green to yellow and brown. It was as if the whole land were dying. Eoferhild leaned wearily against a pile of stones and closed her eyes. She rested, half-listening to the wind howling through the ruins, thinking it reminded her of church bells. Or could she really hear church bells? She opened her eyes and instead of the broken ruins of a place she had loved she saw, superimposed upon the rubble, the outline of vast stone pillars and stained glass windows, with plainsong and the peal of bells in the background, and the ever-present calling of the gulls. Eoferhild smiled to herself. They would rebuild the monastery from stone, a monument fit for kings, the memory of the vicious Norsemen would be erased, the Abbey of Whitby would once again stand proud and tall upon the headland, facing out to sea for as long as stone endured and men believed. The world was not dying. It could be renewed.

This story is set in the Anglo-Saxon era. The Abbey at Whitby was built mostly of wood until the Norman era, when in the eleventh century a stone church began to be constructed. The Norsemen would now be known as Vikings, but that name was given to them after their era, so I have deliberately avoided using it.

The Far Side of the Street

By Kerry Rowe

It was the first of September when Nicholas padded across the room, flipping through the posy of cabinet keys. He unlocked the door and sunshine poured into the room and dazzled him. As he leaned into the display cabinet, he lifted his hand to his forehead, and then juddered backwards as a figure, came into his vision.

Nicholas noticed the woman's graceful hand first, the unvarnished nails, the neat, pale knuckles, and her slender wrist. He flitted up to look at the woman's face. Her green-grey eyes were cast down at the arrangement of wrist-watches. Nicholas gazed at her face, at her smooth, high cheekbones and her claret lips. The woman moved, and Nicholas jolted his head downwards, pretending to search the display for the item that he had been sent to fetch. When he looked back up with the engagement ring in his hand, the woman had gone.

At lunchtime, Nicholas meandered down to The Station Cafe, as he often did. He sat in a corner of the crowded room, with a one-way view of the street from the window. He found himself searching, processing and disregarding each figure that passed. After twenty minutes, his attention was taken by an elegant figure that drifted across the street. She was too far away for him to be sure, and she had passed out of his sight. Nicholas craned to see her, but he slipped back, sinking into his seat, when a woman, who came from behind him, cast a shadow across him. It was the woman. Nicholas watched, until she paced away and continued down the street. In one abrupt movement, he stood and moved after her, but when he reached the street she had moved out of sight.

With his return to work imminent, Nicholas had to give up his seeking of Whitby. But, the woman never left his mind and he imagined her jaunting around the town, in and out of shops, peering out at the harbour, and sipping tea from china cups in tea shops with lace table cloths.

When evening had come and Nicholas had bid goodbye to his boss, Mr Richardson, he walked back down the street towards The Station Cafe. As he approached, the woman, who had served him at lunchtime was locking the door, so he breezed past with his head bowed and without peering into the cafe. Beyond the cafe, Nicholas slowed his pace, as he came to the point at which the woman had disappeared from his view earlier. She could have made her way down the street to the left or to the right, or continued. She could have entered a shop or cafe. Nicholas ran the fingers of one hand up his cheek, then down again. With the shops' closing time passed, Nicholas turned left, to make his way towards the harbour.

In the evening, when the town reclined into tranquillity, the harbour still had a lazy throb of life. The harbour had come into Nicholas's view, so had the sauntering couples and families that walked around the town, immersing themselves in the scenic charm of a seaside town. When Nicholas reached the harbour, he stood, with his hands on the railings, scanning his left and then his right. Turning his back to the sea and leaning against the railings, he searched the vista before him. With the woman gone, vanished into some unknown place, an unknown home, Nicholas closed his eyes to the faces that approached and passed him. He raised his chin and opened his eyes to the cool blue sky, and the pale grassy hillside with the Abbey making a stretch upwards. Nicholas gazed at the magnetic, silent spectacle, and headed towards the 199 steps.

Nicholas, who from childhood had counted each step, did not watch every footstep that he placed. Instead, he kept thinking about the Abbey, determined that the woman was there. A surge of people was coming down the steps; children bouncing from one to the next calling out the number they had passed. Nicholas looked down at his watch, it was ten to six and he knew that closing time at the Abbey was close. When he looked back up, he was near the end of the steps, but he stopped and gripped the hand rail to his side. At the top of the steps, the woman stood, with her back to Nicholas, peering up at the Abbey. As he watched her, she turned and looked down upon him. For the first time, her eyes had fallen upon him, for the first time, she noticed him. Nicholas moved as if about to speak to the woman, but he did not, so the woman smiled at him and whispered hello.

Nicholas fell into step beside the woman, (whom he learnt was Sarah), as she ambled down the steps. By the time the couple had reached the end, Nicholas had told of the two occasions that he had seen her and she had giggled, freeing the way for Nicholas to ask her about herself. Sarah, her tender voice low and honeyed, answered with gracious sincerity. As they stood on the street, with the steps sprawling behind and above them, Sarah turned to Nicholas and said, "Well Nicholas, I have to meet somebody for dinner." As she said this, she glanced down, breaking away from Nicholas's look and held out her left hand to him. He took her hand, in his left and turned his wrist so that Sarah's palm faced upwards. Then he bought her palm up to his lips and kissed it, before saying, "I'll walk you." Sarah paled and again averted her eyes from Nicholas as she explained that it wasn't necessary for him to.

Nicholas's and Sarah's hands were still joined, while Nicholas said, "We could meet after, do something. If you'll give me your number, I . . ."

"No." Sarah removed her hand and used both to grip her purse, but she looked up into Nicholas's face, her eyes contrite as she continued, "I'm staying at a hotel, so . . . I'll meet you tomorrow. At midday. Here." Nicholas tried to insist that she give him something more concrete, a stronger contact, but Sarah moved onto her tiptoes, gripped Nicholas's shirt and kissed him, before she pulled away from him and strolled out of sight.

For Nicholas, who had expected the night to be a torturous torrent of sleeplessness and convincing illusions of Sarah and her kisses, the night had passed rapidly. He had not shaken that kiss, but he had slept with a sense of comfort and serenity. It was eleven when he woke and, as he wanted to set out at half past eleven, he left breakfast and didn't make his bed or pull back his curtains.

As he walked through Whitby, looking up at the Abbey, Nicholas began to wonder about Sarah, and for the first time, he replayed the whole of the previous day's events. Why had she been so adamant in refusing to exchange phone numbers? It had not occurred to him before that she may not show up, that she did not want to be found by him again.

Despite this thought flashing across his mind, he remained relaxed and it didn't stay at the forefront of his mind for long.

By twelve o'clock, Nicholas and Sarah were wandering around Whitby Abbey, with their hands clasped together. They had been holding hands since Nicholas had approached Sarah who had been stood looking out towards the sea. He had put a palm against her back and she had turned to look up at him and asked to go back up to the Abbey. They had turned to the steps together and together they had grasped for each other's hands and they had not let go.

Walking through what would have been the inside of the Abbey, Nicholas asked Sarah why he was not allowed her hotel's phone number or even its name. Once he had said it, he cringed and was about to apologise but Sarah spun around to face him and said,

"I'm married." She shone her grey-green eyes into Nicholas's. "I've been married for four years." They were stood facing each other, their hands still together before the tallest, windowless wall of the Abbey.

"Let me guess," replied Nicholas, "he's a pig, he treats you badly, you get no love, no affection and you need an escape." Sarah was shaking her head.

"That's not it at all. I loved Robert when I married him and I love him now." Her eyes had not moved from Nicholas's face, and they did not flit away from him as he asked,

"What was that kiss last night, and why meet me today?" His voice was low, but he was not upset.

"The kiss and meeting you today, I . . . I just knew that I had to do it. When I turned around on the steps yesterday and you were there I just knew you, knew that I felt comfortable at your side. Since yesterday I've felt . . . fine, calm, at ease with everything." Sarah stepped closer to Nicholas so that she was against him, she peered up at him and he smiled down on her.

"I think I know what you mean," he said.

After walking around the ruins, Nicholas and Sarah made their way down to the town, had lunch and strolled around the harbour. Nicholas did not shy away from asking Sarah about Robert and Sarah did not shy away from answering him. From his questions, he learnt that Robert was an historian and had been sent to Whitby Museum for two months' work and that afterwards he and Sarah were flying to New York for a week. Sarah had told him that she had been a teacher but that Robert's work caused him to travel the world, she had given up her own career to travel with him. With her husband dedicated to his work, Sarah was alone for much of the time in an unfamiliar place.

Almost every day of the one month and three weeks that had passed, Nicholas made his way to the 199 steps at lunch time and after his day at work. Nicholas and Sarah had just an hour together in the evening when Nicholas had to work, but they could spend the whole day together on Saturday. Now that the final week had arrived, a dull grey sadness had begun to hover over the couple, one that each felt but did not mention. On the last Monday, they had met at the steps again but they had not moved from the bottom of them. Nicholas had clutched Sarah to him and for the first time, he pleaded in a frantic whisper for Sarah to stay with him, to not leave with her husband. Sarah didn't reply, but she was hushed for the rest of the day and when Nicholas turned to look at her she was often gazing out in earnest thought. When Sarah had to leave Nicholas, he pulled her close to him and asked, again in a whisper, "Stay with me. Don't leave on Saturday." He kissed her forehead and waited for her reply.

The last day had arrived. At the bottom of the 199 steps, Nicholas was waiting for Sarah, but she was late. Twenty minutes late, and it had been her idea to meet early, at nine o'clock, because the flight to New York was scheduled for ten that night. Nicholas had spent the last week meditating this day, what he would say to keep Sarah in Whitby. As he waited, he considered it now, how he would hold her to him and insist that she stay, that she didn't have to leave, she owed nothing to her husband, she had given up so much for him already. His thoughts were interrupted by Sarah's presence at his side. He slipped his arm around her, without looking down at her.

"Let's go up to the Abbey," she said, and they turned to the steps together, their hands falling into place.

Wandering around the Abbey, Nicholas could not find the spirit to beg Sarah to stay. The hours had been flawless and he did not want to spoil what could be the final moments that he had with Sarah. As Nicholas stood thinking about how the day was faultless, Sarah came up to him, standing at his side with her arm around his waist and she peeked up at him.

"Shall we go to the cafe?" She smiled at him and they wandered to the steps, laughing together.

The steps were busy. At the bottom, Nicholas had to release Sarah's hand so that two women, with five children could get up the stairs together. Nicholas reached the side of the street while Sarah was stranded on the steps, against the rail to let the group pass. When Sarah had left the last step and was in the street, there came a call, "Sarah!" Hearing her name, Sarah and Nicholas turned and both went pale. The man who had called her approached Sarah and kissed her cheek. "What are you doing here, I just came up to see the old ruin before we leave, is it brilliant?" Robert hadn't noticed Nicholas on the far side of the street, staring at Sarah, nor had he noticed Sarah stare back at Nicholas.

Healthy Eating, Healthy Living

By Peter Parrish

It was a surprise to find Count Dracula tending a cliff-top allotment near Whitby Abbey.

"Dracula," I said, "what exactly do you think you're doing?"

The Prince of the Nosferatu twitched beneath his cape at the sound of my voice and turned to face me, eyes full of malevolence. I could not prevent a shallow gasp escaping my mouth as his sneer revealed pointed fangs. His foul maw opened in reply to my impertinent demand, and I recoiled in expectant horror at what dreadful eldritch screed would tumble forth. What untold curses would his dark tongue lay upon my mortal soul? What fetid and malignant—

"Oh bother," he said.

It was a somewhat underwhelming gambit.

"Look," he continued, "I suppose it's too late to suggest that I'm going to drain every drop from your body and leave you a shrivelled, lifeless husk?"

"A bit late, yes," I said.

"Curses."

He fussed briefly with a rake, pushing it down into the soil at the end of a row of lettuce. We stood for a while with just the sound of the waves, our eyes straying as the conversation lulled. I looked back towards the Abbey, watching the clouds creeping their way across the sky above its great ruined structure.

"I saw you coming you know," Dracula said at last. "With my vampire foresight."

"You bloody well didn't, I saw you jump!"

Dracula's eyebrows curved in anger at my insolence and he fixed me in place with a contemptuous gaze. It was contempt that I knew could accelerate into a fury of bloodlust at any moment, awakening the obsidian beast from the depths of his blighted body and pushing this vengeful lord of undeath to terrible feats of—

Well, he looked a little put out anyway.

"The foresight is vague, I didn't know when you would be coming," he scowled. "And please don't use that word, I don't actually do ... that ... any more."

"What word?"

"The 'b' word. Or any variations thereof."

"You don't drink bl ... the red stuff?" I said, perplexed, "But how do you sate your vampyric urges if you no longer drain pale maidens beneath a lavish moon?"

I had hoped my knowledge of vampire lore and scholarly tone would find favour, but Dracula's black eyeballs appeared to be rolling at the tedium of my deductions.

"Oh God, you're one of those awful goths aren't you. If I give you an autograph will you just push off?"

My palms went up in defence. "I didn't even come looking for you, I was just visiting the Abbey and went for a walk along the cliffs." I gestured back towards the arches to solidify my tale. "Sorry," I added.

Dracula ran a hand slowly down the side of his face and looked at his row of lettuce for a spell.

"Fine," he said, "I thought I'd be far enough away here, but it seems not." He looked at me again, "so go on, ask me."

"Ask you what?" I said, a jumble of questions jostling for space inside my brain.

"Oh come now."

"Well ... I suppose I was wondering, how are you able to be outside? In the sun and everything."

"It's not all that sunny," sniffed Dracula. "More overcast if anything."

"You know what I mean," I said.

He sneered again in what may have been an attempt at a smile, then pulled out a plastic tube from the folds of his cape and waved it in my direction. "Factor 50. The skincare industry has been rather busy in my absence. I get an unlimited supply from my sponsors."

"Sponsors?" Now I really was baffled.

"Yes, sponsors," he said, motioning to the allotment "I'm the new face of the Fangs Into Fresh Veg campaign, that's what all this stuff is about. You didn't think you were the first person to stumble across me here, did you?"

"I, uh—"

"Well you aren't," Dracula said, "After I became ... ahh ... active again at the Abbey, word got out. Everybody has a mobile phone with a camera in it. Anyway, once I'd had my fill of freaking out goths and tourists I found myself with some representation."

"You have an image consultant?" My mind was spinning.

"Sure, nice guy. Brian Stoker."

"Did you say Br—"

"That's right, Brian Stoker."

"I see."

"There's a Fangs Into Fresh Veg event at the Abbey tomorrow afternoon, why don't you come along?"

Long before I reached the Abbey, I could hear the band. The unmistakable thump and snare of an 808 drum machine. Lyrics on the wind. Fangs Into Fresh Veg had constructed a sizeable stage in the shadow of the ruins, presumably as close as regulations would allow.

"My dark angels / the blackest surrender / night of horrors / darkened splendour"

Banners strung overhead depicted cartoon Draculas taking a lusty bite out of some tomatoes, two beetroot and a cauliflower. Beneath the stage, a moderate crowd had gathered. Some were spasming in dance, others simply stared up at the black-clad performers and swayed. Further away from the stage, people were enjoying free samples from vegetable stalls or lounging around on the grass.

"I must feed / before I bleed / the perfect flesh / for my other death"

I scooped up a discarded leaflet from the ground. The gothic typeface identified the opening act as My Glorious Wasting Disease, while the reverse featured a complementary recipe for vegetarian 'ghoulash'. As I read, the song concluded in dramatic E-minor fashion. With my attention drawn back to the stage, I caught sight of a caped figure waiting in the sidelines, deep in conversation with a sleek-looking man in a grey suit. I watched the band mope slowly offstage to muted applause as these two figures moved to take their places. The man in the grey suit approached the microphone at the centre of the platform and began to address the crowd.

"Alright! Let's hear it for My Glorious Wasting Disease!"

The crowd responded, there were some isolated incidents of whooping.

"OK, OK. Welcome, everybody, to a very special Fangs Into Fresh Veg event. I hope you've all had a taste of our free samples. If you haven't, get yourself over to one of our stalls and tuck in. Everything you taste today is one hundred percent local. Some of those lettuce have been grown by Dracula himself, ladies and gentlemen, so you don't want to miss out on those."

Mr grey suit soaked in the 'Ooohs.'

"But I've done enough talking already. We're here to listen to the face, the inspiration, the beating heart of the Fangs Into Fresh Veg campaign.

Bit of a local celebrity around here, I'm told. He's the man who's going to help us bite back against obesity ... the former lord of the vampires himself, Count Dracula!"

Huge applause rang out as Dracula took the mic. His arm seemed to be shaking a bit. Probably nerves, I thought. He's not used to big crowds.

"Thank you. T-tha ... yes, thanks."

He paused, allowing the hubbub to subside.

"Lifestyle changes can be hard. Nobody knows that better than me. That's why I'm proud to be spear-heading this Fangs Into Fresh Veg campaign. We're here to help you, the delicio ... the ambitious people of Whitby fight back against the flab."

I thought I'd caught a quiver in his voice, but he seemed to be getting into his stride.

"Once you've tasted our range of magnificent vegetables, you simply won't be able to go back to m-meat. There's nothing like the succulent crunch of an onion, or the ... the j-juice of a tomato running over your jaws after the first bite. That first ... sweet bite ... as the juice ..."

Dracula swayed a little, but regained his poise.

"... the juice, g-gushing ..."

He was staring now. Staring hungrily into the crowd. Sizing up each and every meaty blood vessel like an Hanoverian king at a banquet. Just as I feared he might leap at the nearest exposed neck, he swirled his cape and vanished from the stage.

I pushed my way through the people in front of me, barging through puzzled onlookers until I bumped into the grey suited man, barking into his phone.

"It's a disaster Shelley, a total disaster. Get a press release out, say ... Christ I don't know, just say he was feeling unwell. The moon was affecting him or something. What? Yes I know that's werewolves Shelley, Jesus!"

"Mr Stoker?" I said.

"I've got to handle things here, get that press release out today." The man closed his mobile and addressed me with a certain exasperation.

"... Yes?"

"Is Dracula OK?"

His eyes narrowed a little as he scrutinised me.

"Why, are you a friend of his?"

"Sort of, I—"

The phone rang. The man looked as if he was about to start chewing his own fist.

"Whatever, great. Look, if you see him, give him this. We need to get a few things straightened out." He handed me a business card: B. Stoker, Fangs Into Fresh Veg.

We sat on the raised base of a long-gone pillar in what had once been the nave of the Abbey. A banner from the afternoon's event still fluttered limply in the distance. The dusk breeze had caught some of the leaflets and deposited them haphazardly inside the Abbey grounds. English Heritage won't be too happy about that, I thought.

"I couldn't do it," said Dracula, quiet as dust on a grave.

"Probably wasn't your scene," I said, "you and vegetables ... it's a pretty stupid idea."

"No ... I mean, I couldn't look at them without wanting to feed."

I suddenly felt quite vulnerable. Dracula must have read the disquiet in my silence.

"Oh, don't worry," he said, "I've had a butcher in town hooking me up with animal blood. My thirst is quenched for the moment."

"The vegetables?"

"Never touched them. I think they were imported anyway. Stoker's idea, he said it was cheaper."

"I see."

Droplets of rain started to fall.

"I'm tired," said Dracula, "let's go."

I followed him into a secluded part of the Abbey, away from the breeze and the drizzle. He crouched and ran his hands over the ancient stonework, searching for something. I watched as his fingers found purchase and seemed to peel back a slab, revealing a small entrance.

"My abode," he motioned. "Won't you join me?"

I peered into the gloom and made out the first two steps of a spiral staircase. Together, we made our way down. What remained of the daylight was finding its way into the narrow stairwell through tiny cracks in the masonry, allowing me to find my way. After a few minutes of footsteps echoing on stone, we emerged in a small chamber, which I realised must be several feet below the Abbey. In the centre, raised on a wide, flat plinth was an ornate coffin lined with plush red material. A cardboard pallet of sunscreen tubes lay to one side of the plinth, and tucked away in the farthest corner was a mini-fridge, hooked up to a small generator.

"My blood bank," said Dracula, motioning to the fridge in the dim atmosphere, "the generator is siphoning power from one of the lights outside."

He stepped wearily into the coffin and lay down with his arms crossed over his chest. A clawed finger stretched up and beckoned me closer. I made my way over to the coffin, stooping so as not to brush my head against the low ceiling.

"Stoker," he said, "where might I find Stoker?"

Recalling our brief meeting, I searched my pockets for the business card.

"Here, he asked me to give you this, but—"

"Thank you."

"You're not thinking of going back to all that, are you?" I said, aghast.

Count Dracula gave me a final sneer.

"I'm through with vegetables," he said, "But sometimes when I wake up early I can often feel a bit ... peckish."

The coffin lid closed, leaving me alone with the soft hum of the mini-fridge.

Music and Murder

By Francis Wright

The bell was ringing for Vespers as Will hurried across the market square towards the steps up to the Abbey. The stalls were being packed up and moved away by the traders who bustled between the carts, under a sky that was white, and heavy with coming snow, while the Abbey loomed darkly overhead.

"I can't afford to get into trouble again," Will thought. He wondered whether the side door to the choir room would still be unlocked. He had taken care to leave it slightly ajar, but it would have been just typical for one of the brothers to have closed the door, leaving Will with no choice but to make his way through the West Front, where he would be caught for sure. He looked around for any sign of life. There seemed to be no one around and the side door was still open. Quickly and quietly he opened the door a few inches, squeezed through, and closed it gently.

"Tomkins. What are you doing? Late again, are we?"

"No, Brother Matthew, I was just closing the door. Some idiot seems to have left it open, and there's an awful draft. I noticed it on my way to the vesting room."

"Well, you'd best get a move on, hadn't you? You wouldn't want to be late."

Brother Matthew was right: he didn't want to be late. In fact, he was on his last, last warning, and he could not afford to chance his luck again. Father Pearsall, the head of the choir school, had upbraided him again last week, and some of the other boys were just desperate for him to step out of line. Wouldn't it make their year to see the "street urchin" sent packing? But they didn't have didn't have his troubles, did they? They wouldn't even be able to understand.

"Mr Tomkins, oughtn't we to be in our surplice by now?" It was Brother John, the choirmaster.

"Yes, brother."

"All ready for your solo, I hope. You know, you might not have had the gentle upbringing of some of your colleagues, but never forget that you have the voice.

"But please don't let me down for choosing you to sing the solo this evening."

Will most certainly did not want to disappoint Brother John. But more than that, he did not want to let his father down. The old man had been greedy for news of his progress when Will slipped out after lunch to see him earlier that afternoon.

"Will. Son. God bless you for coming down to see me. At my age, you know, it isn't easy to make it up the hill. I would so like to be there to hear you sing again. No matter, and God bless the brothers for letting you see your old dad. So kind of them to make an exception and let you out on your own. Tell me all about the singing this morning. You can talk while I tuck into some of those leftovers. I don't know what I would do if the brothers weren't able to spare the food. Without then I would never be able to have any meat."

"I can't eat these slops," Morley had said at lunch that afternoon, "It's like being in prison."

"Don't I wish you were in prison!" thought Will, and his cheeks coloured when he thought of how pleased, and grateful, his father would be to receive the leftover "slops" that Will would have to scheme to rescue from the refectory when the other boys got up from their seats.

Will did not tell his father about the solo that afternoon. He wasn't sure why, exactly, just that somehow it might be tempting fate. If it all went wrong, he didn't want to have to lie to his father. And although he knew that Brother John was right (he did have the best voice in the choir) he also knew that Morley and his acolytes would be praying for his voice to falter when the organ began. So he kept it to himself, and after all it would make the old man even prouder of him if (and it was a big "if") he could visit again next week and tell him all about it.

While Will was struggling into his surplice he heard the organ bellows being primed. The service was about to start. Today was Candlemas Day: an especially important feast, and Brother John had chosen some extremely impressive music for the occasion.

Will and the other boys formed into a double line behind the monks, the usual blessing was given by the Abbot, the venerable and ancient looking John Topcliffe, and the procession set off down the Abbey. The organ started. Deep and solemn on the pedals, taking then elaborating the theme, building up the texture and then bursting into fanfare like exchanges as the procession made its way up the nave. The hairs on Will's neck stood on end.

The Abbey was crowded and Will saw, with a shudder, that Morley's father was among the congregation lining the central aisle. He smiled cravenly as Morley went past, but the look melted from his face as he saw Will coming up in line. Will could not meet his eye. He was an important man in the town. The master of the Abbey's estates. A cruel looking man with hair as black as a raven's wing, and eyes to match. And he had always made it obvious that he could not bear that the Abbey and its choir was, as he saw it, being sullied by the likes of Will.

The procession moved on like a white clad battalion, and reached the choir stalls, bowing and filtering off to left and right, into their places. The whole Abbey seemed to glow and flicker with the light of hundreds of candles; on all the side altars, in front of the statues and gilded pictures of the saints, but especially round the massive carved choir stalls and in the great candle sticks on the high altar.

But there were also shadows.

One late afternoon, following vespers towards the end of the previous term, Will had to return to the church to retrieve some music. All the lights had already been extinguished. He knew, or at least thought he knew, that he must be alone: the wardens always did their rounds and made sure that the Abbey was empty before locking the great West

Doors. But he could not shake the feeling that someone else was there, and a shiver ran down his spine. He thought he could hear breathing, shallow and tight, struggling to keep as quiet as possible. A foot seemed to shuffle on the flagstones. Was that the sound of fingers moving nervously on a pew? He did not wait to find out, grabbing the music and running as quickly as he could, the breath burning in his throat, to the safety of the choir room, towards people, noise, and light.

But today the Abbey was busy. The service began, and the monks sang the plainchant for that day. It struck Will that the singing was like a ball game: the first verse being sung by one side of the choir, then answered by the other, passing back and forth and then joining together with great sonority for the final verse of each psalm. And then it was time for the Magnificat, the canticle of the Blessed Virgin, and Will's solo. The organ began and the whole choir rose to sing the first verse. Will was struggling to relax. His lungs felt tight as he followed the line of music on the page. Panic rose in his chest. But then Brother John caught his eye and he mouthed something. He spoke slowly. There was no mistaking the words.

"You...can...do...it..."

And instantly the tension left his chest, like air escaping from a burst ball. He steadied himself, inhaled slowly and steadily, and started to sing. His voice arched over the choir, decorating the lines being sung by the choir and bringing out the text, sometimes gently, at other times high and clear and trumpet like.

He hath put down the mighty from their seat. And hath exalted the humble and meek.

He allowed himself a quick sideways glance in Morley's direction. It was a wonder that Morley could make any sound at all. His face was contorted into a look of sheer disgust; or perhaps hate? He looked at Will like something nasty he had trodden in by mistake, and the thought only spurred Will on to finish the piece triumphantly.

The canticle drew to a close, Will singing his final cadence. He felt enormous relief at having reached the end, having made no mistakes, and – he had to admit it to himself – having sung well, and he was almost sad not to be able to continue. He had the feeling of being able to sing all day long. The choir answered with a gentle Amen like a sigh settling over the church.

There was a scream.

It came from Will's left, and rang down the nave. The choristers started forward in their seats. It would not have been the first time for a crazy person to wander into the church and cause a commotion. But this was different. And then Father Pearsall dropped forward limply from his seat. He seemed to struggle to say something, his face crumpled and pale:

"Why…why…did…you…?"

But the old man clattered to the floor, the words dying in his throat. Will saw with horror that in his back, through the gold cope, piercing the embroidered picture of a pelican, was the hilt of a knife. A hilt topped with the carved figure of a snake.

The Abbey erupted. The realisation of what had just happened passed through the congregation, like a pack of cards being rifled. There was a great uproar of shouting, screaming, people rushing, some looking to see how they might help, others storming towards the door, mothers gathering up children, elderly people, bewildered, being jostled out of the way.

"Boys. Follow me. Quickly!" Brother John called through the din.

A ragged kind of procession formed, and the choir hurriedly exited in Brother John's wake, through the south transept, to safety.

Wraith of the Ruins

By Alison Ryan

I first saw him beneath those majestic arches, the sun streaming through casting long dark shadows, stretched and grotesque. He turned to face me, his stunning eyes sharp and piercing. I caught my breath and my heart skipped a beat. Involuntarily taking a step towards him, I suddenly felt myself falling. The wild sea, thrashing at the cliffs below, roared up fiercely to meet me as I fell...

I woke up with a start, my heart thumping. Sitting up in bed, I tried to calm down. It was only a dream after all. Knowing that I wouldn't be able to sleep for a while, I stumbled out of bed and pulled on my dressing gown. I drew open the curtains and gazed out of the window at the moonlit view. My eyes were immediately drawn to Whitby Abbey, standing dark and mysterious high up on the cliffs opposite. I shivered, recalling my dream, and shut the curtains to block out both the view and the memory. I wondered yet again if it had been the right decision to come here. I was taking time out of my dull and boring life to visit a friend who lives in Whitby.

I'm a writer, or at least I was until writer's block decided to grasp me with its destructive talons. A change of scenery would do me good, I had thought. A lovely place like Whitby with the Abbey, sand, sea and harbour... perfect inspiration. But every night since I arrived, I had been having disturbing dreams about Whitby Abbey. Similar to tonight's dream, except I hadn't seen him before. And I still wasn't free from writer's block. My notebook was blank and my mind a mess. Sighing, I climbed back into bed and wrapped the covers tightly around me and tried to sleep.

The next morning I was slumped over a cup of strong coffee when my friend hurried in, rushing to get ready for work.

"You look terrible!" Kate remarked after glancing at me, and then added mischievously, "scary dreams of the terrifying Abbey again?"

"Thank you very much. And yes, if you must know," I muttered, stirring my coffee. Kate picked up her bag, and checked her watch.

"I've got to go. Look – go and visit the Abbey today. You haven't actually been up there yet, and it's just a pile of old ruins, nothing scary about it! Once you've seen it, I'm sure the dreams will stop."

"Hummm maybe," I mumbled noncommittally. "I hope you have a good day at the office!"

Kate screwed up her face as she opened the front door. "I'll try!"

Left alone, I dragged myself upstairs to get changed. When I opened the curtains, I looked straight across at the Abbey. Yes, I would go and see it today. What harm could that possibly do?

As I crossed the bridge to get to the other side of Whitby where the Abbey stood high up on the cliffs, I felt a peculiar sense of foreboding. It was strange; I had never felt anything quite like this before. My heart was pounding, my head felt as if it was going to explode and irrational fear clouded my mind. I leaned against the side of the bridge to steady myself and breathed deeply, the salty sea air filling my lungs. The dreams must have been affecting me more than I thought. Telling myself sternly to get a grip, I carried on and headed briskly for the Abbey.

I was out of breath after climbing up the seemingly never ending steps, but carried on regardless. The strange feeling still hadn't subsided, and I didn't want to lose my nerve. After paying the entrance fee, I wandered around the museum. Discovering the richly woven and occasionally dark history of the Abbey was fascinating, and I was also encouraged that so many authors had been inspired by these gothic ruins. Maybe this visit would alleviate my writer's block after all. Then it was time to walk around the Abbey itself.

The sun streamed through the majestic arches casting long, dark shadows on the grass. As I gazed around, I felt insignificant compared to the magnificent, imposing ruins. The views from the Abbey were spectacular, but I had to shield my eyes from the sun to see anything clearly. Suddenly I felt calm. All thoughts of my strange dreams disappeared as I looked around the awe inspiring ruins. I wandered away from the Abbey and headed towards the cliff. Smiling to myself, I lifted my face to the sun and closed my eyes, enjoying the warmth that gradually penetrated my skin.

After a few minutes of soaking up the sun, I opened my eyes and noticed a lone figure dressed in black standing near the cliff edge, looking out to sea. As I watched absentmindedly, he slowly turned around to face me. He looked straight at me, and his eyes burned into mine. I felt as if I'd been punched. My heart thudded against my ribs, my head pounded and a feeling of horror filled my entire body. And yet as he held my gaze, I felt something thrilling too. He was handsome, with a chiselled jaw and dark hair which almost fell into his strange, deep black-brown eyes. He was captivating, and I couldn't look away. After what seemed like an eternity, he started to walk towards me, still starring at me intently. Then, the sudden sound of children's laughter close behind me caused him to shift his gaze, and I could look away from him. Breathing hard, I shut my eyes and rubbed my forehead in a vain attempt to disperse the throbbing headache. I felt a cool hand cover mine and I froze, a chill creeping down my spine. It was him.

He gently touched my forehead and strangely the pain instantly evaporated. Seeming to sense this, he slowly drew my hand away from my face. I opened my eyes and gazed into his stunning eyes, which seemed to sparkle with amusement but also curiosity.

"Better?" he enquired, his voice low and soft. Not able to speak, I nodded, trying to concentrate on keeping my trembling hands still.

"So…" he started, looking deep into my eyes curiously, "You can actually see me… and feel me." It was a statement, not a question. Still holding my hand, he gave it a gentle squeeze. Confused, I nodded again. He smiled for the first time and then whispered so quietly that I could barely catch his words. "Well you're the only one!"

Sliding my hand out of his grasp, I became suddenly aware of all the other people around us. Groups of children were laughing and running about, their parents chatting, while keeping a watchful eye on them. One of the little girls ran up and presented me with a daisy she had picked, then smiled at me, and ran off after her friends without a glance at him. Then a couple walked past, straight towards him. He moved swiftly out of their path as they breezed past, not seeing him at all. I gasped, staring after them. They really didn't see him.

This was beyond ridiculous. I could only imagine it was a joke, or some new form of interactive theatre. There was no way it was real. I turned back to challenge him, but he was gone. I spun around, looking for him but he was nowhere to be seen. I quickly scanned the area, and judged that he couldn't have gone far in that brief second I looked away from him. So where was he? Not being able to answer that logically, I started to wonder if I had imaged the whole thing, and had conjured him up from my dream last night. But no, deep down I knew he was definitely real, and my hand was still tingling from his touch. Suddenly feeling claustrophobic, I had to get away from the Abbey, and I made my way swiftly home. I went to bed very late that night, dreading the dreams that I knew would haunt my sleep.

I was at the Abbey again, but this time it was night. The imposing ruins silhouetted in the moonlight towered over me, dark and frightening. I was inexplicably drawn away from the Abbey towards the cliff edge. My heart hammered against my ribs in fright as I noticed a large, deep hole very close to the edge. As I moved closer, I realised there was something in there, but I couldn't quite make it out. I knelt down on the cool grass, leaned over and looked in. I gasped as I realised it was him lying there, his eyes shut and his dark hair shining in the moonlight. As I reached out to touch him, his eyes snapped open, and his cold gaze met mine. I heard a piercing scream, and realised it was my own...

I woke up screaming in a cold sweat and my heart pounding. I couldn't think straight. What did this mean? I sat up and grasped the glass of water by my bed, my hand trembling. Taking a refreshing gulp, I told myself that it was only a dream. But then I thought that last time. When I was reasonably calm, I climbed out of bed and stumbled to the window. Taking a deep breath, I pulled open the curtains and stared fixedly at the Abbey. It looked the same as it always did, dark and foreboding, but also strangely intriguing. I made up my mind to go back to the Abbey tomorrow, just to reassure myself that all my dreams were just twisted nightmares, created by my writing-starved mind in order to torment me. But that wasn't the only reason. As I shut the curtains and got back into bed, a small part of me was hoping I would see him again. If only to discover some mundane explanation for our strange first meeting.

I was up early the next morning, eager to get to the Abbey as soon as it opened. I barely looked at the museum this time, and went straight to the ruins. After wandering around admiring the beautiful scene, I moved slowly towards the cliffs and gazed out over the sea, the salty breeze caressing my face. The ground there was uneven, but I was sure I could make out a darker patch of grass where I had dreamt the hole had been. Intrigued, I walked back to the Abbey, and sat down on the grass in the warm sun. Tired after another sleepless night, I feel asleep.

I woke up shivering a while later, and the daylight was fading fast into evening. Glancing at my watch, I realised I had been asleep for hours and it was almost time for the Abbey to close for the night. I got to my feet and walked towards the exit, frustrated that I was no further forward in finding any explanation. And I hadn't seen him either. As I passed a spade propped up against a wall, I was struck with an idea. I could hide amongst the ruins until the Abbey had closed, and then I could borrow that spade to dig up that dark patch of grass near the cliff. It was a ludicrous thought but I was desperate for answers. Despite my reservations, I headed back to the Abbey to find a place to wait.

A while later I was lying on the grass near the cliff edge taking a break from digging. The setting sun lit up the sky with a beautiful array of fiery colours. I started to pick at the loose soil in my hole and struck something hard. Reaching in, I grasped the cold object and pulled it out. Horrified, I realised it was a skull, and in shock I dropped it back into the depths of the dark hole. Was my dream true – was it his skull? Could he be the ghost of someone who was buried there God knows how long ago? And why was I dreaming about him? My heart pounded sickeningly against my chest as these questions raced through my mind. I desperately started to fill in the hole, but as I glanced up he was next to me, his face inches from mine.

Stifling a scream, I scrambled to my feet and edged away from him.

"Who – or what – are you?" I stuttered, "and what do you want from me?"

His piercing gaze held mine as he replied softly. "I fell from this cliff a long time ago."

He took a step towards me, and I moved backwards trying to keep some distance between, us.

"Stop!" he cried, reaching out to me. But too late I realised how close I was to the edge of the cliff, and not being able to keep my balance, I stumbled off the edge. Terror consumed me as it dawned on me that my dream was coming true. As I fell, I could see the wild sea thrashing at the cliffs below roaring up fiercely to meet me…

I must have blacked out, because when I woke up, I was lying on the grass near the cliff edge staring at the pale blue sky. Confused, I realised that it was dawn. Then in a flash, the memory of falling suddenly hit me. But what was I doing still alive? And back up here? Did he save me? I tried to move but found a thick woollen blanket wrapped tightly around me.

"She's awake!" shouted a woman's voice from somewhere out of my view, and a few people instantly crowded around me. Then I heard a male voice.

"I'm a doctor, please give us some room. You say it looks like she's been here all night?"

A man pushed his way through and stood next to me. I looked up at him and was shocked to realise that he looked very familiar. He had blond hair, but the same face, chiselled jaw and black-brown eyes as the man from my dream.

I stared at him in astonishment, and at that moment, a beam of sunlight flowed over the horizon. Although feeling weak and tired, I felt inspired. I knew I would never find any explanations for these strange events, but I was hit by a sudden burning desire to write again. As he knelt down next to me, the doctor met my gaze, and I could have sworn he winked at me. As he leaned closer, I heard him whisper, "you should be careful near the cliff, it's so easy to trip and fall over the edge."

Breaking the Spirit

By Judith Crow

Age 17-21 category runner up

Well, lad, you heard someone calling the name of Maggie Johnson in the ruins, did you? I'll admit to you it's a long time since I heard that name mentioned in Whitby. It was a man's voice, you say? Well, that's no surprise. I've heard it myself up there many years ago, rushed in on the wind. They used to say that it was only the wind as remembered her name but it's not true.

Come and sit by the fire. You're shivering, lad, and it's not cold outside. Don't worry, Maggie Johnson can't hurt you, she can't hurt anyone but herself.

I can't tell you the story, it's too long ago now. Perhaps I can find my father's book. It's all written down in there, see? Let me read it to you, lad, as it was told to him by his father over a hundred years ago.

They said the harvest was late that year. Farmers waited with bated breath to see what was to become of the hard work and toil they had put into their land throughout the year. And, as the black clouds of the October storms began to break over the small town, the farm labourers worked through the night to secure all that they could.

Their lanterns flickered in the fields around Whitby, casting dancing shadows around the town like the silhouettes of the chorus from a Greek tragedy. Away from their hushed conversations and stolen moments of laughter, the town lay dumb, with each ear and eye closed to the sounds of the small boat that steered its way silently into Whitby's ancient harbour. As the anchor dropped, the Whitby Gentlemen, carrying heavy cases of illicit alcohol, scurried from the boat with their faces covered by thick cowls and their words too muffled to be heard.

And there, standing by the harbour, was fair Maggie Johnson. Proud and glorious, like an angel come down to dwell on the Earth. Her eyes were shining bright as the sun, and her hair like strands of golden thread blew behind her. She watched as the Whitby Gentlemen hurried past her, each one giving her a look of surprise and confusion, but never saying a word. As the last of the barrels of illegal gin disappeared into the dark cellars of the harbour cottages, Maggie Johnson looked at the boat and saw the young captain clamber down, looking nervously around him for fear of the appearance of the excisemen. When he saw the beautiful woman, he looked at her, his eyes burning with anger as hers burnt with love. For a moment, they stood staring at one another, each one with a proud beauty that would not entertain thoughts of a broken spirit.

"In God's name, what are you doing here, woman? When every other God-fearing Christian but ourselves has their senses blocked to the harbour this night?" He raised his hand to strike the woman but she pulled away.

"Is it a crime? A sin to wait here for you? You have been away from me for long enough." She held his arm tightly with her thin fingers but he pulled away.

"It will be more than a crime for you should you do it again." He made no attempt to hide the venom in his words and, with a scowl, he turned his back on her, and the town of Whitby, and returned once again to his ship. As she watched him disappearing into the darkness of his small boat, proud Maggie Johnson, torn by anguish, spun around on her heels and rushed through the streets of Whitby, her heart racing with anger and hurt, both for her unwelcome display of love and for her wounded pride. On the path of a journey that she had taken countless times before, she hurried up the steps to the Abbey, her cold, wet dress hitting hard against her legs with a pain that seemed insignificant compared to the slight she had just endured at the hands of the man she loved. As she caught sight of the church of St Mary's, she paused and looked around her. From her view, blocked somewhat by the eerie tombstones, she could see the lanterns in the fields, tiny pinpricks of light by which Maggie Johnson could just make out the figures who toiled there. She had spent many years playing amongst these gravestones but now they looked like a threatening enemy. It had been from here that she had watched the Whitby Gentlemen sail away a month previously.

She turned around and hurried up towards the Abbey. As she reached the ruins of the ancient building, she fell to her knees and allowed her proud head to bend with the tears that spilled from her beautiful eyes and her shoulders shook uncontrollably.

So many days, weeks even, she had waited for the ship's return. Unsure of her love's safety from the sea, the taxmen... he had so many enemies who would claim his life as they had taken so many others. It had not been easy for her as she fought to defend both herself and her love from the people who hated the actions of the Whitby Gentlemen. But now, with the Autumn, he had come back to her, and she had waited for him at the harbour, hopeful of the loving greeting that she would receive. She had been slighted, and could think of no reason why she should have been treated in such a way.

As she had done so many times before, she plucked a daisy from the ground beside her. In the darkness, it covered its golden face with fine, white petals like a bridal veil and Maggie Johnson sobbed as she looked at it.

"Even the flowers know to close their eyes to the Whitby Gentlemen. Why, why did I not accept that the same rule would apply to me?" Her tears fell more and more until they blurred her sight and she was forced to wipe them from her face with her hand. As she sobbed, the flaming red harvest moon shone a beam of scarlet-tinged light through the high Rose Window on the Abbey ruins. Maggie Johnson raised her beautiful head and looked on in awe as, through the window, shone a heavenly flower. Taking a deep breath of the cold Autumn air, she began to count the petals on the empty window.

"He loves me, he loves me not." Her heart pounded. "He loves me, he loves me not." The wind began to pick up around her. "He loves me, he loves me not." Somewhere, down in the town below, a child began to cry loudly, to Maggie Johnson it sounded thin and torn by the wind. "He loves me, he loves me not." The waves rose and hit violently against the cliffs below the Abbey. "He loves me, he loves me not."

And there, Maggie Johnson knew her life had ended.

Such a sign, the moon shining through the old window, could not be ignored. She would have gladly accepted it had the outcome been different, and would not allow herself to have different rules for a different outcome. Burying her head in her slender hands, she cried and cried, then clenched her fist and shouted curses at the sea, the moon, the Abbey and at the man who had deserted her.

She looked up at the window again and saw the light had ceased to shine through it and now, with the grace of a noblewoman clad in its red silk, the moon was rising higher and higher into the heavens. It had stayed just long enough to show her the truth. But even the ugliest lie could not have been as cruel as the truth that she had just realised.

With a fierce determination, Maggie Johnson began to climb the ruin of the Abbey, oblivious to the loud tearing sounds as her dress caught on first one stone then another. It was difficult to keep hold of the sheer walls with her bare hands, but her anger and determination did not allow her to fall before her time. As she reached a place where she could stand on the ledge of a ruined window, she stood still and looked around her.

There were no lights suddenly. The lanterns that had been burning in the fields since dusk had ceased and Whitby had been plunged into a silent darkness. Maggie Johnson had known the town since her birth nineteen years ago, but never had she seen it look as desolate and unloving as it did now. Then, as she looked around, a single light began to shine. A tear, silver in the moonlight, rolled down her cheek and fell to the ground far below as she realised that the light shining was from The Lady Nyx, her love's boat. With spine-tingling resolve, proud Maggie Johnson decided that it would be by this light that she would leave him, and the world, behind her.

Stone by stone, the Abbey seemed to collapse around her as she moved from the step and time came to a grinding halt beneath the weight of her decision. As she fell, her eyes set upon her love, The Whitby Gentleman whose pale face was torn with the pain of what he was seeing and he rushed up to her too late. As, piercing the darkness, the moon shone through the Rose Window onto his angry tears, he cursed his quick tongue and wished in vain that he had never set anchor in the town that night.

There, lad, that's the story of Maggie Johnson. My father used to say that she was cursed to wander through the ruins of the Abbey for eternity, knowing that she had made the wrong choice.

But it was such a long time ago now. Over two hundred years I would think. Who would have thought that the captain would still be calling for her after all this time? It's a true kind of love as would make a man give up his place in heaven to spend eternity looking for a lost soul.

Under Destiny's Moon

By Julie Heslington

197, 198, 199. I don't think I've ever climbed the steps to Whitby Abbey without counting each one.

I run up the path by St Mary's Church. I clear the church grounds and pause to catch my breath; not just from the exertion of the climb but from the stunning view of the harbour below me and the Abbey peaking out just above. I've been here many times yet the sight of the Abbey standing tall and proud before me - as if being a ruin has always been its raison d'être - still takes my breath away.

Inside the Abbey grounds I walk quickly across the grass until I'm stood in the crossing with the echoes of the past all around me.

My heart races and my stomach knots with nervous excitement. He isn't far away. I can already feel the tension, the anticipation, the electricity. It's always there - hanging in the fierce headland wind - just before we meet. I remember feeling it the first time I came here.

I opened my eyes, threw back the covers, and grabbed the notebook by my bed. I'd had the dream again.

I started sketching. This time I'd seen more detail. At first – a few weeks before - there'd just been a shape; a circle set in a triangle. I'd woken up compelled to draw it, clueless as to what it meant. With each dream more shapes emerged until I finally saw a large and majestic building.

I studied my latest sketch. The circle I'd started with was now clearly a window with detailing that resembled a large flower. Triangular turrets soared either side and there were long arched windows below with detailed stonework round them.

What is it? Where is it? What's my connection to it? There had to be one for why else would I dream about it at least twice a week? I asked my father if he knew of such a place. He looked at me with contempt. 'Don't be ridiculous, Rachel. If it exists – which I doubt if you've dreamt it – then it's outside Derbyshire. Stop daydreaming and focus on finding a husband.'

A husband? My parents were obsessed. I'd upset the balance of Derbyshire Society by daring to pass the grand old age of twenty whilst remaining resolutely single. I knew our family fortune relied on me making a good 'match' but I refused to marry for any reason but love. Alas, love eluded me. With a temper as fiery as my red hair, confidence, ideas and opinions which I freely expressed, I was labelled 'difficult'. None of these traits were welcome in a woman back then.

'It's disgraceful. Nobody will marry her. She needs to stop thinking and stop talking,' I'd hear potential suitors tell my father before they stormed out the house. At first, father lectured me on the importance of a good marriage while his mouth twitched with amusement at whatever 'disgraceful' opinion I'd dared to proffer over dinner. With no son and heir to spar with I knew he enjoyed our lengthy conversations and lively debates. But mother had worn him down. As each year passed with me no closer to walking down the aisle my closest ally turned against me, financial worries overtaking his eldest daughter's wishes.

For all my strong will and outward bravado, I was a hopeless romantic at heart. I wanted to get married; truly I did. I just didn't want to do it for financial reasons or to please my parents. And I definitely didn't want to change into someone I wasn't. I wanted a partnership; not a feeling of being a lesser being.

My 21st birthday was fast approaching when father gave me an ultimatum. He'd throw a ball and invite all society's eligible bachelors. I could choose my husband that evening or he'd choose for me. My objections fell on deaf ears.

Exactly two weeks before the ball I had the dream again. I found myself stood on a cliff top looking at the grey sea pounding below when I heard a man call my name. I didn't recognise the voice yet it sounded familiar and comforting. I turned and gasped as I saw the familiar building on the opposite cliff top. Next minute I was in the grounds. I saw a figure in the distance, arms outstretched towards me. I ran to his embrace, tears streaming down my face. 'I've been waiting for you for a long time, Red,' he said.

I awoke with tears still running down my cheeks and the sound of his voice echoing round my room. 'Who are you?' I whispered into the darkness.

Each subsequent night I had the same dream, more and more vivid each time. Each morning I woke up crying. I could never quite see his face. It was always evening and his face was in shadow but I wasn't afraid. I felt I'd known him all my life. When I ran towards him, I felt complete, like I'd finally found where I belonged.

My 21st birthday and the day of the ball dawned. The September weather was as gloomy as my mood. I watched the rain pelt against the windows, anxiety and tension building inside me. I felt trapped, oppressed and completely lost. I didn't belong there anymore. I had to leave. I had to find that place and him.

I retreated to my room to lie down and think but, instead, sleep overcame me. It wasn't long before I was at the building again. He was there. 'It's time,' he said. 'Meet me at the Abbey under destiny's moon.'

I don't remember the journey. I have no idea how I knew to travel north or how I knew to take the connection to Whitby. I stood on a cliff top two days later looking at the Abbey on the opposite cliff, my dream unfolding into reality.

Like a magnet I found myself drawn into the town and up the steps, oblivious to the rapidly fading light. The Abbey was a black featureless silhouette against the darkening sky yet I could visualise every detail, etched on my mind forever from my dreams. My heart raced with nervous excitement. I knew my life was about to change forever.

Where are you?

I frowned. There was no figure up ahead, arms outstretched, to emulate my dreams and no voice that had called to me at night. Have I made a mistake?

I stand in the North Transept in front of the round floral window, the warm September sun bathing my face with light. My whole body is trembling. It will definitely happen today. The Fruit Moon showed last night. Not long now.

Feeling weak from my long journey and lack of food, the enormity of what I'd done consumed me. While the household prepared for the ball, I'd clambered down the ivy. I hadn't left a note; how could I when I didn't know where I was going? I'd run away and for what? To find the owner of a voice I'd only heard in my dreams at a place I'd only seen in my dreams. Am I going mad? The place is real; surely he is too?

But the Abbey seemed deserted. I slumped to the floor, trembling, and wept with disappointment. I was lost. I was alone. Yet I still felt my stomach clench with nervous excitement and anticipation. Are you here?

I look at my watch. I've been here nearly three hours so far. Be patient! Sometimes I have to wait all day before I see him. Sometimes it's a few days; as long as the full moon lasts. The grounds are closed at night now. We can no longer meet under the moon. I have to hope he gets here before darkness falls or it's an anxious wait 'til the following day.

'Excuse me, miss. Are you lost or hurt?'

I looked up and my heart sank. It wasn't him. The voice hadn't been familiar and neither was the figure before me; an elderly man with a white beard holding a spade.

You foolish woman; chasing a dream. He's not real.

'Miss?'

I brushed away my tears and stood up. 'Fine,' I said feeling far from it. 'Long journey … no food … looking for somebody … not here …'

'Jack!' he shouted. Jack? A thread of hope streaked through me before blackness engulfed me.

I was at the Abbey again. The man of my dreams – literally - was holding my hand and whispering my name. 'Rachel. Red …' Red? Like in my dream.

I opened my eyes.

'Red. Thank goodness. Are you hurt?'

I smiled weakly. 'Just tired.'

'Drink this.' He pressed something to my lips and a warm sweet liquid ran into my mouth.

'Another dream?' Please say no. It felt real but my last few dreams had been so vivid that I couldn't be sure. I tried to adjust my eyes to the dim light. What's that glow? It isn't candlelight. I recalled the same peculiar glow from my dreams.

'No,' he said. 'It's real. Red, do you know who I am?'

I looked at the young man with messy dark hair and warm eyes before me and felt butterflies in my stomach for the first time in my life. 'Jack?'

He laughed softly. 'Yes, I'm Jack. I'm as a groundsman here. But do you know me?'

'Only from my dreams.'

'Your dreams?'

'I know it sounds ridiculous but-'

He tenderly pushed a loose tendril of hair behind my ear. 'Believe me, it doesn't. Same as me knowing you'd come today doesn't.'

He took my hands in his and helped me to my feet. I felt electricity fizz between us at his touch.

As I stood, I spotted the source of the strange light through the window; a full yellow moon.

'It's the Fruit Moon,' he said. 'The pagans believed it held mystical powers; powers that could bring lost souls together and unite them in destiny. I call it destiny's moon.'

Am I a lost soul? Was he? Was it destiny for us to meet? Was that why I'd had the dreams? It felt like it was always meant to be this way. I felt like I'd known Jack forever. I felt I was finally where I belonged.

'I'm so happy you're here,' he said. 'You have no idea how long I've waited to meet you. I have so much to tell you but first I want to know all about you, Red. Do you think you can walk?' He offered his arm which I took, grateful to feel his touch once more. We wandered into the grounds.

'What do you want to know?'

'Everything - your passions, your hopes and dreams, your fears.'

'You really want to know these things?' Nobody else ever has. Except you in my dreams.

'Of course. They're the things that make you you.'

We talked and talked until the moon gave way to a rich red sunrise. We laughed, we cried, we shared, just like I dreamt.

'You do realise, Red,' he said, 'that the Pagans were right. We're destined to be together always; not just in this lifetime but for all eternity.'

'What's the difference?'

'This lifetime is what we have now, Red. Eternity is all our other lives. It's next century and all those that follow.'

I want to believe, but ... 'It sounds like a dream.'

'You dreamt of the Abbey and me and you're here now; proof that dreams come true. You've already felt the magic of the moon and the Abbey. The only proof I can give you is time and experience. We'll meet again in the North Transept under the Fruit Moon of your next 21st year. We'll look different but we'll know each other. Once it's happened once, you'll believe.'

'What makes you believe?'

'I was first here in 1309. You felt far away then but this time, when I found myself living and working here, I knew it was time for us to meet. Sadly, each time I return, there's a little less of the Abbey. The building may not be fully intact now but the magic is stronger than ever.'

A loud ring-tone brings me out of my reverie. I tut at the young man who sidles past shouting expletives down his mobile.

'Nah, it's rubbish,' I catch. 'Just a pile of stones... nothing here... not worth the climb...'

Rubbish? Just a pile of stones? Nothing here? Have you no respect for this place of beauty? For the history? For the magic?

Incensed I march after him then stop. He's young. Actually, he's probably in his early twenties like me, but he doesn't have my experience. He doesn't know what the Abbey really means. Let him go and join his mates for an evening of binge-drinking. He doesn't belong here. Not like Jack and me. We belong here. Together. Always.

I turn to head back towards the North Transept – where I first saw his face and the moon - to wait for him. Instantly I know he's there. He steps out of the shadows. He's taller this time and his hair is blond but it's him.

'Red?'

'Jack?'

We run and cling tightly to each other.

'I'm so sorry I'm late,' he says, voice choking with emotion. 'I never had to worry about traffic and parking when we first met. I thought I'd missed you.'

I shake my head. 'I'd have waited forever. You know that.'

'I see the red hair is back.' He tenderly touches a loose tendril just like he did the first time. 'I like it.'

I smile. 'So what's your name this time?'

'Daniel. But you can call me Jack, of course. Yours?'

'Chloe. But you can call me Red. At least this time I have the hair to match the name.'

'I feel like I've waited a hundred lifetimes for this day to come again,' he says

'Same here. Each year seems longer every time.'

'Remember the first time we met how your parents disowned you for eloping and predicted it would never last? We proved them wrong, didn't we?'

I hug him tightly. 'Four hundred years has to be pretty good by anyone's standards.'

'And the Abbey's still looking pretty good,' he says. 'A little less of it again but still spectacular. And still incredibly special.'

We both look back to where we met under destiny's moon.

'I just hope it looks as good in another hundred years,' I say. 'But, for now, we have this lifetime together so let's start enjoying it. I've heard they do great fish and chips in the town.'

'Sounds like a plan. Race you down the steps.'

199, 198, 197....

Whitby is Calling

By Jan Hills

'So where's this then, honey?' Jo-Jo's deep southern drawl broke through Amy's feverish concentration.

Amy paused, glancing up from her drawing board, pencil point still hovering over her cartoon seal. Jo-Jo had chucked her Sleeping Beauty costume carelessly over the back of the sofa beside Amy's teddy bear outfit and was peering at her friend's latest art acquisition on the living room wall. It was a surprise junk shop find – she'd picked it up in downtown Orlando on her day off. Amy grinned and sighed dramatically.

'Dahling! It's my childhood!' she declared, grey eyes twinkling as she flung her hands theatrically, up in the air. 'It's where I spent every childhood holiday until I was fourteen!'

'It sure looks quaint' Jo-Jo told her 'very English - in an olde worlde, ruined, kinda way' she added, wrinkling her nose. 'You been back there since?' she asked as she peered more closely at the whale jaw-bones that had been sketched to form a natural frame to the picture.

The question reverberated around Amy's head. No she hadn't been back since. Life had just got in the way somehow. After dad's promotion, they'd spent their family holidays in the guaranteed sunshine of Spain and Greece and Italy, before Amy had headed off to uni, and her extended gap year. She'd ended up joining a bunch of friends in Florida. With money tight she'd looked for work. She hadn't been back since.

Dad hadn't been impressed when she called home last year, to tell them she'd decided to stay in the States for a while.

'Doing what?' he'd asked suspiciously over the phone.

'This and that – there's lots of opportunities for artists' she'd said with her fingers crossed firmly as they gripped the phone. 'And Jo-Jo is going to help me get a job with her in Disney World.'

'So the Fine Arts degree we supported you through university for three years won't be a complete waste?' her father's sarcasm shot back across the Atlantic.

Dad didn't understand – he must be getting old she'd decided dismissively.

So it had jolted her when she had come across the picture. She'd been rummaging in the depths of the funny little junk shop, and the painting - with its grubby driftwood frame - had been slumped across a pile of old teapots. It had seemed to reach out to her - and she just had to buy it.

It was unmistakeably Whitby, of course. There's nowhere else with an ancient Abbey like that - with its vast arching windows and solid towers, steadfastly uniting the soft green cliff-top with the stormy grey skies. The centre of the watercolour was dominated by a straggle of cottages, their attic rooms popping through the red tiled roofs like frogs eyes. In the bottom left hand corner, the artist had added a haphazard pile of bright orange lobster pots; to the right, a huddle of fat little fishing boats. 'Kippers' thought Amy and her mouth watered painfully as she remembered their unique, smoky flavour. 'When had she last had a kipper?'

The foreground included an expanse of blue-grey sea, with curling waves and a hint of the vast solid beach - the beach on which she and her sister had built countless sandcastles before they'd devoured mum's 'doorstep' egg sandwiches, carefully wrapped in greaseproof paper, and burnt their tongues on steaming Thermos flask tea.

But the top of the picture featured the Abbey. And it was the Abbey that Amy had always loved the most. One of her earliest memories included feeling her chubby little legs bouncing on her dad's shoulders as he gave her a piggy-back ride up the last dozen or so steps. She remembered her mum telling her about the Abbey's history. That it was an ancient monastery.

'Like a church?' she had whispered.

'Yes sort of,' her mum had smiled down at her.

'So where are the pews?' she had asked, looking all about her for the familiar trappings of Sunday school.

'Oh they've long gone!' her dad had chuckled '– we'll have to sit on the grass instead.' And Amy had plonked herself down and faced the tall windowless arches and told them solemnly that she was waiting for the sermon and 'shushed' them all as it was a-bit-like-a-church.

Amy smiled as she remembered those carefree holidays when pure happiness meant a morning running on the sands – jumping through the waves if it was warm enough - and an afternoon wandering through the Abbey ruins, whilst licking a dripping ice-cream cone.

When she was eight her dad had taken her fishing and they went so far out to sea that they could hardly see the town. The wind had whipped up and the little boat had rocked alarmingly. Dad had wrapped a huge comforting arm around her and pointed out the stark silhouette of the Abbey. He'd told her the Abbey would point them safely back into harbour.

On rainy days, Amy remembered making up stories for her sister, as they huddled up together on the window-seat of their holiday cottage, jagged scars of lightening crackling through the sombre sky.

'The Abbey is our great protector,' she declared solemnly.

'What's a protector?'

'Something that watches over us.'

'What - like a giant?' her sister had whispered, her eyes round as buttons.

'Sort of. Well, more like a big grandparent of the rocks and cliffs…' Amy had expanded '…and best of friends with children and donkeys and seagulls.'

Amy sighed, she could almost hear the seagulls as they flapped lazily on the air currents around the vast stone walls and smell the sea water laced with seaweed, on the stiff north-easterly breeze, as it whistled through the windowless arches and straight up to the sky. She put down her pencil, rested her chin on her hand and leant her elbow on her drawing board. The images swirled around in her head like sea frets, and her brain responded to her awakening memories with sharp pangs of longing.

'No, I haven't been back in a while' she sighed softly 'Dear old Whitby - it's beautiful - part of my heritage, and yes, very English.'

'Looks like it needs fixin'- one of those TV make-overs!' Jo-Jo turned away from the picture, shrugging. 'Now shake a leg girl, or we gonna be late for shift! An' you know Mr Disney, he don't wait for nobody!'

Amy tore her eyes away from the watercolour, abandoning her work and, grabbing her furry costume, she headed for the door.

The day was pure Florida – all blue sky and ocean, carefully arranged clouds and immaculate beaches. As Jo-Jo floored the old Chevvy and started up her non-stop chatter about show-biz gossip, Amy rested her arm on the open window and pulled on a pair of nearly-designer shades. Her hair whipped across as she turned her face up to the golden sunshine, gently closing her eyes.

At one time Florida had suited her very well, with no real commitments, the freelance art work had slotted in well with her Disney job. She had adored the weather, loved her new friends and spent every spare moment on the beach. But just lately, things had started to pall. The sunshine was just – well - so predictable, everyone she knew seemed to be 'in therapy' and if you strayed away from the main thoroughfares of the cities, beggars dotted the streets in sharp contrast to the glitzy show-biz world she had once aspired to.

The freedom she had craved, she was beginning to realise, was built on a flimsy foundation of un-reality TV and trashy magazines. She had two jobs just to pay the rent on a shabby studio apartment in a down-at-heel part of town. Her shopping had become the window-only kind and her Starbucks coffee bill swallowed the last of her meagre income in one gulp of 'lite-cappuchino' froth.

Amy opened her eyes as Jo-Jo started to weave in and out of the traffic. The sunlight made the building blocks stand out in a startling brashness that had Amy squinting despite her sunglasses.

Jo-Jo was pulling on the handbrake, squealing the tyres as she nipped into a staff parking spot. She always insisted on making an entrance.

'Gotta get noticed,' she said, her mouth in a generous grin as a group of maintenance guys whistled at them, 'otherwise you're nobody!'

Amy spent the first half hour of her shift getting used to the cumbersome costume again. The head was the worst part. 'Cartoon characters always have such huge heads,' she groaned to herself and, despite the clever construction, it was still hot and stuffy inside as she entertained the 'line-ups' and helped holidaymakers find their way around the giant complex.

She sneaked under an awning, out of the relentless sunshine, as a family of five, grazing on sugar-saturated drinks and salt-laden snacks, waddled past. Their grizzly squabble spilled onto the busy thoroughfare as they tried to decide where to go next. 'Pa' finally ended the spat by declaring that he wanted a 'real' English beer in a 'real' English pub.

'Yeah! – Epcot – then we can do England and the rest of the world before dinner!' Mom agreed enthusiastically.

As the family wandered off, Amy felt her jaw drop inside the teddy bear outfit. Which was worse – thinking it was possible to 'do' England in half a day, or to think that Disney was real?! Despite the soaring midday temperatures she shuddered. Amy had 'done' England in Epcot months back, with its obligatory Olde English Pub, plethora of Beatrix Potter furry toys and some suspect Wedgewood coasters. She'd not been back.

Amy felt a headache starting at the back of her right eye. She closed her eyes and let her mind drift back to England – to the wide-open North Yorkshire moors and the bracing freshness of the Whitby coastline, quickly losing herself in delightful childhood memories.

She abruptly became aware of a small child kicking her left shin.

'Hey! Stop that!' she cried out through the fur fabric.

'Stupid bear, stupid, stupid, stupid!' the child continued kicking her leg viciously. 'I wanna see Goofy!' he demanded.

'Now Bobby, leave the bear alone an' let's go find you a nice big ice-cream,' cajoled his mother.

Bobby aimed a punch at Amy's stomach. She stepped back rapidly, missing the worst of the impact, and the child swung round and fell over, bawling his head off.

'Mommy! Mommy! The bear pushed me over!' he screamed, his round face turning puce. Amy pulled her costume head off in a flash.

'Hey it wasn't like that!' she yelled just as the supervisor was walking by. Amy scrabbled the costume head back on as the child broke out in an ear-piercing scream.

'Mommy, Mommy! The bear's head came off!' and he ended in a torrent of squealing that seemed to have the entire theme park agog.

Amy had just committed a dreadful sin. 'We never, no NEVER, remove a part of our costume when out on duty,' the supervisor had emphasised on induction. 'It may frighten the poor little kiddies.' Amy had thought for quite some time now that most of the 'poor little kiddies' were vicious little monsters and that the world would be better off if prospective parents had to pass a parenting diploma prior to being given permission to conceive.

Clearly Amy wasn't cut out for Disney work, her supervisor told her in the office half an hour later and since she obviously didn't intend to change her ways, she could hand over her costume and leave immediately. Amy reluctantly accepted her last pay cheque and trudged to the bus stop.

The air-conditioning on the bus was set to arctic and Amy shivered as the scenery flashed by. The bus slowed as a huge crane finished flattening a large empty hotel. The hoarding proclaimed that it was to be replaced by 'The Biggest and Best in all of Orlando!' The hotel had only been three years old. 'It's no wonder they don't have any history,' Amy thought. 'They're obsessed with newer and younger!'

Amy had a violent rush of homesickness that swept up from her stomach and took her breath away faster than the child's punch to her stomach. Suddenly it just didn't feel real. Any of it. The population was transient and disconnected. When had she last been to see a play or a classical concert, or visit an art gallery or a museum? Was the world all make-overs and lunchtime botox-fixes? There was no substance to anything. No history.

As the bus jogged her along, she stopped seeing the beaches of Florida and the huge out-of-town shopping malls as they swept past. In her head she could see the crashing waves of Whitby beach and the solid fishermen's cottages winding up the 199 steps. Instead of the Floridian hot-dog street vendors and the ice-cream parlours, Amy saw the cafés and tea-shops clustered throughout the cobbled streets of Whitby's little town. She smelled buttery toasted tea cakes and the hint of Earl Grey tea, heard the chink of china cups and saucers, and tinkling shop doorbells welcoming visitors.

She had a sudden memory of herself and her sister singing at the tops of their voices in the back of the battered old family Ford. The car laboured round the headland at the start of their annual fortnight and she recalled the shrieks from her sister and herself as they first spotted the tip of the Abbey.

'There it is! We're there!'

She thought back to numerous picnics on the solid, rippled sand, chucking the crusts to the greedy gulls as they hovered overhead. It was all so real that she jumped when a passenger brushed past her. She'd lost all sense of time and yet…. And yet Amy knew that she'd stumbled on a truth. It was as if a prince had kissed her and woken her from a hundred year sleep. She grinned to herself, no that was Disney, what she wanted was something real. It was about her roots, about being English and it was about a long overdue trip to visit the Abbey. She stood up abruptly as the bus pulled to her stop. She had some planning to do. It was time to go home. She started to text her sister – maybe she fancied joining her on a trip back to their 'great protector.'

The Smuggle Run

By David Mills

It was the first time Edward had been out smuggling, his older brother Jack had been doing it for the past four years since he turned fourteen. Jack had told Edward that it was tradition to do all the rowing on your first smuggling trip. Although it was no tradition that Edward had heard before he was just happy to be able to go out and have an adventure, plus of course he was more than happy to be earning some money.

The past few days had been filled with rumours that customs officers were headed for town and ready to arrest anyone caught smuggling and this had been playing on Edward's mind ever since they'd set off from the beach.

"What's wrong Ward? You're not still worrying about getting caught are you?" Jack asked.

"No. Of course not; I was never worried anyway." Edward replied trying to push the thought of the officers out of his mind and focus on the job at hand. All the muscles in his upper arms and belly were starting to tremble and ache with the effort of rowing. "I'm going to have to have a little rest brov, I'm done in."

Edward made sure the oars were secured in their rests then allowed his eyes to survey the coastline. He noticed a procession of lanterns leading their way through the narrow winding streets and down to the harbour and assumed that they were the women of town waiting to receive the smuggled goods. Dominating the skyline was the unmistakeable tall gothic image of Whitby Abbey, well what was left of the Abbey anyway. The Abbey had always given Edward the creeps, but he'd never seen it from the sea at night before and it filled him with a whole new level of fear.

The tall stone work silhouetted against the unusually large moon seemed to leer at Edward in a way that made him feel uncomfortable. Unable to look at the terrible skyline anymore Edward diverted his attention behind him to the huge luger ship that was their destination and also their meal ticket. The ship was still a fair distance away but Edward still found the sheer size of it menacing with its three vertical masts reaching high into the sky. Despite all his best effort Edward's gaze turned back towards the Abbey positioned high above the quiet harbour town. It almost felt as though the old ruins were staring back at him. With that Edward decided to get back to rowing, at least while he was rowing he wasn't thinking about the Abbey.

When they finally reached the ship there was a man waiting to greet them. He was a lot shorter than Edward had thought he would be, but apart from his severe height deficiency he was exactly what Edward had expected. He had scruffy hair and mangy beard matted with the remnants of his last meal and who knows maybe even the meal before that too. A thick layer of dead skin lined the top of his coat and every time he scratched his face (which was a lot) more skin fell off. Although Edward didn't get too close to the sailor he still had to stop himself from gagging on the smell of his breath which was worse than rotting fish guts.

Edward allowed himself to slip into a daydream of Molly Sanders while Jack did what little talking there was to be done. Edward and Molly had been friends since they were children but over the past couple of months their relationship had started to blossom into more than just friendship. Edward was hoping to make enough money tonight to be able to take her out on a date and win her affections for sure. Whilst away in his own little world Edward was vaguely aware of a look of confusion on his older brother's face before being snapped back into reality by the deafening crack of a pistol being fired followed closely by a cry of agony from Jack. The next few minutes seemed to go in slow motion and Edward felt as though he was moving through water.

Jack recoiled and reached for his right leg. Coins fell to the floor of their boat and spiralled wildly to a halt. Edward reached for the oars but they seemed like they were a million miles away. The vertically challenged man was barking something to rest of the crew on board and had now produced a long menacing looking sword. Jack was yelling something but Edward couldn't hear a word of it, it was like he wasn't just moving through water but underneath it as well. The short man lunged off of the luger and landed in between Jack and Edward. Before he could get a firm footing Jack pushed him square in the back and into the water. Edward's hearing returned just in time for him to hear the splash as his body hit the water, he could now hear that Jack was yelling at him to get down under the seat.

"Stay down! We need to get out of here NOW!" Jack shouted.

"Are you alright? Did they get you?" Edward cried.

"Don't worry 'bout me, damn thing just grazed past my leg that's all."

Jack reached for his own pistol, a Queen Anne box lock with a walnut grip and quickly loaded it hoping that it hadn't got too wet to fire and took aim at a man who was pointing a rifle at them and squeezed the trigger. He missed his target and hit the wooden banister that ran the length of the ship. Wooden splinters shot up from the point of impact and Edward thought that the splinters had gone into his eyes but couldn't tell for sure. Jack handed the pistol to Edward, picked up the oars and started rowing as hard as he could. Edward reloaded the pistol without having to be asked but didn't try to shoot at the ship. The distance that Jack had already managed to put between them was far too great for the weapon to have any real effect.

Edward wanted to ask why they shot at him but he already knew the answer. The rumours of the customs officers were obviously true and there was no doubt in Edward's mind that the procession of lights that he'd seen going down to the harbour were more officers waiting to arrest them as soon as they docked. He also knew that Jack had lied about his wound just being a graze he could already see blood pooling around his feet.

Edward didn't know how Jack managed to maintain the pace that he'd set especially with the amount of pain he must have been in. As they neared the shore they could hear what sounded like a riot coming from the harbour. Jack steered their boat slightly south towards the ruins of the Abbey and told Edward to be ready for trouble.

They landed their boat a few hundred metres south of the harbour and made their way into the village hoping to be able to blend into the back of the crowd that had undoubtedly gathered. By the time they'd got halfway down Henrietta Street they could see shadows of people running away from the harbour.

"You ready with that pistol Ward? It looks like we might be running into a little trouble." Jack whispered.

Edward could almost hear the life draining away in his voice. Just around the corner four men in military uniforms were standing in a straight line forming a human barricade, luckily for Jack and Edward they were on the lookout for anyone coming up from the harbour and were all stood with their backs towards them. Jack winced with pain as he tried to hunker down and out of view should they decide to turn around. Edward crouched down behind him trying to conceal himself behind a stack of empty lobster pots. A fifth soldier came running from the harbour and stared straight at Edward. Adrenaline pumped through his veins at such a rate that it was almost deafening in his ears. He was just about to get up and start running back down Henrietta Street and onto the beach when the soldier fell in line with the others facing the harbour.

"Captain sent word from the ship, said there were two of 'em. He shot one of 'em in the leg so be on lookout for someone wi' a limp." The newcomer said followed by a howl of laughter from the other soldiers.

Edward knew that this was the best time for them to try and get past but the only way for them to go other than back down to the beach was up the 199 steps up to the church and the Abbey ruins beyond. He lifted Jack's arm over his shoulder and helped him to his feet. Jack struggled up the first two or three steps but quickly settled into a rhythm using Edward to support his injured leg.

The more steps they climbed the further away the top of the steps seemed to be and Jack's leg was causing him too much pain for him to be able to carry on and he sat down on one of the steps. Edward sat next to him and under the light of the full moon was able to see that Jack's face had drained of colour to a pale lifeless grey. Edward also noticed a thin trail of blood leading from Jack's wounded leg and all the way the down the steps as far as he could see. He knew that if any of the soldiers saw it they'd almost certainly follow the trail.

"Come on, we've got to move." Edward said pulling at Jack's arm.

For a few moments Jack didn't move and Edward was filled with the fear that he was dead and started weeping.

"What you cryin' for? You're not a little girl are you?" Jack said attempting the same mocking tone he'd used earlier. Seeing the look of worry on Edward's face Jack attempted a smile that just looked like the thin and wiry smile of a dead man. "Come on let's move, they won't be able to track us over the grass in this light."

As the top of the steps came into sight so did the dark imposing image of the Abbey ruins. Although Edward knew that this was the best place for them to hide he didn't relish the idea of having to go there in the dark. The tall arches of the Abbey seemed impossibly dark compared to the light of the moon. Edward felt as though a million eyes were watching him from the dark depths.

From far in the distance Edward could hear voices getting closer and the faint glow of lanterns coming over the brow of the hill. Knowing that time wasn't on his side Edward half carried, half dragged Jack to the nearest arch, cast his eye back to the approaching men and decided he had time to move down to the next arch. It wasn't an ideal hiding place, but this wasn't an ideal situation. All that Edward could do now was hope that they wouldn't be found and hope that the soldiers would get bored of looking for them before Jack's condition got too bad.

Lying back as far as he could into the darkness, Edward and Jack listened intently as footsteps steadily grew closer and closer and closer. The tension of the situation was almost suffocating to Edward; it took all of his will power to stop him from screaming. And the footsteps grew closer still, but now they were moving at a steady jog. Edward prayed that the person would be travelling at an all out run by the time they reached them and would simply run straight past.

The footsteps stopped dead just before their hiding place. Jack reached out a trembling hand and gently squeezed Edward's hand trying to reassure him. Edward reached for the pistol but Jack pushed his hand away from it. Edward understood that Jack knew they weren't going to get away and the punishment for killing a soldier is far greater than the punishment for smuggling. A hand sneaked into view and gripped the corner of the wall, closely followed by a chiselled stubbly face.

"Jack, Ward, is that you?" The man that Edward would soon come know as William said "You better come with me quick or we'll all be in trouble."

Edward vaguely recognised the man but didn't quite know where from. That didn't matter, he wanted to help and if anyone needed help right now it was those two. The familiar stranger crouched down and inspected Jack's leg, then without a word swooped him up over his shoulder and started marching off in the opposite direction to where all the noise was coming from. Edward followed without a moment's hesitation.

It didn't take them long to cover the distance of the field and reach the row of houses that sat highest on the hill. William fumbled in his pockets for a key then opened the door to the first house on that row. Once inside William took Jack upstairs and laid him on a bed. From the window Edward could see that the Abbey was now flooded with soldiers carrying lanterns and realised that if William hadn't come to help then they would have been caught for sure. Edward went and crouched down next to Jack and took his hand into his own.

"Ward, I think it's about time me and you have a career change, what do you think?" Jack asked and laughed.

Poetic Ruins

By Sophie Jackson

'Are you ready?' Angel grinned.

'To be frightened or inspired?' I asked grimly.

Angel (or Angela as her parents knew her) was dressed all in black for the occasion with a flowing, lacy cardigan draped artistically over her shoulders. While I huddled in my Winter coat, woolly gloves and bobble hat, Angel floated around the ruins like some gothic Cinderella.

This was Halloween, Angel had said, not a night for being at home. No, Angel had other plans. Among her many quirks Angel was a horror freak, fascinated by all the things that went bump in the night and this October Angel had planned a special event.

Angel danced through an archway in the old Whitby Abbey ruins. Behind, a dark courtyard was formed by the half collapsed walls and this was clearly to become our base camp for the night. Angel was on a ghost hunt, Halloween, she theorised, was the night for spirits to rise up from the ground and Whitby Abbey was the place to be. She loved this place, she said the stone had captured her heart and in daylight I could see her point, though I am not a particularly spiritual person. But at night... at night this place is just damn spooky.

Angel settled on the ground.

'I brought cake and tea,' she announced cheerfully.

Stomping my feet, pretending it was to keep warm rather than nerves, I glanced around the eerie walls. Shadows seemed to linger everywhere. I pulled my collar up higher round my face and felt my warm breath wrap around my chin.

Angel was setting up a small tin lamp. Inside a frail tealight was burning.

'Isn't this better than being stuck in?' she asked me.

I simply shrugged. Right now I felt like being stuck in. I had felt that way since Darren had rung the other day and said those dreadful words; 'Hey babe, look, I've been thinking. We're going nowhere, so let's call it quits, OK?'

And in my confusion and disbelief I had not even thought to argue. But Angel had. As soon as she knew she stormed over to his flat and hammered on the door determined to let him have it. The fact that a scantily clad brunette had opened the door had just been the icing on the cake. Then there I was, single again.

But in some respects that wasn't the worst part. OK, I felt betrayed and hurt, but what worried me more was that since then I had not been able to do any work. I'm a painter, usually quite prolific, but since Darren, my creativity had dried up along with the paint on my palette. With Christmas looming I should have gone into overdrive, instead I found myself struggling to even get started.

I think that was why Angel suddenly announced this evening out, she didn't want me to sit at home and brood.

'This place is good for the soul,' she said fixing me with one of her looks.

'I'm not sure I like it here,' I answered.

'Just close your eyes,' Angel replied as she closed her own, 'just picture the walls solid instead of broken. Imagine candles burning and monks walking about singing Gregorian chants.'

I tried. But instead of monks my mind's eye only made the shadows deeper and the moonlight more sinister. All I could hear was the wind whistling around the walls and I shivered.

When I opened my eyes Angel had produced a book – Dracula – and was managing to read it in the pathetic glow of the tealight. She held out a flask to me.

'Tea?'

I sighed and helped myself to a cup.

We sat together in the darkness for what seemed like hours. Angel started to fall asleep, helpless to the draw of slumber. I was also feeling weary, but my nerves kept me awake and vigilant. I watched the moon draw level with a jagged outcrop of wall and tried to picture the Abbey as it had once been.

The world seemed to grow quiet. I let my eyes half-close as I visualised the scene, and then the music filled my head. The steady, solemn chant of male voices. Singing words I did not understand. Melodic. Peaceful. I might not know what they sang, but I understood the sincerity and a faint smile traced its way across my lips.

Then, suddenly, my head shot up. I had almost fallen asleep sitting upright. I blinked rapidly, trying to jolt myself back to reality and as I took in the deep shadows of the courtyard again I realised the music had not stopped.

The chant was echoing around the walls, but it was fading, slipping away. Slipping back to the past.

I found myself looking around in alarm, trying to seek the source. Some radio perhaps? Or an audio tape automatically set to play when visitors entered? I tried to ignore the improbability of that and looked around until my eyes spotted something.

Not a something. No. A person.

My heart started to race. Someone was stood in a ruined doorway. They had a hood over their head so I could not see their face and their body was masked by the shadows. But they were there alright, and staring straight back at me.

I should have screamed. I should have shook Angel awake. But I didn't. I just sat there. And the figure watched me, the hood moving slightly as he breathed in and out.

Then the wind blew and with it the music seemed stirred up again. The chant sailed out across the grass. The figure suddenly jerked backwards as though the music had woken him from his thoughts. He shot a glance over his shoulder and then turned to move away.

I don't know why but in that instant I suddenly didn't want him to leave. He seemed sad, heartbroken even, just like me and as he fell back into the shadows I was on my feet and following him.

He vanished through the doorway, I went through too. He was running now, across the grass where once an aisle had perhaps been. The bases of pillars still loomed in the darkness. I chased him.

'Hey!' I shouted.

But he didn't slow, he kept moving, rushing forward until he found some steps and skipped down them. I followed this intruder determined to catch him, but as I too raced down the steps intent on the pursuit I didn't see the iron grille. I slammed into it where it blocked part of the staircase and I swore. Loudly.

Slumping back on the steps I had just run down I felt mildly dazed and disorientated. The figure had vanished.

'You've seen the ghost,' a voice said behind me.

I jumped out of my skin, stumbled to my feet and turned around. Outlined in the moonlight that illuminated the top of the staircase a man stood. He appeared to be in a suit, hands tucked in his pockets. Fear now preoccupied my thoughts. If I screamed would Angel hear?

'Ghost?' I said, hoping I sounded nonchalant.

'Yes. A novice who fell in love with a local girl and wished to elope with her. She, unfortunately, spurned him and he threw himself down a set of stairs in the Abbey. Possibly these ones.'

His words made me automatically glance down at the stone beneath my feet. Then back up.

'Who are you?'

'Frederick Davies,' he held out a hand, somehow it seemed rude not to shake it, 'poet and antiquarian.'

'You like local legends?'

'Very much.'

I couldn't quite tell in the moonlight, but I think Mr Davies looked slightly abashed at his last statement. Anyway, at that point he turned and we both emerged from the stairs into the relative brightness of the night.

'Whitby has lots of legends,' Davies continued, 'many ghosts too. This Abbey has a long and intriguing history that has inspired a great many writers and poets.'

'And is that why you come here?' In the moonlight I could see he was indeed wearing a suit and was quite good looking.

He smiled. It was a nice smile.

'Yes,' he answered simply, 'and you?'

'My friend's idea. She fancied a ghost hunt, then fell asleep.'

'Ah, well that is no good. She has missed the monk.'

My gaze went back to the staircase.

'He seemed...so real.'

'Ghosts do, sometimes. You'd be amazed how many people are convinced they have met a living, breathing monk here.'

'I could almost have touched him.'

'I like to think,' Frederick mused, 'that the afterlife is more tangible than we realise. That a spirit can touch, can feel, can think. That in fact, they are not so very different from a living person. That they are waiting, perhaps in limbo.'

'Waiting for what?'

Frederick cast his eyes up to a rising arch.

'Who's to say? Forgiveness? Conclusion?'

'Conclusion?'

'Yes. Sometimes an ending can be...abrupt. It leaves loose ends that some souls find it hard not to try and tie up.'

'You are quite philosophical,' I smiled.

He shrugged.

'I think too much.'

We walked together in the moonlight, giving me plenty of time to study the man beside me. He was tall, with dark hair. In profile his nose could be considered a little long, but when he smiled everything else seemed to fall into proportion. I found I liked him and drew a little closer.

'Do you come here often at night?' I asked.

'Almost every night,' he nodded, 'bit of a habit I'm afraid.'

'Have you written a poem about Whitby Abbey?'

'No. That is my one failure. I want to so badly, but I can't find the words. So I walk here again and again in the hope that one time I might be able to capture this atmosphere in verse.'

All around us the ruins glistened in the moonlight and I could suddenly understand how he felt.

'One day,' I said to him.

'Yes,' he laughed, 'if it is the last thing I do!'

We paused at a broken lump of wall and he sat upon it. I hopped up beside him.

'Listen!' he hissed.

Holding my breath I listened as the chant seeped over the walls again. This time though I felt engulfed by the music. I clung tightly to the stone I sat on, fearful that if I let go I might be swept away with the chant, swept to some other place. A hand touched mine.

'You do not need to be afraid,' Frederick said.

'The music is so...beautiful?'

Frederick gazed across the ruins as the music drifted over us. Suddenly he sighed deeply.

'If only I could capture this feeling with words.'

'If only I could capture this in paint,' I replied.

He looked at me sharply.

'I'm a painter!' I think I sounded a little too eager to laugh at myself.

'A fellow artiste,' Frederick smiled, 'perhaps that is why I was drawn to you. I don't often speak with people, I usually prefer to be alone.'

'No one should be alone.'

'But many of us are.' Frederick's hand was icy cold on mine, it made a shiver creep down my spine.

That sensation seemed to awaken me from some daydream.

'Angel!' I cried.

I had left her alone in the courtyard sleeping. Who was to say what could have happened while I was gone? And she had no idea where I was either. Leaping off the broken wall, I ran back to the doorway. Frederick was beside me, oddly silent. When I reached the doorway I saw Angel sound asleep on the ground. Relief filled me.

'It is nearly midnight,' Frederick said softly.

'Really?' I looked at my watch and as I did I heard a screech and a bang.

Overhead in the sky a firework exploded in a glittering spray of red and green.

'Gosh! That made me jump!' I looked to Frederick, but he was gone, 'Frederick?'

Another shiver ran down my back. Suddenly the atmosphere that had so encircled me a few moments ago instead now felt cold, empty, barren. Shaking violently I went to Angel and shook her awake.

'Let's go home.'

Angel glanced at her watch.

'Yeah, OK.'

Gathering up the little lantern, the flask, cake and book, we made our way out of the Abbey. Angel insisted we take the shortcut through the nearby graveyard, it being Halloween and all. I didn't have the heart to argue. I was wondering where Frederick had vanished to. I had liked him, had wanted to get to know him. Just typical that he should disappear like that.

Angel was reading tombstones as her lamp cast light on them.

'Daisy Smith. Charlie Johnson. Abigail Waters.'

I had my eyes firmly trained on the ground. My hands were still sore from where I had banged into that grille.

'Arthur Humphrey Seaton. That's a good one.'

I was hardly paying attention to Angel's ramblings. It was beginning to cross my mind that what had happened that night might have been some peculiar dream, it seemed too unreal to have been anything else.

'Fredrick Davies.'

I stopped dead.

'What?'

Angel stared at me.

'Frederick Davies.' she repeated, swinging the lamp at a white gravestone.

Breath catching in my throat I staggered towards the grave and stared at the carved letters.

'Frederick Davies. Beloved son. 1924 – 1944.' Angel read, 'The war got him then.'

'He was a poet.' I said, 'But he never got to finish his last piece.'

Angel stared at me peculiarly.

'I don't understand.'

'I...I read about him.' It was a poor excuse.

'Poor chap.' Angel moved off swinging the lantern, 'What did you think of Whitby?'

I felt unable to take my eyes from the gravestone even though without the lantern I could no longer read it.

'It had atmosphere.'

'Perhaps you could paint it.'

'I think I shall.'

Angel smiled at me.

'Good, I want to see you painting again. You are always happiest when you are being creative.'

I was surprised she had noticed. Suddenly feeling emotional I put a hand on Angel's shoulder.

'Fancy a drink?' I asked

'Yeah.'

We wandered off through the gravestones.

'Pity we didn't see a ghost.' she grumbled.

'If we did would we realise?' the words slipped out of my mouth.

'Sure,' said Angel, 'why wouldn't we?'

All I could do was shrug.

'Well, we can try again next year. There's supposed to be this monk.'

Angel began telling me the legend of the Whitby monk, but I wasn't listening. All I could think about was the young poet among the ruins. His face was frozen in my mind. I knew now what I would paint on that blank canvas sitting at home.

My inspiration was back. I could only hope that one day I could return the favour and that Frederick might find peace in his last poem.

The Just in Case Fund

By A. J. Kirby

So there I was with a priceless antique – possibly the Holy Grail - smashed in my jacket pocket, my trousers round my ankles, a blinding pain in my head and an injured unicorn at my feet. And absolutely no idea how I could make things right.

As if to make things worse, a toothless hag with what looked like snakes for hair was screaming dog's abuse into my face so loudly that it was virtually impossible to hear the unicorn's complaints, let alone translate them. The unicorn spoke French for some reason, despite being born and raised in Yorkshire, and I was under no illusions as to the reason for this. He was just trying to be awkward. Just like he was with his horn.

'It hurt me, Monsieur Dawson,' he breathed. 'Make ze, uh, pain go aways.'

His leg, which had always seemed too easily breakable, had finally given up the ghost, and lay at a nasty right-angle to his body. He'd been trying to complete a circuit of the Abbey's grounds. Call it a high-hurdles for unicorns, in which he leaped over each of the beams in the ribcage of the Abbey. Only, he'd over-compensated on one jump, like I'd seen the British athlete do in the Olympics, and had clipped his heel. As soon as he did, I knew he'd fall from a great height. As soon as he did, I knew that he'd be injured. The only doubt in my mind was whether he'd land horn-first. He didn't.

If the unicorn's predicament wasn't so tragic, it would have been funny. But the muffled sounds of pain which escaped from his mouth chilled my heart. He was trembling all over too, like a dreaming cat, but he was awake, wide-eyed, bushy-tailed, red-horned. He'd once told me that when his horn glowed red it meant danger. Back then, I didn't believe him. Back then, I refused to believe the evidence of my own eyes.

'You're a nincompoop,' railed the hag, who I understood to be called Abi, after the Abbey, even though she'd not told me her name. 'A wastrel.'

'Yeah, yeah,' I said, crouching over the unicorn and stroking his mane and then turning to look at her. 'Tell me what I can do for him.'

It was harder to look at her for more than a few seconds without becoming hypnotised by her incredible ugliness, petrified by her weirdness. She was like one of my caricatures; her face an archipelago of warts, her eyes burning sea-volcanoes, her chin a veritable jetty. Her hair was so greasy, it looked like a cow had licked it, but also, in certain lights, writhed like snakes (grass-snakes though: certainly nothing deadly. I understood that).

'If you'd have taken better care of the unicorn in the first place, none of this would have ever happened,' she said.

I broke the spell. Looked away from her. Looked out past the skeletal Abbey and towards the sea. A couple of small fishing vessels trawled into view. Abi interrupted my reverie, impatiently clicking her fingers in front of my face, so loud that it almost seemed like she'd broken them in the process.

'That's right, think about painting. Painting will help at a time like this,' she said.

'If I'd wanted to be nagged at, I'd have got myself a wife,' I moaned, and received a clip round the ear for my pains. I'd not received a clip round the ear since I was knee-high to a gobstopper and I'd forgotten that the word 'clip' was something of a euphemism. Although she struck me open-handed, it was like being hit round the face by a cliff.

'I wasn't being sarcastic, boy,' said Abi, glaring down at me.

'She was, uh, telling ze truth,' said the unicorn, pleading with me with his big brown eyes.

I screwed up my eyes and wished that it would all go away. Gingerly opened them up again and saw that it hadn't. Ah, it hadn't always been like this. Once upon a time, I was happy in my monochrome little world, painting my dull as dishes watercolours for the tourists; sunsets, always sunsets. Once upon a time, my imagination was as crippled as the damn unicorn.

I used to do caricatures. I'd perch outside the glittery, bawdy arcades in Summer, surrounded by pen and ink renderings of celebrities with exaggerated ass-ears and windsock mouths. My celebrity pictures were pretty useless really, and the idea that Pamela Anderson, for example, had one, visited Whitby and two, posed for me to draw her looking so ridiculous seemed unlikely. But the tourists fell for them, hook, line and sinker, just like they fell for the unusable fishing rods from the tackle shops along the front. Being on holiday seemed to do strange things to people; made them more willing to believe whatever line I cared to spin them.

One time - I'll always remember it – this tiny, wizened old woman came up to me during one of my quiet periods. At first, I presumed her one of the homeless travellers which often flocked around these parts in the Summer months, and I shifted my Tupperware money dish further under my stool. She sat herself down on the other stool and made herself comfortable without being asked. What cheek!

'Got any money, love?' I asked her, finding it difficult not to sound rude. 'No money, no dice. No money, no caricature.'

She smiled this gap-toothed smile at me, eyes flickering full of knowledge. And then, flicking her fingers dismissively against the David Beckham caricature, she said: 'You're wasting your talents, boy. You're a wastrel.'

Now, the David Beckham caricature was the one I was most proud of, in a funny sort of way. Sure it didn't look exactly like him. He was a little too perfect looking to make a proper honest-to-goodness destruction job of. But I liked the way I'd managed to turn his body into this writhing mass of tattoos. The unicorns and Whitby Abbeys on his chest seemed almost alive... Almost.

'Do you want your picture done or not, dear?' I asked.

She screwed up her face; wrinkles collapsed in on each other, like it was a Lancastrian gurning competition. I'd have made a good job of painting her, I reckoned. I might not be as polite with her as I was with some of the others.

'You ain't good enough to paint me yet, boy,' she said, and then… And then she seemed to disappear into thin air. At the time, I dismissed it as the after-effects of my drinking session the night before. At the time, I dismissed it as a trick of the light. But her challenge stayed with me. Her dismissal of my talents stayed with me all right.

One day, I'd paint her. I'd prove it.

But in the mean time, the caricatures started to make me cynical. They made me respect that thing we call our imagination less and less. I found that I could make money simply by rehashing what I saw. I never had to pull my finger out to portray anything extraordinary or wondrous. When a madman approached me and asked me to paint his horse – his horse goddamn it – I painted a horse that was so dull he could have been any horse in the world. I resisted that urge which came over me to paint a great whopping horn on the horse's head and turn him into a unicorn. I resisted any urge to give the horse a man's torso and head, and make him a centaur. When I painted the Abbey or the crashing sea, I snapped-happy, as though I was using a fun-camera, not really bothering to lend depth to the images I created. I didn't imagine white unicorns high-hurdling through the sea, nor did I paint the Abbey as I really saw it; as the skeleton of some massive sea creature washed up onto the cliff by some tidal wave. Deep down, I knew that I should have obeyed my urges, but the buyers didn't seem to mind my kind of stereotyped stylings. In fact, the less imaginative my paintings became, the more money I started to make.

And because I acted all-mystical; stared out to sea and told them that I enjoyed the way that the light dappled on the water in Summer and that they should see it in Winter when the sea grew fierce, they opened their wallets and let me select the biggest of the notes. Because I told them, barely keeping a straight face, that painting underneath the crippled skeleton of the once proud Abbey gave me special powers, they begged me to write my own cheques in their battered books.

That was how I really made it as a seaside painter; pretend mystical powers. And in a place like Whitby, full of its Dracula tales and its seaside antiquity, people bought it. I had American dollars, Kenyan Shillings, Euros, locked in a drawer in my lodgings that I'd fleeced from foreign tourists all keen to experience the real England, the real Yorkshire. I never bothered to change them because - I don't know - I suppose something told me to keep these notes in reserve. They were my just in case fund.

After a while, I sold a simple view of the Abbey in the snow, rushed off with barely a second's thought, to a company which flogged prints to new offices, and I made enough money to slap a deposit down on a house on the edge of the town. This allowed me to sit on my rapidly expanding bottom and contemplate nothing in particular for a while. I don't suppose that you could have said I was happy. Not really. But I got by. By filling my time with stop-gap solutions, I never had to worry about what it was that I was losing out on.

After a while commissions started to pile-up, and rather than let them slide and let some other Whitby painter pick them up, I decided to get back on the horse again and start with my art. Only, for some reason, my long period of inactivity seemed to have mucked about with my talent. I'd always been one to imagine that my talent was like a tap, ready to be cranked on or off whenever I felt the need. But now, when I really needed it, it seemed to be deserting me. My painting arm felt like lead. It refused to move with the liquidity that it once had. I longed to paint over every broad brush stroke that I made. I longed to start over. But I couldn't seem to find the will to start, let alone finish a painting. Until that windswept Winter's night when I was up at the Abbey.

I was drunk. Must have been. As usual, I'd staggered up the famous 199 steps to the Abbey so I could find a place to sit and not-think. By the time I got up there it was dark, and the shadows of the tumbledown gothic ruin loomed over me like something out of an old black and white horror flick. I half-imagined Frankenstein's monster, or Dracula himself, to be lurking behind that rumbled pillar, or hiding away in the eaves. I half-imagined... Suddenly, I felt an all-powerful itch in my painting arm. So strong that I imagined I needed claws to scratch it properly. Imagined.

I didn't have my easel with me, but in a trance, I rooted through my pockets and immediately found my old pen that I used for the pen and ink caricatures. I didn't have any paper, so instead, I drew on my left arm, and eventually on my belly, so that once I got back to my pad, I could copy it all down if it was good. If it was good; I already knew it was going to be good. I'd already imagined it would be my best work to date. And because it was so dark, I didn't concentrate on the detail. Instead, I populated those dark places with pictures from my mind. For some reason I sketched a unicorn. For some reason, I inked the snake-haired old crone, half-remembering those words she'd spoken to me, all those years ago.

After a while, I had removed my trousers and was inking right onto my thighs. Every once in a while I would look at the complete picture, and my jaw would drop open in awe. The Abbey was coming alive in front of my eyes. The ribcage was starting to shift in the ground. And its beating heart was starting to come to the surface - the Holy Grail. Despite the unlikely nature of some of the images, it felt so real that I could almost feel the unicorn's wet nose nuzzling on my hands. I reached into the pocket of my jacket and offered it an apple. Not thinking...

But then it started to rain. The pictures started to wash off my thighs, belly and arms. Suddenly, the pictures started to wash into each other. And I knew that my greatest work was going to be lost forever. I climbed to my feet, started to dash towards the 199 steps. And I suppose that's when I slipped. And I suppose that's when I bumped my head. Because when I woke up again, I was lying on top of the damn Holy Grail. It was smashed in my jacket pocket; one shard digging into my thigh. The unicorn was lying at my feet, whimpering away. The old crone, Abi, was railing at me.

'You haven't given the image enough depth yet,' she cried. 'Give us more depth so we can survive.'

'But it's raining... It will wash away!'

She shook her head. 'No matter.'

And so, I took down my trousers once more and started to sketch. I started to give life to the crippled victims of my half-born imagination. And although the rain washed away what I drew, magic did occur. Suddenly the woman, Abi, started to appear beautiful. In time, the unicorn climbed to its feet, shook down his glistening flanks and then trotted off into the hills. As the sun rose over the Abbey, I saw the skeletal ribcage of the long-dead sea creature on the south cliff-top start to grow flesh and skin. And in time, it started to come to life, slip-sliding back over to the cliff, from whence it plunged into the welcoming embrace of the sea.

'Thank you,' it called, as it left.

Finally, I turned to the old crone, now a beautiful lady. She nodded, simply. And I knew what she was telling me. Somehow I understood that she was telling me that my just in case fund was my imagination, not the foreign currency I'd saved. Suddenly I knew I could paint again.

A Letter of Wishes

By Cressida Schofield

The Duke of York pub was situated at the base of the Abbey steps and it was here that they had agreed to meet on New Year's Day, 1986. There had been four of them once. Ashtray and his brother and their two best friends, Dobbo and Oakesy, until the two friends had fallen out some years ago and the friendship had been disbanded. When pressed, one would blame a girl for the grudge, the other would cite a disputed football result. But Ashtray knew the real reason had been long forgotten, trivial and moot.

Ashtray hadn't seen either man since they had stood at opposite sides of the crematorium at his brother's funeral, which had taken place just before Christmas back home in Newcastle. Now he had a duty to perform. Beneath the table he had placed a sports bag. It was not his usual style as he was not prone to strenuous activity but on this night it was required. Now all that could be done was wait and see if the two invited men would show. His optimism was proved by the two pints nicely warming before him and bought in anticipation of their attendance.

They arrived separately but within the same five minutes. Dobbo, as compact and wiry as a terrier and equally tenacious, and Oakesy, a brute of a man with an asymmetrical face that had an overhanging brow and dark, frowning eyes like Sam the Eagle from the Muppets. Different though they were in appearance, they shared similar character traits such as their mocking humour and stubbornness. As each man entered the pub they barely acknowledged each other. Their animosity was evident but at least neither man turned on his heel at the sight of the other, much to Ashtray's relief. He indicated to the waiting beers which were accepted with alacrity. As the two men drank Ashtray amused himself

298

by tearing tiny strips off a beer mat, rolling them into balls and flicking them into the fire.

"What yer deeing that fer? Where's yer lighter?" Dobbo asked in his heavy accent.

Ashtray, like his brother, had smoked since childhood but had quit the habit at his brother's request not long after the diagnosis of cancer had been made. He could think of no better tribute. Since then, to occupy restless fingers, he continually flicked at a fuel-less Zippo, the redundant flint doing nothing more than sparking. Its absence was noteworthy.

"I lost it." Ashtray's tone was dismissive.

For several minutes the three men sat in uncomfortable silence, the only sounds in the almost empty bar being the clink of glasses as the barmaid prepared for the evening's custom and David Bowie singing Ashes to Ashes on the jukebox. Ashtray couldn't help but acknowledge with wry irony the appropriateness of the lyrics.

Before the first round was finished, and the two men could decide to leave, Ashtray produced a plain wooden box with simple but well conceived carvings and a solid bronze fastening. He plonked it amidst the glasses.

"What's that?" Oakesy asked, licking foam off his upper lip.

"That's wor kid." Dobbo and Oakesy recoiled from the table, discomforted, mouths cringing. "Leastways what's left of him. You're here at his personal bequest. When we went through his papers we found a Letter of Wishes. In that was his wish that the three of us meet here to perform his last request."

"And what's that?" Dobbo asked, suspicious. "If it involves skinny dipping I'll say my goodbyes reet now."

"Nothing like that," said Ashtray, and went on to explain the Letter's contents.

His brother had requested that his ashes be scattered on the Abbey headland. The four men had grown up together from childhood as friends and neighbours, almost family. Holidays, school trips and stag nights had all taken place in Whitby. There was no better, or more appropriate, place than Whitby Abbey to perform this task.

"He specifically wanted it to be the four of us," Ashtray concluded.

"Four?" Dobbo asked, still suspicious. Ashtray nodded towards the casket. Dobbo's face was the epitome of horror.

"I'm guessing that's why you instructed us to wear black," Oakesy said. "Out of respect, like."

"Not exactly…" Ashtray said, looking shifty. "Howay, drink up that flat beer and I'll reveal all."

Outside the cold January air curled round them. It wasn't frosty, but bitter enough to ensure that any sensible soul would be safe and warm in his own house rather than wandering the deserted streets of Whitby. Above them the sky had reached full darkness. There was no Hammer Horror moon, just a gently reclining crescent, a wisp of a girl, quietly resting as she slipped in and out of a thin layer of cirrostratus cloud.

"Am nat gannin' up there. It's spooky!" Dobbo protested as they approached the steps that climbed the East Cliff to the Abbey. Normally bold and abrasive, Dobbo was curiously intimidated by anything of a supernatural ilk and it was this fear that Ashtray intended to exploit to his own ends.

"Divven be a wuss, man," Oakesy said scornfully, beginning his ascent of the steps. They were made slippy by the cold night air and the three men were thankful of the sturdy black railings. Behind them the fishermen's cottages, pastel and crooked, faded into obscurity as they continued to climb until all that could be seen were a few Christmas lights, illuminating trees and windows and providing a comforting element of frivolity to an otherwise sombre occasion.

All three men were panting as they climbed the last half dozen steps. Along the pathway that ran beside St. Mary's church filtered lamp posts threw shadows on the tombstones, causing them to glow orange in the night darkness like Jack o'lanterns. Shadow-castings loomed, irregular and face-like, out of the stonework. Beyond the boundaries of St. Mary's, the Abbey headland was dark and undiscovered, and the pathway to the Abbey shrouded in darkness. The gates were locked, Ashtray explained, and there would be security to avoid. Silence was imperative. What they were doing wasn't illegal, but it wasn't exactly encouraged either.

"So this is why you wanted us to wear black," Oakesy said, after they had scaled a low wall and dropped into the Abbey grounds. "Mind you, Dobbo looks more like he's delivering posh chocs in that polo neck. All because the lady loves, eh, Dobbo?"

Dobbo scowled at him."Shut yer face, Oakesy."

Ashtray hissed at them to be quiet but neither man was paying attention. Oakesy, a keen pub quizzer and trivia sponge, had gravitated towards an information board.

"It sez here that there was a monk called Hilda. Ah've heard everything now. Ah no, she wasn't a monk. She was the Abbess of Hartlepool."

"Hartlepool? Eee, the poor lass!"

They all hooted in unison before engaging in a chorus of shushes.

"An' this Abbey had both monks and nuns. That was risqué for the seventh century, eh? I wonder if they ever met up for a few cheeky Vimtos and a game of Twister."

"Aye, an' a canny bagga Tudor," Ashtray added.

"Nah, in monastic circles Tudor's a dirty word," Oakesy continued, well into his stride by this time. Only Dobbo refused to be drawn.

"Ah divven like tae thenk of all them monks, an' that. Ye nah, wondering round all suppressed and barefoot," he said, continually glancing from left to right, keeping an eye out for ghosts.

Oakesy ignored him and instead continued to read from the information board.

"There are one hundred and ninety nine steps to the Abbey – nee wonder I'm jiggered – which are also known as Caedmon's Trod…"

His lecture was truncated as something fast and low swooped above their heads.

"A bat!" cried Dobbo, flinging himself onto the ground in terror.

"Mebbe it was Count himself, who walks with footsteps silent," Oakesy whispered in a sepulchral voice. Dobbo glowered at him as he clambered to his feet.

"It was a seagull," Ashtray said, scathingly. He pointed. "Gan over there, round the back of the ruins where it's darker. You two gan ahead, I need to find me torch."

As Dobbo and Oakesy shuffled off round the north transept, Ashtray ducked into the ruined nave. Satisfied that he was invisible to his two friends he rummaged in the sports bag, drawing out several objects, including the lighter he claimed he had lost. With one swift motion he turned the cog; flame appeared. It was the first time the Zippo had been fuelled since he had promised his brother he would quit smoking.

Whole minutes passed before Dobbo and Oakesy realised that Ashtray was gone. As they scoured the landscape for him, hissing his name to get his attention, Ashtray was ignoring them. Instead he was assembling with deft hands a makeshift paper lantern from a copied photograph, some wire and a tealight. Once he was satisfied with his handiwork he set it upon the ledge of a glassless window, lit the tealight and scuttled off. Still concealed but now several yards away, he threw a small pebble towards where he had set the lantern. The slight rattle of pebble hitting rock caused Dobbo and Oakesy's heads to snap round.

"There's a face. It's him!" The tealight glowed, at head height, behind a thin photo of their deceased friend's grinning face. Half shadowed and disembodied, it proved to be an eerie yet unnervingly lifelike resemblance. "It's him, he's back and he's taken Ashtray beyond the grave," Dobbo wailed, any faint pretence at bravado abandoned. "Ashtray! Ashtray, where are yer, man?"

Terrified, he reversed at speed, then gave a bellow of shock as his foot was submerged in something cold and wet. This new discomfort diverted his attention from the horrors of visitations from the afterlife.

"Aw, man, me foot's drenched," he cried, hopping forward.

"Ye've heard of Caedmon's Trod. Now there's Dobbo's Trod. Ye've trod in the pond, ye fondy," Oakesy said.

Still concealed within the ruin, Ashtray didn't know whether to laugh or yell at them as he eavesdropped on this exchange. Peering out he saw Dobbo balanced on one foot as he shook the other frantically, his face a gurning mask of fury. Oakesy offered no sympathy but stood with his hands on his hips, his back arched as he roared with laughter.

But there was no time for dawdling. Ashtray drew another item out of the sports bag and stabbed it into the ground. Yet again the cog turned on his lighter.

The first thing Dobbo and Oakesy heard was a sinister hissing.

"What's that?" Dobbo asked, panicked, all thoughts of his sodden foot forgotten. The hissing increased in volume.

"Ah divven knaa," Oakesy replied, also inert with fear. Just as he had convinced himself that it was nothing, a projectile of remarkable pitch and volume screamed out of the belly of the Abbey and soared skywards. Jumping violently, Dobbo and Oakesy clutched each other in terror and shrieked for their mammies as the firework exploded above their heads in a kaleidoscope of gold and red. They then realised their close proximity and sprang apart like negative magnets.

Across the headland there was movement in the guard's cabin. A solitary beam of torchlight punctured the navy sky and somewhere in the distance a dog barked in disapproval. Dobbo emitted a second and unflatteringly girlish scream as Ashtray, howling with laughter, launched himself from behind a wall.

"Howay! Security!" he panted as he tore past. "Leggit! Hopefully they'll think it's just kids clartin' aboot."

The three men fled toward the steps. Just as they reached the cusp of the Abbey grounds Ashtray stopped, and turned. He took a few minutes to acknowledge his brother's death: the acute agony of loss juxtaposed with the guilt and acceptance of relief at his brother's release from suffering. There was little comfort to be taken from the knowledge that he and his family had been able to survive the horrendous ordeal of grief, which had been as cancerous as the disease itself, as it mercilessly and indiscriminately invaded their lives, tainting everything, unstoppable and unwanted. But little comfort was better than none. It was time to move on.

"Rest in peace, wor kid. Ah'll be seein' yer."

Watched with sobriety by Dobbo and Oakesy, Ashtray hesitated for a mere fraction before he lifted the lid and flung the contents of the casket into the night. Ashes and shards of bone swirled like a spectre before drifting over toward the Abbey and onwards to the cliff edge and the sea below. A moment was all it took to pay their final respects as the remains dissipated into the elements.

Ashtray had done what he had set out to do, and in every respect it would seem. Dobbo and Oakesy were grinning at each other, hands resting on thighs as they leaned forward to catch their breath. All trace of hostility had been eradicated in the evening's excitement.

"There wasn't a Letter of Wishes at all, was there?" Oakesy panted as they descended the steps at a jog. Thankfully, no one seemed to be following them.

"Oh, there was. Wor kid's final wish was that you two made it up. How I did it was my own deeing. I knew that you wouldn't agree to meet for a mere lads' neet oot but you couldn't refuse to spread your old mate's ashes. Scaring the bejeezus out of you to get you talking was all my idea."

The irony was, he went on, that there had been no need to do it so clandestinely. There was no reason why they couldn't have simply agreed to meet in Whitby, each paid the entrance fee to the Abbey grounds and scattered the ashes under less stressful circumstances. This way had just seemed so much more amusing.

Dobbo shot Ashtray a darting look but the merry glint in his eyes belied any implied enmity. Oakesy was less reticent and prodded Ashtray in his back by way of mock beration.

"Aye, well, mebbe your plan worked a little too well and we'll start talking tae each other but stop talking tae you."

"Aye, well, mebbe that was part of the plan an' all."

The banter continued until they reached the bottom of the steps. Ahead of them the lights of the Duke of York, offering a refreshing pint and anonymity within, beckoned.

The Fugitive

By Jane Tingle

I suppose they'll find me soon enough. There's only so long you can hide out at a heritage attraction. I mean, look at Tess of the D'Urbervilles.

They might not find me easily though. I mean, I'm practically camouflaged up here. If they're going by the description of a sixty-something woman in a pac-a-mac, eating ham sandwiches and drinking from a thermos, it'll take them hours to track me down amongst this lot.

I don't doubt that the woman in the shop will have reported it. She seemed the type. Beady eyes through the humbug jars, peering at you over her mono-bosom. How anyone can manage such a haughty look whilst handling giant marshmallow buttocks is beyond me. That's quite a skill she's got. Oh yes, she'll have been on her crime hotline faster than you can say sherbet dib-dabs, that one.

The others will be packing up their easels by now and Carol will be herding them. She'll be starting to worry about me. Hates it if we're late. Worries that we've been savaged by gulls or had a funny turn on some cockles. She's coming to the end of an NVQ in Enabling Senior People. This kind of thing could scupper it good and proper, I imagine. Still – I had to make a run for it and this is the best vantage point in town.

I haven't even checked my haul yet. What have we got? One packet of clotted cream fudge, rum and raisin. One jar of Mother Sidebottom's Venerable Herbal Tablets. And in here – three sticks of rock: a Fangs for the Whitby Memories, one Doncaster F.C. and a Big Boy. 'Big Boy', I ask you! And the shape of it? I don't know how people can put it in their mouths.

I wonder if they'll charge me this time. I think they have to, don't they? I mean, I've got form at Knaresborough, Pickering and Robin Hood's Bay now. And these computers all talk to each other nowadays, don't they?

The first time it happened, mind, I didn't even know I'd done it. First I knew was when a Security Guard took me by the elbow and led me to a back room. 'Madam,' he says. 'I have reason to believe you are harbouring a packet of stuffing mix up your cardigan.' I said 'Stuffing mix? Bread stuffing mix? Oh, I don't think so, love. Not with Henry a coeliac and me on the Atkins again.' But there it was. Stuffing mix. Apricot, macadamia and thyme, apparently. Get me!

They were very good about it. Just cautioned me. Obviously thought I was having a 'senior moment'. Of course, it helped that the Chief Constable goes to the Mooses with Henry. Took one look at my name and murmured between themselves, then nod, nod, wink, wink, Madam, say no more, just a mistake, happens to the best of us. They made quite a fuss of me actually. Tea, malted milks, a ride home in a panda car. It were quite a day out in the end.

It's a lovely spot this, I've always thought so. There are little signs everywhere, telling you about the Abbey. They have headphones too but I need my wits about me. It was founded by St Hilda apparently, says she was a skilled administrator. Funny that, so was I once, right at the start of the business, before the children. I could do eighty-five words per minute at my peak. I used to love that job, me and Henry working together as a team. I asked him if I could go back when the youngest started school but by then he'd installed the first one, Karen I think it was. I don't like to think what she could reach at her peak.

Not that she lasted long. None of them ever did. Ever do.

I feel a bit guilty about Carol. She'll be fretting. And the others will be baying for their fish supper. It's Thursday, they do free bread and butter and limitless tea. You keep a pensioner from that at your peril. Speaking of which, I'm ravenous, that ham sandwich didn't touch the sides. It's all those seeds they put in the bread these days. I'm going to have to start on the fudge. Not all of it, I'll be sure to leave some as evidence. Or the packet and postcard anyways. The judge will need to know exactly what he's dealing with.

The second time was the Pickering job. I only popped in for some milk but once I got in the supermarket, I came over all funny and before I knew it I was in the Polish specialities aisle. In Pickering! This time I knew what I was doing but I just couldn't stop myself. It felt so exciting, my heart was thumping – I thought they'd be able to hear it – and my palms were all sweaty. Oh, but such a buzz! They stopped me in the car park this time. If I'd have left it at the pickled mushrooms and bilberry jam I might have got away with it but the bottle of vodka was a step too far.

They had to tell Henry this time. The Chief Constable had a 'quiet word'. He went berserk. Said if it got out, he'd be a laughing stock, that he hadn't spent thirty years building his reputation as cheese king of the North Riding for me to ruin it all with a menopausal episode. A 'menopausal episode'? Where's he been for the last twenty years? He was so angry. He was shouting at me: 'If I wanted to eat Eastern European peasant food, I'd dine in the canteen with my factory staff.' He never used to be such a snob. His dad worked fifty years on the bins; he'd wallop him to Hell and Hull if he caught him talking like that. Anyway, he didn't speak to me for a week and then suddenly says, out of nowhere, all frosty: 'You're obviously bored. I suggest you busy yourself this week by hoovering the curtains.'

Well, bugger the curtains, I thought. And that's when I signed up for this painting course.

We go to some lovely places, it's the highlight of my week really - the feel of the brush in my hand and the way the colours all come together. The others are a funny lot mind, mostly widowed, all a bit older than me. There's one old guy, I'm not sure he's all there. No matter what you sit him in front of – lobster pots, moorland train, shaggy sheep – he always paints a naked lady - and a big naked black lady at that. Someone asked him once, gentle like, 'Is that your wife, love?' 'No,' he says. 'It's Shirley Bassey.' And that was that. Not another word before or since.

Another little sign here. This Hilda sounds like quite a woman. Says she drew kings and nobles from afar seeking her advice and counsel. Crikey. I'm lucky if the kids can be bothered to come back from college with their washing.

I wonder how many offences it is before they send you to prison. They all add up surely, even the little ones. I've three points on my driving licence - doing 37 in a 30. I don't mind the idea of prison actually. Irene next door, her lad got two years glassing a man in a pub, came out a trained plumber. I've always fancied the idea of a degree. Daft, I know. I thought about evening classes but Henry likes his dinner on the table. I was good at Art at school and Carol says I have 'an eye'. Henry calls them my daubs and tells me not to get paint in his Audi.

It is a lovely spot though. We used to come here when we were courting. Eat fish and chips, draw hearts in the sand, all that. I remember coming up here in the moonlight once, we were a bit sloshed and he tried to carry me up all them steps. Oh, it was such a laugh. It seemed romantic, in the shadow of the ruins, listening to the waves crashing on the rocks below. Very 'From Here to Eternity'. We got a bit carried away on one of the table tombs and he gave me such a love-bite! Crimson for days, it was. I said to him, 'I'll be for it when my Dad sees that!' He ran away, laughing: 'Tell him it were Dracula!' he says.

Dracula. Funny that now. Because he's certainly sucked the life out of me.

I can see the coach park at the harbour from here. They're still there. It'll be pandemonium, I expect. Geoff'll be wanting to leave by six, runaway or not. The dusk plays havoc with his cataracts.

Anyway, the third time, it was cheese. Predictable, I realise, but it was asking to happen. It's not as easy as you'd think - you're dealing with volatile stuff. The Lancashire Blue in my handbag was fine and a Babybel'll keep in your palm for a good while, but the wedge of Brie stuffed down my cleavage wasn't one of my brighter moves.

This time they called Henry into the station. Explained how serious it was. Talked about counselling. Talked as if I wasn't there really. But then I'm used to that by now. Anyway, Henry leads me to the car by my elbow and puts me in the front – I swear this is true – with his hand on my head, like he thinks he's in The Sweeney. He didn't even get to the end of the road before he lost it. 'Lancashire Blue? Lancashire Blue! What are you trying to do to me? As if it's not bad enough having a klepto for a wife, you go and do that to me. I'll be the laughing stock of the Yorkshire cheese fraternity.' He drives in silence for another five minutes but I can see a nerve in his cheek twitching and his mouth all screwed up like a cat's bum. We stop to let some kids cross and he bangs the steering wheel, scares the lollipop lady out of her wits. 'They don't call me the Big Cheese for nothing, you know!' he's shouting. Thing is, they don't call him the Big Cheese at all, well, not for the reason he likes to think. Let's just say it's less about his skills as a master fromager and more about him trying to get all the typists to bunk up with him at the Nantwich Cheese Fair.

Anyway, he finishes off by saying, 'Why? Why are you doing this to me? Haven't I given you everything you could want?' And I suppose, looking at it from the outside, he has, yes. Three kids, a nice house, never having to worry about where the money's coming from. But, thing is, I'm not sure that is everything I want. I don't even know what I want. But I'm fairly sure it's not spending half of my weekdays cleaning up ready for the cleaner and every evening on my own watching repeats of Coast.

I wonder how Hilda handled all that solitude, stuck up here in the wilds. I suppose it's the difference between being on your own and being lonely. Sounds like she kept herself busy. It says here that 'all property and goods were held in common'. That wouldn't bother me. It's all very well, the house and the pool and the gas barbeque but I'd give anything not to be rambling about on my own all day and sitting in silence whenever Henry is home.

Sometimes I think about running away, starting again. I thought maybe India. I saw a National Geographic at the dentists and the colours were beautiful – the saris and the tiles, even the cows are painted. It'd be wonderful to paint there. Irene said, 'India? All that dirt? Why would you want to go to India with Hutton-le-Hole on your doorstep?' But I said to her: 'No cheese, Irene.' Well, there's paneer, of course, but that hardly counts.

He never used to be like this, Henry. I mean, he used to wind me up something chronic – but just teasing. He used to tell me he wanted to be the first man to bring pig's cheese to Yorkshire. Told me it had a nutty flavour and was nutritionally superior to cow's - the only reason it wasn't already on the shelves was that it was so expensive to produce. Seven years he kept that one going then one day just turned and laughed in my face. A nasty laugh. Told me I was the stupidest woman he'd ever met, that everyone knows you can't milk pigs. I said, 'I don't see why not. I've seen the size of their nipples. They're not inconsiderable.' He tells everyone that one; I've become quite the party piece. I sometimes think, 'Ha ha, very funny. Perhaps I'll tell Mr Chairman of the Dales Cheese Marketing Board how you believed I couldn't get pregnant if we did it in the bath and that's why we've got James, so don't call me bloody gullible!'

The timetable says there's two trains leave Whitby before half past seven. One'll get me home if I change at Leeds. The other goes to Leeds Bradford International. You can fly all over from there now, I've seen it on the billboards. Barbados, Pakistan, Tunisia. Imagine! I've never been outside Europe. Although if I've been to The Algarve once, I've been a hundred times - for the golf, you see.

I've got my passport in my bag. I've got used to carrying it around for when they need to ID me at the police station.

Oh, what am I thinking! Shirley bloody Valentine I'm not.

The man in the ticket office is looking at his watch. I suppose I should be heading down now.

It's a funny graveyard this, very dramatic. There's a tomb in one corner. A couple, both died within days of each other aged a hundred and something. They must have been married for sixty, seventy years. I used to think it was so romantic – that one must have died from a broken heart, unable to think about life without the other. Now I'm not so sure. Most likely they were waiting the best part of seventy years for the miserable old bugger to pop off so they could go on a Saga cruise or whatever they did back then. And then what happens? Bang, it's all over for them.

I can't see Saint Hilda hanging around, putting up with that, waiting at home for a man. She wouldn't let the grass grow under her feet, that one.

Well.

Time's getting on.

I'd best go and get that train.

The Storm

By Tara Chintapatia

Age 11 and under category winner

The rain battered the window and lightning ripped the skies. Below the cliffs the waves were enormous. The Smiths stared in horror as a black boat struggled in the waters. They watched as a small, wet, tired figure emerged and slowly turned towards the old Whitby Abbey and disappeared ……..

10 years had passed and it was a fine day. Susie Smith and her friend Alex Wright ran to their favourite place - the Whitby cliffs. They spotted a floating piece of wood. "Look Susie - there is some writing on it!" They removed the shells from the driftwood and read "Crockey boat".

At home Mr Smith told them the story.

In 1999 a prisoner, Richard Blaxter, had escaped from HMP Leeds. He had been found guilty of murder and robbery. Shortly after his escape the "Crockey boat" went missing from the Hull docks. It was suspected that Richard Blaxter had made his escape on that boat. Then in 2004 there were some incredible headlines:

"Escaped convict blameless."

"Murderer innocent"

But…….the prisoner was never found again.

The children now determined to find Richard Blaxter. Over the next two months, at the library, they searched every newspaper about the escape. They even found his picture. They kept all his cuttings.

The summer holidays had started and it became very busy in Alex's father's bakery. Because of this Mr Wright was delighted when 'Bob the summer helper' turned up. Bob had come every summer holiday for many years. He was a good but quiet worker.

One evening Susie and Alex saw Bob climbing the stairs towards the ruins of the ancient Abbey of Whitby. Bob passed the church, then the Abbey entrance and then walked south along the surrounding wall.

Suddenly he leaped over the wall and walked back along the pond taking care that nobody saw him.

Susie and Alex followed Bob secretly. They entered the tall chilly ruins, and saw Bob move a big carved stone away. Susie was shaking in excitement and fright. They decided to go home and think of a plan.

The next day, when Bob was still in the bakery, Susie and Alex went back to the Abbey. They moved the carved stone. There was an under ground hideaway. Inside there was a mattress, a prisoner's uniform, a desk with a candle on it. And there was a diary...

Susie nearly cried when she finished reading that diary. It was "him".

"He must have missed all the headlines in the paper staying below the Abbey all winter" Susie concluded.

Susie quickly put the headlines of 2004 on the table and left.

After a long time they heard Bob's footsteps approaching and entering his hideaway. When Bob came out the last sun beams of the day shone on him and the children saw the biggest smile ever lit his face.

Susie and Alex came out from behind the columns and shouted in joy "Richard Blaxter".

It was a new beginning....

Dracula Returns

By Ellie Robinson

Age 11 and under category runner up

It started on a cold miserable day. A little girl wandered round the ruins of Whitby Abbey with her parents. She heard a voice. 'Come to me now' it whispered. She shook her head. She must be insane! She walked behind her mum and dad, dragging her fingers across the cold stone, trying to make sense of what she thought she heard.

Up ahead, her parents turned the corner and the girl stood alone. Suddenly, she heard her mum's cries and her father calling for help. She started to run. She rounded the corner and spotted a strange man dressed in a long cloak. She felt so angry and started to shout. The man turned to face her 'I am Dracula'; he said 'you will never survive.' He pulled his cloak round his body and left quickly.

The girl's mother said, 'Don't worry sweet heart, we will save you!' putting her arm across the girl's shoulder. 'No!' the girl cried pushing her mum away 'I have to do it by myself.' She dashed off, running into the old Abbey.

'Dracula, where are you?' the girl demanded. Out of nowhere Dracula appeared. 'Here I am Miss Angel' he hissed. The girl looked around at her surroundings. Bats and black dogs where everywhere. She turned back to Dracula and he was gone. 'Oh great' she sighed. Then, she remembered that Dracula could turn into a bat or a black dog. This is why he came here, she thought, to confuse me! She looked closer at the bats and dogs. The dogs wore collars and the bats had a very dark spot on their left wing. She decided to check all the bats and dogs and found a bat without a dark spot on its left wing. The spot was on the bat's right wing. 'Dracula, I know I'm looking at you' the girl said. She watched the bat closely, but it didn't transform into Dracula.

She thought hard. Maybe, just maybe, if I sprinkle the bat with salt, he would turn into a puddle of water, just like a witch. Reaching into her bag, she found a pot of salt and poured it over the bat. Instantly, the bat turned into water, making a puddle on the floor. Suddenly all the dogs and bats turned into people! 'Thank you for helping us' said one lady. 'Dracula drank our blood! I can't understand or explain how we turned into animals but I am grateful that you saved us all.' The girl felt relieved but had to leave to make sure her parents were OK.

'What an adventure' the girl told her parents afterwards. 'I hope we come to Whitby Abbey again soon.' And do you know what? She did.

Hidden

By Sean O'Grady

Age 12-16 category winner

No wind or rain dared to exercise its power. Serene dark skies, pricked with spots of light, seemed to mock the distress felt by the passengers of a carriage. It was failing to climb the rough path. No one was surprised that this was the case, the carriage after all being designed for the paved streets of London, not the jagged cliffs of Whitby. But tonight pragmatism and the truth were whispers of a far off life and reality. This place, which had inspired Caedmon to write his poem, was now a sanctuary. It should have inspired passion and happiness, however a distinct feeling of anxiousness and foreboding came over the occupants as Whitby Abbey blotted out the stars of the perfect night.

"The house of God? More of a hovel," it was the woman who spoke first, her voice sounding as seductive as the promise of power and land. She was furthest away from the door, clutching at the seat she sat on, her elongated fingers trembling with the exertion. Though she had spoken in disdain, her face revealed nothing. Her auburn hair, beautiful but obviously false, sat perfectly on her head. The only way to describe her face was dazzling, for as the moon shot its light into the carriage, her face of porcelain white made it impossible to look at her.

"It has been abandoned for several years majesty. I am sure the Abbey would have challenged even the palace in splendour before the dissolution," the man, sat on the opposite side of the carriage next to a moving bundle, spoke with deference and an almost fatherly love. His hair was already greying even though he was barely forty, his beard cut into his own personal style, refusing to adapt to the fashions of court. As usual he wore black, a stark contrast to the pearl covered dress of his Queen. The carriage stopped abruptly, almost causing the bundle to fall to the floor. Neither the Queen nor her companion seemed to be worried. The only noise left was a whimper which escaped the bundle, threatening to become a shrill cry.

"Give her to me," the woman reached out her arms to receive the bundle from her companion. He hesitated for a moment but hastily obeyed the order as it started to shake, obviously beginning to cry. Greedily the woman took the shaking form. She let the silk fall away, revealing the head and torso of her child. She began to rock the baby issuing soothing noises. The man focused on his Queen's eyes and was shocked. He was not accustomed to seeing fear on his ruler's face much less what he saw beneath it. Love. Pure, naked, unadulterated love was beneath that fear. The most beautiful sight in the world, it rivalled the Madonna carrying an infant Jesus. A sudden noise interrupted his thoughts; someone was banging on the door.

The person did not wait for a response, instead letting themselves into the carriage. Whereas both the man and woman wore rich clothes, the new entrant did not. She was obviously old, her face gaunt. There were wrinkles too, but it was impossible to tell whether they had been gained by enjoyment or a life of hardship; given who she was the man guessed the latter. She wore the traditional garb of a bride of Christ. A red sash was stretched across her habit marking her as the Mother Superior of Whitby Abbey, this order commonly known as the Fallen Order. The Sister made a bizarre addition to the Queen's company.

"Is that the baby?" A harsh, matter of fact voice emanated from the Mother Superior.

"Yes Sister Hilda, this is the baby," the Queen said, her eyes locked on the woman who was to become the mother of her child. Hatred replaced the fear in her eyes; the man had to look away. Never before had he seen such coldness, and he knew he never would do again. The rules of nature stated that a mother was the most dangerous state to be in, and now he could see why. Hate, fear, love, anger, desperation; the full spectrum of human emotion held in a single instant, Mother Nature was truly terrifying.

"Why have you come to me?" the Queen's companion realised that Sister Hilda had been speaking whilst he had been appreciating the ferocity of nature. The Queen passed her child to the man. "The Abbey has a great history Sister. Several palaces now hold some piece of its stone. I remember a story my mother once told me, she said that if ever a royal woman needed protection then the sisterhood would give it."

It was Sister Hilda's turn to show hatred, "Your mother betrayed us! The sisterhood was almost destroyed when the Abbey was closed. She relinquished your right to the protection." The Queen went to respond.

"I realise you deem yourself above the laws of this state but may I remind you Sister that your body is subject to the rules of reality?" it was the man who spoke, forcing the Queen to stop. Sister Hilda was an intelligent woman and the threat concealed in the man's words was clearer to her than the moon or the stars. "How dare you threaten me! I've seen the peaceful slaughtered by the father of your precious Queen, all because of a woman who wanted more power than she deserved." They both wanted to continue but the baby's shrill cry stopped them. But the tears didn't alone belong to the baby. The Queen, her mask of a ruler now gone, was shedding her first true tears. One would expect her to look like a weak child but she did not. Impossibly the tears made her a woman for the first time, a woman who had seen her share of cruelty and much more. When she spoke her voice was so delicate, it was if a mere thought could destroy it.

"One God, Sister. Not one for Protestants and a different God for Catholics but one to unite us." She paused, the baby quietening down, somehow sensing what to do. "The Bible constantly tells us of the tests the prophets and saints had to undergo. This is a test for you, Sister Hilda. This child deserves a life of happiness, she will not have one if I remain her mother. Anne Boleyn thought that a new religion would make England greater. It may do in years, but my daughter will not be its pawn." The Queen bent down and kissed her baby on the forehead, her eyes taking in every last detail. The harsh lines on Sister Hilda's face now softened. "Whitby Abbey was founded by a King, now it will play home to a Queen. Your majesty, the Sisterhood will raise your daughter." Sister Hilda reached for the baby from a woman who was already assembling herself to again portray an unflappable Queen. Hilda climbed out of the carriage which quickly pulled away.

"Your mother didn't tell me your name." The Mother Superior was rocking the princess, as if she were her own. The harshest woman ever to have walked within the halls of Whitby Abbey would become the surrogate mother to the granddaughter of a protestant tyrant. "I know; your name will be your mother's. Though she is not quite a virgin Queen." The nun chuckled and the child smiled. They made their way to the Abbey, new home to the hidden.

The Stone of Amber

By Emily Castles

Age 12-16 category runner up

It was a dark dismal night in the year of 1468. Three sullenly hooded figures gathered inside a dubious drinkers' tavern known as "The Witch's Black Cat", a pub that was famed for its bloodshed and carnage. It was a bar for the wicked and those escaping the law. It was a somewhat ugly building, the outside décor slightly disconcerting. The walls that, in their prime, had been an alluring, pearly white, were now a repugnant shade of yellow and crumbling forevermore. Indeed, an awful place for a pint.

The three figures sat around a table, two on the right, the other unaided on the left. A barmaid came up to them timidly, her little black note book and pen in hand.

"Three whiskeys, and make it nippy," grunted the man on the left. Obeying his stern wishes she scuttled off and was back with beverages only seconds later.

"So, my good man, have you got it for us?" questioned one of the figures on the right. The man on the left gave a small grunt, and started to rummage around in his coat pocket. He got out a small brown bag and lay it on the table carefully.

"There, you must understand though. I am not giving this to you willingly, I think it would be much more safe in my possession, but I have been informed that you have a secret place where it may lie for eternity without being disturbed and found, suppose it beats my sullied pocket," he mumbled, with that, he took a big swig of the whiskey and strode out of the door.

The two remaining figures pulled down their hoods, enthralled by the confounding package. One of the two was a man in his mid-forties, quite handsome but rather dishevelled. The other, surprisingly, was a girl of but fifteen. Pretty but austere. They were father and daughter.

"Father, I know I came here even though you were against it, but can't you just tell me what this all about. All the private letters and peculiar visitors, and now the exchanging of an anonymous object. Tell me!"

"Oh do hush Emma, you should never have come, you followed me and it a was very juvenile and foolish thing to do. Now you must forget what you have seen and go home. You should not have been here to hear my business, and you most certainly won't hear any more. Now go!"

She scowled at him despising, put up her hood once more, and charged out the door. Ten minutes later her father followed, he turned east and started the journey to the next chapter. Little did he know, there was another figure but a few yards away from him. Following him, step by step.

After several hours a figure came out of the woods, walking towards Emma's father. She darted behind a tree, but so he was still in view and, she soon found out, in hearing distance too.

"You have the stone?" said the tall eerie man.

"Who are you? What do you want?" said my father standing tall, but you could detect his fear through his quivering voice.

"You know what we want fool!" At this point the man got out a large sword, which glistened disturbingly in the moonlight. He held it to my father's throat. My father, so valiant and indomitable, standing so high and fearless. He would give his life to protect this "stone", no ordinary pebble then, thought Emma. The eerie man, getting more and more agitated at her father's silence, edged the blade just a tiny bit further into her father's throat. Blood started to trickle down.

"No!" shrieked Emma running from the trees. Her father's heart sank, "That imprudent girl!" he thought heatedly. As the man's eyes left her father to inspect this prying little girl, he kicked him as hard as he could and yelled for Emma to run. So, holding each others hands securely, they ran. As they looked behind them, more and more men were emerging from the trees, obviously the eerie man's men, hiding in the forest this whole time as back up.

"Emma, you are so aggravating and foolish and irrational and dim."

"Yes dad, OK, but this is not the time," she said interrupting, with that they ran even faster until at long last they finally lost the army of men.

They sat huddled under a large oak tree, for it was awfully cold, eating some food that her father had luckily brought along on his expedition.

"OK then," said Emma. "Out with it. What is this whole thing about?"

"OK, I suppose I have no choice but to tell you since you made it absolutely necessary that you got involved." He sighed a long sigh. "This," he said taking out the brown bag, "is the stone of Amber," he tipped it out of the bag. Emma thought it was rather odd to call it Amber as it looked rather more like Ruby. But still, it was an immaculate jewel.

"It has the power to give eternal life, and in the hands of a villain, can be fatal to us all. It can bring so much anguish and sorrow. Such catastrophes have happened in the past, and the government and I are adamant that they don't repeat. Which is why it was given to me, so I can protect it."

"Is that right?" said Emma. "Eternal life? Well I'll be! But how can you protect it? What can keep it safe?"

"Nothing, which is why I must destroy it," he said holding it close.

"What? But think of what you could do with it! It's all yours!" exclaimed Emma.

"But I must dear girl, people will try and stop me, like those men back there, but I have to, for all our sakes. We will go to Whitby Abbey, and throw it into the flames that lurk beneath. It is the only way to destroy such a thing, it dies where it was born." Soon after, they set off.

Many hours later they embarked. Whitby Abbey stood imposingly before them. The illustrious windows reflected the picturesque town and harbour below. The ancient walls that were the shrine of the foundress,

St Hilda, standing proud. The Abbey truly was king in this little town. Utterly exquisite.

Suddenly, their peaceful analysis of the place was interrupted by a growing sound of a mob. As father and daughter looked behind, they saw the army of men gaining rapidly. Her father grasped her arm, and yelled: "RUN!"

So they did, down countless corridors and numerous doorways. Dearest Emma was far too anxious and petrified to even consider where they were going, but her father seemed calm and at ease, which somewhat settled her nerves.

Eventually they came to a large gothic door. She gasped at what lay behind. It really was a bed of flames. A whole chamber full of hissing fire. The scolding colours of sweltering orange and blistering yellow blasting from each corner. Her father, with a muscular swing, threw the stone into its mouth. Seconds later, just in time to see its demolition, the army of men fled through, foolishly throwing themselves in after it.

The stone was never seen again, though some say it still exists, that a stone so precious can never be destroyed. And that somewhere, beneath the ruins of Whitby Abbey, the chamber still burns, the jewel as bright as ever.